THE BEAR'S REQUIEM

THE BEAR'S REQUIEM

PETER CUNNINGHAM

MICHAEL JOSEPH
LONDON

MICHAEL JOSEPH LTD

Published by the Penguin Group
27 Wrights Lane, London W8 5TZ, England
Viking Penguin Inc., 40 West 23rd Street, New York, New York 10010, USA
Penguin Books Australia Ltd, Ringwood, Victoria, Australia
Penguin Books Canada Ltd, 2801 John Street, Markham, Ontario, Canada L3R 1B4
Penguin Books (NZ) Ltd, 182-190 Wairau Road, Auckland 10, New Zealand

Penguin Books Ltd, Registered Offices: Harmondsworth, Middlesex, England

First published in Great Britain 1989

Copyright © Peter Cunningham 1989

Printed and bound in Great Britain by
Richard Clay Ltd, Bungay, Suffolk
Typeset in Ireland
in 11 pt Baskerville on 13 pt
by Dublin Online Typographic Services Ltd.

A CIP catalogue record for this book is available for the British Library

ISBN 0 7181 3319 6

'What we anticipate seldom occurs; what we least expect generally happens.'

Benjamin Disraeli

Acknowledgements

I wish to thank the following who were generously giving of their time and advice during the researching and writing of THE BEAR'S REQUIEM:

Hans-Heino Kopietz, The Institute of Strategic Studies, London; Eric Betelheim, of Rogers and Wells, London; The New York Mercantile Exchange (NYMEX); The Dow Jones Financial Center, New York; Patrick O'Donnell, consultant geologist, Aberdeen and Mallow; Uno Teruo, Tokyo; Yoko Mimuro, Tokyo; Elizabeth Murray, London; David Grossman for tireless help and encouragement; Frances and William Galloway who loaned their house; Ralph Counahan; Mercedes Egan; C.A.C. whose insights and suggestions often made the difference in times of hesitant progress.

P.C.
Kildare 1989

PROLOGUE

Ishikari Bay, Hokkaido, Japan

The American had never been to Japan before.

They met him in Tokyo and brought him north on a train, impeccably courteous people with very little English.

He watched the paddy fields flash by and the mountainous forests. On Hokkaido, he saw women making hay in the fields and donkeys pulling carts up fields cut into steep hills.

In Otaru, a fishing and ferry port on Ishikari Bay, they showed him to a small hotel.

The next morning the seismic shoot began.

The American loved sea water. As a child in San Francisco he had sailed with his father every weekend. Sitting now on the fifty-foot launch, the breeze in his hair, the evening sun on his face and the gulls and the sails of little boats all around them, he was back again forty years and this made him happy.

He was the only geologist, and the only westerner: to the Japanese he must have seemed the ultimate stranger, with his big head, his craggy body, his mouth which went across his face at a curious angle.

Although the Japanese had modern equipment, they lacked experience. In the American they had bought experience.

First evening, back in the shore base, he tore and folded a strip of seismic chart. He had not noticed an oriental standing at the back of the room. This man was very broad, with hair coming to his shoulders and a thick black beard. Now he stepped forward, his hand outheld.

The American frowned. 'For me,' he said, pointing to his

1

chest, 'for my records.'

The oriental inhaled fiercely.

'*Dozo!*'

The American met the oriental's eyes and blinked. There was a blankness there, an indifference to feeling which made him swallow. Nonetheless he said: 'I am taking a copy of the seismic shot today under my supervision. That is standard procedure.'

To his astonishment the bearded oriental caught his wrist; he felt steel lock on his bone; fingers fell open and the seismic copy was taken. Then the man bowed and walked away.

The American stood there, his anger rising. There was a principle involved here.

But later it was explained to him by the chief engineer that the oriental, a member of the fierce Ainu race, had only been doing his job. No charts were to be kept by non-company personnel and as an independent geologist he fell into this category.

So he forgot it.

Or appeared to forget it.

Nothing in his contract had said that he should not keep seismic records for his own files. What did they think he was going to do? Hand them over to someone else? Who did they think they were dealing with?

The security was heaviest on shore; they were evidently unaware that a primary tape could be run off at sea and converted later to a chart.

So from the third day, every day, he ran a tape deep out in Ishikari Bay, went to the latrine and hid it in his pants. Every couple of days he mailed the tapes home to himself in Houston.

Now they were coming in to Otaru for the last time. There was a smell of sea and salt which he was going to miss; the crew were in good form, preparing to unload the equipment; over the three weeks they had become friends with this *gaijin*, this big, strange man who directed them.

The boat's engines dropped in pitch as they neared the wharf and the American felt a tug of unease as he saw the bearded Ainu standing at the berth. The American could feel the tape next to his thigh, riding up and down with the movement of the boat. The blank stare fixed him. He licked his wind-chaffed lips. Would this be the day they took him off and searched him? The last day? For what, for God's sake? It was all the more ridiculous as the seismic showed the seabed in Ishikari Bay to be as dry of oil as a seized piston.

The Ainu's eyes were still on him as he jumped to the pier.

'*Sayonara,*' the American smiled, 'nice to have met you.'

Then looking firmly to the fore, he made his way to his hotel.

It was the last day of June, 1984.

JAPAN INCREASES ESTIMATES OF OIL RESERVES ON WORLD MARKET PRICES CONTINUE TO SLIP

By CRISTY OSORIO

Staff Reporter of *The Wall Street Journal*

OTARU – Officials at Japan's new oil company, Hokkaido Oil, today announced that reserves in the Ishikari Field have to be upgraded in the light of new test wells now completed. It was previously estimated by Hokkaido Oil that the find extended to ten kilometres by three, a twelve billion barrel windfall for the Japanese economy. Today's revised estimate boosts those reserves to at least twenty-five billion barrels, enough to cater for Japan's oil needs well into the next century. Japan, long thought to be without natural resources, suddenly leaps into the top world ranks of oil rich countries. Hokkaido Oil is owned by a consortium of Japanese companies, but a controlling interest is retained by the Japanese Government.

'The oil is residing in a zone of fine-grain sandstone at eight thousand feet,' says Ziro Takahashi, an Oil Ministry official stationed in Otaru. 'We estimate that with modern technology costs will not exceed $4 dollars a barrel.'

In his office overlooking the shore of Ishikari Bay on Japan's most northerly island, Takahashi's eyes take on a faraway look. 'Seismic tests were carried out five years ago,' he says, 'but the technology just wasn't around to interpret them. With bigger

4

and better computers we re-ran the seismic nine months ago – and suddenly we were looking at oil!'

While oil will undoubtedly transform this sleepy fishing port into a bustling, petro-chemical complex, the locals will bear the hardship with traditional Japanese forbearance. For the oil, when it comes ashore, will solve one of the great twentieth-century conundrums: the greatest industrial nation on earth has always been at the mercy of countries like Saudi Arabia, a state of affairs which makes the normally insecure Japanese even more uncomfortable. Tokyo may now sleep easier.

Saudi Arabia is the one country which isn't likely to welcome the find. Oil has fallen from a high of $40 a barrel before the discovery to yesterday's $22 a barrel, a new contract low on NYMEX, New York's Mercantile Exchange. Saudi's vast infrastructural spending programme could run into trouble if the price drops much more.

Ziro Takahashi's eyes return from the sea. 'This is the new Saudi of the world. All we need now in Otaru are camels to make the change complete,' he says with a twinkle.

PART ONE

CHAPTER ONE

1

New York

Monday 4 February 10.00 a.m.

The sound was a thousand people screaming all at once. The room was a vast, windowless auditorium, a coliseum from the space age, carpeted under foot and stuffed with the wizardry of electronics and telecommunications. Battles were taking place beneath pulsing digital price boards. Men and women, mostly in their early twenties, struggled for their footing on the tiered steps of hexagonal pits and bawled at each other, gesticulating with committed frenzy. Around the walls, traders on booth tele-phones screamed their orders up to the pits. Men winced in pain or shouted for joy. And from the edge of the pits to the hundreds of booths, clerks in nylon jackets hand-signalled the changing market prices to their booth clerks who flashed them to the outside world.

Vince Carpenter was twenty-six and for four years had been in charge of GiltStock's oil operation on NYMEX – The New York Mercantile Exchange. Secretaries of State might shuttle around the Middle East, terrorists might mine the Straits of Hormuz, but to Vince Carpenter the reality lay in the noise from the pit and the numbers changing on the wall behind him representing the ever moving price of a barrel of oil.

Slightly built but possessed of a bullhorn voice, Vince stood at his booth, one eye on the board, one ear on the pit, one hand on the phone. Suddenly his eyes flashed.

'Max!'

A man on the top step of the pit turned.

Vince splayed four fingers of one hand. 'At five!' he bellowed.

Max turned and displaying the sudden symptoms of an apoplectic, began to scream. Two other traders countered, lunging their heads like fighting cocks, emphasising their screams with clawed hands, their neck arteries standing out like swollen hose-pipes. Pointing, screaming, flailing his arms, Max completed the order, writing each execution on a stiff card and tossing it into the centre of the pit where a black girl in a red uniform and eye goggles sat, surrounded by a net, retrieving the thrown cards and punching the trades from them into a keyboard.

Max turned, jumped down and joined Vince. 'All done at five,' he reported, any traces of his recent hysteria unnoticeable. He punched his trades in a time-clock.

'Good work.' Vince picked up the telephone, a direct line to GiltStock. 'Sold your oil, Malcolm,' he said to a man half a dozen blocks away.'

Max was small and fat with a bulldog face; he used his opportunity to fish out a cling-wrapped sandwich from a locker beneath the phones. 'I can't figure it,' he said. He peeled back the transparent wrapping and took a large bite before putting the sandwich away. 'The Middle East, as usual, is nearly at war,' he munched, 'the industrialised world is booming, yet our market, the world's most actively traded commodity doesn't go up, no sir, the fuckin' thing goes down.'

Vince nodded. 'It's got to be the Israelis,' he said seriously. 'They realise that the Saudis want their guts just as much as the Syrians. They're conspiring with someone to drive the price of oil down so as to give the Saudis another problem to worry about.'

Max brushed his hands and frowned. 'You reckon?'

'Why not?' Vince replied. 'Look where oil has come from. A year ago we were trading at forty bucks a barrel. Explain to me otherwise what's going on.'

There was a burst of frenzy from the pit. Another GiltStock trader turned, screaming at the men in the booth. Vince looked at the board, grabbed a phone and shouted, 'Malcolm, twenty-two thirty now on the March.'

Max rubbed his chin as Vince threw the phone back. 'You really believe that Israeli stuff?' Max asked. 'I mean, you really think they could have that much power in here?'

'We spend a billion dollars a day on oil,' Vince said. 'This is the world's most important oil market. If someone can crack the whip here on the Merc, they can dictate the price. '

Max shook his head. 'All I know,' he said, 'is that any time I try to make a buck I lose my ass.' There was renewed clamour from the pit and Max clenched his teeth. 'Look at that fuckin' market!' he said. 'Twenty-two forty-five. That's twenty fuckin' cents up from where we sold that four hundred thousand.'

Vince smiled ruefully. 'Are you short?' he asked.

'Of course I'm short,' Max rasped, bustling out of the booth towards the pit. 'Isn't everyone?'

Vince's head was shaking. 'Steve isn't,' he smiled.

2

Monday 10.15 a.m.

Steve Osorio nodded in approval. Standing between gold and silver, his eyes took in the volume indicator at the other side of the auditorium: it was ten-fifteen and of the fifty thousand crude oil contracts already traded on NYMEX that morning, GiltStock had done seven thousand of them. Osorio nodded again. The aggressive marketing methods and cut-throat commissions he had pushed over the years had paid off – in commodities GiltStock was still the fastest growing outfit on Wall Street and that was the way Osorio intended it to stay.

The crowd noise rose further and Osorio's eye went to the board once more. March oil was being strongly bid. He glanced to the pit where the traders were shouting at each other like madmen, then he did a quick calculation. That morning, on the opening, he had purchased two hundred and fifty March oil contracts at twenty-two dollars and fifteen cents a barrel, the equivalent to a quarter of a million barrels of crude. The trades had been nominally intended for the large discretionary fund which GiltStock managed and now March oil was suddenly trading at twenty-two forty-five.

Osorio made his way briskly to a booth where he whispered to Vince Carpenter. Vince turned to the pit and bellowed at Max. Max dived headlong into the screaming throng. There was no discernable break in the noise level, but a few seconds later he emerged and tic-tacked the result of his foray back to the booth where Vince nodded once to Steve Osorio. Osorio spoke again. Vince indicated that he understood and picked up the tie-line to give the trade to GiltStock's accounts department.

A nominee account with an address in Miami would that evening be nearly fifty thousand dollars better off. Osorio smiled and brushed ink-black hair back from his collar. It was a good start to the day by any yardstick.

'Nice play, Steve,' said Vince.

'Thanks, Vince,' Osorio responded. 'I see volume is holding up pretty well.'

'Volume is fantastic,' said Vince, 'but trying to guess the direction of the next fifty cents is the problem.'

A roaring from the pit brought both men's attention to the board. March oil had slipped back three cents from where Osorio had sold minutes before.

'See what I mean?' Vince said. He looked at Osorio in genuine awe. 'We're down here the whole goddamm day, we're meant to be the experts. How the hell do you do it?' he asked.

Osorio's eyes for the briefest moment took on a faraway look. 'Call it feel,' he said, then he grinned and touched Vince on the arm. 'See you later,' he said and walked into the throng.

3

Monday 10.30 a.m.

Vince Carpenter looked after Osorio in unconcealed admiration. Where would he be without Osorio? Without the faith which Osorio had placed in him? Vince had started out in sugar as a clerk for GiltStock, eight years ago, aged eighteen. Those days, he still lived with his parents on East 14th Street. Vince had a big bellowing voice which made him a natural. You stood your ground, you opened your mouth and you willed the other guy to trade with *you*.

He could not remember when exactly he discovered he could trade for his own account, but it was a Friday evening in summer, after the markets, in a bar someplace, and he had suddenly come to realise that he was the only one not doing it.

So easy. Everyone wanted business, you opened an account with another firm, no one knew and anyway most of your trades would be opened and closed the same day. It made sense. If money couldn't be made watching the big boys on the floor, handling their own goddamm money for Chrissakes, how could it be made?

He lost his ass. He sold his car. He sold his tv set. He sold a stamp collection which he had inherited from his grandfather. He went prematurely grey. He had to go see a guy, in an office on Broadway and 89th, who'd never once stopped smiling as he wrote Vince out the cheque.

The goons had been around twice, once at night, once on a Sunday morning, thankfully each time Vince's parents had been out. Vince had felt terror as he had never imagined. He couldn't eat or sleep. He lost weight. Then he plucked up the courage and went to see Osorio.

'How much are you into them for?' asked Osorio coolly.

'It's fifteen grand now, with interest,' Vince whispered, his ears screaming, his eyes on the carpet.

An eternity had passed, then he made himself look up. Osorio was sitting like a statue, waiting.

'I'm going to write you out a cheque for fifteen grand,' said Osorio softly when their eyes met. 'But first I want to hear your promise.'

'I promise I'll pay you back,' Vince said, overcome with relief. 'I swear to God I will.'

'That's not the promise I want to hear,' Osorio said quietly.

Vince gulped as he suddenly realised what the other man meant. He closed his eyes, then took a very deep breath.

'You have my promise,' he said slowly, 'that as of this minute,

I'll never trade for myself again.'

Osorio had shrugged, taken out a personal cheque-book and written out the amount.

'It's so simple,' he said, handing the money across.

'I can't tell you how much I appreciate this,' said Vince with feeling.

'Forget it,' Osorio had smiled. 'That's what friends are for.'

4

Monday 10.45 a.m.

Osorio prowled around the far side of silver. The supple leather of his crocodile footwear crunched discarded litter, a good inch deep even at this early hour. Any morning he was in New York he made a point of spending time down here on the floor. He had two traders and eight clerks working gold and silver alone, as well as others in cocoa and coffee and sugar.

Brent had taught him everything. Everytime Osorio traded he felt it was really Brent at work. In the last ten years they'd talked a few times, long distance. Osorio wondered whether Brent had changed; he rubbed his jaw reflectively; if they ever bothered to do an autopsy on Steve Osorio, they'd find a bump the size of a marble on his jaw where his old man had hit him the morning he said he was going away.

Funny that, the way people think they own you. He would have died for Brent. More like brothers, which they physically resembled, than a father and son. Lean, hard bodies. A way of walking on the balls of their feet. Olive eyes like the Kiowa Apache, hand-downs from great-grandma Osorio who Brent said great-grandpa had bought on the Oklahoma border for two cases of fire-water and a stainless-steel knife. Osorio remembered her, ancient, smoked black skin, gutting chickens in Amarillo, she didn't mind the blood on her bare feet.

Osorio's nostrils picked up the smell of expensive perfume. A lady broker in shimmering blue and gold bracelets was making her way past him.

14

'Morning, Steve.' Her smile would melt butter.

'Hi, honey,' Osorio grinned and watched her swing by, all curve and leg and clanking jewelry. From the gold pit someone let out a low wolf-whistle and Osorio turned away in laughter. He looked at the board and the surging throng beneath it. While most of them traded oil from the short side, hoping it would fall so they could buy it in cheaper, his instinct was always to be long, to buy oil as it rose. That was his legacy from Brent. 'Cheap oil ain't worth a sheet, little fellah. What d'we want drill holes in the ground for to pump up barrels of piss?' Osorio scratched his head. Unlike the people here, he understood oil. Oil, clean and black, squirting out of the earth, you ducked your head and let it wash you.

He had used this understanding first to start GiltStock, then to build it into what it now was; nowadays when GiltStock moved, particularly on oil, the markets were beginning to notice. And people who hadn't heard of Steve Osorio would soon realise that a new voice existed on Wall Street. Osorio nodded. As vice-chairman-elect of NYMEX he had the perfect platform to make his voice heard, to say something interesting, to ask penetrating questions. His forthcoming accession speech at the NYMEX annual dinner would be one he intended to be remembered.

There was money but there was also privilege. Until you had the first you didn't know how badly you wanted the second. Osorio sighed and looked at nothing in particular: with the same determination which he had used to build GiltStock, he was now on the verge of giving himself something which Brent never could: he was about to get class. If a year ago anyone had told him that in three weeks time we would be married, he would have quicker believed that The Gulf of Mexico would freeze in summer. He had always considered himself too obsessive, too ambitious for the domestic ties which a marriage would involve.

But here he was, Steve Osorio, with three weeks to go.

Monday 12.00 noon

Like a mote in a sunbeam the squash ball licked through space and into the back corner of the court. The bigger player went for it: although the angle was all against him, he managed to scoop a shot out to the playing wall, but it was weak and recognising it he began to scramble forward for position. His opponent who had never once left the centre of the shining deal floor slammed his reply with such force that the black ball ended its rebound again behind. Caught off balance, the bigger player lunged back, but too late.

'Well done, Steve,' he panted, tearing off his wide headband. 'My lunch, as usual.'

Steve Osorio wiped his arm across his forehead. 'You made me work, Ron,' he said.

They shook hands and walked through the small door of the squash court. Side by side, their physical types contrasted: Osorio the more mobile of the two, his body gracefully powerful as he peeled off his sports shirt; his friend, Ron Spirakis, also powerful, but strength achieved by mass, by the width of his shoulders, by his height and by the obvious strength of his limbs.

'How're your markets today?' Ron asked as he stepped under a steaming shower.

Water sluiced down Osorio's gleaming body. 'Pretty much unchanged,' he answered. 'Oil tried to rally earlier, but as usual, it got zapped. Anything new in the world of banking?'

'Nothing inspiring,' Ron said.

'How's Cristy?'

'She sends her love. She wants to know why a brother and sister who both live on the same little island only see each other once a year.'

Osorio laughed. 'She's a good kid,' he said. 'She still wants to become the most famous financial reporter in New York?'

'That's her,' Ron replied. 'Talk about marriage to her and you get a wall.' He rinsed himself. 'But talk to her about a plot to destabilise the Fed and you won't shut her up for a week.'

The members' bar was wood-panelled and portrait-hung with

fine views of New York Harbour.

'Mr Osorio.'

The barman held his hand over the phone's mouthpiece.

'*The New York Post* . I didn't say you were here.'

'I'll take it,' said Osorio, sitting on a stool. 'Steve Osorio.' He looked at Ron as he listened. 'Yes,' he said, 'I understand both the governor and the mayor will be there.' He shook his head from side to side. 'Yes, and Elizabeth Taylor, she's an old friend of the Tremaine family. But can I suggest you call Mr Tremaine's office direct? Thank you. No, I've no comment except to say that we're both extremely happy.'

A steward in a crisp, white jacket placed a platter of pink, open-faced beef-on-bread and a pot of mustard on a low table. Osorio drank deeply of sparkling water and sat back; in the sun shining from over the Verrazano Narrows, his face glowed.

'I guess you're talking about quite a production out there in Lloyd's Neck,' said Ron, smearing mustard thickly on meat.

'Work has been going on for six months,' Osorio said. 'Dutch has built a ballroom in the garden, the exact replica of one in Vienna, so that everyone can waltz at the same time. He's refurbished the entire house. He's block booked the local hotel one month ahead of the wedding and insisted that they redecorate it completely to his specification.'

'Hey, ah, excuse me,' said Ron in a good takeoff of Dutch Tremaine, 'my daughter's route takes her past the Brooklyn Bridge, do you think you could have that painted by Wednesday next?'

They laughed together.

'Carly is Dutch's only daughter from three marriages,' Osorio said. 'He's crazy mad about her, adores the ground she walks on, literally. I thought he was going to hit me when I told him we were getting married.'

Ron wiped his mouth with a linen napkin. 'He's an extraordinary guy, isn't he?' he said seriously. 'I mean, the Tremaine's have had wealth for generations, he could have sat back and lived a life of zero hassle, yet what did he do? Rolled his sleeves up, grabbed the old family bank, turned it into Manhattan First and himself into a legend.'

'We bank there, always have done,' Osorio said.

'He's okay to deal with?' Ron asked.

'It's hard to really know a man like that,' Osorio said. He paused. 'I mean he's not just a loveable daddy.' He looked at the big man. 'Let me ask you something,' he said with interest. 'What's it like to work for one of these guys? I mean, I've heard it said that Abel Eller is the most difficult guy on Wall Street. If that's true, then you must have the most difficult job in New York.'

Ron's eyes were thoughtful as the steward removed plates and presented porcelain cups and a silver pot.

'Abel Eller runs a tight ship,' he said. 'Each member of the Durst Bank crew knows his place.'

'Which is to say, bankers don't discuss ship's details with squash partners,' Osorio smiled.

Ron's face was enigmatic. 'Abel Eller invented the saying, "loose lips sink ships", to continue the metaphor,' he said. He poured them both coffee. 'Steve, this is changing the subject, but there's something I want to mention.'

'Go right ahead,' said Osorio.

Ron's big face showed concern. 'Cristy is worried about Brent's position for the wedding.'

When Osorio frowned, his eyes immediately became defensive, dangerous.

'What position?'

'You know what I mean, Steve.'

'I don't know.'

'He's her old man too, Steve,' Ron said gently. 'She doesn't want him hurt.'

Osorio looked away. 'Does she think she knows him any better than I do? Do either of us know him? I haven't seen him for nearly ten years, last I heard he was living with some teenage girl south of Abilene.'

'I'm only a messenger,' Ron said, 'but I know and care for your sister.'

Osorio eyes were cold. 'Brent wouldn't fit in up here, Ron,' he said. 'It wouldn't be the right thing to do to make him feel out of place. Cristy's lost touch.'

'Come on, Steve,' Ron said. 'You and she are close. She told me.'

'How, told you?'

'About how you looked after her when she first got to New

York; about how you found her a job before she went to work for the *Journal.*'

Osorio let himself relax. 'Let me think about Brent, okay?' he said.

'Sure,' said Ron as they both got to their feet.

At street level they stood for a moment before going their separate ways.

'I meant to mention it,' Ron said, 'but it looks as if I'm going to have pass on your big night at the NYMEX dinner. Sorry, but work keeps interfering with my social life.'

'I'm sorry too,' Osorio said. He smiled. 'I'm tired of endless speeches at these dinners. I've got something to make them all sit up – especially the oil bears.'

'Oh yes?'

'I'm going to talk about information,' Osorio said. 'Information is so crucial to our industry, to what we do. A lot of the time we're operating on imperfect information, facts that may be fed to the market by people with a vested interest. It can cost us tens of millions.'

'Sounds interesting,' said Ron. 'Where does oil come into it?'

'I've come across an article written by a geologist down in Houston,' Osorio said. 'The guy is probably crazy, what he says sounds off the wall. But it's interesting. He challenges the Jap estimates on their oil find. He challenges the accepted information which is exactly the type of provocative angle I want to get across in my speech.'

'I'm sorry I'll miss it,' Ron said. Osorio looked at him for a moment, then reached to an inside pocket.

'There's no need to,' he smiled, 'here it is. Read it and let me know what you think.'

'I'm no oil expert,' said Ron, taking the speech.

'Just give me your opinion,' said Osorio. He laughed. 'But Ron, don't show it to Cristy. I don't want it on page one of the *Journal.*'

19

6

Osorio had to ring twice before the apartment door was opened. The girl standing there had black hair, tied up, and was wearing a waistcoat with clusters of pins stuck in the lapels.

'Are you Steve?'

'Yes.'

'Miss Tremaine said to come on in. She can't move, we're fitting her.'

Osorio walked into the familiar lobby, marble underfoot, modern art at eye-level and a ceiling all inlaid with mirrors. The theme was repeated through to the expansive living-room, two apartments knocked together with floor to ceiling glass which gave unforgettable views over Manhattan. There was a white piano, white leather chairs and sofas, a raised bar, deep pile rugs, pieces of sculpture and, on a dais at the extreme other end, surrounded by kneeling people, Carly Tremaine. In a snow-white, cascading gown, she stood like some priceless icon, her very blonde hair tumbling diaphanously around her shoulders, an escutcheon for her very pretty face. At her hem a man and a woman worked while to the boa of lace at her neck a further man made adjustments. As Osorio came into view this man stood back, clasping his hands.

'Am I seeing something I'm not meant to?' Osorio called.

'Of course not,' Carly replied. 'I think we're nearly through.' She turned herself sideways to a full-length mirror, raised her breasts and smoothed the line of her stomach with both her hands. 'What do you think, Maurice? A little higher lift?'

Maurice, fully a foot shorter than Carly and clearly wearing a wig, pouted.

'No, no, darling; just so is fan-tas-tic. You embody fantasy. Any more would be . . . over.'

Carly sighed. 'I haven't the energy to argue,' she said. 'Get me out of this thing, will you?'

The hem pinchers doubled their efforts as Maurice peeled open the back of the dress from Carly's neck down to the floor and the girl who had admitted Osorio held a robe for the future

20

Mrs Osorio to step into. Large boxes frothing with tissue were produced, the dress was packed reverentially away and Maurice minced out backwards after his troupe, murmuring confirmation that he would be back again in four days.

'Hi,' Osorio smiled. 'How is the big world of publishing today?'

'I think we're getting the formula about right,' replied Carly, brushing her hair. 'Women's magazines is a jungle, but I'm frankly not just publishing *Mirror* for just any woman, you know what I mean? I guess what I'm saying is, *Mirror* isn't just a magazine, but a way of life.' She straightened up and smiled at Osorio. 'The way of life I know, I guess,' she said. 'How was your day?'

'Not too strenuous,' Osorio smiled. 'Oil went the right way for once; I played Ron at squash and got my lunch paid for; I gave a telephone interview to some woman columnist from *The New York Post.*'

Carly leaned her head to one side so that her hair cascaded, then began to brush it underneath.

'So what did they want?' she asked.

'The usual. It is true the governor is coming ? And the mayor? And Elizabeth Taylor?' He paused for effect. '"Is it true, Mr Osorio, that you're the happiest man in New York?"'

Carly stopped. 'To which you replied . . . ?'

Osorio made a face. 'I asked her to be more specific. I mean "happiest" is a pretty subjective term. I mean . . . '

Carly put her brush down. 'You said *what?*'

'Come here,' Osorio murmured. 'Do you know how beautiful you are?'

She came to him, her arms out. She caught the back of his head and licked all around the outside of his mouth. 'Did Daddy get you?' she murmured.

'I was meant to call him back,' Osorio replied.

'Naughty, naughty,' she mumbled, her tongue now at his throat. 'One thing we must always do: when Daddy calls we must right away call him back.'

Osorio undid the belt of her robe and slid his hands inside and under the elastic of her knickers. Carletta's mouth continued its downward creep until she had to kneel.

'What going on down here?' she cried.

Osorio closed his eyes and smiled as she unzipped him, then popped him out, taut and straining, in front of the cheval mirror. 'Mirror, mirror,' Carletta intoned, shrugging off her robe, 'tell me, your queen, truthfully, if ever you have seen anything as beautiful before?'

'Isn't the mirror meant to reply?' Osorio asked.

'It is,' Carletta whispered, 'but it can't because it's busy.'

Osorio drew in his breath as she took him.

'Oh, Christ,' she gasped after two minutes, 'I live for this.'

Osorio began to slowly undress, throwing his clothes to the ground, watching the golden head in the mirror as it bobbed, feeling her fingers as they began to work. Eventually, she caught him and like someone in a daze, led him to a long leather couch directly in front of an enormous window through which most of night-time Manhattan could be seen.

'I hope no one is using binoculars tonight,' he said.

'If they are,' Carletta whispered, 'they'll never have seen anything as big as this.' In full view of the window she sank down and took him again, working him up and down, faster and faster. Osorio held back her hair: Carletta pumped with frenzy.

'Come on,' Osorio growled.

She slid beneath him; just at his moment of entry she arched, then locked her long legs around him. Osorio finished it. At the final moment, he saw not the perfect face beneath him, nor the hundred thousand eyes which he imagined looking in, but the changing prices on the board of NYMEX, which registered light, sweet Texas crude.

CHAPTER TWO

1

Houston, Texas

Eric Gerhardt was a big man. Forty years before there had been a physical presence about him, an unrefined rawness which people found interesting. They related his size and strength to his work: they saw, or thought they saw, geology as a man.

But time had changed all that. Now there was size without elegance. A big head, square shaped and topped with some strands of greying hair. A mouth, crooked as a fissure, and above it erratic patches of hair, not joined, never really a moustache.

His office contained, on shelves and in boxes, the rocks of his trade. Many years before, so far back that he could not remember when, those rocks had been Gerhardt's pride. He had had them mounted on stands with plaques which gave their age. Shale: 300 million years. Sandstone from the Jurassic era: 200 million years. Limestone: 700 million years, formed before life itself had come to earth. The stands of rock had been either boxed or shoved to the end of dusty shelves to make way for the tide of papers and periodicals that Gerhardt never seemed to get around to. He ran his finger inside his collar and peered to the outer office.

The girl at the typewriter had long, dark hair and looked about twenty-two. When the work mounted up Gerhardt called one of the downtown agencies and they sent out a girl to do it.

This one had worked hard all morning; some of them tried to stretch the work out, but not this one. As he looked, she flicked a page from the typewriter, said 'phew!', then looked in at him with a smile. For the first time, Gerhardt noticed her brown eyes.

'That's it,' she said.

'You're through?' he asked, looking at his watch.

She nodded.

'Well, thanks,' Gerhardt said, getting to his feet. He watched her as she got up and reached for her bag. She wore jeans and had very long legs. She wore a short-sleeved, white blouse. Probably a student, working her way through college.

'Goodbye, and thanks once more,' Gerhardt said.

'My pleasure,' she replied. At the door she paused. 'By the way, Mr Gerhardt, I enjoy the work here. Anytime you want, just call.'

Gerhardt stood as the door closed, blinking. Then his face lit up.

'Hey!' he called and opened the door.

She was at the elevator.

'If I want them to send you again, who do I ask for?'

'Just ask for Jen,' she smiled as the elevator opened.

2

Gerhardt checked the empty mail-box in the lobby. Although his apartment was on the first floor, he rode the elevator.

Alone. All his life alone. It should have got easier but it never had.

He let himself in, walked to a side table and poured two fingers from the scotch bottle. Picking up an open magazine, he sat and gazed towards the window. Night-time Houston outside, a world full of people with whom he no longer had any contact. He fingered the pages in his lap. For six months he had tried to get someone to publish the article. First bemused, he had become increasingly depressed at each new letter of rejection. It became a matter of supreme importance.

Then a shaft of light: a publication in New York he'd never

24

heard of called *Key Stone* said they would buy it. The result was on his knees.

He smiled as he read the article. It was essential that it should have been written. There was a principle here. He had swallowed his pride all those years ago but now it was too much. Twenty-five billion barrels? It was outlandish, brazen, it was . . . obscene!

Gerhardt looked to a sideboard and his smile widened. At least there was one other person who had found the whole thing interesting. From where he sat Gerhardt could read the lettering on the invitation:

The President of the New York Mercantile Exchange requests the pleasure of your company.

What had the broker's name been again? Gerhardt frowned, then nodded. Osorio. He'd called three time for details, whatever his interest was. Then the invitation to the oil dinner had come, out of the blue. A nice gesture. It was good to be appreciated again. It was years since he had been to New York.

Gerhardt picked up the magazine and held it out before him.

'The Myth of Ishikari Bay,' he read aloud.

Outside, Houston slept.

CHAPTER THREE

1

New York

Thursday 7 February 9.00 a.m.

The elevator doors hummed open and Osorio walked past a large, gold-coloured sign saying 'GILTSTOCK', through a carpeted lobby, past a receptionist and in through double doors to the trading room of the firm which he had started nine years ago in a ten-by-six rented office over a drug store.

The scene sizzled with activity. Traders sat, grouped according to their markets, each of their positions a half-mooned console containing three touch monitors linking them to every financial centre on earth and a recessed keyboard to access GiltStock's thousand megabyte computer.

Osorio made his way through, heading for the boardroom on the far side. To his left was a section, rounded for the exchange of information, where base and precious metals were traded. An attractive woman in her middle twenties sat, a telephone in each hand; as Osorio passed she looked up and caught his eye. Osorio smiled and kept going. He passed groups of threes and fours, back to back, where the edible commodities and oil were traded. At the desk reserved for the trading of financial instruments a man with a shining, bald head was shouting something into a telephone. Nearly everyone was smoking. Over fifty traders sat in this windowless room which every day turned over more than the GNP of a fair-sized country. While most New Yorkers slept as copper opened in London or gold closed in Hong Kong, in GiltStock the endless trading continued with scarcely a lull for the cleaners to hurry in and clear out the debris of the day before.

'Steve!'

A trader was waving a phone.

Osorio shook his head. 'Not now,' he shouted. 'I'll call back.'

'It's Vince,' called the man over the noise of the room.

Osorio stopped. He sat down at an empty console and pressed a switch.

'Yeah, Vince?'

'It's twenty-two fifteen again on the March, Steve,' said the voice of Vince Carpenter. 'You asked me to keep you informed.'

Osorio thought for a moment. Over the telephone he could hear the noise of the oil futures market at work.

'Any reasons?' he asked.

'The usual word that there's a big seller around,' answered Vince, 'but no clues yet as to who. If I get a glimpse through the wall I'll let you know.'

Osorio's eyes went to a screen where March oil had just traded again at twenty-two dollars and fifteen cents a barrel.

'Buy a hundred thousand of the March at twenty-two fifteen or better,' he said and disconnected.

Osorio liked the space of the boardroom; although he had his own office he rarely used it, preferring to work from one end of a vast, sweeping table from where he could see the skyline of the city that was now home. A stand on wheels beside his chair carried a duplicate batch of the communications devices used by each trader outside. In addition, three wall-mounted monitors which swivelled directionally in response to a hand-held remote, flickered continuously with market data. Osorio sat and the intercom came to life.

'Steve, Vince again on six.'

Osorio hit six. 'Yeah, Vince?' he asked, his eyes now on the wall screens.

'Steve, filled that hundred order,' said Vince Carpenter.

'Thanks,' said Osorio.

A door at the far end of the boardroom opened and Osorio's secretary came in.

'Marilee, hi,' Osorio said.

'Hi,' she smiled.

Marilee's legs, good legs, extra long today with her tartan skirt.

'What have you got?' Osorio asked.

'Well, the usual calls,' she said, 'most of which I've been able to deal with.' She handed Osorio a sheet of paper. 'Other than those, Miss Tremaine says she'll be at home from six. Mr Dutch Tremaine wonders if you'll call him. And the travel agent has been on, those reservations for Egypt in three weeks' time are just fine.'

'Okay,' Osorio nodded.

'Now to your nine-fifteen appointment,' said Marilee. 'They arrived five minutes ago, I gave them coffee, they're in the waiting room.'

'They?'

'A gentleman and a lady.'

'Okay,' Osorio said again.

Marilee opened her top file. 'They represent a company called Gabriel Holdings, Caymen registered with offices in Geneva. As you know, they called a week ago, didn't want to see anyone but you. I've tried to find out something on them, as instructed, but other than what I've told you, no one has ever heard of Gabriel Holdings – and that includes Manhattan First Bank and Dun and Bradstreet. But now that they're here, there's one thing I can tell you about them.'

Osorio's eyebrows arched.

'They're Arabs,' Marilee whispered.

Osorio watched Marilee's legs again as she walked through the end door; Marilee was safely married to a tv company sound engineer, but sometimes her inflections left Osorio wondering. Now, for example, she was striding back in, smiling enigmatically, beside a fat man in a grey, mohair suit and a woman.

'Mr Ahmed of Gabriel Holdings, Mr Osorio,' Marilee announced. 'And Miss Ahmed.'

Osorio stepped forward, clasped the man's soft hand, smiled into his pudgy face, then turned to the woman and immediately understood Marilee's game. He saw very brown eyes, shoulder length black hair and an amazingly attractive face.

Osorio took air in sharply through both nostrils.

'Pleased to meet you,' he said. He indicated chairs, pulled out one for himself, sat and crossed his legs. 'I'm sorry I have not been able to see you before now,' he said, smiling to them both, 'but I'm sure you'll understand the pressures in this business.'

The girl had also crossed her legs; Osorio noticed her hands, joined in her lap, and a gold bracelet on a wrist which showed a sheen of fine black hairs. Spontaneously, he felt himself distend; pointedly, he locked his eyes on the man. 'So how can GiltStock help you, sir?' he asked.

'Mr Osorio.' Ahmed sat back, both hands across his belly, a gesture which sought to bring the pace of conversation down to a slower gear. He spoke English in a stilted, slightly sing-song manner. 'Your company, GiltStock, is greatly admired,' he said. 'In all the commodities markets, you have people. You publish research which is sensible and often quoted. GiltStock Voice, yes?'

Osorio nodded.

'Your reputation in executing orders is high, your commissions reasonable. You are, as they say in America, people to watch,' Ahmed said.

'Thank you,' Osorio replied. His eyes kept deserting Ahmed's oily face for the girl's, in profile studious as it watched her father, if father he was.

'We are particularly impressed,' Ahmed continued, 'with what GiltStock Voice has had to say over the last twelve months about the price of oil.'

Osorio could smell the musk of her perfume. 'We?' he enquired.

Ahmed held up an admonitory finger. 'We find your view very close to our own, Mr Osorio. Very high rates of industrial production and consumption in the West, controlled output by OPEC, a situation in the Middle East which continues to be far from stable, and yet – oil, each month, loses new ground.'

Osorio nodded and reflexively checked a wall monitor: March oil last traded at twenty-two ten. He looked at the girl whose eyes were now on him; she wore a white blouse up to her neck, but there was no hiding her figure which was full and firm and collected at her waist with a gold-coloured sash. She had star quality.

Ahmed had taken from his pocket what Osorio saw to be a back issue of GiltStock Voice. He fitted spectacles and began to

read: ' "A market which continually refuses to recognise fundamentals is a dangerous place to be, even for day-traders. Oil in
the low. twenties is a slumbering giant which will one day come
to life." ' Ahmed beamed. ' "Slumbering giant." That is the
expression which, Mr Osorio, meant more to my people than
anything.'

'There are factors which the market chooses to notice,'
Osorio said patiently. 'The most obvious is the recent Japanese
oil find.' Osorio's practised eye saw March oil tick at twenty-two
twelve and the tip of the girl's tongue as briefly it pressed her
lower lip. 'I for one feel the selling is overdone, but that is not to
say that I think I can always beat it. These markets are living,
dangerous things. They devour good men.' Osorio brushed his
hair back. 'So how, sir, can I be of help to you?' he asked once
more.

Ahmed leaned forward. 'You asked, Mr Osorio, about "we". I
am here as the representative of powerful people. Very powerful. If you insist on knowing their identities, then I regret that we
will not be doing business together. But please accept my word
when I tell you that we are talking about men for whom money
does not represent a problem.'

Osorio smiled. 'In my experience, Mr Ahmed,' he said reasonably, 'money is always a problem. But please go on.'

Ahmed also smiled, the smile of the desert fox. 'Gabriel
Holdings is named after a figure in mythology,' he said. 'The
angel Gabriel, an avenging angel, a saint with a sword, a warrior
in the battle against evil.' He paused. 'This time, Mr Osorio,
Gabriel will do battle for oil.'

'You want to buy oil?' Osorio asked impassively.

'Yes, sir.'

'A lot of oil?'

'Yes, sir.'

'You want to buy a lot of oil using the futures markets in the
belief that you'll push the price up?'

'That is nearly correct.'

Osorio waited.

'We intend to buy a lot of oil on the futures markets in order
to make a great profit *when* the price of oil goes up,' Ahmed
said. 'Draw your own conclusions from what I say, Mr Osorio.
Naturally we expect our buying to help push up the price, but

essentially the action of the people whom I represent is motivated entirely by profit.'

'You mean, they expect the price to rise?'

'That is correct. Not just a rise of a dollar, or even two, but a dimensional rise, Mr Osorio, a surge in price which will mean that oil will never be the same again.'

Osorio scratched his head. 'And you want GiltStock to act?'

Ahmed inclined his head. 'We would be honoured.'

Osorio got up and went to the window where he turned. He concentrated on Ahmed's face; the girl's had an amused expression.

'You're correct to assume that I'm a bull of oil,' Osorio said, 'but I don't have access to anything other than my judgement and a good team of people to implement it. That I'm a bull of oil doesn't mean that I'm involved in some sort of crusade, I simply hold an opinion.'

Ahmed was smiling. 'We have acknowledged that you are a true professional,' he said, 'but we also think that we can recognise passion when we see it.'

Osorio couldn't keep his eyes off the girl; there was live chemistry at work between them across the room.

Osorio dragged his eyes away from her and said, 'Mr Ahmed, may we talk for a moment about futures? Most people who come in here for the first time don't understand how quickly these markets move. This is the fastest game in town. It's not just a matter of buying or selling commodities for future delivery, where you only have to put down a small margin and sit back. In a market which moves with the speed oil does, you can lose all your money, and I mean all of it, overnight. It's not like the stockmarket where you can sit for a year or two and wait for things to improve; in here, sir, what is lost is usually lost for ever.'

The girl was smiling at him. He could see the line of her legs and thighs beneath her skirt.

'Mr Ahmed, I'm a broker,' Osorio went on. 'There's an old saying which has served brokers well down the years: it is, know your client. Let's speak frankly. We've only just met. It would seem that you are talking about investments of a very significant nature for Gabriel Holdings.'

Ahmed nodded and the girl put her hand to her neck and flicked out her hair.

31

'Let me explain how GiltStock operates,' Osorio said. 'First we will not act for anyone unless we have all the financial data in place – and I mean all of it. Second, we need a recommendation on your behalf from a class one bank in this city. Third, there are significant account opening procedures to be followed, including your notarised acknowledgement that you understand all the risks inherent in these markets. Finally, there's money. We need all our initial margins, plus fifty percent in the case of a new client, up front. When margin calls occur, they must be paid into our bank same day, even when more than one call in a day may be made. In this area it must be perfectly understood that if there is a delay in transferring cash to us which may be no fault whatsoever of the clients – a bank error, for example – we will, on non-receipt of the cash, cut that client's position like you'd slit a porker.'

Ahmed had sat politely, now he reached towards the girl, rasping his fingers. From a bag she took a white envelope and handed it to him; Ahmed ferried it onwards to Osorio.

'Please conclude your enquiries, Mr Osorio,' he said, rising to his feet. 'We do, of course, understand perfectly well everything you have said.' He gestured to the girl. 'All our instructions will be made through Laisha.'

Osorio looked at her, also on her feet, slit the envelope and withdrew a banker's cheque in favour of GiltStock for fifteen million U.S. dollars.

'Any correspondence should be sent to this address.'

Osorio blinked and realised that Laisha had spoken for the first time. He took the card.

'My father likes to work with people he trusts,' she smiled. Her English was Americanised and perfect. 'You notice he has just trusted you with fifteen million of his dollars without any notarised acknowledgement of the inherent risks involved.'

Osorio could not help himself smiling. 'I'll send the necessary papers on,' he said as they walked to the door. Marilee appeared with coats.

Ahmed bowed, offering his hand. The girl's hand was warm and stayed for just the briefest instant too long. Osorio felt himself surge.

He watched Marilee escort them out, then he walked back the length of the boardroom and stood by the window where he shook himself. The attraction had been immediate: two animals, visceral and intense. Osorio breathed deeply, looked down at the small card, smelled the musk of her which seemed to have attached itself to him. He stood for some minutes, waiting for his blood to fall. He looked at the screens. Twenty-two twelve on the March. He walked to the table and slid the cheque out of its envelope. He bit his lip, shook his head and went to the intercom. 'Malcolm,' he said, 'could you get in here for a moment, please? Bring Cheryl and Jay with you.'

As they came in Osorio looked at each carefully.

Malcolm Finch, white, wavy hair framing a face pale from many thousands of hours of drifting cigarette smoke and squinting up at flickering screens. Loyal to the last.

Jay Cox, disaffectionately known as Suck, had earned his spurs in the financial futures area.

And Cheryl. What a face, what a figure. So poised, so professional . . . but so cold. As cold as the precious metals she traded. Could she really be that cold?

Osorio put his feet up on the boardroom table.

'What do you think of oil?' he said.

Malcolm Finch screwed up his face. He took a packet of cigarettes from his shirt pocket and offered one to Cox, then to Osorio who declined but selected himself a long, thin cheroot. As Cheryl sat and watched, all three men lit up and blew smoke into the boardroom air.

'I wouldn't want to be long of it,' replied Malcolm eventually.

Osorio nodded.

'The March is on its way down to twenty-two this morning,' Malcolm continued. 'That's the third straight decline this week. It's looking lousy on the chart, it looks certain to test lower levels.'

'Reasons?' said Osorio.

Malcolm stretched. 'Fundamentally oil has been in trouble for a year now,' he said. 'It seems many moons ago that oil was forty dollars a barrel. Why the decline? Smaller cars, nuclear energy, even goddamm wave power, they're all working against the market. Then there's the oil find in Japan – that really put the cap on it. Me, I'd want to trade it from the short side.'

'Although that is the accepted wisdom,' said Cheryl crisply, 'there may be some grounds for thinking that the selling has been overdone.' She felt Osorio's eyes on her and involuntarily smoothed the collar of her jacket. 'I was looking at the chart last night; oil is approaching a point of major resistance – the twenty dollar a barrel mark. It could bounce quite strongly from there and might be worth buying. I do, however, agree with Malcolm on the fundamentals. Nowadays, there are oil people out there in a lot of trouble.'

Jay Cox resembled in almost every department a series of eggs: a white, shining dome of an egghead incorporating an almost perfectly oval face sat upon a rotund body, its chest encased in an ovum of a waistcoat. His eyes, his wire glasses, even his nostrils resembled a basket of *oeufs à la coque*. Now he ground out his partially smoked cigarette. 'I agree,' he said. 'OPEC is a thing of the past – those assholes dug their own grave.' He shrugged his round shoulders and offered both upturned hands to the room. 'So they dug their own grave.'

Osorio controlled his irritation. 'I've just met with some potential new clients,' he said. 'They're Arabs. They appear to be fronting for an operation based in Geneva, goes by the name of Gabriel Holdings. They say oil is going to rise. They want to buy it and they want us to act for them.'

'Geneva is where OPEC's headquarters is located,' Cheryl said.

'That's right,' Osorio nodded.

'What sort of introduction do they come with?' asked Jay Cox.

'At this point, a tellers cheque for fifteen million,' Osorio replied.

Jay Cox spoke: 'What bank is the cheque drawn on?'

Osorio thumbed the cheque into view. 'Durst Bank,' he replied.

'And what did you tell them?' Cox asked.

'I told them we need all their stats before we agree to anything,' Osorio replied.

'Could they be OPEC?' Malcolm asked. 'Shit, is there a chance they could be OPEC?'

'They could be anybody,' Osorio replied.

'Jesus, imagine GiltStock acting for OPEC,' Malcolm said and rubbed his hands. 'You know something?' he said seriously. 'I really believe that if they tried they could steady oil by buying into this market. NYMEX is big enough now, it's liquid enough.'

'Do these people understand position limits?' Cheryl asked.

'Did you explain to them that they can't just buy huge quantities of oil and not tell anyone? That we have reporting procedures to comply with?'

'I'll inform them of that if and when we decide to do business with them,' Osorio replied.

Jay Cox shook his head. 'I get a chill when I hear about OPEC and the like,' he said. 'I don't like them, especially the Arabs, they're sovereign governments who up to the other day have been wandering around in the sand looking for two flat stones. They invented reneging. They screw their camels. I don't like them.'

'You can't confine doing business to people you like,' Osorio said.

'We've made rules to deal with these situations,' said Cox standing up. 'Remember our famous Chinese friends who went long of gold at seven hundred?'

'That didn't cost GiltStock a red cent,' said Osorio drily.

'But there were moments in the game,' Cox said, 'when the palms of all our hands were a little more than moist.'

'Jay, I think that's unfair,' said Osorio.

'Steve.' Cox was resting his hands on the back of the chair he had sat on. 'I work my ass off out there in the financial futures markets,' he said with what went for a smile on his face. 'Personally I don't give a fuck if they start giving oil away in the morning; all I'm interested in is that at the end of the day GiltStock is able to pay me my bonus.'

Cheryl Leinster also rose and was smoothing her skirt. 'If you gentlemen will excuse me,' she said. She looked at Osorio. 'I'll have a fresh look at the charts tonight, Steve,' she said.

'Thanks, Cheryl,' said Osorio. He turned to Malcolm as she left the room. 'I've made some notes on my conversation with the Arabs. I'll have Marilee do them up and give you a copy. See if you can come up with anything on them from your end.'

'Sure, Steve,' said Malcolm Finch.

Osorio scratched his head. 'Why do I put up with that shit from Suck?' he asked.

Malcom Finch shrugged. 'Because he's the best bond trader either you or I have ever come across,' he said. 'Don't let him get to you – he's like that, it's what makes him able to make money.'

'Did you know that when Suck buys a book he buys two copies?' Osorio asked. 'One he keeps and the other he actually writes comments on and sends to the author. I'm serious, he told me himself.'

The intercom blared as Finch left the room.

'Yeah?' Osorio said.

'Steve, Ray.'

'Hi, Ray.'

Ray Leonard, GiltStock's accountant, two storeys below, was a bearded, hulking man who looked like a country and western singer. A considerable computer expert, Ray has written most of GiltStock's programmes himself.

'Did you see the Bears last night?' Ray asked.

'They were pure shit,' said Osorio.

'Is this an appropriate moment to discuss our small outstanding wager?' asked the accountant.

'You son-of-a-bitch,' Osorio grinned. 'You want to let it roll?'

'Hmmm,' came the reply. 'I think I'd like to turn some of my position into cash.'

'Like how much?'

'Fifty percent?'

'Okay,' said Osorio, reaching for his wallet. 'Ten dollars is on its way down to you – and you've ten rolling against the Broncos.'

'*Exquisito,*' Ray Leonard said.

'By the way, Ray,' Osorio said, 'I met with some potential new clients this morning, I've made some notes, they're on their way to you.'

'Okay, José,' Ray said, 'I'll make the enquiries.'

'Wonderful,' Osorio said, looking at his watch. He had an outside meeting in ten minutes with a floor broker called Tony Quagliano, known to everyone on Wall Street as Tony Quacks.

'Just one thing, Steve,' Ray Leonard said. 'I got a hundred thousand barrel buy execution for March oil at twenty-two fifteen from Vince. He says you put it in. Who is it for?'

'What's oil now?' Osorio asked even though he knew the answer.

Ray Leonard could be heard tapping a keyboard. 'Twenty-two o-five,' he replied. 'The position is losing ten grand at the moment.'

Osorio swore to himself. 'I'm late for a meeting with Tony Quacks, Ray,' he said. 'Sell it out for a day-trade.'

'Understood, Steve,' said the accountant. 'And the loss? What do I do with that?'

Osorio shook his head. 'Oh, put it into the fucking fund,' he said and left the boardroom, slamming its door behind him.

2

Thursday 3.30 p.m.

At her desk in the trading room, Cheryl Leinster opened her handbag, took out a small mirror and looked at herself. Her big, grey eyes looked back, eyes framed by thick off-blonde hair.

To many people she looked serious. She *was* serious, in the way that her father, a Cincinatti businessman, interpreted the word. Serious was not someone who couldn't enjoy life, but meant the opposite to lightweight. To be a serious player meant that people took you . . . seriously. No softheads here, no sir, that's the way it is, and if you don't like it, then goddammit get out of my way!

Wall Street via Harvard and still her father had been the only man who measured up: his only child, he had taught her to fish and to trap and to drive stock-cars like a man, flinging them up inclines with him beside her, holding the torque until she thought her wrists would break. Then came Steve Osorio.

Cheryl had taken the job, base and precious metals. She wasn't disappointed. Osorio in action was something to be appreciated, savoured by people who understood such things. It wasn't just that he was a trader from when he was born; there was something extra, a supplemental equation to Osorio, an aura of something akin to magic which touched everyone every day in GiltStock and which Cheryl knew she wanted to be part of.

He had moulded her and a bunch of talented people into something cohesive. There was intense excitement, you held your head high and when someone asked and you said, 'I'm with GiltStock', you could see it from their eyes that you were scoring in there, that you had attained a piece of that extra equation yourself, just by association.

Cheryl lived in SoHo in a studio apartment off Broome Street which her father had bought for her. The building – squat with a cast-iron, neo-Grec facade – faced a small park. Cheryl was serious, and she was also solitary. She had painted since she was a child: sensitive, peaceful watercolours, mainly with water as their theme, although from the big bay window of her studio the only water visible was when it rained.

As she brought depth to streams, or white fluff to a wave's cap, Cheryl's mind saw those upward eyes, Slavic almost; she saw him walk, rolling and mobile; he would have a body lithe and supple like a salmon's; he would have perfect strength in his arms and hips and legs; he would be a joy to paint.

But at the end of the day, there was something about them both that she found incompatible: Osorio was invulnerable. This thirty-three-year-old guy with the Indian eyes and the body made by God on a good day, he was complete, total, he had no chink, no want or need, no flaw which would let Cheryl in. This was a flaw in her, she accepted, but that was the way she was. Her man, when she found him, would have an imperfection, however small, that Cheryl could recognise and say to herself, he needs me to put that right, without me he will remain less than whole. But not Osorio. He did not need anyone.

Cheryl put her mirror away and checked out her screen. Anyway, quite apart from need, Osorio was now getting married to Carly Tremaine, known as *the* Carly Tremaine if you bothered with the columns which dealt with such things, although what Osorio saw in her Cheryl couldn't fathom, he had brought her in a couple of times and she'd walked around like the queen of someplace visiting a correction centre.

Cheryl tapped her keyboard and brought Comex gold flashing up. Quiet as a graveyard. She looked at her watch. Osorio's wedding to which she had been invited but to which she did not intend to go, was in less than three weeks. Would it change him? Would it sap his dynamism, GiltStock's? He was entering a new world where money meant something entirely different to what her father had taught her.

Cheryl sighed. To everyone his taste. She picked up her brief-case and reaching for some chart books she put them in and stood up. She wanted to be home early: her father was in town and they were going to the Met together.

As she left the trading room Cheryl could see March oil on a screen, last traded twenty-one eighty.

3

New York

Thursday 8 February 6.00 p.m.

Five blocks from the athletics club, Osorio increased his speed a notch, exhilarated by his own well-being. Ron Spirakis would at this moment be leaving Durst Bank and making his way to their appointed game.

Cristy Osorio had sounded relieved the night before when Osorio had called her.

'I haven't spoken to him yet,' Osorio said. 'I don't know if he'll come.'

'Brent?' Cristy laughed. 'Of course he'll come. Think of how proud he'll be.'

'Why don't we get together, sometime middle of next week?' Osorio said. 'I'd like you and Ron to meet Carly and be my guests at dinner.'

'Sounds wonderful,' Cristy said.

'Then you can tell me what it's like to be a hot-shit financial reporter,' Osorio had laughed, and hung up before she could reply.

After the game, usual result, there was only the two of them and an attendant in the changing room. Standing under the scalding jets next to Osorio, Ron lathered his hairless head.

'I'm intrigued about your speech,' Ron said. 'I read it and it kills me that I'll have to miss it.'

'You liked it?' Osorio laughed. 'It'll make 'em all sit up, especially the oil bears.'

Ron pivoted, water bouncing off him. 'How exactly does a person become an oil bear?' he asked.

'You sell the oil futures market,' answered Osorio. 'It's as easy to sell what you haven't got as to buy. You just put up a percentage of the value of the contract – we call it initial margin – and give your sell order to a broker on NYMEX. When the market goes down you buy in cheaper than you sold and take your profit.' He grinned mischievously. 'Durst Bank have some big new oil clients, Ron, but as you probably know, they're more of the bull variety.'

Ron's face was a pleasant blank.

'Where did you get your information for the speech from?' he asked, as they sat swathed in towels.

'I want to say something at the oil dinner that will make an impact,' Osorio said. 'About six weeks ago I came across this article.' He leaned back. 'It's called *The Myth of Ishikari Bay*, a great title, when you consider that Ishikari Bay is where the Japs say they've found this huge oil field. It's written by Eric Gerhardt, a geologist down in Houston. Gerhardt says that current Jap claims of a huge find there have to be wild exaggerations. What's more, he can prove it.'

'That's what it reads like,' Ron said.

'Gerhardt did the seismic testing in Ishikari Bay back in '84,' said Osorio.

'Seismic, that's wavy charts, right?' Ron said.

'You send soundwaves down into the earth and they travel different speeds as they hit the different type of rock,' Osorio said. 'It's like fingerprinting the earth.'

'Why would the Japs want to exaggerate the find?' Ron asked.

'Search me,' Osorio said. 'Political reasons? I've spoken to Gerhardt a few times and he seems to know what he's talking about. He says he's known this for six months but no one would listen to him. I mean, it's probably crazy but it's interesting crazy. It underlies the point I'll be making about how these markets react to information.'

'Won't you be accused of market rigging?' Ron asked.

'Who's market rigging? I'm just going to ask some pointed questions and see what happens,' said Osorio.

'You know your market,' Ron said, his eyes concerned, 'but is something like this not a bit provocative?'

'Sure it's provocative,' Osorio replied. 'It's meant to be'. He slapped Ron's shoulder. 'You lawyers are all the same: if you had your way you'd have us all wearing lead diapers.'

They dressed, then took the elevator down to the dark street.

'I spoke with Cristy about Brent,' Osorio said as they stood outside.

'I know,' Ron said, 'you've made her happy.'

'I suggested we all get together for dinner next week – you've never met Carly either.'

'Sounds a great idea,' Ron replied.

'How about The Oracle in Brooklyn, Wednesday next? About eight, if that suits everyone?' Osorio said.

'I look forward to it,' smiled Ron.

He stood for a moment looking after Osorio, pinching his spherical chin, his expansive brow furrowed where seconds before it had been smooth. Then sighing, he turned and made his way towards the Staten Island Ferry.

CHAPTER FOUR

1

Lloyd's Neck, Long Island.

Thursday 12.00 noon

From the drawing-room of the house the butler could see Long Island Sound. It was a cold, early February sea of spuming white tops which every so often the wind hurled across the Tudor-style windows. The butler, dressed in quiet livery, moved from the window to check the fire – real logs, leaping flames – and then to a small, low-beamed dining-room, where a table set for four awaited luncheon. From this room, through windows at the other end, the butler could see men at a distance of fifty yards, removing scaffolding on to long trailers and other men, in white overalls, painting the outside finishing touches to a newer building.

From a sideboard the exquisite chimes of an ormolu clock proclaimed noon. The butler checked the time with his own wrist-watch, then made his measured way back through the drawing-room and out to an oak-panelled hall. Here traditional black and white marble echoed underfoot and glass-eyed bison and moose stared down from the walls they shared with serious men done in oils. The butler proceeded to the back end of this entrance hall. There, in a room entered through another door, he picked up a walkie-talkie.

'Base to one, over,' he intoned.

There was a crackle. 'One to base, I read, over.'

'It is noon, sir,' the butler said, 'over.'

'I'm coming up, over and out.'

The butler waited patiently. This room was small, on the face of it a box-room, little used, whose single window overlooked an internal courtyard, dark at this time of year. At one end of the room stone steps ran down, as if to a cellar, whilst around the walls were piles of neatly cut, four by four cedar boards.

'Goddammit, it's cold up here!'

Dutch Tremaine's head hair was snowy white, that on his chest fading ginger. He had very large, grey eyes which gave life to a face whose normal complexion was a pasty white. Over six feet and dressed in scuffed blue jeans and old boots, his bare upper body shone with sweat. He had once been in remarkable condition, but now maintenance was the objective. He drew on the thick-knit which the butler had handed him.

'Just four inches,' he sighed, 'but I'm getting there. I reckon that right now I'm under Hannah's Wood.'

'Very good, sir,' remarked the butler.

They made their way through the hall, upstairs and into a large bedroom from which not only the sea, but the cliffs of that part of the North Shore could be seen.

'Miss Carletta call, Oliver?' Tremaine asked.

'No, sir.'

'How's work on the ballroom coming?'

'The outside painting is nearly complete, sir.'

Leaving his clothes lying in a small heap, Tremaine proceed-ed to the bathroom where Oliver had activated a steaming show-er. His mind was never idle: short-lists kept popping up which needed continual up-dating as anybody who worked on the fifti-eth floor of Manhattan First Bank knew. Even down in his tunnel under Hannah's Wood, whilst he concentrated on the slow ero-sion of the sticky soil and the careful fitting of each cedar board, his mind was sorting and solving the dimensional problems of the bank he considered his own.

He stepped from the cubicle, accepted the towel and began to pummel his skin until it was glowing red. He was sixty-five. They had changed the rules at the bank in order that his tenure could be extended. He rubbed his skin vigorously; he had dealt with most problems that way all his life, vigorous up-front confrontation of the issue as if sheer force and willpower would move mountains, and it usually did.

But sometimes willpower alone did not work. Sometimes even Dutch Tremaine's great confidence deserted him – and the night before, when Wall Street closed, and the call came through, he had found himself alone, staring into space, an old, nervous man.

Wall Street was suddenly sour on Man First. For years the darling of commentators, Tremaine was now reading daily phrases such as 'stale', 'unexciting', 'flat earnings caused by injudicious loans'. Since he was associated so personally with the bank, the inference was that the loans which Man First was being forced to write off were his mistake. He felt a tremor of doubt: had he overstretched them in his race for growth? Anger replaced doubt: like hell, he had! Jesus, he's built the place with his own hands!

In such times he took to the tunnel: running from the cellar of the mock Tudor house where he had been born and into the hill behind, one day he would emerge at the other side. Each four by four cedar board represented agonising hours of toil and tons of earth; but when he emerged, invariably it was refreshed and cleansed and ready for action.

Dry, he walked across the bedroom and bent to look out of the window to Long Island Sound. In his mind he began once again to go over the problem that he had been tossing around all morning, and all the night before, ever since the moment he had got the call. He breathed in, swelling his big chest out to the full.

'Over my dead body,' he snarled.

Behind him, his butler waited to dress him in formal clothes.

'Sir?'

Still looking out, Tremaine could see the speck, growing every second in the grey sky.

'Never mind,' he said. 'They're here.'

Jacob Landey, President of Manhattan First Bank Corp, said very little. Fifty-three, tidy, popular, and widely regarded as Dutch Tremaine's principal yes-man, Landey had survived where many hadn't. His taciturn demeanour belied an ambitious nature; a consummate tactician he awaited his shot at the top job: Landey

44

now had the feeling that his chance might not be very far away.

The lunch of salads and salmon was over and coffee was being served from an antique pot. Dutch Tremaine had spent lunch elaborating on the details for the forthcoming wedding of his daughter, a device Landey recognised as saying to the seated men, gentlemen, I'm not worried, I've got everything right under control.

Two other men sat, listening patiently to a description of how Tremaine ran campesinos off his ranch in Brazil. William Maldonado, forty, heavily shaven, thin and fit, was Manhattan First's Executive Vice President for Corporate Finance. Executive Vice President for Development, Joseph Pappas, was a lawyer in his mid-forties, eyes light blue, hair steel grey.

'So, anything else on our conversation last night?' Tremaine asked Landey casually.

Jacob Landey smiled slightly and nodded his head towards Maldonado.

'Further confirmation, sir,' Maldonado nodded, glad to get down to business. 'Someone is definitely building up a significant shareholding in Manhattan First.'

Tremaine's eyes had telescoped into tiny points. He made a point of slowly sipping some coffee before he spoke again. 'What are the numbers?' he asked.

'About a two percent stake as of last night,' Maldonado replied. 'Taking our capital's wide spread, if that figure nudges over toward three, it would be enough to get whoever it is a seat on the board.'

'I see,' Tremaine said.

'That's assuming they stop at three percent,' Maldonado said.

'What are we traded this morning?' he asked.

'Thirty-five even, sir,' answered Maldonado, 'down another dollar.'

Tremaine breathed in deeply. 'So who are the candidates?' he asked.

The men exchanged glances.

'The most likely, sir,' responded Maldonado gently, 'is Abel Eller of Durst Bank.'

'Over my dead body,' Tremaine rasped.

'His views on Manhattan First's recent performance are well known,' said Joseph Pappas. 'There are three or four other people we can mention, but Eller looks the overwhelming likelihood.'

'Dealing with Eller is like arm wrestling a rat,' Tremaine snarled. 'He plays by different rules and the rat always wins.'

'He certainly plays by different rules,' said Maldonado. 'I can't think of another bank that has lower bad debt provisions on their balance sheet – if they're for real, that is.'

'Eller is sitting on a crock of shit,' Tremaine said. 'That's why he has to buy profits.' He turned to Landey. 'What do you think? Is Eller the one buying our shares?'

Landey shrugged. 'Could be. Problem is, Dutch, if he moves fast now, he might be difficult to stop.'

Tremaine looked derisorily at his number two. 'Stopped he will be,' he said. 'I've spoken with Broadhurst Colridge just this morning. They're putting their best men on this right away: I told them I want alternatives, to consider everything, from buy back of our own shares to poisoned pills.' He looked to see how Landey had taken it, but the neat bank president turned again to Maldonado.

William Maldonado cleared his throat. 'No matter how hard Broadhurst Colridge work,' he said, 'with respect, they won't solve the basic problem.'

'Why not?' asked Tremaine.

'We've known we've been vulnerable for six months,' Maldonado answered. 'Our income is flat, two hundred million last year was only up two percent on the previous.'

'It's those goddamm loan provisions, Dutch,' said Landey quietly. 'I know we pushed them when we needed growth, but now they've come back to haunt us.'

'What you mean is, I pushed them,' said Tremaine.

'Manhattan First's shares are trailing the bottom of the first division,' Landey said with apparent sincerity. 'We need spark. We need earnings.'

'We've got a strategy to give us just that, goddammit,' Tremaine replied, his colour rising.

'With respect, sir, we need earnings now, not strategies,' Maldonado said.

Tremaine was quietly working the fingers of his right hand in and out of a fist.

'So you're saying . . . ?'

'That we should consider bringing forward as many development strategies as possible, in time to consolidate them in our next quarter,' Maldonado replied.

Tremaine turned his head to Pappas. 'What have you got that we can push the starter button on, Joe?' he asked.

Joseph Pappas looked down at the open file on his knee.

'The first name I've got here is GiltStock,' said the bank's development strategist. 'They're a perfect fit. We estimate GiltStock will earn as much as ten million this year. Plugged into our structures, into our worldwide operation, that gives us a presence in futures which we just don't have at the moment. There are a whole host of other synergies: there are also substantial savings where costs, such as accounting costs, would be absorbed by our existing operations. We reckon that in Manhattan First's hands, GiltStock's ten million dollars could become twenty million in the first year.' Pappas looked at Tremaine. 'That alone would add ten percent to our bottom line.'

'But they're not for sale,' Tremaine said. 'Steve Osorio owns eighty-five percent of the common stock and wants to build them up into a global trader.'

'It's six months since we've made any soundings,' Pappas said. He coughed delicately. 'Perhaps, given your new ties with Mr Osorio another probe might be opportune.'

Tremaine's grey eyes were thoughtful.

'They bank with us,' he said, 'we can't appear to be using privileged knowledge.'

'Precisely,' Pappas said. 'That is why the soundings by . . . one of the family, is far more appropriate than anything formal.'

Tremaine's face had resumed its usual colour, that of poured wax.

'What should I know?' he asked quietly.

Pappas looked at Maldonado. 'It's a quiet time of year for GiltStock,' he said. 'They've gotten very quickly into a new league: new premises, expensive personnel, fancy hardware. Mr Osorio is probably the kind of man who is insecure unless they're making money the whole time. He's about to get married, he may be under more pressure than he was six months ago. A figure of, say, fifty million, may look eminently attractive.'

'How do they stand with us?' Tremaine asked.

'Up near their limits,' Maldonado replied. 'We're not worried, but it does mean something.'

Tremaine nodded. 'Anything else?'

'Well,' said Pappas carefully, 'I mentioned the soundings we took six months ago. An outfit like GiltStock is essentially just a bunch of talented people with contacts – their cohesion is what gives them their value.' Pappas looked momentarily uncomfortable.

'Say what you have to,' Tremaine snapped.

'I just got the impression at the time,' Pappas said, 'that there might be . . . discontented elements in there. Let's say, if things ever took a serious downturn, I don't know how much Osorio could depend on the team he has.'

'You're saying maybe we could steal it?' Tremaine said.

'There have been signals coming out,' Pappas said. 'Some of the GiltStock people are ambitious.'

Tremaine thought for some moments.

'Okay,' he said, seeming to come to a conclusion. 'I'll talk to him. What's next?'

'Opportunities for Manhattan First Equity Trust Corp,' Pappas replied, turning to another page. 'You know this oil find that's been made off Japan? The Ishikari Field?'

'Sure, I've heard about it,' Tremaine said.

'We think that there may be good investment bargains in that whole area out there,' Pappas said. 'Not many people from here are looking at it yet, but the shares of exploration companies have started to move in Tokyo. We could make a killing pretty quickly.'

'What have you in mind?' Tremaine asked.

'Selective equity investments,' Pappas replied, 'say not more than five million in any one outfit.'

'Do it,' Tremaine said. 'I'll go to the board retroactively.'

He looked outside; the sun had come out, changing the colour of the water on the Sound. He turned back to the men, his jaw set.

'Manhattan First is not going to become part of Abel Eller's harem,' he said. 'That, gentlemen, will not happen as long as I'm in this saddle.'

As the men filed out to their helicopter, the butler moved quietly in to clear away.

CHAPTER FIVE

1

New York

Friday   12.30 p.m.

Osorio slipped into the chair at the head of the table. He checked the screens, mentally noted the prices, then turned his attention to the four people sitting at the table.

'Okay, our weekly review,' he said. 'How're things?'

'Pretty flat, to be honest,' replied Malcolm Finch. 'Edibles are doing nothing. Oil went up a dollar, some say helped by your piece in GiltStock Voice, but it lost it again.' Malcolm screwed his face. 'There are trade figures on Monday, maybe they'll have some surprises.'

'But in the meantime we're not busy.'

'When things don't move,' Malcolm said, 'we're not busy.'

'Cheryl?' said Osorio.

'Same story,' Cheryl replied. 'Quiet, quiet. Gold is stuck at five hundred, so any interest there was has dried up. Copper . . . lead . . . zinc? Cobalt, that's something that might move on developments in Zaire, but otherwise . . . '

'We're trading Chicago every time it blinks up there,' Jay Cox said, 'but I can't pretend we'll smash any records this week.'

Osorio nodded his head quickly, half a dozen times. 'Ray?' he asked.

Ray Leonard favoured t-shirts and jeans at all times.

49

'It's that time of the year,' he said, looking at a print-out on his lap. He shrugged. 'Halfway through the first quarter and we're holding our own on last year; but like Malcolm says, nothing's happening.'

'Holding our own?' Osorio snapped.

'There's one hell of an overhead now, Steve,' Ray said, 'and it's risen substantially since we came in here. It costs two hundred thousand a week before we earn a cent. When things are quiet, those numbers begin to bite.'

'So how will the first quarter net out?' Osorio asked.

'We're only halfway through it.'

'If things don't pick up?'

'If things don't pick up, we'll break even,' Ray replied. He looked down. 'Last year we made nine hundred thousand.'

'So on the bottom line, we're not holding our own,' Osorio said.

'Come on, Steve,' Malcolm Finch laughed, looking at Osorio's urgent face. 'We've been here before. Things always pick up. It's just unusually quiet, that's all; matter of fact, it's so damn quiet I think if next week stays the same, I'm going to go north and catch myself some trout.'

'What about problem accounts?' asked Osorio, ignoring Malcolm.

'This morning, just our old friends, Metal Base,' Ray answered. 'They took a position in copper last week and it's gone against them. Not much, mind you, but I made a twenty-five thousand dollar margin call on them four days ago and we still haven't got paid.'

'Stop them out,' said Osorio. 'We can't afford to carry these sort of people.'

'They've always paid up before,' Ray said.

'Metal Base have been with us a long time, Steve,' ventured Cheryl. 'They're little guys. You could hurt them bad if you take them out. I mean, you could put them over the edge.'

'I said, stop them out,' Osorio repeated. 'I'm going to be away from this place week after next for nearly a month. I want to sleep every night, not lie awake worrying that there's money going out the door here because you guys can't take tough decisions. How do you think people like Merrill and Tony Quacks got where they are? By being pussy-cats? You agree, Malcolm?'

50

'They're not my account . . . ' Malcolm said.

'Of course stop them out,' Cox snorted. 'Why the fuckin' discussion?'

'If their money hasn't arrived by the time London opens, they get stopped,' said Ray quietly.

Osorio looked pensively at the screens. 'What news of our new friends, Gabriel Holdings?' he asked Ray.

'I've put their money into an escrow account,' Ray said, opening another file on his lap. 'I've been up and down Wall Street a few times and if Gabriel have an account with anyone else, well, nobody's talking about it.'

'You've asked Manhattan First?' Osorio queried.

'Sure. They don't know them.'

'Durst Bank?' Osorio asked. 'It was their cheque.'

'You know Durst Bank,' Ray said. 'I spoke to a guy I know in there, but all I got was a wall.' Ray shrugged. 'I guess the fact that Durst are acting for them means something, but as to pedigree . . . '

Osorio was drumming his fingers. 'Money is pedigree in this business,' he said. 'What about the forms?'

'The forms are all back, all signed up,' Ray said.

'Notarised?'

'All notarised.'

'By whom?'

'By Herbert, Allen and Goldberg, Park Avenue.'

'They're big,' Malcolm said.

'They're the biggest,' said Osorio. 'But no bank reference?' he asked, turning back to Ray.

Ray shook his head. 'We just know they used Durst Bank, nothing more.'

'No accounts? No data?'

'*Nada*,' Ray replied.

'Forget them,' Jay Cox said. 'We all had the shit scared out of us by the Chinese incident that I know isn't popular to mention, but nevertheless, we sat down and drew up criteria for new clients. There's no point in agonising every time someone comes in the door and hands us a sackful of money. We stick to our own rules, and as far as I'm concerned that's the end of it.'

'I've been asking around about them,' Malcolm said tentatively.

Jay Cox looked at his watch and sighed.

'Hold on there, Jay,' Osorio said, his face clouding, 'let's hear Malcolm out. Okay, what have you come up with, Malcolm?'

Malcolm Finch rocked his hand a bit. 'They're certainly not known in London or in Rotterdam and whilst none of the majors have ever heard of them . . . '

'But,' Osorio pressed.

Malcolm winced. 'Okay, but, and this is pure crap-shooting . . . '

'Go ahead.'

' . . . there's this whole Saudi business,' Malcolm said, shaking his head. 'I only know what I read and what I hear in the trade, but whereas six months ago there were no question marks over Saudi, today there's . . . uncertainty, you know what I mean.'

Osorio was nodding.

'It's no secret that the royal family out there are under a lot of pressure due to falling oil prices which they seem incapable of correcting,' Malcolm said. 'Saudi's a modern country now, with all a modern country's problems and a feudal government system.'

'Go on,' said Osorio.

'Well,' said Malcolm slowly, 'I've been thinking about it and it just struck me as funny that Arabs should walk in here out of the blue and hand you a bundle of money. Is it possible that the Saudi situation may change? Mind you, my opinion is that oil is still going to fall.'

Osorio drummed his fingers. 'These guys are like that, you know,' he said. 'I mean here we've got an open society, there are laws to make information available. But over there it's the opposite.'

Ray Leonard grimaced and made a little gesture with his head to show that he wasn't impressed.

'It may be the case, Ray,' Osorio said, 'that they're simply not in a position to give us any data because there isn't any to give.' He spread his hands. 'If you take Malcolm's scenario, an emerging regime, trying to put a whole lot of pieces in place . . . These guys don't want to get beheaded, you know, they can't spew out profit and loss accounts.'

'We're making a lot of assumptions,' said Ray, unmoved.

'We're making a lot of money on their fifteen big ones,'

Osorio retorted drily. 'Like nearly a hundred and fifty grand a year if they stay with us – like nearly enough to pay the expenses for a few days around here.'

'That's fine,' Jay Cox said, 'and let's hope they keep it coming in – I mean they're lending us money interest free, isn't that what it amounts to?' He laughed and looked down at his waistcoat. 'Arabs,' he said. 'No way would I trade with an Arab unless I had his balls tied to the furniture.'

Osorio sighed. 'What do you say, Cheryl?' he asked.

Cheryl tossed back her hair. 'I came here after you drew up these rules,' she said, 'but I've always thought them pretty reasonable.'

'Okay,' said Osorio in resignation. 'But let's keep up the hunt for information. We'll look assholes if this business goes someplace else and Malcolm's theory turns out right.'

Ray got to his feet. 'I'm waiting on a couple more calls back,' he said. 'Let's see what they produce.'

'So if they come on, no trade, right?' Malcolm said.

'That's what's been agreed,' said Jay Cox.

Osorio sighed and nodded. He left his chair and went to the window as the others made their way from the boardroom. He could see cold light reflecting on moving colours, miles below; the sound of car horns wafted upwards; the sun began its slip behind Staten Island.

He picked up the telephone and punched a number.

'Cristy Osorio, please.'

'Steve?'

'Oh, hi sis. Sorry if I'm interrupting some Pulitzer Prize project.'

'I got through that an hour ago,' Cristy laughed. 'What's on your mind?'

'Let me ask your advice on something,' Osorio said, 'hypothetical question, of course.'

'Of course.'

'I get a big new account, dealing in big numbers. Routine bank enquiries seem okay, but I want to probe a little deeper, you know, if we make a mistake on something like this, get landed badly, it could hurt a lot.' Osorio paused. 'I know this account deal with Durst Bank. Could I press Ron to give me an inside track?'

'You could,' Cristy replied, 'but I doubt if it would get you anywhere. You know Ron works directly for Abel Eller?'

'Yes.'

'That's the greatest bitch of a job there is,' Cristy said. 'Eller is paranoid about secrecy. One whiff that Ron even dreams about business and he would be out – and believe me, he can't afford that.'

'Meaning what?'

'I shouldn't be telling you this,' Cristy said, 'but you know Ron was married before?'

'Sure.'

'He's got two kids at expensive schools and fancy payments to his ex,' Cristy said. 'Add to that both his parents whom he adores, who are very elderly and who he has in the best old folks home in Vermont and you begin to see why he needs every penny he gets from Abel Eller.'

'Forget I ever mentioned it,' Osorio said. 'Listen, I'm really looking forward to seeing you both Wednesday next.'

'Me too,' Cristy said. 'Take care.'

Osorio bit his lip thoughtfully.

'Some coffee?'

Marilee was placing a porcelain cup at the head of the table.

'Mr Dutch Tremaine called,' she said. 'I told him you were in conference. He wants to know if you can meet him tonight for dinner: Tante Leslie at eight,' she said.

Osorio made a face. 'Tell him yes,' he said. He looked at the screens. 'And Marilee, can you get me Iqbal, Miss Singer, and, let me see, yeah, Duffin, right away, any order.'

Osorio sat and sipped coffee. Within a minute the phone flashed.

'Miss Singer on two,' said Marilee's voice.

Osorio pressed two. 'Miss Singer?'

'So at last he calls.'

A smile split Osorio's face. 'Miss Singer, how are you today?'

'You were meant to visit me.'

'I'm going to,' Osorio said.

'You're always going to. Give me a date.'

Osorio smiled. 'It will be in the next two weeks,' he said, 'I promise. I'll bring red roses.'

'You're not coming to a cemetery,' Miss Singer said. 'Just bring yourself.

'Now let's talk business. How are the markets?'

Osorio narrowed his eyes and looked at the screens.

'March bonds look sexy,' he said, 'up fifteen on the day, they could go higher.' He could hear Miss Singer's stiff fingers tapping on a keyboard in her apartment somewhere on Fifth Avenue.

'I think interest rates are going to soften,' Miss Singer said. 'I've had all the fun I'm going to have in bonds for the moment. You're the broker, you're meant to be the one with the ideas.'

'That's why I called you.'

'I'd never have guessed.'

'Have you looked at oil recently?'

'Just a minute.' The fingers tapped again. 'What month should I look at – the March?'

'Right on.'

'I have it, let me see, twenty-two thirty last traded and a seller. Let me look at the chart.' Papers rustled. 'Looks like a heap of trouble to me,' Miss Singer said.

'I agree,' Osorio responded. 'But things are never as they seem.'

'I know what's coming,' Miss Singer said. 'I read that little piece this morning in your newsletter. No way, if I want to scare myself I'll hang-glide.'

'That's fine by me,' Osorio said, 'but don't blame me if you get left out.'

'What are you talking about?'

'I can't say for sure,' Osorio said softly, 'but we've reason to believe that the market we're discussing may be about to move – up.'

'You reckon?'

'I do.'

Osorio could imagine an old, lined face, pinched up in thought, probably staring out at the park she'd last walked in God knows when.

'I'll buy fifty,' Miss Singer said.

'You should buy a hundred,' Osorio replied. 'You'll make a killing.'

'Seventy-five.'

'Take a hundred,' Osorio said.

There was a pause.

'Okay, buy a hundred of the March,' Miss Singer said. 'At twenty-two thirty or better. Money's on its way.'

'One hundred thousand barrels of March oil, understood,' Osorio smiled, scribbling down the order. 'We'll be in touch.'

'I love you, kid,' said the old lady whom he'd never met.

'I love you too,' he said and disconnected.

Almost immediately Marilee was on. 'Jerry Duffin in the Bahamas is holding on one, Steve.'

Osorio hit one. 'Jerry, hi, hard at work?'

'Busy keeping the flies off my spritzer,' said the man who two years before had sold out his software house for three hundred million. 'What gives?'

'A little play maybe in oil.'

'Uh-huh?'

'There are some Arabs in town,' Osorio said softly. 'They've got a lot of cash they want to change into black gold.'

'I like it.'

'Nothing firm yet, but I think we'll be acting.'

'I like it even more. What do you think?'

'Well, I'm just about to take on some of the March – it's holding the twenty-two thirty pretty well.'

'Include me in,' Jerry Duffin said. 'How much do you think?'

'I'm buying five hundred thousand barrels,' Osorio said.

'In that case, I'll do a hundred,' Duffin said. 'Where should I put the stop?'

'Just over twenty-two,' said Osorio looking at the oil chart.

'Then go ahead.'

'Got it,' said Osorio. 'We'll be back.'

He was noting Duffin's order when Marilee's voice came on. 'Steve, Dr Iqbal in Jo'burg on two. The line's bad and I think he's kind of busy.'

'Iqbal, can you talk or will I call you back?' Osorio asked over six thousand miles of static.

'In a minute, in a minute,' the voice of Dr Iqbal could be heard saying. 'Steve? This line is bad.'

'Iqbal, I think you should be in some oil.'

'Some oil? You think some oil, Steve? I presume you mean short?'

'On the contrary, we're about to buy,' Osorio shouted as the line faded. 'I can't say too much, but the information is right.'

'Buy oil?' Voices could be heard behind the South African doctor, who now half-cupped the mouthpiece. 'Yes, yes, two three times a day. Hello, Steve? I'm sorry, but I live in a madhouse.'

'So do I, Iqbal,' Osorio laughed, 'so do I.'

'What is oil today?' Dr Iqbal asked.

'Twenty-two twenty-seven on the March as we speak,' Osorio said.

'And this is red hot? Oh my God, don't drop him, lie him down over there. Steve, you still there?'

Osorio shook his head. 'I'm playing a hunch, Iqbal, but it may be right to be in.'

'Should I plunge?'

'Why not start building a position?'

'Buy fifty thousand barrels, then,' Iqbal said. 'Sorry, Steve, but I've got to go.'

'Bless you, Iqbal,' Osorio said, writing the order. He hit the intercom. 'Malcolm!'

'Yes, Steve?'

'Take an order. Buy two hundred and fifty thousand barrels of March oil up to twenty-two thirty. Details later.'

'Sure thing, Steve,' Malcolm said.

'And Malcolm?'

'Yes?'

'Can you tell those fifty or so people out there that the little plastic instrument they see in front of them with holes in both ends is called a phone; and that if they pick it up and punch little numbers into their keyboards they get to talk to other people out there in the world, who might just agree to buy some of this shit that we merchandise.'

Without waiting for a reply, Osorio clicked off the intercom and made his way to Saldi's for lunch.

2

New York

Friday 2.30 p.m.

Malcolm put down the phone and gazed at the flickering monitor. Malcolm was sixty-five. This was not widely known; in fact had people been asked they would have put Malcolm's age at fifty something. The truth was that Malcolm ten years ago, at fifty-five, looked little different to Malcolm at forty-five, or for that matter, the Malcolm now mid-sixty. But sixty-five was Malcolm's age and it was a fact which in recent weeks he had thought about a lot.

He had arrived in Wall Street after the war by accident. He had been just a youngster, a mere twenty-three-year-old, who demobbed in '48 having spent three years, first in Hawaii and then in Tokyo with the old OSS, the Office of Strategic Services, the precursor of the modern CIA. Malcolm never forgot that time; the camaraderie, the sense of achievement, the belonging which they had all enjoyed. Lieutenant Finch had never seen action, just kept his head down in the huge office which he shared with thirty others on Nijubashi, right across the road from the Imperial Palace, home of the God Emperor. But it had been the Emperor who had crossed the road to be interviewed by MacArthur, not the other way around.

That was a lifetime ago. Malcolm had come to Wall Street, got married, had two kids, changed his job half a dozen times, each time rising another small notch on the totem pole.

They lived five minutes from Dobbs Ferry, an hour up the Hudson from Manhattan. His wife and he divorced when the children left home; she had been replaced by Malcolm's sister, a deaf lady, a widow from Poughkeepsie who sailed around in her private silent world, smiled when anything was said and dutifully came up with an evening meal every day. It was Malcolm's grandson who occupied his fondest thoughts, an earnest eight-year-old for whom he had high hopes as a fly fisherman.

Ten years ago Malcolm had started to think about retiring. He had more than enough put by, he didn't need the hassle of markets anymore. Then one day he met Osorio. Malcolm had experienced a sense of wonder. The sheer blinding confidence, the energy, the utter unacceptability of defeat. Malcolm had come along for the ride, for a couple of years at the most, he had promised himself.

'We'll need a few grey hairs around,' Osorio had grinned.

At the start Malcolm was wheeled in to meet clients who might judge age as an asset; in some cases Osorio behaved as if it were Malcolm who was the boss.

The memories of those days were the ones which Malcolm really cherished. Budgets were skinned to the bone. In their old, cramped offices where they were piled up one on the other and all ordered once a day from the local deli, there had been a comradeship which had never quite survived to the new GiltStock.

The new GiltStock was different. Osorio grew in stature, Malcolm remained the trader he had always been. He knew that his grey hairs now probably caused more irritation than anything else.

He looked at the screen. There was no excitement anymore, just a daily function, the pursuit of budgets, the worry of new overheads, the realisation that he was older than all of them, the feeling that he was slowing down, a catch in his chest when he should have been enjoying himself. And for what? All for what?

Malcolm shook his head.

It was time to think of getting out.

3

New York

Friday evening

Dinner at Tante Leslie proceeded as it did every evening, with the quietly controlled confidence of a show that had been running to full houses longer than anyone could remember.

They had walked in across the dining-room and had been

stopped half a dozen times by people whom Dutch had to stop and shake hands with and whose wives he had to kiss and to whom he then introduced Osorio.

'Oh, he's beautiful,' one of them remarked, making Osorio feel like a boy slave. 'Dutch, where did you find him?'

'I got washed up one morning out at Lloyd's Neck,'Osorio replied and the old dowager blinked as if taken by surprise that he could talk too.

Osorio ate half a lobster, then half a duck; Dutch Tremaine picked a salad, then a minute steak with the life beaten out of it and grilled with nothing.

Now there was another visitation, this time from a small man whom Osorio knew to be the owner of enough of the upper west side to need a car for inspections. Dutch stood just out of earshot, nodding gravely; Osorio looked at him. This man could have had a life of social glitter and ease, a man who traced back in an unbroken line to the 'Mayflower', whose family for generations had meant wealth, power and selective breeding.

Osorio saw the big, hairy hand briefly catch the property man's arm for emphasis. The world saw Dutch Tremaine as an urbane, handsome man, carefully groomed, affable, carrying his power and wealth easily, a man who turned women's heads, his white hair shining, his grey eyes sparkling, someone whose yacht wintered in Nassau Sound and then made the long journey to spend the summer waiting off some island of the Dodecanese, waiting for Tremaine to scream out of La Guardia at a moment's notice in his private Gulfstream and bring his companion of the moment to wherever they might have some fun.

But things changed. Not even Napoleon had managed to stay on top forever and now there was talk, on the Street, in the media, in the back booths where real information was exchanged: the king was getting old, losing his grip; earnings were flat, flat; the shares were down and the rabble were beginning to get uneasy. Would the king survive, and if so, for how long? Osorio toyed with a tiny porcelain flower vase and wondered why he had been asked to dinner.

'Be in touch, Sam,' said Tremaine, pressing flesh and resuming his seat. 'Sorry about that,' he said to Osorio, 'you meet one, you've got to meet them all.'

'I understand,' Osorio smiled.

A waiter appeared with menus.

'Desserts, gentlemen?'

Dutch Tremaine shook his head.

'What's the mousse with chocolate and macaroons?' Osorio asked.

'Eggs are beaten with melted chocolate, sir,' the waiter explained, 'and then mixed with syrup. The resulting mousse is served chilled with a rum-soaked macaroon.'

'I'll have that,' Osorio said, handing the man the menu.

'Steve, there's something I just have to say,' Tremaine said.

He began rearranging items near him on the table: the tiny vase of flowers went from Osorio's side to centre, a sugar bowl to the centre from the right.

'Let me level with you, Steve. Upfront. Let me say how very happy I am about you and Carletta. No bullshit. Frankly, I'm thrilled. Not just because I look at you and I like what I see, but because she's happy. And let me tell you, that for me is better than money after tax any day. Okay?'

'Okay,' Osorio said as the sugar bowl was adjusted to align with the flowers.

'I didn't give her much of a family life. I guess I was too busy putting things together. You know yourself what I mean, you're probably at the same stage, building, adapting, changing. Rolling every day with new circumstances? Wondering who's going to try and slip that old knife between your shoulder blades?'

'Sure,' Osorio said as his mousse arrived.

Dutch Tremaine's eyes had become almost soft. 'She's the only kid I've got, as you know,' he said and moistened his lips. 'I'm crazy about her.' He nodded quietly, repositioning his empty coffee cup. 'Couldn't stand her mother, but I'm crazy about Carletta.'

'So am I, Dutch,' Osorio said. 'And I'll look after her.'

'I'm sure you will,' Tremaine said. He held Osorio's eyes, deep brown and vital. 'You know, something,' he laughed, 'in a funny sort of a way, I'm as jealous as hell. Is that wrong?'

Osorio shrugged disarmingly as he ate. 'Of course not. I can try and guess how you feel.'

Tremaine leaned forward, dividing flower vase and sugar bowl with his hands.

61

'I've never had a son, alright?'

'Alright,' said Osorio cautiously.

'But I'm about to have a son-in-law,' Tremaine said. 'I feel about that very deeply. I feel about this extended family almost religiously. Can you understand me?'

'I think so,' Osorio replied.

'So . . . just for a moment . . . can I talk like family?'

'Sure,' said Osorio, scooping the last of the dessert into his mouth and leaning back.

'You're ambitious,' Tremaine said, smiling knowingly and nodding. 'You've told me your plans for GiltStock, for yourself, where you see the operation in five years' time. What you tell me is exciting. It turns me on. Because I know you and your ability, I see in many ways a mirror image of myself twenty-five years ago when I set out to build something, and goddammit I was going to do it and no son-of-a-bitch was going to get in the way.'

Osorio nodded, his face pleasantly expressionless.

'There were times I didn't know if I was going to succeed,' Dutch said. 'In those times, Steve, I was always grateful that I had a father to turn to, someone I could trust, someone I knew could understand and to whom having money was as natural as breathing.' He paused. 'Are you with me?'

Osorio nodded again.

'Up to now you've had no such luxury,' Tremaine said gently. 'But you're marrying Carletta; you now have such a father. Do I make myself clear?'

'I appreciate it, genuinely, thank you,' said Osorio.

'But,' Tremaine said quietly, 'you're in a pretty wild business. You're playing in the fastest game in town, I think you'll agree.'

Osorio raised his eyebrows and brushed black hair back from his collar. 'That's right.'

Tremaine's hands were no more than six inches away, finger-tips joined and pointed at Osorio's belly. 'Just suppose for a moment,' he said very softly, 'just suppose, out of consideration for Carletta and you and this wonderful new family unit that we all devoutly want to succeed, just suppose that I were to suggest to you, purely hypothetically, that GiltStock might be a lot safer in a bigger tent, what would you say?'

'Bigger tent?' said Osorio enquiringly as all his nerve ends went on alert.

Tremaine was nodding. 'Manhattan First is a transglobal financial institution,' he said. 'It's got total assets of nearly twenty-five billion dollars.' He chortled. 'With that sort of muscle behind you, GiltStock could become the international number one in its field.'

Osorio leaned back from the large man opposite him.

'Dutch,' he said carefully, 'are you making me a proposal?'

'I'm putting my neck on the line,' Tremaine said in a fierce whisper. 'I'm not going to be running the bank for ever. If I could get them interested in GiltStock, you could walk away with forty, fifty million bucks and you'd never have to worry about money again.'

'What makes you think I worry about it now?'

'Don't be flip with me, Steve,' Tremaine said. 'I'm offering you a chance that most people ever only dream about.'

Osorio closed his eyes briefly and sighed; then he smiled brightly.

'I'm very flattered by your concern, sincerely I am,' he said. 'I love your daughter and I know she loves me. I'm going to give her a good life and I hope you'll be proud of me.'

He signalled a waiter for coffee.

'That's all?' Dutch Tremaine's face showed wounded puzzlement.

'That's all there is to say,' Osorio responded. 'You're a man who understands independence, I'm sure you'll understand my position.'

'You're turning your back on fifty million?'

'On the contrary, I would expect GiltStock to be worth multiples of that figure in five years' time.'

Tremaine sat back, declining fresh coffee.

'At least think about it,' he said smiling again. 'I genuinely want to try and be of help.'

'I know,' Osorio replied. 'Again, thank you.'

Tremaine motioned for the cheque. 'By the way,' he said, 'something I want your view on. We are thinking of investing in Japanese oil. What's your feeling there?'

'I don't know,' Osorio said. 'The main effect of Japanese oil to date has been to depress the world oil market. I take the view that it has been overdone and that oil at these levels is undervalued. I've even spoken to a man, a geologist, who claims that the oil find is a fabrication.'

'That's interesting,' Tremaine said.

Osorio's smile was that of an exotic cat. 'Isn't it?' he said.

Tremaine scribbled his name on the cheque and got to his feet.

It was raining and they both stood waiting inside the door: Osorio had given his driver the night off; Tremaine's limousine would take the banker to the downtown heliport.

'Just remember,' Tremaine said, 'regardless of how you feel about our talk tonight, don't be short, you hear? You don't ever have to die of thirst if you live beside a well.'

Before Osorio could reply, Tremaine had stepped through the revolving doors and ducked under the doorman's umbrella into the back of a long car with black windows.

'Have a nice night, sir,' said the doorman as Osorio pressed him a five and dived into the back of a cab.

'Where to?' asked the cabby.

'Go to Fifth and Seventy-fifth,' Osorio said. He looked at the cabby's face; the man was black, fat and completely bald. For some reason Brent's face popped into Osorio's vision.

'What would you say,' Osorio asked the cabby, 'if a guy told you he wanted to give you fifty million bucks?'

'I'd tell him go screw himself,' said the cabby without hesitation.

Osorio's grin was from ear to ear.

'Right on, man,' he said, 'right on.'

CHAPTER SIX

Houston, Texas

Eric Gerhardt parked in the lot two blocks from his office. He hauled himself from his car and sucked in air. It was ten, later than his usual time, but the evening before he had dropped off at the tv and when he had woken to the blank screen, his head hurt, and his back. Two capsules had put him away for seven hours.

He stood by the car, pressing his hand to the small of his back which still twinged. Two girls in mini-skirts flicked along, left to right, on the sidewalk outside the lot.

'Jesus!' exclaimed Gerhardt and felt a sudden rush of excitement, all the more thrilling and confusing because it was so novel.

The office was as usual in the mornings: stuffy. He stepped over the sheaf of mail which lay inside the door and went to the window which he opened. He breathed deeply, the process tickling some long-forgotten memories somewhere. The girls' legs . . .

Gerhardt picked up the phone and with a marvellous headiness, dialled the number.

The agency answered.

'This is Gerhardt Geology in North Bayou,' he said. 'I've got some work I need done today.'

'Sure thing, we'll have someone out to you,' the girl said.

'I'd kind of like it if the lady who came the other day,' Gerhardt said, 'her name was Jen, I believe, she seemed to, ah, get into things quickly, if she might . . . '

'You'd like Jen?'

'If she was available.'

'I'll call her and let you know.'

The restaurant was very French, two blocks from the office. He wondered if people thought him a father taking his daughter to lunch.

'Call me Eric,' he said.

'Well, tell me how you became a geologist, Eric,' Jen smiled.

He told her: about growing up in San Francisco, about his interest in things old, things which told you how the earth had started.

'So you got into oil,' she said.

He nodded as a waiter poured white wine.

'I was an innocent,' Gerhardt said, 'I knew nothing about business, and what I did know, I didn't like. Geology was – is – my interest, not business.'

'Are they incompatible?' Jen asked.

'Not always,' Gerhardt replied, 'but sometimes. It's the some-times I have always objected to.'

'Like what you describe in your article?'

'You read it?'

'Sure, there's a copy of the magazine in your office. I got a buzz reading it,' she said. 'Some of the geological terms were beyond me, but the main thrust was absorbing.'

'It just contains my observations,' Gerhardt said.

'"The Myth of Ishikari Bay"' she said, tilting her head to one side and looking beyond him. 'It's sort of like the plot for a movie.'

'Oh, I'm sure it's not as dramatic as that,' Gerhardt said. 'What I'm really just trying to do is to provoke discussion, that's all. It's just a technical paper.'

'I know,' Jen persisted, 'but even so, it was absorbing. I could visualise it as I read: the bay out there, you surrounded by little yellow men with slit eyes.'

'A big oil broker in New York has read it,' Gerhardt said. 'He's called me half a dozen times.'

'I'm not surprised.'

'He's asked me to come as his guest to a dinner in New York.'

66

'There you go,' she said. 'Don't laugh when I say it could be a movie.'

'The next thing you'll tell me,' Gerhardt smiled, 'is that I'm going to be famous.'

'You could be,' she said.

He shook his head. 'I'll never be anything other than what you see here,' he said quietly.

He stood watching as she prepared to leave the office.

'Thank you for everything,' she smiled warmly. 'I don't often get taken to such a nice lunch.'

'I enjoyed it greatly,' he said.

'In case I don't see you,' she said, 'enjoy your trip to New York.'

Gerhardt felt himself struck by panic.

'Jen,' he said recklessly, 'can I ask you something?'

She turned, her lips parted, her eyebrows raised.

He said: 'Would you care to join me on my trip to New York?'

For a moment anything could have happened, then she came and kissed him, her lips on his cheek the sweetest, softest experience of his whole life.

'Let me think about it, okay?' she said as she went to the door.

There were evening shadows now in the small office suite. Gerhardt sat at his desk, the room unlit. It was three hours since she had gone, yet he didn't dare to leave in case he might disturb the memory. She had lit a flame in him that had made the years fall away. He closed his eyes as a great yearning swept him. He could visualise her so vividly that she could be beside him. He felt he knew each contour of her body, each perfect rise and fall, each knob of her back, right up to where her neck plunged between her shoulder blades. As one of his hands rubbed the other he was stroking her length, smoothing the honey of her flesh.

He jumped as the phone on his desk rang.

'Eric Gerhardt?'

The voice was not familiar.

'Yes, this is Eric Gerhardt.'

'Mr Gerhardt, you have upset a great number of people.'

'Who . . . ?'

67

'You will kindly listen,' the caller said in a voice of steel. 'Tonight, and no later than tonight, you will compose a letter to the editor of *Key Stone* magazine in New York.'

'What is this . . . ?'

'Listen, Mr Gerhardt! In the letter you will explain that you have been grievously mistaken. That your article entitled *"The Myth of Ishikari Bay"* was based upon a mistaken analysis of seismic data. That you have now revaluated the information available and conclude that there is no reason why the Japanese claims cannot be true. Is that all clear?'

Gerhardt was speechless.

'You will then assemble all the seismic data in your possession on Ishikari Bay and leave it tomorrow on the driver's seat of your unlocked car, parked as usual in the lot. An envelope containing five thousand dollars in cash will be left in it's place. Do you understand?'

'Sure I understand,' Gerhardt cried, 'but . . . '

'Good,' the caller said. 'The letter to the magazine must be mailed by special delivery so as to be published in the edition due out next week. On publication you will receive, in cash, a further five thousand dollars.'

'And if I don't write the letter?' Gerhardt managed to say.

'Then there will be no place on earth that you will be able to hide,' the caller said.

Gerhardt tried to talk but found he could not.

'I suggest, Mr Gerhardt, that in order not to waste any further time you put on your office lights and begin writing.'

As the phone line went dead, Eric Gerhardt began to tremble.

CHAPTER SEVEN

1

Brooklyn, New York
Wednesday 13 February 8.00 p.m.

'"No, no, daarling; just so is fan-tas-tic. You emboh-dy fantasy."'
Carly Tremaine looked around at the laughing table.

'If a dress by Maurice is not worth fifty thousand,' she said, 'then he certainly makes up the balance in entertainment value.'

Osorio looked at her proudly and then beyond her, out through the expansive windows of the riverboat restaurant, over Governors Island to Manhattan where the Twin Towers twinkled comfortingly. A waiter hovered.

'Dessert, folks?'

'Just decaff for me,' Cristy Osorio said.

'Regular coffee,' said Carly.

'And for me,' said Ron.

Osorio considered the menu. 'The glazed strawberries with shortcake biscuits sound fine,' he said.

'Now tell me *exactly* what you do,' said Carly addressing Ron. 'I should warn you that my principal and only hobby is other people.'

Ron's face beamed – Carly had him eating out of her hand. Osorio looked across to Cristy. Small and mobile-looking like all the Osorios but that was as far as the likeness went. None of the upswept eyes or other legacy of plainsmen from northern

69

steppes that the rest of us exude. Strawberry blonde, very American, white, even teeth and the kind of freckled, unmade-up skin that glowed fresh and healthy, that was Cristy.

'So how have you been?' he asked her.

'Fine,' she replied.

'Your work okay?'

'I'm having a ball,' she said.

'I've read some of your pieces.'

'No kidding?'

'Yes, I . . . ' He stopped himself and smiled as he saw her eyes laughing at him. 'It's great you both could get here,' he said quietly. 'Expecially you. It means a lot to me.'

'Thanks,' said Cristy.

'I even promise I'll call Brent and ask him to the wedding,' Osorio said.

Cristy's face was happy.

'I hear you're becoming part of the permanent Wall Street furniture,' she said. 'Vice-Chairman-elect of NYMEX?'

'You hear right,' Osorio confirmed.

'Are we to expect any major changes down there?' Cristy asked. 'Off the record, of course.'

'Off the record,' Osorio said, 'I hope to ask some questions in my speech about the media and information and how they both crucially affect the markets we work in. As a case in point I plan to instance oil.'

'Sounds interesting,' Cristy said.

'It is,' Osorio replied.

Ron whooped with laughter and Osorio turned back to them. Cristy watched him. Big brother. Warm pool of water outside the caravan. Nearby thump of a donkey-rig, a noise that none of them felt comfortable without. Hot sun. Cristy don't wear nothin' in this weather. She wants to go out. At the door she turns, kneels, hot floor at her knees, reverses one step, two step, hot earth under her feet, waddles over and sits plop in the water. He comes round the corner. Black to her brown. Injun, she heard boys call him. Now the black and fair again contrasted for Cristy, here in a Brooklyn restaurant on the river. She saw Osorio's fond looks at Carly's perfect face, saw Carly's exuberance which made her the centre.

The waiter arrived with Osorio's dessert, delicate tiers of round biscuits and plump strawberries.

'Am I alone?' he asked.

'Enjoy,' Carly beamed as with a shrug Osorio began to spoon shortcake mouthwards.

Ron's hand went to wine in a cold bucket, topped Carly's glass first, then the others.

'This is superb,' said Osorio as he fed himself shortcake. 'You people don't know what you're missing.'

'My God,' said Carly with amazement, 'I don't know how you do it and stay in shape. I mean, if I ate what you're eating it would be bread and water for the next week.' She turned to Cristy. 'Was he always like this?'

'Always,' said Cristy happily. 'He takes after Brent, our father.'

'Whom I haven't yet met,' Carly said.

'I hope you'll have that opportunity in just two weeks,' Cristy said.

'Oh, is he coming? Oh good,' Carly said. 'I haven't really been told. But if he is, then I especially want to meet the man who's responsible for this hunk of the species,' and as they laughed, Carly twined her arm through Osorio's and bared her teeth.

'To the hunks of the species,' said Ron jocularly in the booming voice of a toastmaster and raised his glass.

Carly shrieked and turned to Osorio.

'Are all your friends as amusing as this one?' she asked.

'Whadayusay, Hunk?' Ron asked.

Osorio smiled briefly, then turned to Cristy as Ron began to make Carly laugh again.

'Cristy,' he said cleaning his plate, 'I need your help.'

Cristy looked at him openly. Carly flirting with Ron. Steve was annoyed now. Carly would always have been the pivot in men's company. As a little girl, brought downstairs in a party dress, a bow in her incredibly blonde hair, to smile at Daddy's friends, or to sing, or to poke at the keys of a piano. She would always have moved up a gear with men around, a flattering word for each of them, a hundred daddys to be seduced anew. Stop analysing her.

'Let me ask you something.'

'Sure,' Cristy said

'Your knowledge about most things makes encyclopedias redundant,' Osorio said.

Flatter 'em, then fuck 'em, as Brent used to say.

'Tell me in language that a fool can understand what's happening in Saudi Arabia today beneath the surface.'

'A lot of oil, I'm told,' Cristy said.

'Come on,' said Osorio.

'You mean politically?'

'Yeah. Is it still our steadiest ally out there, for example?'

Cristy made a face. 'You really want a run-down?'

'Sure,' he said, everything about him wideawake.

Cristy looked briefly over to Ron, still embroiled with Carly.

'The present situation in Saudi,' she said slowly, 'like nearly all problems which arise out there, can be traced back to the descent of power from the 1920s. King Abdel-Aziz, the founder of the kingdom, left forty-two sons from his numerous wives, and grandchildren in the hundreds.'

When Osorio was concentrating hard, as now, his breathing seemed to cease.

'One of these grandchildren,' Cristy continued, 'is called Prince Saleem who is from a hitherto obscure branch of the Saud family. Saleem is undoubtedly bright. For the past seven years he has worked hard in Riyadh and kept a low profile. Two years ago he was appointed in charge of the Air Defence Forces, and a year ago he was made number two man at the Ministry of Oil.'

'Could he seize power?' Osorio asked.

Cristy considered the question. 'Possible, but unlikely,' she answered. 'It depends on the power base out there and how it's changing. In a country like that, of course, when the power base starts to shift, anything can happen.'

'Why should it shift?' Osorio asked.

'Money,' Cristy replied. 'The Saudis are spending money at the moment in truly gargantuan amounts. Defence, roads, health, you name it, they're spending over a hundred billion U.S. a year. Such expenditures are hard to curb. If oil falls much more they may be forced to cut back and people will become angry.'

'So what's so special about Saleem?' Osorio asked.

'Prince Saleem, for some reason, has his knife into the Japs,' Cristy replied. 'You know how dependent the Japanese are on Middle East oil and equally how paranoid they are about it?

Well, over the last year, Saleem has been making noises which are very anti-Jap. He has expressed the view, for example, that Japan's domination of world industry is undesirable and that Saudi oil should not be committed to this purpose. I bet that caused a bit of head-banging in Tokyo.'

'Why is he so anti-Jap?' Osorio asked.

'Search me,' Cristy said. 'Maybe his Sony compact is tripping on the left amplifier.'

'What are you two conspiring about?' Carly asked.

'Arabs and oil,' Osorio said. He turned mischievously to Ron. 'I expect you come across both pretty regularly in Durst Bank, Ron,' he said.

'Across what?' asked Ron pleasantly.

Osorio could see Cristy give him daggers, but he said: 'Arabs and oil. I hear Durst Bank act for some key players in that area.'

Ron offered both palms to the ceiling and made an elaborate shrug.

'Arabs, Jews, Christians, Hindus, as long as they have the money, I guess we're happy to take it.

'And Prince Saleem?' Osorio asked. 'Do you act for him?'

Ron's face never twitched.

'I told you, Durst Bank would act for King Kong if he had the money.'

Carly let out a little laugh.

'Lawyers.' She pointed at Ron. 'They're all the same. We've been here two hours and all I've managed to find out is that he works for that awful man Abel Eller.'

'You're lucky you got that out of him,' Osorio grinned.

Cristy asked quietly: 'Why is Abel Eller so awful?'

'Daddy describes him as a predator by necessity,' Carly said. 'He says that Durst Bank's balance sheet is so weak that he has to buy other companies' profits to survive. He says Abel Eller got where he is by climbing over the bones of dead men. Seriously,' she added as Ron's beaming face remained unchanged.

'Dead men's bones?' Cristy said. 'What does that mean?'

Osorio grinned. 'It means that Dutch is scared out of his pants that Man First Bank is going to end up in Abel Eller's back lot,' he said.

'Steve! That's not funny!' said Carly sharply. 'Neither is it even vaguely true. Everyone knows that Abel Eller stops at nothing to

73

get what he wants. I'm sorry, Ron.' She threw down her crumpled napkin. 'I need to freshen up,' she said getting to her feet.

'Let me come with you,' said Cristy.

Osorio watched them across the room.

'Women, Jesus Christ,' he said and took a cheroot. 'You need to be a fucking magician.'

'So we're both in the same business,' Carly smiled. 'We're both animals of the media.'

'I'm flattered as a lowly reporter to be included in such a description,' Cristy laughed.

'I envy you,' Carly said.

Cristy raised her eyebrows.

'No, I mean it,' Carly went on. 'I've never really worked *for* someone, you know what I mean? I was given a magazine and told, this is yours, go run it. Immediately I was in charge. But it must be comfortable not to be right up there, to be part of something big and solid, yet to have no *ultimate* responsibility.'

Cristy saw them both in the big gilt mirror of the rest-room.

'I think that's a bit too general,' she said gently.

'Of course it is,' Carla agreed. 'I'm sorry, I didn't mean to make it sound as if I thought you had a lightweight job or anything . . . '

'Don't worry,' Cristy said.

'I shouldn't have jumped up like that out there,' said Carly. 'But I just can't bear that sort of talk about Daddy.'

'You're completely right,' said Cristy. 'Steve sometimes goes too far.'

'I adore your brother,' Carly said, 'believe me, I've never been in love like this before. But I also worship my father. Is that wrong? He's put his whole life into his bank. He's given me everything since I was a baby. He is my life. I can't bear to hear people make fun of him like that.'

'If it were my father I'd be the same,' Cristy said.

Carly flicked out her hair and bent down for a final look in the mirror. The she straightened up.

'I have this nightmare,' she said. 'It's me, sitting on a wall someplace. Steve is one side, Daddy is the other. They both want me to go with them. I have to make a choice.'

'And do you?' Cristy asked.

'Of course,' Carly smiled. 'I choose Steve. Isn't that the choice I made when I decided to marry him?'

The men stood as Cristy and Carly returned. Osorio looked at his watch. 'Folks, this has been real fun, but I told the guys back at the ranch I'd look in there on my way up town – there may be some action in the Far East I'd like to follow.'

They waited for their coats in the small vestibule.

'You want to come and see some of the action?' Osorio asked Carly.

She shivered and shook her head. 'I want my bed,' she replied. 'I'll drop you off and your car can take me home.'

The GiltStock Cadillac swung up to the door.

Osorio turned to Cristy. 'It's been good to see you, little sister,' he said as they touched cheeks.

'Take care,' she whispered.

'I will,' he retorted, slipping into the long limousine after Carly.

Cristy linked Ron as they walked across the yellow lighted parking lot.

'What's all this about Abel Eller and dead men's bones?' she asked and squeezed his arm.

'It's a load of bullshit,' he laughed.

She leaned her head against him. 'What are we doing tonight?' she asked.

'Tonight, my princess,' Ron said in a booming voice, 'we drive across the Verrazano Bridge in all its splendour, to my castle on my island in the sea. I carry you across the drawbridge, up to my turret room and there I make sweet sweet love to you until the stars are driven from the sky.'

'You're such a lyrical asshole,' Cristy said, bursting out with laughter. She reached up both arms around his neck and pulled his mouth to hers.

Over Ron's shoulder Cristy could still see Manhattan's lights, twinkling with their cold comfort.

2

Osorio used an encoded card to enter the building and to activate the elevator. In the trading-room on the thirty-fifth floor half a dozen men sat in shirt sleeves, smoking and watching the screens. Some of them turned as Osorio entered.

'Hi, Steve.'

'Hi,' answered Osorio. 'What's on the move in the Far East?'

'Not much. Gold is firm and the dollar's getting hammered, but we're not doing anything.'

'No news anywhere?'

'Nah, not really. Three hundred people drowned in India when a ferry capsised, one in eight Russians is an alcoholic, it's one of those evenings.'

'Steve,' called a trader from another console. 'There were calls for you earlier.'

'Yeah?'

'Some lady, left her number, I put it on your desk.'

'Thanks,' said Osorio and made his way to the boardroom.

The message was spiked on a pencil over his phone. Osorio looked at it, shrugged and tapped out the number. As it rang he could see New Jersey across the Hudson, shimmering like a fantasy.

'Hello.'

'This is Steve Osorio.'

'Mr Osorio, I'm so glad you called.'

'I'm sorry,' Osorio laughed, 'who is this?'

'You're speaking to Laisha Ahmed,' came the reply.

'Ah, Miss Ahmed,' Osorio said, 'sorry, I just dropped in here on my way home and got a message with the number but no name. How are you?'

'Mr Osorio, I got on to GiltStock earlier today and tried to use our account,' Laisha said, 'but I was told it wasn't yet opened. Can that be true?'

Osorio grimaced. Then he saw the memo from Malcolm on his desk, two short paragraphs, confirming what the girl was saying.

'Unfortunately, yes,' he replied. 'You see, there are procedures which we are forced to follow, and in this case . . . '

'Mr Osorio!' Laisha's voice stopped Osorio dead. 'I want to

see you about this, tonight. It's important. Things are about to happen.'

Osorio looked at his watch. It was nearly eleven.

'Can't it wait . . . ?'

'I'm on the top floor, suite A, 300 Park,' she said and hung up.

Slowly, Osorio replaced the phone, then drew in air through both nostrils. The vision of her which in the past days he had succeeded in diluting came rushing back. Somehow it was the contrast: her dark against Carly's blonde, hot and cold, and the sheer electric field that had buzzed when she was there . . .

Osorio shook himself and turned out the boardroom lights.

'Early to bed now, Steve,' called a trader as Osorio made his way out through the trading-room.

'You bet,' replied Osorio.

The cab wove uptown, bumping into and out of great dips, the chassis scraping, the cabby swearing and Osorio being eyed all the while from the front by a panting German Shepherd.

He was goingto see a client who had deposited fifteen million dollars with GiltStock. But he knew as little about Gabriel as when Ahmed and his daughter had walked into his office six days ago. Osorio hit his fist into his hand causing the dog to growl. No matter what Laisha Ahmed's information, the committee in GiltStock, particularly Jay Cox, would have to be satisfied with Gabriel's credentials. An entity like GiltStock was fragile, something made up of men and women, all held together by no more than common purpose and his leadership. No one in GiltStock was manacled to their desks: the door was always open and they were always free to leave.

The doorman at 300 Park opened the cab door. In the spacious lobby, a dark-suited concierge wrote Osorio's name into a book then spoke quietly into a telephone.

'The thirty-third floor, Mr Osorio,' he said. 'Turn right out of the elevator.'

In the ascending mirror, Osorio examined his face: except for a darkening of stubble on his jaw he looked as fresh as he had fifteen hours before. This won't take more than twenty minutes, he said to himself as the doors opened.

The door was oak panelled; Osorio sensed that he was being examined through a peephole, then it swung open.

His first impression was the smell of incense. As a kid he had once been to a Catholic high mass and as he stepped inside he was back there, for all around the dimly lighted room were thuribles wisping with their fragrant gums. Osorio walked to the middle of the room and blinked. Silks, dozens of them, blues in twenty different shades, fell from points above his head to provide tented cocoons; lights positioned behind the silks threw magical shadows up the walls and along the ceiling; there was no conventional furniture, just beds of cushions, hundreds of them, scattered on fine rugs. Then Osorio saw her.

He could not remember her as tall as she now appeared. She was standing to one side, wearing a striped, sleeveless t-shirt which came right to her neck, a black mini-skirt and no shoes. The mini was what gave her height; it made her legs go to the moon.

'Please take off your shoes,' she said, and shook her hair to one side.

Osorio slipped one shoe off, then the other, never for a moment allowing his eyes to leave her face. Some process beyond his control was at work deep within him. She was incredibly ripe, luscious, ready; unmindful of his tumescence he stepped towards her.

'Can we go through here, Mr Osorio? It's easier for business.'

Osorio bit his tongue and followed. Laisha carried a file which he hadn't noticed and they entered a carpeted room with a large central desk, leather chairs and some filing cabinets.

'Thank you for making it so quickly,' Laisha Ahmed said and drew the cord to bring down venetian blinds on the window. She sat behind the desk, indicated a chair for Osorio. 'I know it's late, Mr Osorio, but I've been trying to get you since I spoke to Geneva.'

'I had a dinner appointment,' Osorio said, 'and my friends call me Steve.'

She looked at him, then smiled pleasantly. 'I'm Laisha,' she said. She opened her file, scanned it, then looked up. 'It's time to fish or cut bait, Steve,' she said. 'Will GiltStock act for Gabriel or not?'

Osorio took a deep breath. If she had deliberately walked him under a freezing douche she could scarcely have been more successful.

'Laisha,' said Osorio slowly, 'I've no doubt you people know your business, and certainly I know mine. We have procedures which must be followed and they include definitely not acting for new clients, however distinguished they may appear, unless we have maximum information. In the case of Gabriel we have almost no information, so we have a problem.'

Laisha put both her hands behind her head, caught her long hair and wound it swiftly into a plait. The gesture showed kisses of jet black silk under each armpit.

'Let me try and explain a few things to you,' she said, returning her hands to the desk. 'Firstly, why we chose GiltStock. You want to know? It's because you're smaller than the others, alright? We chose you because we want maximum discretion, not the whole street talking about our business the way it would if we went into someone big like Merrill. Okay? That's the first reason. The second is because we've heard you're hungry. Hungry people are often good.'

'I understand,' Osorio said.

'Now let's try and clear the air about Gabriel Holdings.' She smiled slightly. 'Obviously the fact that we handed you fifteen million didn't cut any ice, although I doubt if it's an event which happens in your boardroom every other day.'

Osorio shrugged. 'We appreciate business,' he said.

'Who is Gabriel?' she asked rhetorically. 'Gabriel, Steve, is a company which has been formed by people who have a very substantial interest in the price of oil.' She laced her hands and put them under her chin; although her mouth was smiling, her very brown eyes were not. 'We're talking dynasties here, Steve,' she said softly. 'We're talking not just about the price of a commodity, but about the integrity of a nation.'

'I need to know specifics,' Osorio said. 'What company? What people? Which nation? I'm not asking for it in writing.'

'A fool who opens his mouth too wide, risks losing it to a hawk,' Laisha said.

Osorio's head went from side to side.

'Give me facts, not proverbs,' he said.

The girl looked at him, then reflectively around her. Then she made a decision.

'In the Kingdom of Saudi Arabia there is a prince of the house of Saud whose name is Saleem,' she said very quietly.

'Okay,' said Osorio.

'Gabriel is Saleem.'

'Okay.'

'Events are about to happen involving Prince Saleem. Oil will rise in price. Do I make myself clear?'

''Perfectly.'

'When the rise begins, certain high-placed people – known to you as Gabriel Holdings – wish to cement the financial position for themselves, and their children, and for their children's children, in a land far from the desert – just in case, you understand, that these events do not unfold as well as planned.'

'I think I understand,' Osorio smiled.

'You are privileged,' Laisha said, 'to be chosen as the instrument for a plan from which you will undoubtedly make yourself a lot of money – and I don't refer only to commissions.'

Osorio raised his eyebrows.

'Let's not fool around,' Laisha said. 'Big orders like we'll give you are a licence for a broker to print money.'

Osorio inclined his head. She was sharp on a scale higher than he could have imagined.

'What's the plan?' he asked quietly.

Her eyebrows arched. 'Only the broker knows the plan,' she said. 'So you agree to act?'

'First I need to know the plan.'

She thought for a moment, then appeared to make a decision.

'On one condition,' she said.

'Which is?'

'That whether you agree to act or not, that the overall details of our strategy will be known by you and you only.'

Osorio thought, then shrugged. 'You're the boss.'

'That if you act, that you and only you will be involved in actually dealing with the business. We don't want to talk to anyone other than you.'

'Agreed.'

Laisha leaned back, her hands in her lap, her cotton shirt tight against her body

'Gabriel has two hundred and fifty million dollars at it's disposal,' she said. 'All of it will be invested in oil futures within the next ten days.'

Osorio whistled. 'That's a lot of oil,' he said.

80

'It's over a hundred and twenty-five million barrels,' she replied, 'or five billion gallons, or a week's production of all the OPEC countries combined.'

Osorio's mind raced. 'What's your target price?' he asked.

Laisha pouted for a moment. 'It depends on how seriously coming events develop,' she said. 'But a minimum price of thirty dollars a barrel would be a reasonable expectation.'

'That's a rise of nearly ten bucks a barrel,' Osorio said. 'Your friends are going to make themselves over a billion – clear?'

'Plenty of people nowadays are worth that kind of money,' Laisha remarked.

Osorio drummed his fingers on the arm of the chair.

'It could just happen too,' he said, half to himself. 'This market *wants* to go up, but it can't.'

'It will rise,' she said, 'of that there is no question. The only question which now remains, Steve, is whether or not you will act. And I need to know the answer to that right now.'

'There are position limits to be considered in this thing,' Osorio said. 'You just can't go out and buy a huge quantity of oil futures of the magnitude you're talking. The rules say the position must be reported and only *bona fide* hedge positions of that size are permitted.'

Laisha smiled. 'Both you and I know that rules are made to be broken,' she said, showing the tip of her tongue. 'Anyway, whoever said that we're not – what was the expression – *bona fide?*'

Slowly Osorio got to his feet. He went to the window and prised the blind open: midtown gleamed in at him, other penthouses all around, no doubt full of people all hatching political coups and billion-dollar safety nets in Switzerland. He laughed aloud, then turned around.

'I'll do it,' he said, 'but with one proviso.'

Laisha raised her eyebrows.

'I will need complete freedom to work an order this size,' Osorio said. 'There will be no question of you or anyone else looking over my shoulder or pinning me down with impossible price limits.'

Laisha smiled. 'Of course,' she said with understanding. 'Incidentally, although my father handed you fifteen million the other day,' she said, 'we are, by nature, suspicious people. When we start to trade, you can expect at least one request for our

81

money to be returned before we go in for the next trade – it's a kind of test: he's given you his money, he will want to see if GiltStock is as good at giving it back.'

Osorio shrugged. 'Sounds reasonable,' he said. 'He'll have it.'

'That's settled then,' Laisha said, standing and smoothing her skirt. 'You already have the signed papers – all that remains is the money, and we quite understand the thrust of your little lecture to us in your boardroom: you'll get it as you need it.'

They walked from the office to the muted, scented outer room.

'Just remember,' she said. 'On this, we deal exclusively with you and no one else.'

'That's quite clear,' Osorio said.

The room they had returned to was dark after the office; Osorio narrowed his eyes as he cast around.

'What are you looking for?' she asked.

'Just my shoes,' he smiled.

'Why do you want your shoes?'

'I normally like to wear them when I'm going home,' he replied. Then he found it hard to breath. He straightened up: while he had been bent, she had removed the t-shirt, so that now she stood there, dressed only in the mini, her hands joined before her, her marvellous body exactly as he had imagined it, only better.

'Who said anything about going home?' she murmured.

Osorio swept her off the ground and carried her to the cushions. He sank them both down and then took the nipple of her breast in his mouth, sucking and circling it with his urgent tongue. He heard her gasping, he felt her fingers tear at his shirt buttons, then his belt, then his zip. His mouth went to her other breast and sucked so hard that she yelled. He caught the waist of the skirt and in one movement brought it down to her ankles and off, then he knelt up, freed himself from his jacket and shirt, sat and wriggled from his pants, then turned back. She was kneeling, her elbows on the ground, her twin mounds thrust towards him, her hair all around her, hiding her head. He caught her waist, pulled her to him, and then took her the Arab way, hard, ten times. She gasped for breath. He pulled out, turned her over and went back in, finishing it a minute later, his mouth on hers, his hands crushing her breasts.

They lay back, exhausted, panting. The sounds of their breathing and the smell of incense filled the room.

3

Cristy Osorio walked straight from the elevators on the ninth floor of *The Wall Street Journal* to her cubicle. Shelves on either side of her chair overflowed with papers, books and periodicals, hemming her in. Her desk held further stacks of books, notepads, an old typewriter, a mug full of pencils, a mound of *Journal* back-issues, a telephone, and a grey AST screen and keyboard which also accessed the Dow Jones News/Retrieval system. Either side of her position other reporters worked, keyboards in their laps, quietly typing. Either end of the room were glass-fronted offices where the editors sat.

Cristy flicked through some messages, nothing that couldn't wait. She switched on the AST and sat back as it hummed to life. If she had been asked, Cristy would not have been able to describe precisely how she felt: like a well, rumbling before it gushed, she felt potent, heady. Cristy felt she was on the brink of a story.

Something was happening, she was sure of it. She read it in the falling price of oil, she read it in Steve's face when he had questioned her. She had gone back and turned her Middle East sources inside out; she had scoured the Journal files; two nights in a row she had woken up at three a.m., sat up in bed and stayed that way until dawn, still the rising feeling, still no closer. She had gone down Wall Street and talked to the people she knew: brokers, chartists, oil men, fund men, account executives, people who worked with banks. Sure, oil was going down, half what it was a year ago. Bad for Texas, Cristy, but good for the Union.

But there was something else, a dimension she was missing.

83

She re-read every single piece on oil that she had ever written; weary, she got out the files she kept at home and read them all.

She bit her lip in frustration: the story was there alright, maybe the biggest she would ever get, she was standing right on top of it, but she was damned if she knew what it was.

She decided to call Steve. The phone in her cubicle rang before her hand touched it.

'Cristy Osorio?'

Cristy frowned. The voice was new to her, very thin with almost a whistle in it.

'This is Cristy Osorio.'

'I've read your pieces on oil, Cristy.'

'Who is this?' Cristy asked, feeling sudden fear.

'You are so near the truth, Cristy, so near,' said the voice.

'Near what?'

'You know almost everything: all you need to do is connect them.'

Cristy swallowed.

'About . . . ?'

'Yes, about oil.'

'What do I know?'

'You know about the Arabs; you know about Japan,' said her caller. 'Now look at the market itself. There's an interaction. Catch it and you have the story of a lifetime.'

Cristy's frown was deep.

'Be more specific,' she said. 'Hello . . . ?'

In the busy office, the whining dialtone seemed oddly loud.

CHAPTER EIGHT

1

New York

Monday 18 February 6.45 a.m.

Daylight was just beginning to creep into the canyons and crevices of Wall Street, but high above, in a hundred offices, some traders had already been in for an hour, following the markets in Europe where the day was already half over.

Osorio pounded the path that wound through Battery Park, his hair collected in a luminous headband before flying out behind him. He wore a bright orange Addidas tracksuit and running shoes with luminous stripes on their heels and uppers. He passed a bench which for the night had been bed to a body encased in garbage liners and ran on, into a flock of scavenging pigeons, sending them fluttering out of his way.

Healthy body, healthy mind. To his left, tug boats were working the river and Liberty was gradually coming into view as day began to burn away the mist. Osorio was in love with New York. At times like these when everything stretched out ahead and anything was possible, his love was something real, an exhilarating affair which knew no bounds. On his very first day on Wall Street, years before, he had known that it was exactly right for him, that it was here in this space-age village he would make his fortune, it was here in New York that he would carve his name in a way that would make Brent proud.

He left the Park and pressed uptown on a sidewalk where the second thin phase of earlybirds were hurrying to their desks. He accelerated cheekily across the fender of someone's limo, leaped on to the sidewalk of the next block and began to push himself at double speed for the final half mile.

Oil. Goddammit. He pumped, his face creased with effort. Was he doing the right thing? Risk. Sometimes you had to take it. Remember the Chinese who wanted to buy so much gold that they'd have need a freighter to ship it? But that was different. Money up front, okay, like these Arabs, but the Chinese had been so obviously crooks. He pumped. And GiltStock had been different. Younger. More a target in those days for such people. Now GiltStock had controls, nearly twenty people doing nothing else but monitoring, monitoring, a computer system which had cost a million. Where could there be risk with such controls?

GiltStock. His creation. Nothing must happen to harm it. And yet it had to *earn*. With people like Tremaine sniffing around, the upward momentum had to be maintained.

Osorio came to the final block and pushed with everything. Oil. Christ, what a fuck she was. Jesus, he hoped she was alright. Arab men were filthy. What had Cox said about their camels? His legs were coming high, to his waist, powering up and down like engine parts. Oil. Arab men liked it both ways. So the odds were . . . Hell! He saw the GiltStock building two blocks away and went for it, head down, neck rigid. Oil. Nine months since he'd touched anyone but Carly. Now he'd screwed someone he'd met just once before every night for nearly a week. *Shit!* The oxygen in his chest screamed to be replaced, but he pushed even more, denying it, denying himself, trying to cauterise his very essence with pain.

'Morning, Steve. Trying to kill yourself?'

Osorio pulled up, emptied, at the entrance to the cavernous lobby, his hands on his knees; Cheryl Leinster was standing there, smiling.

'Hi, Cheryl,' Osorio panted. 'I guess it looks like it.'

They walked together to the elevators. Cheryl wore a coat which was black and shining and covered in thousands of multi-coloured sequins.

'Anything new?' asked Osorio when he got his breath back.

Cheryl inclined her head to one side to say could be. They

had the car to themselves.

'You holding out on me?' Osorio grinned.

Cheryl looked at her shoes, then back at the exotic, sweat-lined face.

'There're some rumblings upstairs I guess you probably know about,' she said quietly.

Osorio stopped breathing for the second time in three minutes.

'Such as?'

'Cox is really mad you took on that big account and told no one.'

'Cheryl,' said Osorio, exhaling at length, 'some things can't happen by committee and this is one of them, okay?'

She nodded and smiled. 'I'm not complaining,' she replied and looked away from him, up at the panel to the changing floor numbers. 'By the way,' she said, 'I've been looking at those oil charts like you asked me.'

'Oh yeah? How do they look?'

'Interesting,' she replied.

'When can you see me?'

'I'd like to follow the first metal rings in London,' Cheryl replied. 'Say in thirty minutes?'

'Thirty minutes is fine,' Steve said. 'I'm going to get some breakfast.'

Osorio understood traders. His great-grandfather had traded skins and patent medicines from the back of a horse-cart from Abilene to Corpus Christi. His father's father had begun by trading horses, changed to autos, then moved through leases on tracts of barren land to oil. Brent was a trader in the modern sense: a hardbitten, incorrigible charmer who when he said 'sheet, everythin's for sale', wasn't joking. Osorio who knew rocks and drillbits almost before he could read or write was just one in a long line.

He realised that it took one to know one. The kids who came to work for GiltStock, raw kids from Brooklyn and Queens with clothes that looked as if all their elder brothers had worn them first that day, they were the people he knew; he could tell in a week flat if they were going to make it or not. Confidence was the key. They either got confidence fast, like a bolt of lightning straight up the ass, or they went home and worked behind the counter in a hardware store. The ones that stayed changed so quick, it was hard to recognise them: their clothes, the way they spoke, the way they smelled, it all changed in a matter of weeks. Kids became men, stopped staring like campesinos on a market day and launched themselves with relish into the biggest pool of ready cash on earth. But come the end of the day, Osorio understood, many of them still returned to homes where admiration for a rising twenty-year-old might be tempered by the demands of items like kids or the whines from a too-early marriage.

Osorio understood. It was the main reason why in GiltStock's dining-room he had tried to give them something extra so that the fantasy of excitement, not to mention the hours they worked, would be sustained.

The dining-room had cost a hundred thousand just to design. It was split-level front to back, window all along one side and the wallpaper pure silk done in emerald green. The chairs and tables were good repro Chippendale, traders wiped their mouths with real linen napkins, leaned their elbows on real linen cloths and ate with ebony-handled knives and forks specially designed by someone in England. There was a chef whom Osorio had hijacked from The Pierre, and a team under him who could, if the occasion demanded, produce a grass-fattened Charolais steak and a bottle of Dom Perignon at seven in the morning. There was a little Frenchwoman who did nothing except make desserts: tarts and pies, puddings and pastries, art works in themselves, which appeared each day on a central podium and were the objects of intense competition. This woman had a daughter who came in at three every morning and made croissants, beautifully crispy, weightless wafers with hearts of buttery gold which exploded in the mouth.

One detail had Osorio superimposed on the design: clusters of market monitors, wall mounted every five yards, winked eye-catchingly to remind those below of the ever-present reality which paid for it all.

There were no special tables in the room, you sat wherever was free, yet the corner table at the window from which you looked straight out at the Verrazano Bridge always stayed empty for Osorio when he was around.

He sat, still in his tracksuit, ankle on knee, *The Wall Street Journal* folded lengthwise in half before him, a beaker of fresh orange-juice at his elbow. Commodities and stock-markets the world over were quiet, even the dollar had been let off its daily beating. His eyes checked the closing prices of oil the day before: March had closed at twenty-one dollars and ten cents a barrel, down twenty cents on the day in lightish volume: sixty-five million barrels traded.

Through the door at the far end Osorio saw Ray Leonard shuffle in, untidy even this early, and Malcolm Finch at his side. Malcolm's usually pale face had a varnish of colour; true to his word, he had taken some time off last week to fish with his grandson near Buffalo. Good, thought Osorio, Malcolm's been looking as if he might be getting too old for this game.

'*Buenos dias,*' said Ray and sat next to Osorio, placing a bulky computer printout on the floor beside him.

'Hi, fellas,' Osorio said. He leaned over to Malcolm who had sat on the other side and clapped his shoulder. 'Goddammit, Mr Finch, if no one else has said it, then let me be the first: you look like a hundred million bucks, you old son-of-a-bitch.'

Malcolm beamed brightly.

'I thought I'd miss all you guys when I retire,' he said. 'Well, let me tell you something, in the presence of a six-pound brown trout you're just a distant memory.'

'Six pounds?' Osorio leaned back. 'Get outa here!'

'I swear to God! It took me a half hour to get him in the boat.'

'You're not talking to a bunch of kids, you know,' said Osorio, winking to Ray Leonard's enormous grin.

'Anticipating such a reaction,' said Malcolm triumphantly, 'I took the precaution of bringing my Polaroid along.'

He slapped a colour shot on the tablecloth and sat back.

'Is this the kid?' asked Osorio seriously. 'He's a real fine boy, Malcolm. He really helped you catch that fish?'

'Sure did,' Malcolm nodded. 'Had one of the most beautiful days that I ever remember.'

A waiter in a crisp, white jacket came along, pencil and pad in hand.

'Morning, gentlemen.'

'Good morning,' Malcolm answered. 'I'll just have coffee and croissants, please.'

'And I'll have oatmeal, English style, English muffins and English kippers,' Ray said.

The two men looked at him.

'It's part of a diet,' Ray said, scratching his stomach. 'You work your way around the world. By the time you get out of China you should have lost thirty pounds.'

The other two laughed.

'Anything of note whilst I was away?' Malcolm asked. 'Markets appear to have stayed quiet.'

'Too goddamm quiet,' Osorio said.

'Did anything come through on those enquiries we were making, the Arab enquiries?' Malcolm asked. 'I've checked my messages, nothing has come back to me.'

Ray closed his eyes briefly, then swivelled them in Osorio's direction.

'Yeah, I made some enquiries and I got some answers,' Osorio said.

'And?'

'They're okay,' Osorio replied quietly.

'Well, that's good,' Malcolm said, 'Who are they? OPEC? The King? The Queen?'

'I've established that they represent one hell of a lot of money,' Osorio replied. 'No more than that. They want to deal directly through me.'

Malcolm made a face to say that he was impressed. 'Good, good, good,' he said again. 'That should have no problem getting through.'

Osorio and Ray exchanged glances.

'It's already through, Malcolm,' Osorio said. 'They traded last week.'

Malcolm blinked, tilted his head first to the right, then the left. 'Okay,' he nodded, 'okay. What did they do?'

Ray lifted the printout on to the table, thumbed it to the page, then put it down again as breakfast arrived.

'Two million barrels of the March,' he said

'What did they go in at?' asked Malcolm.

'Twenty-one dollars and thirty cents average,' said Osorio.

'And oil closed at twenty-one ten,' said Ray, anticipating the next question, 'so they've dropped two million times twenty cents, or four hundred thousand bucks.'

'We've got margins way over that figure,' Osorio said.

'Did they pay on time?' Malcolm asked.

Ray made a little movement with his shoulders. 'A fraction slow, if you had to be critical,' he said, 'but, no, I'm happy.'

'Did you tell them to buy?' Malcolm asked Osorio.

'No,' Osorio replied, shaking his head, 'these people have ideas of their own.'

'What on God's earth makes *them* think oil is going to rise?' Malcolm asked. 'Why does everyone always want to buy something that's going down?'

'Not everyone thinks you're right, Malcolm,' said Osorio coolly.

'It was dropping when I left here last week,' Malcom replied. 'I come in here this morning, it dropped again on Friday to its lowest level for three years. It's going down, Steve, believe me.'

Osorio's mouth was a straight line. 'I wouldn't call a twenty cent drop in a commodity with a twenty dollar range the end of the word,' he said tightly.

Malcolm Finch shook his white head.

'Steve,' he said. 'At these levels oil is as dangerous as a rattlesnake in a tight boot – and you know it. I just hope these Arabs have a lot of cash.'

'We've got normal deposits plus fifty percent from them,' Osorio said. 'Right, Ray?'

Ray nodded as a silver spoon disappeared under his moustache. 'Right.'

'It's been explained to them that any wrinkle in the cash flow and we cut,' Osorio said.

'What happens if we can't get through to wherever these people are based to call for the cash?' Malcolm asked.

'They have someone right here in New York,' Osorio said. 'We make a local call.'

'Who have they got here?' Malcolm asked.

'A woman,' Osorio answered and immediately began to feel something happen to the surface of his skin. 'Their head guy's daughter.'

Malcolm stirred sugar into black coffee whilst Ray leant back to allow the waiter to remove his empty porridge bowl and to place two rust coloured kippers on a salver before him. Osorio looked up as the unmistakable figure of Jay Cox approached them across the dining-room.

'Here comes Suck,' Osorio murmured.

'Gentlemen.' Without invitation Cox sat in a free chair and placed a thick, computer printout, a copy of the one at Ray's feet, on the table. Cox thumbed the pages.

'I just wanted an explanation on something in this morning's printout,' he said, ostensibly to Ray Leonard. He found the page and swivelled it around. 'Do we really have a three hundred thousand barrel March oil position in the fund?' he asked, frowning as if he was the village idiot. 'Or is the printout a victim of an error, or worse, some distasteful joke?'

Ray Leonard's eyes flicked to Osorio who looked briefly at Cox, then tossed his head back defiantly, a creeping glow colouring his cheeks.

'I put the fund in,' Osorio shrugged. 'I felt what was good for the Arabs would be good for the fund.'

Malcolm's frown caused the ends of his eyebrows to spike upwards. 'For three hundred thousand barrels, Steve?'

Osorio nodded and wiped hair from his forehead.

'At what price?' Malcolm asked.

'Twenty-one thirty, same as the two million barrel order,' Osorio replied.

'That's a sixty grand loss for the fund, Steve,' Malcolm said. 'Shit, the whole thing only made two million last year – we can't afford decisions like that.'

'I've put a fucking stop in at twenty-one,' snapped Osorio.

Jay Cox shook his head in a show of exasperation.

'First we take on a major major account without observing our own rules for vetting it,' he said, 'then we follow it blindly into a market that is clearly going down, using money entrusted to us in good faith by other people.' He offered his hands to the air. 'What's going on around here? We've all got our reputations, you know, Steve, every one of us has played our part in getting money into the GiltStock Fund.'

Osorio sighed very deeply. 'I don't need a lecture from you on ethics, Jay,' he said. 'I can't reveal exactly what I know – but I do believe that events may shortly move in oil's favour and I therefore think that to have omitted the fund would have been a far more gross error than to take on the relatively small position which I have.'

'There are very well established house procedures for any fund positions over twenty-five thousand dollars,' Cox said. 'If I recall, the consent of either Malcolm or myself is specifically required to take a position such as this. Is that not so, Malcolm?'

Malcolm's head was shaking anew. 'I would never have agreed to this, Steve,' he said. 'If you had asked me . . . '

Osorio turned like a conger-eel. 'I couldn't ask you, Malcolm,' he snapped, 'because you'd gone fucking fishing.'

A waiter had wheeled a communications console to the table whilst they spoke; Ray wiped his mouth of kippers and took the call.

'Steve.'

Osorio turned his head.

'Vince on three,' said Ray.

Osorio leaned and pressed a button. 'Morning, Vince.'

'Hi, Steve,' came the voice of Vince Carpenter on NYMEX. 'I thought in view of these new oil positions you might like to hear the first indications before the market opens.'

Osorio felt the muscles of his stomach contract as the three other men looked at him. 'Sure,' he said and lighted himself a cheroot.

'Well, we're calling it up, Steve,' Vince Carpenter said, 'anywhere between thirty to sixty cents.'

Osorio began to smile. 'Just a second, Vince,' he said and pressed another switch on the table console which connected the call to a conference speaker. 'I didn't quite catch that, Vince, could you run it past me again?'

'Sorry,' said Vince, now broadcasting to the dining-room. 'We're calling oil anywhere between thirty to sixty up, that should make the March twenty-one fifty minimum.'

'Now why is that, Vince?' asked Osorio.

'A couple of reasons,' Vince replied. 'There's a rumour doing the rounds that Syria are moving troops nearer Israel's northern border, although no one is admitting it.'

Osorio grinned cheekily at Jay Cox whose egg-head was tilted impassively.

'There's also talk of a very big buy order in the market,' Vince said. 'Maybe you can contribute something on that, Steve?'

'Damned if I can, Vince,' Osorio smiled, 'damned if I can.'

'I'll keep you in touch, Steve,' said Vince as the call was disconnected.

Osorio was still smiling as the three men at the table rose to their feet.

'Better get down to the engine room,' said Ray.

'See you later, Steve,' said Malcolm.

'I want to say one thing very clearly,' said Jay Cox tightly. 'Just because you've got it right once doesn't mean that you can run the fund and this firm like a cowboy.'

So saying, he turned and strode from the dining-room.

'Fuck you too!' said Osorio under his breath.

He signalled to the waiter for hot coffee, reached to the basket of croissants which Malcolm had left and peeled one open, then spearing a pat of butter from an iced dish he coated the opened bread of the croissant, added two spoons of thick, chunky marmalade and popped the whole thing into his mouth.

'That looks sinful.'

Osorio looked up. Cheryl was standing there, a large pad in her hand. He made big eyes that his mouth was full and pointed to a chair.

'How was London?' he asked, munching.

'Flat,' she replied. 'Lead is looking as if it wants to go somewhere, but who wants to trade lead?'

She opened out the pad on the table: it showed in blown up detail the price gyrations of oil over eighteen months. Osorio peered at it, using the handle of a knife to trace the trend lines which Cheryl had drawn in. Oil's fall, although obvious, had slowed considerably and the movement for the past month was now more sideways than down.

'It's forming a triangle,' Osorio said.

'A perfect symmetrical triangle in fact,' Cheryl said.

Osorio's eyes flicked between her and the chart.

'So what way is it going to break?' he asked.

Cheryl threw the pencil down and put her hands behind her head.

'Conventional wisdom suggests,' she said, 'that following the breakout from a symmetrical triangle, the price follows the trend which preceded the triangle.'

'That means it'll go up,' Osorio said.

'It *should* go up,' she said carefully. 'The triangle is saying to me that all the price movement in the last twelve months is simply an aberration within a much more long-term up-trend. We are approaching the most crucial band of support on the entire chart. The price has soon got to break. It should go up, with the emphasis on should.'

'But,' Osorio said.

'But,' Cheryl said, 'the more I look at that market, the more I dislike it. I don't know, I just get the feeling that there's something *extra* going on, you know what I mean? I can't explain it, I'm sorry.'

'Extra?'

'Take all the important points which oil has broken on the way down from forty dollars a barrel,' she said and pointed. 'Thirty-three, thirty, twenty-six. Would it surprise you to know that before each of those breaks there was a major announcement by the Japanese about their big oil find?'

Osorio looked at her.

'Market reaction to fundamentals,' he said and shrugged. 'Who knows? This Jap find may not be all it's cracked up to be.'

Cheryl weighed her hand unhappily. 'Markets like facts,' she said.

Osorio put a match to a cheroot. 'Shit, you said it should go up, but you dislike what you see,' he said. 'What are you trying to be? Neutral?'

'Steve,' she said gently, 'I'm old enough to know that if it doesn't go up, it'll go down.'

Osorio leaned back and looked at her through narrowed eyes, making her colour slightly.

'"If it doesn't go up, it'll go down,"' he repeated quietly. 'Is that all the best brains in this organisation can produce?'

'The market is on the brink,' said Cheryl, colouring more. 'I'm aware, as is everyone, of your views on the matter, but if you want to stand on the edge of a cliff when there's a big wind coming, then I guess that's your business.'

Osorio burst out laughing.

'Cheryl, did you ever go to a cock fight?' he asked.

'A cock fight?'

'Yes, you know, they have them down south, we went to them all the time as kids, you get two cockerels and put them in a ring and they fight each other to the death?'

Cheryl shook her head and looked bemused.

'Well, my grand-daddy, his name was Percy, he had these chickens all over the place,' Osorio said. 'Come the day of a big fight, everyone knew Percy's cock was the best. You only had to look: Percy's bird was the tallest, the strongest, he had the meanest eye, the thickest legs, boy when they put the spurs on him everyone knew where to put their money down. Except, one person. You tell me who.'

Cheryl shook her head.

'Except grand-daddy Percy,' Osorio said. 'He'd be there at the back of an old van, grooming this bird, trimming its hackles and *worrying*, my goodness did he worry! He knew more about that chicken than anyone else, but come the final moment would he go and make himself some money? No way. Percy would find a million excuses to disbelieve what he could see with his own eyes.'

Osorio got to his feet.

'I guess I better go change,' he said. 'Thanks for the chart insight.'

'You're welcome,' Cheryl said and raised her hand for a waiter. 'I'm having some coffee.'

She sat and watched as Osorio walked from the table, down through the dining-room, greeting people at different tables.

'Be careful,' she said, but he had gone too far to hear her.

2

Monday 12.00 noon

A big ship was nosing upchannel, slowly but relentlessly. Osorio paused at the window to watch her. For all her grace there was something sinister too, something . . . intrusive about a big sleek pile of metal slipping in from out there at sea and nosing right into the bowels of the city. Osorio bit his lip. What did the ship remind him of? Something phallic? Christ, the shine from Laisha's rump kept popping in and out of his mind. I'm becoming a sex maniac, he thought. I'm about to marry the most gorgeous creature in New York and all I think about is Arab ass.

I'm forty years of age and

96

It sure ain't very funny,
That all I ever think about
Is ass and makin' money.

He shook his head as the words of Brent's favourite song came into his ears. He looked at his watch: twelve noon. What was Brent doing now – right now? Probably stripped to the waist, fit as a boy of twenty, cussing and swearing at some god-damm whore of a drill-bit that had just gone and cost him five hundred bucks.

Osorio left the window and sat at the head of the boardroom table. There was a folder open containing neatly typed columns of figures, a statement of GiltStock's assets at the previous month end, meticulously prepared by Ray Leonard. Osorio stared at the figures. Suddenly he understood what the big ship had put him in mind of: nudging its inexorable way it looked just like Dutch Tremaine, always advancing with implacable momentum.

Osorio ran his eye down the list of figures. Seats on various exchanges, two and a half million; lease on office at cost, half a million; office fittings and furniture the same. The lease was worth over a million now, easy. Cash at bank, six and a half million. Investments, two. Twelve million. Osorio picked up a pencil. GiltStock had at least twelve million bucks worth of assets, of which he owned eighty-five percent, Malcolm owned five percent and the share-option scheme took the rest.

What about his personal wealth? His apartment off Fifth was worth a million and a half. The house in Boca Raton that he never used, two. Art, racehorses and odds and ends came to another one point five. Investments, four, cash on deposit half a million. Total, nine and a half million. Less monies he owed. About two and a half million. Net, seven. Add to that eighty-five percent of GiltStock.

Osorio scratched his nose. The great intangible was the value of GiltStock – of course it was worth a great deal more than the list of its assets, its value would be based on a multiple of its annual earnings, targeted this year at ten million, an all time high. So how much was it worth? Dutch Tremaine had mentioned fifty million and that was only at the small-talk stage. Dutch was as much a philanthropist as Attila the Hun. If Dutch opened at fifty, then he would go much more. Osorio rose and began to pace. Eight-five percent of fifty million was forty-two and a half. Added to his existing assets he would be worth fifty in cash, aged thirty-three. But the instinct which had guided Osorio when he dismissed the banker's approach was still strong: was independence worth fifty million? GiltStock would no longer be Steve Osorio's baby – it would become a division of Manhattan First, part of Dutch Tremaine's great banking empire, albeit run by Osorio, Tremaine's son-in-law, another of Dutch's great finds.

Osorio paced, the adrenalin pumping. Life with Manhattan First would be heady stuff – he would be able to virtually write his own contract. With the muscle of a major bank behind them, GiltStock could immediately begin the international expansion which Osorio dreamed of.

'Dutch, we need offices in London, Frankfurt, Hong Kong and Tokyo – and we need them in place by the end of this year.'

'You want them, Steve, you got them. You want me to put the Gulfstream at your disposal?'

'Hell, no, Dutch. GiltStock should have its own jet.'

Osorio nodded as he paced. It would happen like that. And it wouldn't end there either. Dutch Tremaine was sixty-five years of age. He ran Manhattan First like it was his own, but who was going to take it over when he retired? Osorio had read an article about the absence of anyone in the ranks matching Tremaine in stature; the article had suggested that Manhattan First might headhunt someone from outside the bank to take over. Osorio nodded. He could see the scenario developing. As son-in-law, married to the daughter Tremaine doted on, Osorio would move closer and closer to the centre of power. Running a big brokerage, running a big bank: what was the difference?

He went to the window. The ship had passed upstream, out of sight. Fifty million for GiltStock was out of the question; it was worth closer to a hundred. The telephone rang.

'Steve,' said Marilee's voice. 'Miss Ahmed on two.'

Osorio hit two.

'Laisha, how are you today?'

'I'm just fine, thank you.' Her tone was all business. 'Steve, are you on your own there?'

'Just me.'

'Things are starting to move,' Laisha said, speaking quietly. 'What is March oil right now?'

Osorio looked to the screens. 'Twenty-one fifty,' he said, 'that's the last trade. I can get you a quote from the floor.'

'Look,' she said urgently, 'this is what we want to do. We already have two million barrels, right?'

'Right,' Osorio said.

'Here is the order: you are to buy a further ten million barrels with a limit of twenty-one seventy, understood?'

'Understood,' said Osorio, tingling. 'We'll have to work that order to get the best price.'

On the console, the house intercom light had begun to flash.

'Please get back to me without delay with the results,' Laisha said and disconnected.

Osorio made a face, then turned to the intercom.

'Yeah?'

'Steve, it's Ray.'

'Yes, Ray?'

'The bank have just been on. Another ten million bucks has just hit our account from your Arab friends, I thought you should know, it looks like they're going in again.'

'They already have,' Osorio smiled. 'They sure aren't slow with the money. Thanks, Ray.'

'See you, Steve.'

'Ray!'

'Yeah?'

'Where did that ten come from? Durst Bank again?'

'No, as a matter of fact, this ten came from Bank Geneva.'

'Thanks,' Osorio said.

He flexed his fingers, thought briefly, and then hit the tie-line to NYMEX.

'Vince?'

'This is Max,' came a voice over the usual swell of noise, 'I'll get Vince.'

Osorio looked at the screen: March oil was showing last at twenty-one fifty-two. Osorio pressed the intercom.

'Marilee, get me Miss Singer, then get me all the names on my short list. Tell Malcolm to get in here.' He released the intercom and pressed his ear to the phone. 'Vince, you there?'

'Right here, Steve.'

'I want you to start buying oil,' Osorio ordered quietly, 'March, you can pay up to fifteen cents above these levels, but work it real sneaky.'

'Quantity?'

'Start with five million barrels,' Osorio said.

'Got it,' said Vince and hung up.

Malcolm came in as line three began to flash.

'Miss Singer on three,' Marilee said.

Osorio nodded Malcolm to a chair, lit a cheroot and pressed three.

'Miss Singer, buy oil,' Osorio said, 'it's going up, I can't tell you why, just buy it.'

'The March?'

'Yeah, the March.'

'Buy a hundred thousand,' Miss Singer said.

'Got it, got to go,' Osorio said and threw the phone down. 'Malcolm, now listen to me.'

Malcolm's eyes darted in his face.

'The Arabs have just given me a buy-order for ten million barrels of oil,' Osorio said. He hit the flashing intercom. 'Marilee, just hold whoever you've got for a minute.' Osorio leaned forward, his two hands readied in front of him like someone waiting to catch a football. 'Malcolm, we've just got to go in again for the fund and with any spare cash we've got. We've an opportunity to put the GiltStock Fund head of its class on Wall Street. It'll outperform anything else. I want you to get out there and talk some sense to Suck. There's a rocket about to take off and we want to be on it.'

Malcolm looked uncomfortable. 'I hate these impulse things,' he said. 'Okay, you know of some action in the Middle East, we may be working very big orders, but the market is still out there, Steve, and it's bigger than anyone.'

'Jesus,' Osorio said, 'what do I have to do? Does no one out there want to make money anymore?'

Malcolm got to his feet. 'I'll go talk to Cox,' he said. He paused at the door as Vince Carpenter's voice came over the intercom.

'Twenty-one fifty-eight trading on the March!' Vince sang. 'Bought two million, working the balance.'

Osorio had picked up another phone.

'Iqbal, is that you?' he was calling.

As he closed the boardroom door, Malcolm Finch suddenly realised that he was too old.

3

Dutch Tremaine was pacing the turf. In leather chairs near the bank chairman's enormous desk sat Maldonado and Pappas. Business had taken Landey, the bank's president, out of town.

'Roll it again,' Tremaine said.

'Seven hundred thousand shares in Man First, Mr Tremaine,' Maldonado said. 'Bought directly from a bank in California for thirty-four and a half.'

'No names?' Tremaine asked, his jaw working.

'Just a Caymen Island trust,' said the younger man.

'You've seen the preliminary Broadhurst Colridge report?' asked Tremaine, indicating a thick document which lay on his desk.

Both men nodded.

'What's your opinion?'

Pappas drew in his breath. 'Broadhurst Colridge have produced a very detailed report outlining exactly how Man First Bank can defend itself from a predator,' he said. 'But it's cosmetic. Okay, give all the top management golden parachutes so it's going to cost any predator a fortune; revalue all our assets worldwide; fill the bank with any other type of poisoned pill you care to mention. It's all cosmetic. Profit is our problem, profit – or not enough of it – is what has our share price where it is.'

Tremaine glared at Pappas, then turned to Maldonado.

'I'm afraid I agree with Joe, sir,' answered William Maldonado. 'If you'll excuse the expression, Man First isn't sexy anymore. Further write-offs from a static profit base which might actually cause earnings to dip will bring the share price substantially lower.'

'There's a rumour that *Barrons* are doing an article on us,'

Pappas said. 'There's a possibility they may talk of our shares hitting thirty soon, that's fifteen bucks off last year's high.'

Tremaine paced up and down.

'I saw Osorio,' he said. 'I talked fifty million and he laughed at me.'

'Now that you mention GiltStock,' said Pappas, sliding in, 'there's been another . . . approach.'

Tremaine's eyebrows shot up. 'From . . . what's his name?'

'His name is Jay Cox', Pappas answered.

'And what did you say?' asked the bank chairman.

'Well,' said the other man, 'I didn't feel free to say anything. I mean, next week we're all going to be out at Lloyd's Neck, celebrating with you and Mr Osorio's bride.'

'But you told him you'd get back to him?' Tremaine pressed.

Maldonado nodded quietly.

'Do it,' said Tremaine. 'We've got to keep all our options open.'

The two men left the room and still he paced. Like a man walking quicksand he kept on the move, fearful of any check in momentum. That people were saying his bank wasn't sexy anymore caused him to feel deep resentment. Sexy! There had been a time when he could have lined the board of directors up and knocked them down with one swing of his phallus. Sexy! Christ had he been sexy! Money and power produced sex like rabbits from a hat. He had picked and chosen like a medieval king and eaten his fill.

But now at sixty-five the urge had almost disappeared. An occasional flicker, a call from the past, but essentially, gone. With it, to some extent, had gone the real, high-bore drive and the clarity of decision. Osorio had all those things in abundance and would have for another thirty years. Jesus! Tremaine's envy made him gasp and stop. In thirty years Osorio would still be riding high, and Dutch Tremaine would just be a name on some damp tombstone somewhere.

He paced anew, covering the whole length of his enormous office, twenty-five paces in each direction. As if his whole life had rushed into one point, Tremaine now had one single objective in view. He saw it as the High Note. He had to leave on an upbeat. No matter what else happened, the day he left Man First had to be a day when the bank's stock was standing proud, when

102

profits were soaring as never before, when the bank was once more . . . sexy! That was it! The image was clear in his mind. That was the note he would leave on, and not before.

But time rarely acquiesced in such arrangements. Tremaine felt, for the first time in his life, time running against him. Landey was distancing himself, probably having talks with members of the board. Someone – in all likelihood, Abel Eller – was building a stake, a prelude to an outright bid if the signs were to be believed. The stock was falling and Man First was no longer sexy. Tremaine paced. The bold stroke was needed. The move which would make people look afresh and say, how about that, it's old Dutch on the warpath again!

Sexy. Osorio. Osorio's creation. GiltStock. GiltStock was oozing sex. In Man First's hands it would seduce every motherfucker on Wall Street. Ten percent, straight to the bottom line. More if they squeezed it hard enough. Fifteen! There was a sexy number! GiltStock will add fifteen percent to Man First Bank's bottom line. The bank's shares jumped five on the news.

Tremaine stopped at his desk. Carletta's photograph, framed in silver, smiled at him. The banker sighed. He had never been able to stand her mother, but he was crazy about Carletta.

CHAPTER NINE

Houston, Texas

Gerhardt's humour was effervescent, positively fizzy. The two blocks from the parking lot to his office had often seemed something to be endured; now he noticed things previously hidden: the window of a chocolate shop, artfully fitted; a colourful window-box high in a building; the deep blue exquisitness of the Texas sky. His legs, often tired, now bounced. He felt fresh, his clothes clean, his mind alert.

He brought his hand up, patted the pocket of his coat and felt the envelope there. Two tickets, supersavers, round trip Houston – New York. And a rooms' confirmation in an hotel on 33rd Street. Two rooms. But side by side. Eric Gerhardt made a little skip. Jen had agreed to come.

Gerhardt thought about the New York trip, then he thought about the whole reason for his going to New York and clouds began to cross his constellation.

For after the telephone call, nothing had happened.

Sure, he had been very scared and sure, he had taken the precaution of removing all the seismic evidence; he had done it the very next morning; it had taken twenty-four hours; if anyone had asked, he planned to say he had been taken ill. But no one asked. And no one knew he had left town. Except Jen. He had told her, but not why.

Gerhardt crossed a traffic intersection.

Then as the days went by he came to think that he might have imagined the call. The very idea was absurd. A letter of retraction! The surrendering of all the evidence! Absurd. He had thought of telling the police, then decided against it. There had been no specific threat. If whoever it was called a second time, then he would tell the police. Gerhardt sighed. This was probably the price of being published, of being in the public domain. After all, his name was in the magazine for all to see, any weirdo could have read it and called him up.

And anyway, nothing had happened.

Gerhardt's office was on the seventh floor. He opened the door, it swung in and he bent as usual for his mail. From this position he became suddenly aware that something was wrong. Then the back of his collar was grasped and he was jerked into the room. Hands out to protect himself, he flew forward. Blinding light exploded as his head connected with the corner of a desk, rocking it. He rolled over, his hands to his face. The toe of a hard boot drove into the peak of his stomach with anatomical precision; Gerhardt doubled, his speechless mouth seeking air like a banked fish.

He was hauled upwards, retching, and dropped into a chair at the desk. Strong hands held his arms. The room came into focus.

Gerhardt first couldn't believe it. You hear of violence, of break-ins, but they always happen to someone else. The room was wrecked. Presses and filing cabinets had been forced open; files and papers were thrown everywhere. He looked sideways into his own office. Ruination. Desks smashed. Boxes overturned. His rock samples lying where they had fallen.

'I keep no money here . . . ' he began, then screamed as a knee found the side of his rib-cage.

Another man was approaching. He had bad skin. He was taking papers from an envelope. He placed them on the desk.

'Sign here,' he instructed, handing Gerhardt a ballpoint.

'Sign . . . ?'

The man stood back and Gerhardt's head was slammed down, six times in succession against the desk-top. His head was then pulled back. He felt gristle and blood from his shattered nose flood into his mouth; he spat out raw, red phelgm.

The man with the mottled skin approached once more.

'Sign here.'

Aware of nothing but the pain and the need to end it, Gerhardt grasped the pen and scrawled his signature. The paper was withdrawn. Carefully it was replaced in its envelope. The man looked in Gerhardt's direction and nodded.

Gerhardt felt himself released. There was a moment of incomparable relief. Then there was a white-hot stinging at his neck, and he was staring at the lights in the ceiling, and regardless of any pain his back might have ever known, his legs were up over the desk, kicking for the sky.

CHAPTER TEN

1

New York

Friday 22 February 2.30 a.m.

Osorio could not sleep. In the dim light of the bedroom he could see the outline of Carly's body beside him, face down, blonde hair spread in a torrent of curls down her golden back. Silently Osorio slipped to the floor, eased through the door and padded across the rugs of the vast living-room to the kitchen. He plugged in a kettle, took a robe of Carly's from behind the door, put it on and sat on a stool, staring out at the spires and conicals and pyramids of Manhattan at plus three hundred feet.

A digital wall clock showed o-two-thirty. Impulsively Osorio grabbed a telephone and from memory punched out a thirteen digit number. At the other side of the Atlantic, in Rotterdam where it was eight-thirty in the morning, the phone rang in a firm of commodity brokers on Coolsinger.

'Piet Seydlitz,' Osorio said.

After a hum and a click, a man's voice said, 'Piet Seydlitz.'

'Piet? Steve Osorio, GiltStock.'

'Steve, what are you doing up at . . . two-thirty, you randy old goat?' asked the continental broker.

'Just checking up on guys like you,' Osorio replied. 'How's the weather in Holland?'

'Cold and wet. How about New York?'

'Warm and sleepy,' answered Osorio as the broker laughed. 'Anything I should know?'

'Nothing much,' said Seydlitz. Osorio could hear him tapping a keyboard. 'Middle East is quiet. King Hussein says the United States should cut its aid to Israel unless the Palestinians get sorted out. Your President says King Hussein should look to put his own house in order first. There's a strike of copper miners in Peru, any help?'

'Nothing on oil?' Osorio asked.

'Thought you might ask that,' Seydlitz said. 'We're hearing that you fellows tried to buy the whole Saudi production yesterday in New York. What's behind that?'

'Just acting for a client,' Osorio said. 'What are you calling oil this morning?'

'Basically unchanged on your close,' Seydlitz said. 'A couple of spot cargoes were done basis New York in the Far East last night, so right now I would call your March twenty bucks seventy cents a barrel – as I say, unchanged.'

'Thanks, Piet,' said Osorio.

'Steve?'

'Yes?'

'Which way are you calling the next dollar in oil?'

'Up,' Osorio said and unplugged the steaming kettle.

He sat on the stool, cradling a mug of hot apple-juice between his hands. Carly had spent the evening before at the Helmsley Palace covering a fashion show for *Mirror Mirror* and Osorio had gone along and watched starved girls swirling up and down a dais before an invited audience. Afterwards there was champagne and a lot of kissing and they'd gone down to the Village for dinner with an art designer from Carly's magazine. Osorio sipped and stared. He was on the verge of great events, but for once, instead of intense excitement, he felt oddly dull.

Event one: oil. Twenty minutes before the close the day before, Laisha had come on and unloaded ten million barrels of oil back into the market, making Gabriel Holdings a profit of twenty cents a barrel, average, or two million dollars.

Five minutes later Ray Leonard had come through.

'Steve, just thought you should know that the lady from Gabriel has been on and told me to take twenty million from their account and to send it to a bank in Switzerland.'

'That was quick,' Osorio said, 'but it's alright, I was told to expect it.'

'Are they pulling out?' asked Ray.

'No,' answered Osorio, 'it's a kind of test. They gave us their money, now they want to see that we're able to give it back.'

'Strange,' Ray said.

'They're into many strange things over there,' Osorio said. 'When you repay the money, how do they then stand with us?'

Ray could be heard accessing his mainframe. 'They've got their original two million barrel open position of March oil at twenty dollars twenty cents a barrel,' he said, 'so as of now, that's making fifty cents, or a million bucks. They've got cash with us of seven million which includes two they made on their big deal.'

'Make sure you pay them their cash on the button,' said Osorio.

'Sure thing, Steve,' Ray replied. 'By the way, today was one of our better ones, as I'm sure you might guess. We made over half a million in commissions.'

'Good,' Osorio had said. 'We need it.'

He put down the mug and listened; at the periphery of his hearing range two things were audible: Carly's even breathing and the siren of a cop car or ambulance far below. Event two. He had decided in principle that a deal for GiltStock with Manhattan First could be the hottest sweetheart affair he was ever likely to be presented with. *If* it was on his own terms. Osorio rasped his jaw with his knuckles. There had been a vulnerability to Dutch Tremaine that Osorio had not seen before. And a certain honesty. It was possible that Tremaine actually meant part of what he said when he spoke about family and Carly and never having had a son. Osorio's head went up and down with certainty. He had called Dutch and suggested lunch. That would be today, the day that was still four hours away from the sleeping city. Osorio stood and stretched. If he wanted a hundred million for GiltStock he would have to ask a hundred and twenty. At the top of his stretch the figure of one hundred million dollars seemed to crystalise and he exploded in laughter. A hundred million bucks, he laughed as he came down. What would they say to that down in Abilene?

He flicked out the kitchen lights and walked into the living-room with Carly's inlaid mirrors everywhere, causing the nocturnal walker to drift through a succession of ghostly reflections.

Abilene. Event three. He had at last done it.. He had called Brent the afternoon before.

'Hi, this is Steve.'

There was the thump of machinery and the squeal of truck brakes; the number he'd eventually got through to must have been a rig-site God knows where.

'Who did you say?'

'Steve, your son, Steve.'

'Shit, Steve, why're you callin' me and I got a test flow goin'?' Brent shouted.

Osorio bit his tongue. 'I can call you back.'

'I'm here now. What you want, little fella?'

'Brent, I'm getting married next week. It's been hard to really plan everything, but I'd like you to come on up here and be my guest for the day.'

'What you want to get married for, boy? Take my advice, women are better changed; like cars, they wear.'

Osorio grinned as in the background oiled parts kept up their deafening din. Suddenly he was back down there, part of the sweat and the heat and the intangibilities that had kept everything together.

'I'm glad you can come,' he had said. 'I'll send you down a ticket just to be sure – you can settle with me later.'

Osorio leaned forward until his forehead touched cool glass. From that position it was a straight, giddy drop, fifty hurtling floors to spattering concrete. He smiled. Imagine Brent's face when he got the ticket, first-class return, sent Federal Express the evening before with a note to say that there was a room in the Plaza. Some room. A suite with two bathrooms and beds big enough for ten people to sleep in. Knowing Brent, nothing would go to waste.

In the bedroom, Carly had turned on to her back, one arm flung in his direction. Asleep she was most beautiful, a sort of childlike, angelic innocence captured in her unlined face, her beautiful mouth, partly open now in sleep.

Beside her, Osorio made no noise, waited for his sleep to come. In the closing years of the century, things happened at such speed. He put his hands behind his head. Instant communications, Piet Seydlitz at this minute in Rotterdam, joking about horny old Steve, at this minute lying awake in New York, thinking of a hundred million bucks. And somewhere else in New York, a sexy Arab girl with an incredible body, probably waiting for word from the deep Middle East, where in the scorching heat, a renegade prince was planning his move, but first waiting to give the word to New York, to buy oil in New York that was pumped out of Brent's Texas sandstone, waiting to give word to the girl who would call GiltStock, who would tell Osorio that the time had come.

In the kitchen, the digital showed o-three-ten.

In the bedroom, Osorio slept.

2

Friday 7.30 a.m.

Rain was driving in, east to west. Ron Spirakis shut the door of the wood and shingled house, clicked up his umbrella and began the ten-minute walk to the ferry. Slim briefcase beneath his arm. Rubber overshoes on his feet. Head covered with a broad-rimmed hat which Cristy said made him look like Eliot Ness.

Black overhead clouds rumbled over Staten Island as Ron walked downhill. Where would Cristy be now? Getting up, showering, getting into her clothes. From the first time he spent five minutes in her company he knew he had something special. Solid. Genuine. And then, very much a woman.

Ron joined a line of people boarding. Cristy's femininity wasn't a protracted affair like with some women, like with her brother's bride-to-be. Ron frowned. Carly. Osorio . . . Osorio. Red zone. Cut.

The ferry cast off; Ron sat inside. Despite the weather, some people were out on the forward deck.

Ron had stayed at home the night before: Cristy was researching something, she had stayed in her apartment on the upper west side. His father had called from Vermont. Wondered when

111

he was coming up this year. Mother was down with a cold. When she recovered they were thinking about a week in Florida . . .

Ron saw Manhattan bob up and down as they approached. In the glass an inch from his eyes he could also see himself. What did other people see there? Authority, yes. Integrity, certainly. The ability never to show surprise. In college he had won a fortune at poker. The ability to keep confidential information without ever sharing it. Conversely, the inability to share a secret. Whichever way you looked at it, it had enabled him to last longer than almost anyone else in Durst Bank.

'Cry, holler, let it out!'

Thirty years ago Mama Spirakis knew about such things, but to her Ron had simply smiled.

'You can't always keep a cork in – someday, the cork's got to fly out, else what's inside rots, you wait and see,' she had said.

Okay for his mother, for someone like Cristy, to be upfront, straight from the shoulder all the time, they could in their own way afford it. But when billions, yes *billions*, were at stake, amounts of money that men killed for, that empires fell because of, that shifted the very balance of power, when these were involved, what did you do with the cork? Ron blinked his eyes. Loose. Lips. Sink. Ships. Abel Eller's cardavorous eyes loomed over Battery Park.

You spent your whole career striving for the top; when you got there you saw things going on that appalled you, that ordinary men and women would never believe.

Abel Eller.

Ron shook himself within his heavy coat.

He wanted out. Soon. As soon as all this was over. As soon as he had somewhere else to go. As soon as he could afford to.

But would they let him go, knowing what he knew? There was the danger. Ron shuddered. He must never expose Cristy to all that. He must never let them make the connection. He began to empty his mind, and joined the line to disembark.

In a very rudimentary way, Ron believed in para-psychology. Just as you communicated your inner feelings by the expression on your face, he also believed that feelings and ideas could be transmitted by simply thinking about them. It happened the whole time. People lifted a telephone, knowing in advance who exactly was on the other end. People dreamed the night before

112

of someone they hadn't seen for twenty years, then next morning received a letter getting back in touch. Therefore Ron had trained his mind as well as his face to empty at strategic times: dangerous times like right now: Steve Osorio. Danger zone. Erase. Exit.

In the tunnel to the subway which would bring him uptown, Ron concentrated on Cristy's face. The more he concentrated, the lighter his step. Love filled his mind, took him over.

When he got in, he would call and tell her.

3

Friday 8.30 a.m.

'Cristy?'

'Hello? Steve, is that you?'

'Yes, hope I'm not disturbing you.'

'No way,' Cristy Osorio said. 'How are you? Last minute jitters, eh? Wondering if you're *doing the right thing* next week? Am I right? Come on, come clean.'

Osorio laughed. 'Trembling as I sit here,' he said, 'reassured by nothing more than hi-technology.' He put his feet on the boardroom table. 'What did you think of her?'

'She's knockout, really gorgeous.'

'Yes, but what did you *think* of her.'

'A very capable lady,' Cristy said. 'I look forward to getting to know her better.'

Osorio felt a twinge of doubt. 'Listen, I thought you might like to know,' he said. 'Brent's coming up.'

Osorio could almost see his sister's smile.

'Now that's good news,' she said.

'I thought you might think so,' Osorio said.

'There are only a few really special days in life,' Cristy said. 'The day you get married for the first time is one of them.'

'I'll try to remember that,' said Osorio, affecting seriousness.

'You know what I mean.'

'Sure,' he said, looking out the window where rain was beating in squalls from the sea into the city. 'Cristy, there's something else.' He took his feet down and pulled the daily print-out to him. 'You remember our dinner conversation in Brooklyn – when I was asking you about Saudi?'

'Of course.'

'Well, my questions weren't exactly academic.'

'I might have guessed.'

Osorio lowered his voice. 'This is hard to be precise about,' he said, 'but I'm given to understand that something very imminent is going to happen there – probably along the lines you spoke of, okay?'

'Okay,' said Cristy cautiously.

'There's a lot involved here,' Osorio said. 'I'd feel happier if I could get a cross-check, know what I mean?'

'You want me to make some calls?' Cristy asked.

'Only if it's not a hassle.'

'What's the hassle? If there's a story, I want it as much as you. As a matter of fact, at this moment, I probably want it more.'

'You working on some angle about oil?'

'Don't be nosey.'

'I'm only kidding.'

'Look, I've got contacts, I'll call them when I get into the office. Then I'll call you.'

'Thanks, sis,' Osorio said.

Marilee buzzed as soon as the phone went down.

'Gabriel Holdings on two.'

Osorio picked it up and sat upright. 'Laisha?'

'Mr Osorio?' asked a man's voice.

'This is Osorio.'

'Mr Osorio, this is Ahmed.'

'Mr Ahmed, good morning,' Osorio said.

'Mr Osorio, I speak to you from New York to where I arrived last evening,' said Ahmed in his thick voice. 'My daughter has told me of the business you have done for us – we are pleased, Mr Osorio, the eminent persons we represent are very pleased.'

'Thank you,' Osorio replied. 'That makes us all pleased, Ahmed, everyone except Jay Cox and if you keep trading the way you did yesterday, even he'll be pleased. Thank you, Mr Ahmed.'

'Mr Osorio,' said Ahmed, 'events are moving swiftly, almost too swiftly. Those of us involved, we do not eat, we do not sleep, there is no time. I therefore give you Laisha.'

Osorio smiled to himself. There were background noises, then Laisha came on.

'Mr Osorio?'

Osorio guessed that in front of other people, including maybe even Saleem himself, familiarities were out.

'Good morning, Miss Ahmed.'

'Mr Osorio, we must move today,' said Laisha in a crisp voice. 'Here therefore are your orders. Are you ready?'

'Go right ahead,' said Osorio, taking a pencil from a cluster.

'Buy thirty million barrels of March oil,' she said, 'with discretion up to twenty-one dollars a barrel. Please repeat.'

Osorio blinked. 'If I heard you right, Miss Ahmed, it's buy thirty million March up to twenty-one, right?' he repeated.

'Affirmative,' she replied.

'Miss Ahmed,' said Osorio slowly, 'I'm sure you realise the huge size of this order? I'd like your father to hear this call.'

'I hear you, sir,' echoed Ahmed's voice.

'We can try to do it,' Osorio said, 'but there's grave danger of pushing the market up beyond our reach. This would be the largest single order ever worked on NYMEX; a far better strategy would be to let us work it over a few days. Besides, there are position limits to be considered.'

'Mr Osorio, this is Friday, no?' said Ahmed. 'Your markets close this afternoon for the weekend and do not open until Monday. On Monday next the basics of this market will have been transformed and people all over the world are going to start remembering again what it is to sit for hours on end in an automobile, waiting for a few litres of gasoline.'

Osorio felt himself quiver.

'I'm with you,' he said.

'The money is on it's way,' Laisha said. 'I'll be in touch.'

Osorio put back the telephone and sat for some moments. From the top of his scalp to his ankles, something was happening: his belly and his scrotum had contracted and all the fine hairs on his arms and legs were standing like the teeth of a rake. The biggest order ever. In oil. The black gold he'd been reared with. A change in the basics. Of oil. And world affairs. The centre. And he was moving it.

He snatched his private phone and tapped out a number. No reply. He jammed the phone to his ear, thumbed open a desk directory and stabbed again.

'*Wall Street Journal.*'

'Cristy Osorio,' he said, looking at his watch.

There was a delay and piped music. Osorio's fingers drummed.

'I'm sorry, but she's not here as yet.'

'Ask her to call her brother, immediately she gets to you, okay?' he said, threw down the instrument and hit the intercom. 'Malcolm? Got a minute? Thanks.'

Osorio was at the window when Malcolm Finch came in.

'Malcolm,' he said, turning, 'what would you say if I told you someone was going to buy thirty million barrels of March oil – and all today?'

Malcolm scratched his head and sat down. 'My response would be, "and have you heard I'm running for President?"'

'Malcolm,' Osorio said, 'you're on the ticket.'

4

Friday 9.30 a.m.

Cheryl Leinster leaned back and crossed her legs. From the telephone she held to her ear came a continuous commentary from a broker in London on the progress of afternoon copper on the London Metal Exchange. Cheryl watched the chart: copper was retreating from rather than attacking the price point she had identified as an upside breakout. The trading session ended.

'That's it then, my love,' said the man in London.

'Thank you,' she replied.

'Do you want the second ring?'

'I don't think so,' Cheryl replied. 'Speak to you Monday. Have a nice weekend.'

Cheryl had split a nail that morning, on the unsanded surface of an old door she'd just had hung in her studio; now she took an emery board and began to file, her eyes interchanging between the flashing screens in front of her and her finger.

Ten minutes before Cheryl had seen Malcolm entering the boardroom. Now he came out and Cheryl looked at him. It was nine thirty-five. Malcolm was standing absolutely still, unaware that he was being observed, rubbing his right hand continuously over and back across his chin in a gesture which Cheryl had seen him use once before and that was the day everyone had taken a bath in gold. Still rubbing, Malcolm hurried to his desk. Looking down the line of trading positions, Cheryl could see him heave open that day's printout, then grab his telephone.

Cheryl picked up her bag, rose from her chair and casually made her way down the desk; Jay Cox, at the other side of the room, must also have registered Malcolm's demeanour, for Cheryl could see his eyes flashing behind his oval, rimless glasses. Behind Malcolm there was a free console and Cheryl leaned on it, appearing to access one of its screens, but in reality, listening behind her to what Malcolm was saying. She listened, and as she did, she felt a surface chill spread over her. Systematically, Malcolm Finch was selling off enormous blocks of positions which Cheryl recognised as belonging to the GiltStock Fund and other discretionary accounts.

Cheryl made her way onwards, out of the trading room and into the powder room. She closed the door, then leaned against it, suddenly drained. What was happening in GiltStock? Why did she feel such foreboding?

She looked at herself in the long mirror, an extravagant, gilt affair. She took out a lipstick and ran it along her mouth. She stood sideways to her reflection, brought up the collar of her yellow blouse and shook her hair out. She had hair that had many years ago been bright blonde and had faded but stopped just short of brown. Many women would have retrieved the blonde, but Cheryl liked the natural colour, which anyway gleamed and was thick and abundant and still contrasted fantastically with her jet black eyebrows.

She turned heads, and she knew it. She sighed. Normally she had the ability to totally detach her personal feelings from her work, but now the two, for reasons she could not comprehend, were inexorably merging.

At the door into the trading-room, Cheryl stopped and stared. At the back of the financial area Jay Cox was remonstrating heatedly with a dejected Ray Leonard. From his desk, Cheryl could see Malcolm looking at the door, his face `pale, then resume whatever business he was transacting.

'Gerry, what's going on?' Cheryl asked a young trader who worked with Jay Cox.

Gerry shrugged. 'Somethin', I guess,' he replied. 'I just hear Jay ranting on about oil.'

Cheryl's foreboding went up a gear as she approached Malcolm's desk.

5

Friday 9.45 a.m.

'Cristy Osorio on four,' said Marilee.

'Got it,' said Osorio and hit the button. 'Yes, Cristy?'

'Well, I may or may not have something,' Cristy said. 'I've called all the people I know and the main thing I can tell you is this: Saleem seems to be missing.'

'Missing?'

'That's what I've been told.'

Osorio's mind raced. 'That could mean a lot of things,' he said, half to Cristy, half to himself. 'If he's about to instigate some sort of major trouble, a *coup d'état* or the like, he could have withdrawn to some neutral point to watch the fun, then plan to swoop in, the returning hero, when it's all over. He'll grab the throne when the fighting's finished. Or maybe he's instigated some third party to lead a revolt and because Saleem's outside the country he can't be blamed. Or then again maybe he's in all this just for the money.'

'Or maybe they've taken him out,' Cristy said.

'I'm pretty sure that's not the case,' Osorio replied. 'Look, thanks, Cristy, keep in close touch, won't you? I'm pretty sure what we're seeing here is the start of something big.'

118

'You realise, don't you,' asked Cristy, 'that the U.S. has a very strong policy on the place we're talking about? Any funny stuff and we go in and take over the oil fields.'

'I hadn't forgotten,' Osorio responded as he disconnected. A U.S. invasion of Saudi Arabia would drive the Soviets insane and send the price of oil up by ten dollars a barrel. Ten bucks! Osorio felt a wave of excitement course through him. All his life he had relished the really big moves and now he was about to orchestrate a monumental one.

He reached and pushed the switch that connected him via a loudspeaker to NYMEX. Deliberately, although he had now had the Arab order for over an hour, he had not communicated it to Vince Carpenter for fear of someone stealing the price. The Arabs had allowed a thirty cent discretion in their order: with luck, using that margin alone, GiltStock could make five million dollars.

'Vince?'

'Yeah, Steve, hi.'

Vince sounded tired.

'Just thought I'd like to know what you're calling the market,' Osorio said

'Unchanged to five cents up,' Vince said. 'That would make the March twenty dollars, seventy-five cents a barrel. There seems to be a feeling here, though, that she'll drift back towards twenty.'

Osorio frowned briefly. 'How long to your opening?' he asked.

'We're counting down,' Vince said. 'Thirty seconds.'

Osorio made a fist of his hand. 'Okay,' he said, 'here's your order: on the opening, buy fifteen million barrels of the March.'

'Christ!' Vince cried. 'Shouldn't you wait?'

'Go to!' Osorio ordered.

There was a sudden explosion of noise as the light crude oil market opened. Malcolm Finch came in holding a long strip of paper.

'As per instructions,' he said evenly. 'I cleared out everything I could – killed some nice positions, mind you – but I've done it. There's at least ten million bucks here to play with. You should know that Jay Cox almost certainly knows what's happening and has left the building.'

119

'Fuck him,' Osorio said.

'Steve!'

'Yeah, Vince?'

'We're mopping up some fairly persistent selling down here,' came Vince's voice. 'The market is just slightly up, twenty seventy-three. We've got about five million barrels on board – in case she turns, shouldn't we wait to do the rest?'

Osorio looked at the list which Malcolm had handed him. 'Complete the order, Vince,' he commanded harshly, 'like now.'

'Is there war in the Middle East or something?' Vince cried.

'Do it,' Osorio rasped.

Osorio's internal phone buzzed. He snatched it.

'Yeah, what is it?'

'I'm sorry, sir, but I've got Miss Ahmed on two. She insists on letting you know she's holding.'

Osorio pressed two. 'Laisha? I was waiting to complete the order before I called you – oil is slightly up, but the market hasn't really got going yet.'

'Steve, I couldn't speak before, but now my father has gone out to arrange the money. He said to tell you that he prays for our success.'

'Thanks, honey,' Osorio said.

'And so do I, my lovely Steve.'

'Good girl,' said Osorio, glancing in Malcolm's direction.

'You must not delay. At any minute things will happen.'

'We'll be on board, don't you fret,' he said.

A direct line into Osorio's office rang and Malcolm answered it and held it up.

'Laisha, I'll call you back,' Osorio said and grabbed the other phone,raising his eyebrows to Malcolm.

'Miss Singer,' Malcolm said.

'Miss Singer, I've been thinking of you,' Osorio said. 'You know those oil positions you took?'

'Of course I know them,' Miss Singer replied. 'So now, I suppose, you want to churn me out of them?'

'I want you to double them,' Osorio said.

'Double them?'

'That's what I said.'

There was only a brief pause. 'Then double them,' Miss Singer said.

Malcolm was holding up the phone again. 'Vince,' he mouthed.

'Got it, Miss S,' Osorio cried, 'got to go.' He hit the sqwaak button. 'Vince, speak!'

'We're filling too easy, Steve,' Vince shouted above the background din. 'I've just bought seven million barrels at twenty eighty-five and there are sellers over. My gut instinct tells me to hang back for the balance.'

'Vince, no discussion, fill the rest!' said Osorio. He stood there, the electrifying noise filling the room.

'Bought your remaining three at twenty-ninety,' said Vince.

'Good work,' Osorio said, his eyes sparkling. 'Now buy another ten million – and fast!'

'Steve, are you certain . . . ?'

'For Christ's sake, Vince, do as I tell you.'

'Hold it, Steve! There's something coming over Reuters with a Saudi dateline.'

'Fill those fucking orders!' Osorio cried and threw down the phone. 'Something on the Reuters,' he said to Malcolm Finch and jumped to his feet. Both of them went to a wall-mounted screen and stood as silently the words came tapping out. It was a one-sentence report, details unconfirmed, which said that there had been an explosion in Riyadh, Saudi Arabia.

Vince beat Osorio to it. 'Steve! It's gone fucking mad down here,' the floor trader shouted. 'We've just filled five million barrels, but at an average price of twenty-one bucks, repeat twenty-one. Still working five, did you get that?'

Osorio could hear the frantic screaming that was the New York light crude market.

'Increase your remaining order from five to twenty million barrels,' he instructed, scribbling his order on Malcolm Finch's list.

'It's bedlam!' bawled Vince Carpenter. 'You'll have to pay maybe twenty-one ten. Why not wait?'

'Fill the order,' said Osorio curtly.

'Jesus, the Israelis must be at the Suez Canal!' said a jubilant Vince.

The house phone rang. 'Steve, it's Ray.'

'Ray, it'll have to wait.'

The telephone rang again immediately.

'Miss Ahmed, sir.'

'Laisha!'

Osorio could see Malcolm's secretary put her head around the door and beckon Malcolm out.

'Oil is moving up strongly, Laisha,' Osorio said. 'There's been an explosion in . . . '

'Steve, I know,' said the girl's voice. 'My father has just been on. You are to buy another ten million barrels at the best price you can.'

Osorio sat bolt upright. '*Got it!*' he cried. 'You're arranging the cash?'

'It's on it's way,' Laisha said.

Osorio snatched at a ringing phone and hit the intercom speaker simultaneously.

'Steve, this is Ray,' said Ray Leonard's voice over the intercom. 'I need to talk to you.'

'Not now, Ray, not now.'

'Steve!' Vince sounded raw. 'All hell's broken loose down here, a major move on the upside. You've filled ten million at twenty-one twenty-five, repeat twenty-five. It's thirty bid now and no sellers. We'll hit limit shortly if we keep going like this!'

Osorio punched air. Let's hope, he thought. Oil was permitted a move of only a dollar in either direction from its previous day's close. If it reached that limit then trading stopped until the next day, unless someone wanted to trade inside the limit, then the market would open again.

'What's limit?' Osorio asked.

'Twenty-one seventy,' shouted Vince.

Osorio could hear him turn away from the phone and scream something at the floor, then he was back.

'Twenty-one forty bid March oil!' Vince bawled. 'There isn't a seller in sight! Volume is a record, all the stops are going and the shorts are getting screwed!'

Osorio felt so powerful that he reckoned at that very moment if he wanted to he could fly.

'What are you working?' he called.

'Ten million barrels,' came Vince's shouted reply. Then he could be heard in an exchange with someone else, probably Max. 'Bought five million at forty-two,' he screamed, 'working five.'

'Buy another ten million!' ordered Osorio, looking down at Laisha's last order. 'And buy them quick!'

'Holy shit!' shouted Vince. 'They must be in Cairo by now! I'll be back!'

The boardroom door closed quietly as Malcolm came back in. 'Take a look at this, my old friend!' said Osorio jubilantly. 'Have a look at a fortune in the making.'

Malcolm nodded grimly.

'Steve, there's something going on outside,' he said.

Osorio caught his breath. 'How, going on? What do you mean?'

'Cox has disappeared,' Malcolm said heavily. 'Ray was out there talking to him and suddenly Cox jumped up and left the building.'

'What does Ray have to do with it?' asked Osorio, suddenly dangerous.

Malcolm shrugged. 'Ray's worried. He says he's been trying to talk with you all morning. The clearing house are hassling him in a big way – none of this Arab cash is in yet.'

'How do you mean, not in?' Osorio snapped.

'Ray says that we've received no cash,' Malcolm shrugged.

Osorio looked slowly at the screen, then he turned. 'Malcolm,' he said quietly, 'what price is March oil?'

Malcolm looked up. 'Twenty-one forty-five last traded,' he said.

'Twenty-one forty-five last traded,' echoed Osorio, 'and we've got over forty million barrels on our books since this morning, mostly below twenty-one, giving an open profit as of this moment somewhere in the ballpark of twenty-five million, with the market heading for limit.' He stared straight at the older man until Malcolm dropped his eyes.

'I'm only telling you what's going on, Steve,' he mumbled.

'Jay Cox is becoming more trouble than he's worth,' Osorio said. 'This money took time to get to us before. Of course they'll pay, and if they don't we'll close them out and make a fortune.'

'Steve!'

Osorio turned up the sqwaak-box: the noise behind Vince Carpenter sounded insane.

'You've filled your last ten million,' Vince shouted, ' but wait for this – you've filled them right on limit! Twenty-one seventy!'

Have you got that?'

'Got it, Vince,' Osorio smiled. 'Good work. She's trading at limit?'

'Right on the seventy,' Vince replied. 'Jesus, what a morning! I've lost track of what ballpark our commissions must be in.'

'We'll try and figure them out,' laughed Osorio.

As the intercom went silent both he and Malcolm turned to the knock on the door. The shuffling figure of Ray Leonard came in.

'Sorry to interrupt, Steve,' he said awkwardly.

'Come in, Ray, sorry I couldn't talk, but it's been all hell broken loose up here,' Osorio said. 'You've been getting the trades, I imagine.'

'That's just it, Steve,' Ray said. 'Our position has increased enormously. The clearing house have been on to me on and off all the morning. Now they've been on again about the business just done. They want seventy-five million dollars instantly or they close the positions.'

Osorio struck his intercom. 'Get me Miss Ahmed,' he said. 'Where's their money coming from?' he asked Ray Leonard.

'That's part of the problem,' Ray answered. 'It's come from different banks each time before – Durst Bank, Manny Hanny, Bank Geneva.'

Osorio shook his head. 'I don't know what we're worrying about,' he said. 'The overall position is over twenty-five million in front.'

'The clearing house have got to have their funds, Steve,' said Ray. 'You know that as well as I do.'

Osorio turned to Finch. 'Malcolm, you know people in the clearing house. Get on to them and see if you can buy us a little time. This is ridiculous.' He turned back to Ray Leonard as Malcolm left the room. 'What are our options? What happens if this money is delayed on a Federal Wire breakdown?'

Ray looked unhappy. 'That's still unhelpful to GiltStock.'

'The money will come in,' Osorio said through his teeth. 'It has before and now, with oil soaring, of course it will again.' He turned impatiently and hit the intercom. 'Goddammit!' he yelled, 'where's that call?'

'I'm trying, Steve,' said his secretary, 'but the number is continually busy.'

Osorio exhaled in a long stream of sound. 'You know what's happening here, don't you?' he asked Ray.

'I'm really not too sure,' replied Ray mournfully.

'There's a *coup d'état* taking place in Saudi,' Osorio said grimly. 'We're acting.'

Ray's eyes were wide as Osorio hit the phone again. 'Get me Cristy Osorio at *The Wall Street Journal*,' he snapped. He turned back to Ray. 'Options,' he said, 'give me options.'

'Sell them out,' Ray said without hesitation. 'Anything can happen. The rules of the game are that you pay up and Gabriel haven't. To hell with the fact that the market is roaring ahead. Sell them out, take the profit and argue later.'

'Their money has taken time to get to us before,' Osorio said through clenched teeth.

'There wasn't as much involved,' Ray responded.

'Steve, Cristy Osorio has left the office for an hour and will call you back,' Marilee's voice said.

'What about Miss Ahmed?' he asked.

'Still busy.'

'Get somebody to call every news agency in New York, every newspaper, use all our contacts, try and find out more on the Saudi situation,' Osorio said.

'Will do, Steve,' answered Marilee.

Osorio took a deep breath and walked to the window.

'They are probably all up there right now,' he said, looking north towards midtown Manhattan, 'waiting to form the next Saudi government.' He swivelled. 'What's our own cash position?' he asked.

'Tight,' Ray replied, 'don't forget you've taken positions for every discretionary account in the house, including the fund.'

'What about our position with Manhattan First?' Osorio asked.

'Use our own money?' said Ray.

'That's what I said.'

'Steve, we've got about seven million – but even if we had seventy, which we don't . . . '

'I can get that sort of money,' said Osorio, half to himself, again looking out the window.

Ray stepped forward. 'Steve, I strongly recommend that you sell these undeposited positions immediately. Don't stay open like this.'

Malcolm came quietly in.

'Well?' Osorio and Ray's face were both enquiring.

'No good,' said Malcolm, his head going from side to side. 'I spoke to their head guy, he and I have been buddies for years. It's no use – they don't see what the hassle is. They're just about to cut us out. Also, the Exchange Surveillance division are looking for confirmation that this is a *bona fide* hedge position.'

'Steve, that number is now ringing out no reply,' said Marilee's voice from the intercom.

'No reply?' Osorio said, his face suddenly perplexed. 'Keep trying,' he snapped and swore aloud. He turned to Ray. 'You get out of a market like this and you spend the next three weeks trying to climb back on board a rocket.'

'Steve?'

Marilee's voice.

'Yes!'

'Vince asks can you put him on the box?'

Osorio leaned forward and pressed the switch. There was a sudden blare as NYMEX came over the loudspeaker.

'*Steve!*'

There was the noise of men whooping and of someone blowing what sounded like a bugle.

'STEVE!' Vince Carpenter's voice had almost gone.

'I'm here,' Osorio said.

'LIMIT UP OIL!' cried the triumphant Vince. There was a great cheer behind him. 'We did it, Steve, you hear me baby? We did it!'

Osorio's glance at Ray was that of a ruffled eagle. 'Get on to the clearing house,' he said, 'and tell them that they'll have their money in ten minutes.'

He swivelled in his chair and hit a button on the desk intercom.

'Marilee,' he said, his smiling eyes still on the men. 'Get me Dutch Tremaine.'

His smiling eyes were still on the men when the call came through.

'Dutch, it's Steve.'

'Steve, I'm seeing you for lunch, right?'

'It couldn't wait until then,' Osorio said. 'You remember our conversation two weeks ago? When you told me just to ask if I needed anything?'

'Of course,' said Dutch Tremaine.

'Well, I need seventy million dollars for twenty-four hours maximum,' Osorio said.

'When?'

'Like now.'

There was an almost undetectable hesitation.

Then Dutch Tremaine said, 'Tell me where you want it paid, Steve.'

6

Friday 11.00 a.m.

Cristy Osorio turned left past reception and into the newsroom. She had been out to cover a statement issued by Morgan Guaranty on behalf of a major client involved in a takeover battle, now she threw her coat on the back of the chair, put her handbag on the desk and scanned her messages.

Ron called, please return. Steve Osorio, same. Sean Kirby, Saudi, will call back at eleven. Cristy looked at her watch. Sean was an old friend, formerly a Middle East stringer, now a Gulf watcher for Press Association in Riyadh. If anything was happening in Saudi, Sean would know.

Cristy picked up a phone, punched a number, and as it rang, ran her eyes over the AST monitor which she had left on news earlier. There was nothing new on the explosion in Riyadh, no update.

'Hi, there,' she said as the call answered.

'Hi there to you,' answered Ron Spirakis, several miles uptown. 'Where were you?'

'Oh, covering a boring press briefing on the battle of the giants,' Cristy replied.

'I called,' Ron said, lowering his voice, 'just to say, that other men are poor creatures indeed if they haven't experienced the happiness which I've had since I met you.'

He hung up.

Cristy blinked, looked at the phone. Me too, she said, her body floating she felt so good, me too. A simple call, a simple message. It was the spontaneous nature of his kindness and love that was so delightful. Unexpected gifts in a treasure hunt. Cristy threw her head back and in a spontaneous impulse, opened her mouth and whooped.

Bill Warner, Cristy's editor, was passing the back of her chair.

'Things must be good today,' he remarked.

'They are,' Cristy smiled.

'Lucky guy,' said Bill, and he meant it.

The telephone rang.

'Cristy?'

The reed-like voice made her palms go moist.

'How are you today?' she made herself say.

'You're stuck, aren't you, Cristy?'

Cristy swallowed and looked around her. 'Kind of,' she said.

'Think of a see-saw.'

'A see-saw?'

'Yes,' the voice wheezed. 'The plank is balanced on a barrel – maybe an oil barrel.'

'Go on,' Cristy said.

'Sitting on one side is Saleem,' said the caller, 'and on the other is Japanese industry.'

'Alright,' Cristy scribbled. 'So what . . . Hello? Shit! Hello?'

But the dead line whined mockingly at her.

7

Friday 11.15 a.m.

'Steve, just wanted you to know that we've paid over that seventy million bucks to the clearing house,' Ray said.

Osorio nodded at the intercom.

'And Gabriel . . . ?'

'Still no cash,' Ray replied. 'We've been on to every bank in town that I can think of, but none of them have made a large transfer to us.'

'It must be coming from Switzerland,' Osorio said. 'Have you asked Federal Wire?'

'They said they would come back, but haven't,' Ray replied. 'What about the Ahmed lady? Have you spoken with her?'

'She's not there,' Osorio said. He looked at the screen where the New York light crude oil market was closed, limit up, the March showing twenty-one dollars seventy cents a barrel. 'Okay, Ray,' Osorio said, 'this is what I've decided. We wait another thirty minutes, at that time over three hours will have passed since they gave us the order and the banks will have been open for over two hours. No cash in thirty minutes and we sell those positions out.'

'You'll have to offer them at limit,' Ray said. 'You'll re-open the market.'

'That market will absorb anything the way it's gone this morning,' Osorio said. 'That's the plan. Stand-by, okay, because I want that cash back from the clearing house by the end of business.'

'Understood,' said Ray.

'Steve?' came Marilee's voice. 'You had a lunch with Mr Dutch Tremaine?'

'That's right,' Osorio said. 'Saldi's at twelve-thirty.'

'He's just called to cancel,' Marilee said, 'something's come up.'

'Why didn't he tell me that when I spoke with him ten minutes ago?' Osorio frowned, then smiled. 'Marilee now I'm as hungry as a fat child. Can you organise a hamburger, medium rare, with a salad, buttered carrots and some sort of mineral water? Here in the boardroom?'

'Sure thing – one medium rare hamburger on its way.'

'Marilee, any suggestions in the dessert department? I haven't had time to look today?'

Marilee laughed. 'Let me see. How about choux pastry wrapped around lychees in cream, or maybe chocolate mousse?' she said.

'I think chocolate mousse,' Osorio replied.

He checked the screen again. Why was there no reply from Laisha's number? What was happening in Saudi at this moment? Osorio made a mental note to contact Sol Ansbacher, GiltStock's lawyer, *after* they sold out the Arabs, if that was what had to be. Although GiltStock would be perfectly within their rights to close the positions, clients became notoriously litigious when such rights were enforced. Sol Ansbacher would provide the ammunition necessary for any defence.

The door opened and Marilee came through, shutting it quietly after her. Osorio looked up.

'There's someone to see you,' she said. 'From Manhattan First.'

Osorio frowned. 'I'm not expecting anyone,' he said.

Marilee shrugged. 'It's Dean Abercrombie, their chief comptroller,' she said.

Osorio made a face. 'You'd better bring him in.'

Marilee returned to the boardroom, followed by a middle-aged man still in his overcoat, carrying his hat and a briefcase.

'Steve,' he smiled, removing a glove.

'Dean, nice to see you, although you've picked one hell of a day . . . '

'This won't take a minute,' said Dean Abercrombie, removing his other glove and opening his briefcase. 'It's just that these forms have to be completed.'

'What forms?' Osorio asked.

Abercrombie looked up blandly. 'Forms of guarantee,' he said. 'For the credit lines you requested this morning.'

Osorio's frown was deep. 'That credit was for GiltStock,' he said.

'Sure,' Abercrombie smiled, 'I know.'

'When I spoke with Dutch he never mentioned anything about guarantees,' Osorio said.

'Dutch,' chuckled Abercrombie, shaking his head as if recalling an incorrigible child. 'Dutch never for a minute considers the paperwork which follows on from these things. Now, Steve, just sign it there, where I've marked it, and initial each page in the box at the bottom right-hand corner.'

'Steve! Vince on the box!' said Malcom's voice.

Osorio checked oil, still limit up.

'I'll come back to him,' Osorio said and switched off the intercom. He turned to the banker. 'Normally I'd have my lawyers check these things out first,' he said. 'What do these guarantees cover?'

130

'Just the monies drawn down by GiltStock this morning,' Abercrombie replied, 'seventy million dollars plus a provision for interest accrued.'

'And what are you asking me to sign?' Osorio queried.

'A personal guarantee, underwriting the loan for the company,' said Abercrombie pleasantly.

'None of this was ever mentioned,' Osorio said. 'I told Dutch that of course I'd stand over everything, but . . . '

It was Dean Abercrombie's turn to frown.

'I understood from Dutch that there would be no problems here, Steve,' he said. 'We've already bypassed all the normal lending procedures on Dutch's say-so. We're a commercial bank, we lend money on security, we've got at least to have something . . . '

'It's for a few hours at most,' snapped Osorio, grabbing a pen. 'How much is it for?'

'The draw-down was seventy million . . . ' replied the once more amenable Abercrombie.

Osorio signed his name four times with a flourish and then began initialling as Marilyee re-materialised to witness his signature on the forms of guarantee.

As Osorio straightened up he could see March oil still limit up, but the spot month, February which was unaffected by limit rules, had begun to flicker.

'Sorry to rush you, Dean,' Osorio said, extending his hand.

'Always a pleasure, Steve,' the banker retorted, gathering his papers.

Osorio saw Dean Abercrombie smiling as he left and Malcolm Finch coming in quietly, closing the door behind him.

'Steve, speak to Vince,' Malcolm said, 'he's on the box.'

Osorio froze. 'Anything wrong?'

Malcolm nodded to the box and Osorio switched it on.

'Yes, Vince?' he asked calmly.

'Steve, I just wanted you to know that the spot has lost ten cents in the last few minutes,' Vince said. 'No big deal, I know, and the volume's tiny, but it could mean *something*.'

'Anything else on the Middle East?' Osorio asked.

'Nothing down here,' Vince replied.

Osorio looked at Malcolm and he spread his hands in the air.

'I just don't have a great *feel* for it anymore,' Vince said.

'You're spooky, Vince,' Osorio said. 'But keep me informed.

I'll keep the box on low.'

Osorio adjusted the volume right down to where only the cries from the other markets could be heard and turned to Malcolm.

'What do you think?' he asked.

'You know me, I'm an old man,' Malcolm replied, 'too old for these numbers, they've gotten too big for me.'

'Our open positions are making a fortune,' Osorio said, 'unprecedented, something like forty million dollars.'

'We had a saying in the army,' Malcolm said. 'Reinforce success, but never risk your ass if you don't have to.'

Osorio laughed and snapped off a salute.

'Yessir . . . what was it? . . . General Finch?' he said.

Malcolm shook his head. 'Come on, Steve, I'm telling you, I'm nervous.'

Osorio laughed again. 'Wait until tomorrow when we've calculated the bonuses General Finch,' he said, 'then you'll feel fine.'

'You shouldn't be supporting other people's positions with what is essentially your own money,' Malcolm said.

'That is true,' Osorio said, 'and to put your mind at ease, let me tell you that since these people's money hasn't hit us, we're just about to take the positions out and grab the profit.'

Malcolm's face brightened.

'But not,' Osorio said, 'before I have something to eat.'

Malcolm turned as a white-jacketed waiter from the dining-room was escorted to the boardroom table by Marilee.

'Malcolm, you want to order something?' Osorio asked as the waiter set out the single place.

'I'm not hungry, thanks,' Malcolm said.

'I'll be right back,' Marilee smiled. 'Chocolate roulade was all that was left when I got there,' she said in a stage whisper before leaving the room.

'What's the news on Cox?' asked Osorio as he began to eat.

'I don't know where he is,' Malcolm replied. 'Thirty minutes ago there was a call for his secretary, and now she's gone too.'

Osorio shook his head. 'Looks to me like we're going to need a new bond trader,' he said, munching.

'*Steve!*'

It was Vince.

'*Look at the Reuters!*'

Osorio turned and with Malcolm began to read the Reuters one-line Riyadh update.

'FOLLOWING THE EXPLOSION OF AN OIL TRUCK OUTSIDE THE OFFICES OF THE MINISTER FOR FINANCE, AUTHORITIES HERE REPORT THE ARREST OF A KOREAN NATIONAL. SOURCES . . . '

'Steve, Cristy Osorio on three,' said Marilee said.

'Steve, it's me, are you looking at the Reuters?' Cristy asked.

' . . . CLOSE TO THE MINISTER FOR THE INTERIOR SAY THAT THE MAN HAD BEEN REFUSED A VISA EXTENSION . . . '

'I see it,' Osorio said. 'What do you make of it?'

'For the moment, nothing is happening out there,' Cristy said. 'Off the record, though, I can tell you that Saleem is back in Riyadh – the great mystery seems to be solved: he was in Cairo getting treated for venereal disease.'

'Thanks, Cristy,' said Osorio quietly and put back the phone. 'Okay,' he said to Malcolm, 'we take everything out, but we've got to be as quiet as mice or we'll bring the house down.'

Malcolm nodded. 'We mustn't spook Vince anymore,' he said. 'I have a suggestion: why not let me start feeding out the position to him as if it was another order completely?'

'Good idea,' Osorio said.

'I'll start with five million barrels,' said Malcolm and hurried from the room.

Osorio looked at the screen where oil was still limit up, sliced through a still-pink piece of hamburger and popped it into his mouth. He didn't want to even begin to think now of why the Arab money wasn't in; they had broken the rules and GiltStock was going to take them out. The profit possibilities in such a situation were enormous: since the sales would amount to forced sales, the actual price at which GiltStock reported the transactions back to the Arabs were subject very much to creative accounting. In a market of such high turnover and multiple transactions, GiltStock could easily add ten cents a barrel to all the buy transactions and, equally, take ten cents from every sale, keeping the resulting twenty cents for its own book. Twenty cents on forty million barrels was eight million dollars, plus commissions. GiltStock would make ten million that day. A licence to print money. The Arabs knew the rules. Laisha was smart. Fuck her. Too goddamm smart. But where the hell was she?

Osorio was sinking his teeth into the last piece of hamburger when Vince Carpenter came on. By the background swell of noise Osorio abruptly realised that New York oil was open again.

'Steve, there's something going on!' shouted Vince. 'She's just popped out of limit. There's been a fair bit of business done at twenty-one sixty-eight, but there are sellers over.'

'Any reasons?' Osorio asked, his mouth full. On the screen, oil showed at sixty-eight – limit was only two cents away and the market was still way over the average price of this morning's purchases.

'Not that I know of,' Vince replied.

Osorio glanced at the wall-clock: it was twelve noon.

'Have you got any sell orders?' asked Osorio casually, thinking of Malcolm outside.

'Yes, as a matter of fact I have,' Vince replied. 'Malcolm's just come on with a five million barrel sell order, but I've told him to hold back for a few minutes to see what happens.'

'I think, Vince, if Malcolm gives you an order you should work the fucking thing instead of always trading your own opinion,' said Osorio.

'I don't know, Steve,' the floor man said. 'Suddenly she's really unsteady, spooky. I get the feeling that the market has absorbed this morning's news and in the absence of any further news . . . '

The noise over the loudspeaker rose in pitch, drowning Vince Carpenter out.

Malcolm came in and sat down two chairs from Osorio.

'Shit!' came Vince's cry. 'Christ that can't be . . . Steve! *Steve!* March just traded at twenty-one forty and a seller!'

Osorio felt half-digested meat stick in his gullet. He coughed it up and spat it out on the plate. The noise from NYMEX seemed to fill the boardroom in a way which it had not earlier.

'We've got to take those positions out,' Malcolm said, his white head going from side to side.

'Vince, sell ten million barrels for what you can get,' Osorio ordered harshly.

'You'll send it lower,' warned Vince Carpenter.

'Do as you're goddamm told,' snarled Osorio. He held on, mesmerised by the background swell of noise. Ray Leonard had come silently in to stand in front of Osorio's desk. He made a thumbs down sign with his hand.

'I'm taking them out, for Christ's sake,' snapped Osorio.

The noise coming out to the three men from the market was like the combined hallucinations of a million lunatics.

'Steve! It's a rout! We're offering at twenty-one ten and there's no bid!'

'Why?' Osorio managed to ask.

'Just a moment.' Vince could be heard holding a shouted conversation with another broker. Then he was back on. 'Evidently some asshole somewhere has come out and increased Japan's oil reserves by thirty percent,' Vince cried.

Cold fear hit Osorio's belly.

'Twenty dollars ninety bid March oil!' shouted Vince.

'Take it,' Osorio shouted.

Further frantic noise ensued.

'Sold a million at twenty-ninety, working nine,' Vince reported. 'It's like trying to catch a falling knife down here.' There was a pause, then: 'Steve! *Holy shit! Steve!* Are you there?'

'I'm here.'

'Twenty dollars fifty cents is now the best bid, repeat twenty-fifty!' Vince bawled. 'I don't know what's going on, but there's a wall of selling like I've never seen before and she's heading for the twenty mark, fast.'

'Sell,' Osorio said. 'Call me back when you've filled.'

'Steve?' said Marilee's voice.

'What?' answered Osorio harshly.

'Miss Carletta Tremaine is holding on two.'

Osorio sighed deeply, closed his eyes, then took two. 'Hi, treasure.'

'Hi, sweet,' Carly said. 'This is kind of sudden, but do you remember Laurie Frazer, Steve?'

Osorio tried to drag his eyes away from the screen.

'Who? Oh, yeah, yeah, sure.'

'They've got a yacht, it's off Acapulco right now,' Carly said. 'Laurie and her sister Betty, they were sort of wondering, being my last weekend and all, if the three of us mightn't take off down there until Monday. Daddy's said the jet's okay.'

There was a pause. In GiltStock's boardroom the door crashed open and Jay Cox arrived unannounced through it, his secretary close behind him.

'What the . . . ?' said Osorio, on his feet.

'Please may I go?' Carly was asking in her little-girl voice.

'Carly, go. I'll speak to you later,' Osorio said and hung up. 'What in God's name do you mean coming in here like that!' Osorio snarled at Cox.

'You just hear me out, Steve,' said Cox, his face dark. 'I have a good idea of the circus you've been conducting in here this morning.'

'Hold it right there . . . ' Osorio began.

'You listen, goddamm it!' Cox shouted. 'It's my job, my reputation on the line here. People trusted me when I told them that GiltStock were reputable people to give their savings to. I've just been to an address I think you're familiar with on Park Avenue, the same address that this Arab account is registered at.'

'You bastard . . . ' said Osorio stepping forward.

But Cox held his ground. 'She's gone, Steve,' he said, bringing his lips back so that his pink, shining gums were revealed, 'gone, vanished into thin air, evaporated, flown the nest, no forwarding address.' Cox took a deep breath. 'The little whore didn't even pay the rent.'

Osorio hit Jay Cox as hard as he could on the point of his egg-shaped chin. The treasury-bond expert went up and back and landed quite unconcious on the wide boardroom table, Malcolm Finch rushed over and stood in front of Osorio, trembling.

'Jesus,' he cried, 'for the love of Jesus, has everyone gone mad?'

Osorio, his nostrils flared, turned to the secretary.

'It's true, Mr Osorio,' whispered the pale woman, 'everything Mr Cox says is true.'

Ray Leonard was standing grim-faced, his hand covering the telephone. 'This is the clearing house,' he said quietly. 'They want more money, or they're calling us in default.'

'Stall,' Osorio said and ran his hands through his hair. 'You've just got to stall.' There was a chaotic sequence of noise streaming into the boardroom from NYMEX. Osorio placed his hands over his ears, whether to blot out the wall of noise or to think, he was not sure. 'Malcolm,' he said, his head shaking, 'we've got to get this position out.'

Malcolm Finch appeared to be having trouble with his breathing.

'Is there any way at all that I can help?'

Osorio swung around. Cheryl was standing there, both hands clasped before her, only her eyes showing any concern.

'Oil . . . ' Osorio began and tried to moisten his dry lips.

'Let's take a look at the chart,' Cheryl said clamly and spread a chart out on the desk between her and Osorio. 'It's all down to whether or not it will hold twenty,' she said, 'If the market breaks twenty dollars a barrel we've got to accept that we may not be able to get out for another couple of dollars. We've got to accept that these Arabs are out of the picture as of this time and that effectively their entire forty million barrel position now belongs to GiltStock.'

Osorio stared at her for a second, then he grabbed the phone. 'I'm stopping everything out through twenty-fifteen,' he said. 'Vince? Vince for Christ's sake where are you? I want you to take an order.'

'Steve!' Vince Carpenter sounded ragged. 'Before you say anything, we've managed to get another three million barrels out, but I hope you're sitting down.'

Osorio closed his eyes.

'It came out at an average of twenty dollars and five cents a barrel,' Vince was saying.

For a moment Osorio was speechless. He sat staring at the loudspeaker from which endless noise was pouring. He wondered if he imagined it hard enough whether he might be transported to another place.

'Sell everything,' he said thickly. 'Stop out every other position we have.'

'I don't think I can!' Vince yelled. 'The fucking thing's gone tits up! It's now trading at nineteen-eighty and a seller over!'

Osorio found the noise hypnotic. He looked at Cheryl's anxious face and wondered why he hadn't realised before that she was so pretty. He saw but did not comprehend Ray Leonard running towards the desk. He saw but did not register the slowly moving, groaning figure of Jay Cox, now coming to on the boardroom table. Osorio's knuckles hurt. He saw the remains of his own lunch, suddenly abhorrent, and the crockery tub of untouched chocolate roulade, strangely surrealistic. The boardroom door opened and Marilee appeared, carrying a glass of water. Outside the door, for the moment before she closed it,

Osorio saw but did not discern the large group of anxious faces peering in at him.

Suddenly all was quiet.

'Steve.' It was Vince's voice, now oddly clear as if he was in the room. 'Limit down oil, Steve,' said Vince quietly.

Ray Leonard who had been kneeling beside the desk, now sprang to his feet.

'Get a doctor!' he shouted to Cox's terrified secretary. 'Malcolm's having a heart attack!'

PART TWO

CHAPTER ELEVEN

Monday 25 February

OIL AT $18 A BARREL IS LESS THAN HALF WHAT IT WAS A YEAR AGO

NEW YORK BROKER MAY FAIL

By CRISTY OSORIO

Staff Reporter of *The Wall Street Journal*

Last week saw a dramatic change in the fortunes of GiltStock, the high-flying commodities broker, rumoured to be caught with a mega-long position in the falling oil market. Word has it that GiltStock is faced with considerable cash flow problems as it tries to fund its positions.

The fall in oil – down to a new contract low of $18 a barrel – has been led by NYMEX, The New York Mercantile Exchange. It has been strongly criticised by Saudi Arabia which claims that powerful sectional interests are at work. Oil at these levels threatens to push high-spending Saudi into deficit for the first time in modern history. The Saudis say that oil is grossly undervalued and should soon rise.

Last week saw changes in personnel in Riyadh. Gone, for health reasons, Prince Saleem, Harvard-educated number two man at the Saudi Oil Ministry. His replacement, Sheikh Abdul

Ormuz, is described by sources as a skilful negotiator and a 'moderate'.

The reshuffle will please many observers, particularly those in Tokyo. Prince Saleem had an uneasy relationship with the Japanese, often voiced by him in public.

As for the oil market itself: floor brokers in New York were saying that further falls could be seen in the coming week.

'These things acquire a momentum of their own,' said Tony Quagliano, a floor broker on NYMEX. 'The market now has to find a bottom.'

Until the bottom is found oil producers like the Saudis – and the Japanese with their new find – will look on with apprehension.

CHAPTER TWELVE

Fear hit him, square between the eyes. Naked fear. Which scarcely allowed him to walk a block for fear of being recognised. Or for fear of someone from a newspaper taking his photograph. Or asking him questions. Fear of the telephone, so he had ripped it out, of the door buzzer, the daily paper, the television news. Fear and revulsion of an entire infrastructure where a week before he had been a crown prince. Fearful to sleep in case he should dream; to wake, for what might await. Fear covered him like a shroud.

Steve Osorio awoke to a millisecond of relief, then plunging, omnipresent despair.

He stared. Even anger was gone. Twenty-four hours since he had shaved. No point. A day since he had eaten. No hunger. He sat, the blinds of the apartment kitchen drawn, staring. Thin. He had lost seven pounds. He was purging. Taste. Something dead in his mouth. Thought. Something dead in his mind.

His mind. No coherent thoughts in there, just flashing pinheads of recall, each hurtful. Hands to his face he sighed, long and deep. Some things were not meant to be endured. He had to forget. He rose and began to search the kitchen. Never a drinker, there was never alcohol around. He opened cupboard doors with effort, the movements of an old man. Eventually, high in a press, he found a bottle of champagne, a gift from times past. Disregarding the irony, Osorio opened it and then drank it down like water in enormous gulps, spasm causing him to sit upright and retch as the gas caught him, but he persisted, bottle on his head until it was empty. Then he sat back and in a feeble gesture flung the empty bottle across the kitchen where it bounced harmlessly off the refrigerator and rolled back to him over the floor.

To forget would be charity; but the wine in its initial phase made Osorio remember.

It had been four-thirty on Monday morning when Osorio awoke. His body and bed clothes were drenched in sweat. The weekend had been a nightmare: of lawyers, of selling off GiltStock's assets so that the clearing house could be paid, of trying – unsuccessfully – to contact Carly, of failing to talk with Dutch Tremaine, of coming to terms with the fact that Gabriel Holdings had vanished. Durst Bank said that they had no further instructions from Gabriel: to get the bank to reveal any more would take a court order.

If there was a bright spot it was the news that Malcolm was fine, the victim not of a heart attack but of an anxiety attack which he would soon be over.

Osorio stood for ten minutes under a scalding shower. He put on shorts, thick-soled socks, a sweat-shirt, the top and bottom of the Addidas tracksuit and running shoes. He pocketed a roll of notes and a bunch of keys. It was pitch dark outside as he paused on the steps of the brownstone, then walked the fifty yards to Fifth Avenue where he waved a cab.

'Downtown,' he said and instinctively looked back to see if there was any activity near his house. Instinctively. This just the third day of a nightmare and now he was doing things instinctively. Now Osorio's single objective in life, one he was prepared to die for, was that GiltStock would be open for business as usual on Monday morning.

They raced downtown, lights with them, limos waiting outside nightspots like cattle around water holes. Through Chinatown, still asleep, they reached Chambers.

'Let me out here,' Osorio said. He got out, handed the man a ten and waited for his change.

'The early bird,' the cabby said.

'Sure,' Osorio said, gave him back a one, then began to jog.

144

He cut a block east so that he could run down Broadway, past the Criminal Court Building, lengthening his stride. To his left the Park was silent, bathed in yellow light which reflected from a heap of garbage bags. A car came towards him, dipped its lights, then swung off left. He was running well as he passed City Hall, pumping along. He had been set up. But by whom? Who would want to set up either him or GiltStock? The blocks slipped by as he ran easily, the oxygen clearing his head, refreshing him. There was a squeal to his right and he saw a garbage truck swing into action. New York was waking for another week. At the next lights he turned right. People in suits and overcoats were suddenly materialising out of the night like mushrooms. Osorio ran flat out for four blocks until he could sense rather than see the river; the final two blocks downtown to GiltStock he walked, he did not want to arrive out of breath.

'Mr Osorio!'

Osorio turned, feet running somewhere behind him, a woman's.

'Mr Osorio!'

A girl was running behind him, a bag on her arm. She was pale, slight, Osorio didn't know her.

'Yeah, what do you want?'

'I'm Veronique,' she said, 'Madame Pelo's daughter.' She sniffed as she saw Osorio frown. 'I make the croissants, Mr Osorio.'

Osorio let out air in a long hiss. 'Veronique, I'm sorry honey, I didn't know you.' He put his arm around her shoulders and they walked on. 'Are you coming to work?' he asked.

'I've just been there, but I couldn't get in,' Veronique said, 'my keys wouldn't open the door.'

'That's okay, Veronique,' Osorio smiled. 'I've had to take some precautions over the weekend, the locks have all been changed.'

'There have been no deliveries,' Veronique said. 'Normally every Monday they leave fresh butter, flour, cream, so that I can bake. But today there's nothing.'

'Do you know where to get ingredients at this hour?' Osorio asked.

'I think so,' the girl replied.

Osorio handed her a fifty. 'Is that enough? Okay, you get a

cab and go buy what you need – and don't waste time. I've never been more goddamm hungry.'

In the lobby the night-shift porter was on duty.

'Good morning,' Osorio sang as he hit the elevator.

The man had been reading a newspaper, now he looked up, quizzically. 'Hi there,' he said.

Osorio used two new keys from the bunch in his pocket to open the door on the thirty-fifth floor. Inside, the trading-room was as quiet as always on a Monday morning and the cleaning ladies had been in, Osorio had seen to that, the place was spotless. He went around, clicking on monitors, bringing the heart of the operation on stream. He would miss the floor action, regretted having to let go people like Vince Carpenter who had run good operations for years. Vince was an exception – there would be a place for him up here trading oil if he wanted it. The thought of oil made Osorio's belly crawl.

In the boardroom, the centre of so much drama the Friday before, Osorio flicked his own screen alive, went into Marilee's office where he plugged in a coffee machine, then returned to his place at the boardroom table. It was five-fifty, ten-fifty in London, ten minutes to noon in continental Europe. Scribbling a list of names, Osorio then went to a desk diary, matched numbers to the names and began to make calls.

Piet Seydlitz in Rotterdam was the first.

'Piet, Steve Osorio,' Osorio said. 'Good morning.'

'Good morning, Steve,' responded the Dutchman, who sounded his usual self. 'Still in bed, I suppose?'

'Regrettably, no,' Osorio laughed. 'How does oil look this morning?'

'Weak after Friday,' replied Seydlitz evenly. 'We're calling your March nineteen dollars.'

Nothing in the Dutchman's tone betrayed any knowledge of Friday's debacle at GiltStock, but Osorio knew the system, he knew that Seydlitz and any other broker with a telephone would have heard the news on Saturday morning before they drank their orange juice.

'Piet,' Osorio said, 'I'm just calling to say that there have been a few items in the media over the last day or two about me and GiltStock which may have come to your notice. The purpose of my call is to let you and your company know that GiltStock is alive and well and open for business. We are looking forward to handling your business with the same efficiency as I hope you agree we've always done.'

Osorio thought he could detect a slight pause on the other end, as if Seydlitz was speaking to someone else.

'Now that you mention it, I did read something,' Piet Seydlitz said, his voice echoing.

'It's a purely personal matter,' Osorio said, realising with a jolt that he was hooked into a conference speaker on the other end. 'GiltStock is completely square with everyone, we're all here and we're ready to go.'

'You're no longer floor members of either NYMEX or COMEX, I understand,' said Seydlitz carefully.

'That's true,' Osorio replied, closing his eyes, 'but it's only temporarily true. Sure we had a cash problem on Friday so we sold our seats. But you can relay your orders to us in the normal way, we have arrangements with colleagues on the floor, commissions will be unchanged.' Osorio realised that his hand hurt from his grip on the phone. Outside, a glimmer of light was creeping into the morning sky.

'We'll be looking at all our options, Steve,' said Seydlitz calmly. 'We'll let you know, okay?'

'Sure, no problem, you know where we are,' said Osorio, preparing to hang up. 'And on a personal note, thanks for your support, Piet.'

'Steve.'

'Yes, Piet?'

'You might like to learn that you're not the only one in New York up early this morning,' the Dutchman said.

Osorio blinked. 'Oh yeah?'

'That's right,' continued Seydlitz smoothly. 'I've been speaking a full three hours ago with Vince Carpenter.'

'Vince?' Osorio said and swallowed. 'Three hours ago?'

'Seems he's moved to a new floor outfit called First Com, they've bought your seat on NYMEX,' Piet Seydlitz said. 'Vince says the whole thing is being headed up by another guy whose name I don't know: Jay Cox, mean anything to you?'

Osorio sensed his balance going as he replaced the phone. He put one hand flat out on the table surface to steady himself; the other hand he bunched until it nearly burst. First Com.

147

Vince. Jay Cox. NYMEX. Forty minutes later he was sitting in the same place, wondering if his head was going to disintegrate. The boardroom door opened.

'Malcolm,' Osorio said, dazed. 'You've come in.'

Malcolm stood there, then shrugged. He looked to have shrunken in two days. 'I figured you'd be here,' he said.

'You shouldn't be here,' Osorio said. 'You're not well.'

'It's hard to kill a really bad old thing like me,' Malcolm said and tried to smile.

'You know what's happened?' Osorio asked faintly.

'I can guess,' Malcolm answered. 'This place is deserted.'

'Cox is heading up an outfit called First Com,' Osorio said as if he hadn't heard Malcolm's reply. 'Every broker in London and on the Continent had this letter on their desk when they got in this morning.' He pushed the letter towards Malcolm who began putting on his glasses. 'Holst Stein in Frankfurt faxed it back to me,' Osorio said. 'It lists the people, all GiltStock traders now working for First Com, it lists the floor seats they've acquired, all GiltStock floor seats, it gives its paid up capital, fifty million, and it's signed by Dutch Tremaine.'

Malcolm shook his head as he read. 'They've cleaned us out,' he said. 'Chief financial officer, Ray Leonard? Shit, so much for loyalty.' He looked up, bemused. 'I must be too old,' he said, 'they never asked me.' He saw Osorio's face. 'The Arabs . . . ? ' he began.

'They don't exist,' Osorio answered. 'I've spent the weekend trying to find them, but it's been like trying to catch the wind in a bottle.'

'Have you managed to speak with Tremaine?' Malcolm asked. 'To ask him for a break?'

Osorio shook his head. 'He won't take my calls. Would you if you'd set this whole thing up?'

Malcolm's mouth fell open. 'You mean . . . ?'

Osorio nodded. 'He couldn't buy GiltStock, so he set us up, then stole it,' he said.

The two men sat in silence, looking at each other.

'It's over, isn't it?' said Malcolm quietly.

The effect of his words on Osorio was electric: his hand went up in the air and came down so hard on the table that everything on it hopped a foot in the air.

148

'I'm *damned* if it's over!' he cried. 'Years and years of building, sweating, licking ass, making the right decisions, scraping, saving, working, working, working – that's all for nothing? That's all over? What had we ten years ago? We had you, me and a girl, that's all. We're still here, you and me. No way is it over!'

The door opened and Marilee came in.

'Good morning,' she said quietly.

'Hi, Marilee,' said Osorio and attempted a smile. 'Have you heard . . . ?'

The girl was nodding. She looked down at a pad, then handed Osorio over a sheet of paper. 'These are the people in so far,' she said.

Osorio read, the corners of his mouth curving down. 'Twenty people,' he said, 'but they're just kids, all kids.' He looked up and laughed. 'I see, however, that we've a full turnout in the kitchen,' he said.

Marilee nodded grimly.

Osorio stood up. He looked at Marilee. 'I guess morale out there is a little low?' he said.

'They don't really know what's happening,' Marilee said.

'Right,' Osorio said and set his jaw, 'this is what's happening. Get on to Sol Ansbacher, tell him I want him. We're suing Man First for fraud, wilful conspiracy, setting us up with phoney Arabs, you name it. Then go to the kitchen and tell the chef I want him to prepare thirty of his best fillet steaks. Get tables arranged in a square so that everyone can sit down together, get a dozen bottles of vintage champagne put out in buckets and then tell everyone outside to meet me in the dining-room at eight sharp, that's in fifty-five minutes.'

Marilee wrote busily.

'You can let the word out in the trading-room,' Osorio said to Malcolm, 'that they can expect *good* news. Those kids all showed up. Despite all the shit they must have read, they showed up. Each one of them jumps fifty percent in salary as of now.'

'I'll get on to the chef,' said Marilee.

'That fifty percent goes for you as well,' Osorio called as she left the room.

'We've no cage, no back office,' Malcolm said. 'That ass-hole, Ray . . . '

'There's no point in getting sore at Ray, or Cox or anyone,'

149

Osorio said. 'Our mission in life is now to stay in business, that's the way to tell all those guys, fuck you, we don't need you, we did it without you.'

Malcolm, on his way out the door, paused. 'This has nothing to do with me, Steve,' he said, 'but are you still getting married on Wednesday?'

'Yes, I am,' replied Osorio matter of factly. 'Yes, I am.'

2

The trading-room was empty at seven fifty-eight. Osorio walked across it, smelling the usual cigarette smoke, taking in prices from the screens. He waited at the elevator to go down to the dining-room, one floor below. People, he thought. Although every experience in life should prepare you for the fact that people are complete bastards, when you came face to face with the genuine article it was still a shock. Tony Quacks with whom Osorio had just spoken was a good example of the complete bastard class.

'I got my problems, Steve baby, you got yours,' he quacked.

'All I want to ascertain, Tony, is that we still give you our trades today.'

'Steve, this is the picture: tomorrow I take your trades, okay? Today, I'm closed.'

'Fine, Tony, no problem,' Osorio responded. 'Talk to you tomorrow, have a nice day.' He slammed the phone down. 'Little cocksucker!' he cried.

Osorio stepped into the elevator, then kept its doors open as Marilee hurried in. He took a copy of the faxed letter from his inside pocket and ran his eyes over it.

'You saw that Cheryl has joined First Com?' he said quietly.

Marilee's eyes were concerned. 'Yes, Steve,' she answered.

Osorio looked at the letter again, shrugged and put it away as the doors opened.

Osorio could smell meat grilling and hear the noise of animated conversation. He paused at the inner door, before anyone saw him. There was one long table, dead centre, its length punctuated by ice buckets with their champagne bottles. Young heads without a speck of grey, nodded in discourse. Osorio stepped firmly into the room and the volume died.

Slowly he walked to the raised section, to the long window, to where his table, Steve's table, now stood, strangely bare without its usual white linen cloth. There was no sound, nothing. Even the kitchen had stopped. Background sounds of traffic and car horns miles away, below, somewhere, but in here everyone was doing without breathing.

'Ladies and gentlemen,' Osorio said quietly, 'I am very proud.'

He tried to look at each one of them in turn.

'I don't have to tell you about the events of the last few days, except to say that GiltStock has discharged all its debts to the clearing house, and apart from a few minor changes in personnel,' – there was nervous laughter – 'nothing has changed.'

Osorio could see a huddle of white uniforms, just inside the kitchen door.

'I am proud. I see you all here, ready for work despite everything, and I suddenly know the value of loyalty. You have rewarded me beyond my wildest expectations and be assured that, if I can, I will in my turn reward you.'

He made fists of both his hands.

'The people who tried to do this to us, mark my words, they're not going to get away with it. But in the meantime, all of you here, your basic salary is increased by fifty percent over what it was last Friday. We're going to prove to this town that far from being dead, GiltStock is more vibrant than ever. For this is the new GiltStock, made up of the men and women in this room. You have my word: no one is going to be hired in over you. You came in this morning – this is your show. Hold up your heads – you should be proud too! Get out there and teach the Street a thing or two about trading! My door is always open. Now let's have some champagne!'

There was a spontaneous outburst of applause, then as one the room came to its feet, clapping and cheering for the man with the Indian eyes who could make anything happen. They kept cheering. At the door of the kitchen GiltStock's chef in his tall hat came out, smiling and clapping, as smiling waiters rushed to the table and began uncorking champagne. Now everyone had a glass and someone started up 'For He's A Jolly

Good Guy' and Osorio stood there with his glass as Malcolm, a bright red spot high on each cheek, climbed up beside him.

Malcolm spread out his hands for hush. 'As the *senior* trader,' he began with mock emphasis, 'I would like to propose a toast.' He raised his glass. 'To Young GiltStock!'

There was a loud cheer and everyone including the chef drank. It was when he had drained his glass and put it down that Osorio saw the man. He stood at the back of the room. He wore a dark suit, gleaming black shoes and his black hair was parted down the middle showing a track of pink scalp.

'Stephen Osorio?'

Osorio felt something catch him, near his centre shirt button. Everyone turned.

'Stephen Osorio?' the man repeated.

'I'm Steve Osorio, who are you? Who let you in here?' said Osorio stepping down.

'Stephen Osorio,' said the man thinly, 'you are hereby served.' So saying he stepped forward and pressed a white envelope into Osorio's hands.

'Just a moment . . . ' Osorio began angrily, but the man turned abruptly and left the same way he had entered.

Thirty pairs of eyes flicked between Osorio's face and the envelope. Reaching for a knife, Osorio slit it and removed the letter. His breath shortened as he read. The words swam in and out of focus.

'Steve, are you alright?'

Malcolm followed Osorio from the totally silent room, through the tiny lobby and out into the corridor.

'Steve, what is it?' Malcolm asked. 'You look ill.'

Osorio's face as he raised it up was that of a man on a rack.

'Carly's called it off,' he managed to say.

3

From his place at the head of the boardroom table, Osorio could see New York Harbour enjoying a morning of pleasant sunshine. He looked up at the clock, eleven, than at the door as Malcolm came in.

'There's no point in not letting you know it exactly,' Malcolm said. 'We're up against a wall out there. The kids are trying their damndest but it's the same response over and over: sorry, but it has always been our policy not to tie ourselves to one broker, thank you, goodbye.'

'What about their existing positions?' Osorio asked.

'They're being transferred to . . . other brokers,' Malcolm replied, 'with a commission adjustment in our favour.'

'Other brokers?'

Malcolm's grey head was nodding. 'First Com, mainly,' he said gently.

'Have you tried our private clients?' Osorio asked wearily.

'Just old Miss Singer; she wants to talk with you, personally,' Malcolm replied. 'Steve?'

Osorio looked up.

'I know you're in bits,' Malcolm said. 'I know how badly you feel about your wedding being cancelled. But you've got to pick up that phone and talk to people. Kids can trade, but they can't talk to the chairman of a billion pound food empire who wants to know if he should still be hedging his coffee through GiltStock. If we don't start to get business, we won't open tomorrow.'

Osorio looked at Malcolm as if he wasn't seeing him. 'The NYMEX people have been on to me,' he said flatly. 'Now that we've sold our seats, they don't want to know me.' He shook his head. 'Here I was with the oil speech that would make them all sit up and take notice of Steve Osorio,' he said bitterly. 'God, I feel so small.'

'Take it easy, Steve,' Malcolm said.

'Just give me a little time, okay?' Osorio said.

'Sure,' said the older man and made his way out.

Osorio looked at the telephone, down the long table, out the window again. The letter lay in front of him on the table. So utterly final. The language of severance. The detail, down to the ring, delivered with other possessions to the safekeeping of Manhattan First. They would even stoop that low.

'Steve.'

The language of forced restraint. *Our client Miss Carletta Tremaine. No contract or further obligation. Attempts to visit will be*

153

treated as harassment. Will be immediately reported.

'Steve.'

Marilee was there, her forehead all puckered up.

'Steve, there's a man outside to see you,' she said.

'I'm not seeing anyone,' Osorio said.

Marilee looked uncomfortable. 'I told him that,' she replied, 'but he insists. He says he's your father.'

'*What?*'

'He says he's Brent Osorio, your father.'

Osorio jumped to his feet, then covered his face with his hands. 'Oh Jesus,' he said, 'he's here for the wedding.' Osorio looked around him like someone searching for a way out. 'Where is he?'

'I put him in my office,' Marilee replied, 'but he made his own way into the trading-room.'

On the balls of his feet, Osorio went to the boardroom door. He opened it a crack. Over the consoles, talking pleasantly to a girl who had taken over Cheryl Leinster's position at the metals desk, was a deeply tanned man, late forties or so he looked, whip-lash slim, wearing a brilliantly white jacket, a blue open-neck shirt and carrying a stetson the same colour as his coat. As Osorio watched, the head of black hair bent to near the girl's face as she gave him a lesson in how the screens worked.

Jesus, Osorio thought. Ten years have just evaporated. We're back again, working a rig outside Abilene. I've never escaped.

'Bring him in,' he sighed to Marilee.

Osorio positioned himself near the window. It was farcical. Ten years of growth and progress. Ten years of building, hoping that one day he could show Brent what he had created. Now the very day had come and GiltStock was being sucked down the tubes.

'Thank you, my dear.'

Stetson in hand, Brent Osorio entered the boardroom. They were of a size, but his father was slighter, wiry, his legs encased in rigorously pressed blue jeans, leather boots with chunky heels on his feet. Osorio just knew that each boot would have a scroll embossed over the ankle. Brent looked around the room, a smile on his face which said it all, his head going from side to side.

'Hi, Brent,' Osorio said.

'Well, well,' Brent said. 'I take my hat off to you, little fellah. Sheet, I have taken my hat off!' He laughed and tossed the hat on to the boardroom table. 'What are you trying to do out there? Send people to the moon? I bet they ain't got anythin' down in NASA like what I seen out there. Your grandaddy would die laughin'.'

'You got here early,' Osorio said.

'First class ticket?' Brent's face suggested that the ticket had been acquired other than by cash. 'I'm staying down in this hotel you put me into, listen while I tell you, Stevie, they must have thought there was a monkey comin'. There's more fruit and nuts in the room than I ever seen before.'

'Why don't you sit down?' Osorio said, drawing air from the very bottom of his lungs.

'You should know I never sit,' Brent replied, pacing the room in wonder. 'I like to lie down on occasion, but I sure hate sittin'. Say, do all these people work for you?'

Osorio nodded. He wondered if he imagined hard enough whether he might not be transported to another place.

'I don't believe it,' Brent was saying. 'When I get home and tell them all this, no one will believe me.' He looked at Osorio in admiration. 'To think that our own flesh and blood have come this far.' He took out a packet of cigarettes, slit the top with his thumbnail, rapped two filters into view and offered them to Osorio. 'Mind if I . . . ?'

'Brent,' said Osorio, fighting for air, 'I got something to tell you.'

Brent's head was back and he was blowing smoke-rings at the ceiling. 'Sheet, I can't take any more surprises, little fellah,' he laughed. 'Before you say anythin', let me tell you somethin'.' He sat lightly on the edge of the table. 'You know Martha Jalowski?'

Osorio shook his head.

'Of course you know her,' Brent said. 'Mrs Jalowski? Big chest, used to run the laundry in Crooked Wood? Sure you do. Well they sold that out soon after you left home, started up a dry cleaners, 'smatter of fact, Martha got all these dudes gussied up for me afore I came up here.'

Osorio thought he was going mad.

'You know what Martha told me two days ago?' Brent asked. A grin cracked his face and made his mouth open. 'She told me that Elizabeth Taylor is goin' to be at your weddin'.' Brent's head went back and he whooped incredulously. 'Sheet, Stevie,' he cried, his whole face alight, 'until I walked in here ten minutes ago, I figured the ol' bitch was off her head and lookin' for a ride.'

'Steve.'

It was Malcolm on the intercom.

'Yeah?'

'I know you got company, but I need you out here,' Malcolm said.

'Be right out.' He looked at Brent. 'I'll be just a minute . . . '

'You go right ahead, son,' Brent said somberly. 'I understand business.'

Osorio left him staring at a monitor; Malcolm was waiting immediately outside the boardroom door.

'We got a problem,' he said gravely.

Osorio's eyes closed briefly. 'Let's hear it,' he sighed.

'National Sweet?'

'The sugar people?' Osorio said. 'What about them?'

'Almost alone of all our major clients, National Sweet don't appear to be affected, or maybe they just haven't heard what's been going on,' Malcolm said. 'At any rate one of the boys five minutes ago got a sell order, five thousand tons, it's a hedge against a cargo they've just bought from Cuba.'

'So what's the problem?' Osorio asked.

'We can't place the business, Steve,' Malcolm said. His face was approaching last Friday's colour range. 'Nobody will take it. They want money up front. We don't have it, we need the money from National Sweet, but of course they won't pay it without an execution. And their guy has already been on once to find out what's happened.'

'What did you tell him?' Osorio asked.

'I told him we were working it,' Malcolm replied, 'but you know them, every grain gets hedged, if they suspect for a moment we're not getting on, they'll go wild.'

'Who have you tried?' Osorio asked.

'All the usuals.'

'Have you tried London?'

'Same story,' replied Malcolm grimly.

Osorio sat down at an empty trading position. 'Who's our best hope?' he asked.

'Shit, I don't know,' Malcolm said. 'If you'd asked me fifteen minutes ago, I would have said that this couldn't happen.' He looked at his watch. 'National Sweet are going to be back on any second looking for fills.'

'I'll try Tony Quacks,' said Osorio and hit a tie-line.

'I already tried . . . ' Malcolm began.

'Is Tony there?' Osorio was asking. 'Steve Osorio.' He leaned back and loosened his tie. He looked at Malcolm. 'You know what this means, if we don't get on, you know what it means, don't you?' he said, his mouth tight. 'Tony? Hi, how are you? Tony, you've spoken with Malcolm, I know, however maybe he didn't explain it to you right.'

'He explained it to me fine,' said Tony Quacks, through his nose. 'I listened to him, then I explained it to him, Steve. This morning I explained it to you. Now everybody has explained it to everybody else, why don't you leave me alone until tomor-row?'

'Tony,' said Osorio, trying not to plead. 'This is for National Sweet. We got to get on. Their money is a formality. They have a cargo of sugar bobbing around on the sea, they need the cover, now come on, I'm trying to give you business.'

'Saudi Arabia was also a formality,' said Tony Quacks, as Osorio imagined the man's face, gathered to the snout like something that lives near water. 'We need money before we move.'

'Goddammit, we haven't received it yet!' Osorio cried.

'Then get it from them,' said Tony Quacks. 'Tell them money makes the world go round.'

'Tony,' said Osorio, his free hand gripping the console ledge, 'sell five thousand tons of sugar and double whatever your com-mission is, we'll trade it for nothing.'

'No dice,' said Tony Quacks.

Osorio could hear a trader call Malcolm's name.

'Tony,' said Osorio, 'we're going to loose a five thousand ton order.' By the panic on Malcolm's face it was clear that National Sweet was on the line again. 'I can't imagine that you're going to turn it down.'

'Can I make a suggestion?' said Tony Quacks.

'What?' asked Osorio.

'Call National Sweet,' said Tony Quacks calmly, 'and tell them to call us direct. We'll do the business direct and pay GiltStock an introduction commission on the business done.'

'Go and screw yourself, you little shit!' roared Osorio, then with all his strength he fragmented the plastic telephone into a million pieces against the surface of the desk.

As Malcolm went ashen-faced to take the call, Osorio had turned and seen his father staring at him in puzzlement from the open boardroom door.

The influx of the champagne on an empty stomach suddenly brought bile into his mouth. His legs going, Osorio made it to the kitchen of his apartment. Collapsing down at the sink, only his elbows supporting his weight, he threw up. Finished, cold sweat swimming from him, he staggered back to a chair. Glassy-eyed he sat until another spasm took him and forced him back to the spattered sink where the cycle was repeated.

At the back of his mind, he had always known there was an option. He looked at his face. Was that really him? How soon everything changes. On the surface and under. He walked out of the kitchen and looked back. The usually well-ordered kitchen, now shuttered, stinking of vomit, debris everywhere. It was a mirror of his life. And Carly somewhere, on assignment, or at her desk, fresh flowers in a vase, probably a dinner date that evening, or a party given by a friend to say, welcome back.

In the bathroom, its blinds also drawn, the fluorescent flickered alive. High in a corner he yanked open the door of the medicine cupboard and reached, finding the plastic bottle with his fingers.

Next would come the hearings. More than he could endure. They would come out of the woodwork to nail him. His career now over, all that was left was juicy copy for the tabloids.

Osorio uncapped the bottle and shook its contents, over twenty dark green capsules into his hand. He looked around for something to drink from. Buzzing in his head made him light-headed. He threw the empty bottle down and went to the kitchen. His left hand clutched the capsules; with his right he searched until he found a cup, then went to the fetid sink and turned the tap. Lightheaded and deliciously uncaring. No more pain. If he had cancer he would have done the same. He filled the cup and the buzzing persisted. Concentrate on a fixed object. Perform the act with detachment. Mechanically. Where would he lie down? His left hand was halfway to his mouth when he stopped.The buzzing wasn't in his head but outside it. Insistent. He blinked as he realised that someone was at his door, had been for several minutes, buzzing with determination.

Putting down the cup, but still clasping the tablets, Osorio made his way to the hall. Through the peephole his eyes could only barely discern an indistinct form. Get rid of whoever it is.

He opened the door.

'Sweet God in heaven, look at you,' said Cheryl Leinster.

CHAPTER THIRTEEN

1

New York

Thursday 28 February 9.00 p.m.

Tinkle of notes, Franz Listz. Twinkle of lights, the Palisades. Warmth. The nose of an '82 St Julien. Ron smiled and watched as Cristy came through from her kitchen carrying three cheeses on a wooden platter: runny Camembert, a Pont l'Eveque and a Cambozola studded with herbs. Beside him on the big sofa, Cristy sliced Pont l'Eveque and popped it into her mouth. She leaned back, her eyes closed, the cascade of music part of the room.

'Tell-ah the people outside-ah,' said Ron in a broken accent, 'that tomorrow they no-ah work-ah, okay? National-ah holiday, their emperor has spoken.'

Cristy smiled at him, caught his hand, then looked away as they sat with the music.

'Manhattan First Bank succeeded in freezing all Steve's assets today,' she said. 'They're also going for bankruptcy in the Federal Court.'

Ron spread white cheese on a biscuit and shook his head grimly.

'I tried to call him at home earlier,' Cristy said, 'but his phone has been disconnected.'

'It's really tough,' Ron said.

Cristy clenched her small fist. 'I know business is business,' she said, 'but those Tremaines are really something else. Dutch Tremaine has now got himself the trading outfit he's been looking for for years, and Carly's off the set, just like that. There's tough and tough, but that's just . . . '

'I know,' said Ron gently.

'I don't know about you,' Cristy said, 'but I really asked myself what Steve saw in her.'

'I expect he's asking himself that, right now,' Ron said.

'Did he actually love her, do you think?' Cristy asked.

Ron considered the question. 'I think Steve thought he loved her,' he replied eventually. 'I think she fascinated him, her looks, the way she was at ease anywhere, the wealth and privilege she represented. But he may have loved her image more than her, he may not have been able to distinguish between the two.'

Cristy looked at him fondly. Wise old owl. So solid. Yet he has a private place where he also goes without me. Like now. He's not letting me hear what he really thinks. Like ten days ago when I painted his bathroom and the car-hire people called from Houston. He told me later he'd been to Vermont to see his parents. So what? It's better people keep a little of themselves. At this stage anyway.

Cristy savoured the music, the rich wine.

'I don't really believe that Steve hasn't tucked away a million or two someplace,' she said.

'I hope he has,' was Ron's reply.

'He'll need it,' Cristy said. 'Wall Street has a particularly nasty way of dealing with failures.'

Cristy's apartment reflected her personality: there was emphasis on uncluttered space, polished floors with quality rugs, bookshelves with books and periodicals. In one corner, a word-processor and printer stood on a table.

'You know what I think?' Cristy asked.

Ron shook his head.

'I think this oil story that I'm following and the GiltStock business are connected.'

Ron made a face.

'I really do,' Cristy said. 'You read my piece on oil and Japan on Monday?'

'I read even the commas when you write them,' Ron said.

'Well my feeling is that GiltStock is tied in there somehow,' Cristy said. 'On Saturday I met Steve and told him.'

Ron smiled admiringly. 'I bet your article has caused some alarm bells to go off in high places,' he smiled.

'I hope it does,' Cristy nodded. 'I hope other people take up the message and run with it.'

'But how could GiltStock be tied in?' he asked.

'As a reporter I was trained never to talk about these things,' Cristy said mischeviously.

Ron shrugged, 'As you wish'.

'I'm kidding,' she said, then bit her lip. 'I'm getting these calls. A guy. Creepy voice. Won't give his name. He's nudging me along in a certain direction.'

Ron frowned.

'Most calls you get are garbage,' Cristy said, 'but this one is somehow different.'

Ron's face was enquiring. Cristy smiled, leaned over, caught his hand in hers again and held it there.

'This caller,' she said quietly, 'first pointed me at Saudi, then at Japan. Now he says there's an awful lot more to oil than meets the eye. He said if I wanted a real story to look at NYMEX, The New York Mercantile Exchange.'

Ron's face was sceptical.

'So what are you going to do?' he asked, eventually.

Cristy sliced a piece of cheese and chewed it.

'I guess I'll do what I'm paid to,' she answered. 'Dig a little more, see if there's anything there.'

'Where will you start?' Ron asked.

'On the oil market, NYMEX,' Cristy said. 'My anonymous informant said he'll call me in a day or two.'

'Real Deep Throat,' Ron laughed. He revolved his glass, scenting the wine with pleasure.

Cristy brought her feet up under her, twined her arm through his and leaned her head against him.

'Steve so very nearly made it, didn't he?' she said quietly. 'An Osorio in the big time. Brent would have been so proud.'

'Don't write him off yet,' Ron said. 'Things often come right.'

'I wish he had a good woman beside him,' Cristy sighed. 'It would make all the difference.'

'They're hard to come by,' said Ron softly, looking for her lips.

CHAPTER FOURTEEN

1

SoHo, New York.

Friday 1 March 1.00 a.m.

The sound of even breathing filled the studio. Everything was quiet, inside and out, except for the sound of his breathing. Cheryl put down the book she had been reading and walked barefoot to her bedroom. The studio's bay window, floor to ceiling and without a curtain, allowed a certain yellow light in: often she sat in the semi darkness, part of her own, special world; in the summer she slept on a mattress there so that she could wake early and paint at the window with the birds.

In her bedroom she undressed. Naked, she reached for a white nightgown, then paused. She looked back at herself from the wall mirror. You rate. Your hair might have some money spent on it, it's losing bounce, but otherwise you rate. Face-wise, your lines are clean and unflawed. You've always had good, firm breasts, good, wide shoulders. She put her hands to her breasts and cupped them, then stood sideways to her reflection. Stomach almost but not too flat, blessed with a metabolism like father, is my backside beginning to spread just a little? She faced again. Legs and thighs still good enough.

Cheryl pulled on her nightgown, took a brush to her hair and stroked it vigorously for five minutes. Then she slipped out of the room and into the one next door from where the even breathing came.

163

She stood by the bed and looked down. In sleep, he appeared unworried, although he was different somehow, older. People would say she was a fool. But this was the man of magic and this was now the man at the brink. Where before there had been a perfect reflection, now there were clefts which split the whole into precarious pieces. It had been his face in the boardroom during the crisis, at the moment oil had gone limit down, which had struck her in a way she would never forget. In place of confidence and poise there had been a look of utter bewilderment, a cry for help which she had heard every night for the last three nights from the depths of her troubled sleep.

This morning she had woken, knowing that now he needed her, now she could not leave him on his own.

On her way back to her own room, Cheryl paused in the centre of the studio so that the yellow light captured her, dissolving the flimsy nightgown, making the outline of her body the only thing discernable in the quiet night.

2

Friday 12.00 noon

'You slept nearly ten hours.'

Osorio looked at his watch. 'So I did.' He looked at Cheryl, sitting near a window, reading. At another window a small table in the sunshine was set for breakfast.

'This is Friday?' Osorio said.

'Yes, it is.'

'It's after ten. Why aren't you at work?'

'It's too nice a day to work,' Cheryl smiled, getting to her feet. 'Have some orange juice while I get the coffee.'

Osorio sat and looked around the sparse room, its rough walls whitewashed and hung everywhere with her watercolours. He drank the tumbler of fresh orange juice down in one long swallow. Cheryl came from the kitchen carrying a coffee pot and a basket.

164

'Croissants and coffee,' she said, placing them.

'Croissants? Where did you get croissants?' he asked.

'This is New York, you know,' she said. 'Eat up.'

Cheryl sipped the strong coffee and sat quietly as Osorio worked his way wordlessly through the basket of five croissants, larding thick butter on each piece and piling it high with marmalade. She refilled the coffee pot, refilled his cup, sat down again. He was dressed in jeans and a sports shirt; she had brought along his shaving gear and he had used it.

'Why aren't you at work?' he repeated.

'I told you.'

'I heard what you told me, that's why I'm asking again,' he said.

Cheryl shrugged. 'I'm old enough to take a day off, I guess,' she said.

'Not if the job is new and you're trying to impress the shit out of everyone,' he replied. 'Not in the first week.'

Cheryl lowered her eyes and smiled.

'I'm not sore with you,' Osorio said. 'But what's it like working for Cox? What kind of a set-up does he have over there?'

Cheryl sighed and looked away. 'I'm not working for Cox,' she said at last.

Osorio blinked. 'If not for Cox, for who?' he asked.

'I'm not working for anyone,' she said.

Osorio looked bewildered. 'Your name was on their letter . . . '

'Steve, I could have gone to work for First Com and Jay Cox ten times over,' Cheryl said. 'And I could have gone for twenty-five thousand a year more than GiltStock was paying me.'

'But you didn't?'

'That's right.'

'But also, you didn't come back to GiltStock.'

'Steve,' she said, her face kind, 'I knew what they were doing. All last weekend they were setting it up. Cox assumed I would come over. I knew everything that was happening. They spent all Saturday and Sunday setting up a trading room in the Man First building, crews of people, telecommunications people, carpenters, electricians, all working around the clock. Printers worked through the weekend to produce notepaper, cards, contract notes, settlements. Ray Leonard had a team of computer experts setting up systems. A special group targeted every broker, trader and client that GiltStock ever dealt with and hit them with a package first thing Monday. Commissions were dropped. All the key players on Wall Street were called at their homes on Sunday morning, personally, by Dutch Tremaine.'

'We didn't have a chance,' said Osorio in a shuddering sigh. He covered his face with both hands and leaned forward. 'Jesus, we didn't have a chance.' He looked up at her, his eyes small. 'What stopped you?'

Cheryl put a cigarette into her mouth. 'I didn't think I could work for Jay Cox,' she said. She lit up, blew a cloud of smoke around her, then looked away.

'Yet you didn't . . . '

'Nor could I bear to see GiltStock just dry up,' she said. 'I have good memories of GiltStock, I want to keep it that way.'

There was a square of green outside, more like a village scene than a big city. Women with strollers and old men sat on wooden benches.

'You know what the worst part was?' he asked her. 'It was putting my old man in a cab for La Guardia. He couldn't even begin to understand what I've been trying to do up here for ten years, the firm I'd built GiltStock into. He thought he was coming up to a fancy wedding – but he never really believed it all, the whole thing to him was like a trick.' Osorio shuddered. 'He wasn't disappointed. Do you know what he did just before the cab pulled away? He shoved something into my pocket. He'd gone before I could look at it. It was a hundred dollar bill.'

Cheryl's eyes were steady.

'That was hard to take,' she said.

'It's a difficult feeling to describe,' Osorio said simply. 'One moment you're up there, flying with the eagles, the next . . . '

His voice trailed off and he looked out the window.

'The next moment you're down in the gutter, or trying to wipe yourself out with an overdose,' she said.

Osorio's head came up with a jerk, his eyes drilling again.

'Shut up, will you?'

'What do you want to hear? Some harangue against Jay Cox? What do you want me to say? That this has all been a bad dream?'

'I said, shut up!'

'Why should I shut up? I'm only telling you what this whole

166

town is talking about. It's the juiciest story of the year.'

'You bitch!' he snarled.

'Was the Arab lady a bitch as well?'

'I was set up by Man First!' hissed Osorio, his teeth bared.

'Sounds like an epitaph,' Cheryl said, 'you know, something you write on a tombstone. Here lies Steve Osorio. He was set up.'

'GODDAMMIT!'

Osorio hit the table making it crash over and all the breakfast things rolled on the floor. He was on his feet, fists clenched, nostrils dilated.

'It was a bad idea for me to come here,' he panted. 'I'll go now and let you get back to your friends the sharks at First Com.'

Cheryl hadn't moved.

'Is that who you really think set you up?' she asked quietly.

'What a fool question,' Osorio said. 'Who else is there?'

'Steve,' said Cheryl, standing, 'that's exactly what you have to try and find out.'

3

New York

Monday 4 March 12.00 noon

'The letting was strictly a short-term arrangement,' said the manager of the Park Avenue apartment building. 'They came to us through our usual agent and paid cash. They said they were part of a U.N. delegation, in town for two weeks,' the man shrugged. He was mid-thirties, plump, impatient to be about his business. 'It looked a good deal at the time,' he said.

'And they paid cash?' Osorio asked.

'Dollar bills.'

'But not enough,' Osorio persisted.

'The agreement was six thousand dollars for two weeks,'

167

replied the manager. 'They paid three thousand down, but never paid the balance.'

'What about all those drapes and cushions they had up there?' Osorio asked. 'Where did they come from?'

'They moved them in as soon as they signed up,' the man said. 'They're still up there. The total value, which we'll be taking, comes to five hundred bucks. You can buy the shit in any one of a thousand stores in New York.'

Osorio shook his head in exasperation. 'You'd do business with people who just walked in like that? Without getting any further references, home address, without even establishing what country they came from?'

'Our agent makes these decisions,' said the manager coolly. 'I suggest you go and talk to him.'

'I already did,' Osorio said. 'He knows nothing. He just took their money. He sent me here.'

'Are you sure you're not a cop?' asked the manager.

'I told you who I am,' replied Osorio. 'I'm a broker and these people have cost me my business.'

'It would appear,' the man said, 'that our agent may not be alone in failing to establish the *bona fides* of new clients.'

4

Monday 5.00 p.m.

'You look like a million dollars,' said Sol Ansbacher. The little lawyer held his saucer at chest height and sipped lemon tea.

Osorio swept his eyes around the Hilton. Sol, as always in yellow waistcoat, blue striped suit and brown suedes looked mildly toasted after five days in Palm Beach.

'I'd prefer to have it in the bank,' Osorio said dryly. 'So how do we look.'

'Well,' said Sol putting down his cup, and drawing his breath in between his teeth, 'it's been pretty heavy down there in court today.' He took papers on to his knees. 'Man First have got the court to issue a garnishee order against you, plus a writ of execution. That means the bank can intercept monies due to you personally from third parties, and it enables the sheriff to take physical custody of your assets.'

'That's already started,' Osorio said, shaking his head. 'Some thoroughbreds I had down in Saratoga got seized this morning.'

Sol's eyebrows went up and down. 'They also petitioned the court under chapter seven of the Bankruptcy Code to have you declared bankrupt,' he said gently. 'The Bankruptcy Court fixed a date for the hearing. It's twenty-one days from now, March 25th.'

'What about my action against Man First Bank?' asked Osorio.

'Although you can countersue, which is the course we're taking,' Sol replied, 'the court is unlikely to set the bankruptcy hearing aside unless we can give them a damn good reason.'

'How good a reason is the fact that an outfit called Gabriel Holdings caught GiltStock for a hundred million?' Osorio asked.

Sol Ansbacher winced. 'Brokers commonly get caught by their clients,' he said. 'Anything further on the Arabs?'

Osorio shook his head. 'I've been trying to follow up some leads,' he said, 'but as of now they've vanished.'

'GiltStock's contract with Gabriel Holdings is one thing; your contract with Man First Bank is another,' Sol said.

'They end up with my fucking business,' said Osorio.

'I haven't missed that point, Steve,' Sol remarked, 'and it's one we'll pursue like sons of bitches, but ultimately the court will want to ask: are the events connected? Is Man First in any way responsible for your misfortunes? Is there any connection between Man First and Gabriel Holdings? Or between your ex-trader Cox and Gabriel Holdings? Was Cox in anyway responsible for introducing Gabriel Holdings to GiltStock, for example?'

Osorio shook his head in disgust.

'We'll still make a hell of a noise about the whole First Com thing,' Sol said with the air of someone quite used to daunting obstacles, 'but between us, doesn't it look as if Man First followed rather than led?'

A waiter came and put a leather wallet containing the check on the table.

'Mine,' said Sol, then smiled as he saw Osorio's gritted teeth. 'Don't get angry, Steve,' the older man said, 'get even. If someone has screwed you, then they're out there in the jungle and no one knows that jungle better than Steve Osorio.'

5

Monday 6.00 p.m.

Osorio took out a cheroot.

'Malcolm's found us new offices off Fulton Street,' he said. 'We're opening there tomorrow.'

'Good for Malcolm,' Cheryl said. 'He won't let you down.'

She sat beside him and unfolded a chart.

'Two things actually happened that Friday,' she said quietly. 'One, you got caught with a mega position, but two, oil cut through the twenty dollar a barrel marker like a knife going through sugar-paper.'

Osorio blew smoke towards the open window. 'And the whole thing happened during record volume,' he said.

Cheryl pointed to the chart. 'Unprecedented volume,' she said, 'over two hundred and fifty million barrels.'

Osorio looked at the volume spike on the chart. 'So much for being a bull of oil,' he said. 'It's lost over another dollar fifty in the last couple of days. It's down to seventeen.'

'Look at that day's volume and think,' Cheryl said. 'Alright, this was a set-up, but who did it? Whereas nothing would surprise me where Dutch Tremaine is concerned, would he really do that? Would he know how?'

'With Cox, he'd know how,' Osorio said.

'Do you really think Jay Cox set you up for Man First?' Cheryl asked.

'Look at what's happened,' Osorio replied. 'Man First have got GiltStock.'

'But that's only one side of it,' Cheryl said. 'Do you honestly believe that Man First Bank are going to hit the oil market with literally hundreds of millions of dollars of sell orders? That they would risk everything going against them and losing hundreds

170

of millions? All to get a broker a fraction of their own size?'

'They'd be insane,' said Osorio softly.

'Exactly!' Cheryl cried. 'They'd never do it! Anymore than I think they'd dare try and set you up in the first place. It's far too risky, they're a big bank, they'd be crucified if they were caught.'

'So what happened?' asked Osorio in mystification.

'Man First Bank simply responded to events as they unfolded,' Cheryl said. She stood and began to pace, her fists clenched. 'Okay, they tied you up with guarantees, but they're bankers, that's what they do. Oil started to slip and Cox saw what was going on. He also saw the dangers to GiltStock. He felt no personal loyalty to you so, being a bright guy, what does he do? He goes to Man First as fast as he can, goes right to Dutch Tremaine who everyone knows wants his own commodity set-up. For all I know Cox may have approached them already, maybe months ago.'

Osorio got up and went up to the window.

'Why are you helping me like this?' he said quietly.

When there was no reply, he turned; he saw the cool, cold Cheryl he remembered from GiltStock, not the warm-blooded Cheryl of seconds before.

'Why?' he repeated.

'I believe in certain principles,' she replied evenly. 'I'm proud to have worked in GiltStock.'

'That's all?'

'I don't like what happened.'

He came over to her chair.

'I've looked at you for two years,' he said softly, 'and wondered what the real Cheryl Leinster was like. A few moments ago I think I saw her.' He reached up to her face. 'Now she's gone again.'

'Please, Steve, no,' she said and turned her head away.

'I want to be close,' Osorio said.

'No. Not now.'

Slowly he got up and went back to his chair.

'Okay, what do I do next?' he asked wearily.

'You go down to NYMEX,' Cheryl said.

'NYMEX?' Osorio said, his face contorted. 'You think I'm going down there after what's happened?'

'Call Vince Carpenter,' Cheryl said, 'get him to find out who

171

the big sellers were.'

'Vince?' Osorio shook his head. 'He's not going to lift his little finger to help me.' He laughed and looked at Cheryl's fine face. 'Guys like Vince can't be seen talking to me. I'm like contagion. You stay away.'

'Steve,' said Cheryl, 'yesterday is over. Today is what we're talking about. And tomorrow. Swallow your pride, and find out what's happened.'

In her eyes, caught by sunlight, Osorio could see his own reflection.

CHAPTER FIFTEEN

1

New York

Tuesday 5 March 12.00 noon

Osorio made his way down three flights of stairs to the street. There was a small glass case in the lobby and Marilee had put their name in it: GILTSTOCK COMMODITIES BROKERS 3RD FLOOR. The new office was less than two blocks from where they had started out, he and Malcolm, ten years previously.

In the street Osorio walked east, his eyes to the fore. Some things were learned easily. Like when men saw you and turned their eyes away, you didn't give them the opportunity anymore. Like cash. Before, the world had been a cashless place where his signature had been enough for anyone; suddenly the spectre of rejection now sat at every turn and cash was everything, there was nothing more vital to him than the thick wad in his pocket which he could finger.

Like Saldi's the day before.

'Just the two of us, Fernando,' Osorio had said, Malcolm by his side. The Maitre d' turned to his reservations book and Osorio became conscious that conversation in the restaurant had ceased. Then he frowned. What was Fernando looking for? Steve Osorio didn't need a reservation in Saldi's.

Fernando's face, when he raised it from the book, said it all.

'Sorry, but I don't seem to have . . . '

173

'C'mon, Malcolm,' Osorio had said, turning on his heel. 'This place is so friendly it's smothering me.'

Osorio walked across a wide plaza; he could see a man in an overcoat approaching: he was a broker named Reilly and the last time they had met he had offered Osorio his yacht for a week. At twelve paces Reilly saw Osorio, covered his face with his hand and made a ninety-degree turn.

Bastard! He had actually covered his face! Brent had always said it. He'd been up and down so often he should know. Your best friend might in the end of the day be a twenty-dollar whore, he had said. Uncomplicated, kind to you when you wanted them, on the same side as you against the world. Not like the namby pamby assholes who put suits on every day and had it going steady with their fist.

The bar which Vince had nominated wasn't a usual watering hole: two blocks east of the Chambers Street subway, Osorio found it and sat at the back, but with a view of the doorway. He raised his hand as the grey-haired floor trader came in.

Vince Carpenter was wearing shades, looking uncomfortable. They shook hands, formally, as if it had been twelve years, not twelve days.

'Good of you to come, Vince,' Osorio said.

Vince nodded grimly and slipped into the seat opposite. 'I can only stay a couple of minutes,' he said, looking back to the door.

'How's oil?' asked Osorio as if nothing had happened.

'Still wants to go down,' Vince said, 'sixteen seventy last traded on the March.'

They sat in silence.

'We had some good times,' Osorio said.

Vince sighed, looked nervously around him, then shook his head. 'Shit,' he said, 'I asked myself, who gave me the breaks? I asked myself, who did I go to when the goons were outside my parents' house?' Vince's face was awkward and he fingered his dark glasses. 'Look, Steve, I owe you one so I'll try and help you if I can. But you're hot, understand?'

'I understand,' Osorio said.

'I'm sorry about this, but it's not me,' Vince said. He ordered a beer from a waitress. 'Jay Cox is paranoid right now. Absolutely crazy paranoid. He's made everyone sign a fucking document

174

this length as a pre-condition of employment. We're not even allowed talk to ourselves at the head.'

'Vince,' said Osorio, 'I sold the floor seats. You would have been an asshole not to get on board First Com.'

'I'm glad you don't take it personally,' Vince said, taking his beer from the girl's tray. 'I'll try another,' he said to her and took the first one down in half a dozen thirsty gulps. 'Jesus, I needed that,' he said. 'All the way up here I imagined I was being followed.' He looked at Osorio. 'I'm sorry about all this, Steve, but . . . I got really scared that weekend. On the Friday morning I had a job at a hundred and fifty grand a year; that-evening I went home and thought I had nothing.'

'I'm sorry for you,' Osorio said.

'I can't afford for Cox to think, even for a second, that I'm not totally his man, you know what I mean?' Vince said. He closed his eyes, rested his head against the back of the booth, then opened his eyes again. 'What's happened to GiltStock?' he asked.

'It's sort of still there,' Osorio replied. 'We've moved to a temporary office off Fulton Street. Malcolm's holding it together, I don't know what I would have done without him.'

'We'd heard you were down to four people,' Vince said. 'Can that be true?'

Osorio nodded. 'Three right now since I'm here,' he said.

The second beer arrived and Vince drank from it. 'I, ah, I got something on what you wanted,' he said, then could not stop his head from turning again to the door.

'Relax,' said Osorio, 'I've never been here in my life, no one is going to see you.'

Vince composed himself, then chanced a crooked smile. 'I'm off the wall to do what I did today,' he said. He ran a hand through his shock of grey hair. 'I went into two other guy's booths for you and looked up their positions, you know that?' he said. 'I'm a fucking screamer.'

'Who?' Osorio asked.

'Shea,' Vince answered. 'Also Benvenuto.'

'They did the selling that Friday?' Osorio asked.

'Most of it. You know there was record volume?'

Osorio nodded.

'Most of it came *after* the market came out of limit,' Vince said, 'in other words, after all our, your, long positions were established. After twelve-thirty.'

'I had that figured,' Osorio said.

'The selling came mainly from them,' Vince whispered, his perspiration beginning to run despite the air-conditioning.

Osorio nodded encouragement.

'Steve, before I tell you this, I want you to promise me something,' Vince said.

Osorio raised his eyebrows.

'After this, we're quits, okay?' Vince said. 'After this you and me don't talk anymore, you don't call me again, ever, agreed?'

'Sure, if that's what you want,' Osorio said.

'It's what I want,' Vince said. He took a deep breath. 'The big sell orders,' he said, 'were all done for Durst Bank.'

2

Wednesday 1.00 p.m.

Cristy Osorio sat back in her chair. She had switched off her AST system, taken a pad from her desk and turned it to a blank page. With a felt-tipped pen she wrote a number of words: the first was OIL. Beneath it she wrote SAUDI and MERC. In another column she also wrote OIL and beneath it JAPAN. A third column was headed GILTSTOCK. Beneath GiltStock Cristy wrote OIL.

On her desk were three files, each an inch thick, from the *Journal* library, containing photostats of any news stories over the last twelve months where any of the above headings interrelated with each other.

Cristy's telephone rang, breaking her concentration. She reached for it.

'Cristy Osorio,' she said.

'Cristy.'

Her flesh crawled at the sound of the now familiar voice.

'Yes,' she said, grabbing a pencil.

'Cristy, this is our last conversation.'

'Why, is there something . . . ?'

176

'Just listen, Cristy.' The voice contained within it almost a whistling sound. 'Everything I have told you, you must now forget, do you understand?'

'Forget?'

'Yes, forget!' said the voice impatiently. 'The game has changed.'

Cristy looked around her, then swallowed, her hands suddenly moist with fear. 'How changed?' she asked. 'I'm following the leads you gave me – I can't just forget everything now.'

'I regret having ever called you,' the thin voice said. 'You must now realise that there is grave danger for anyone who goes poking into this affair.

'Back out, now, whilst you can. Goodbye, Cristy.'

'Just a minute . . . ' Cristy cried, but the line had gone dead.

She looked to her left, to the glass-fronted booth, where Bill was speaking to someone on the telephone. She stared down at the notes on her desk.

'Shit,' Cristy said aloud, 'what do I do now?'

3

Wednesday 1.30 p.m.

Marilee looked up and smiled as Osorio came in.

'Mr Ansbacher was on,' she said. 'He wants you to call him.'

'He'll have to wait,' Osorio said, his jaw rigid.

GiltStock's new premises consisted of a tiny outer office which doubled as a waiting area and two small rooms behind it, one of which was now a trading-room. Malcolm Finch sat in his shirtsleeves across a table from a youth with freckles. Between them were a couple of telephones and, at eye level, a flickering monitor.

'Malcolm,' Osorio snapped and nodded towards his own office.

Osorio's office was the size of the big, walk-in cupboard they'd had in old GiltStock for the coats and umbrellas. Immediately outside the single window, blocking fifty percent of the daylight, were the letters of a large neon sign which ran horizontally across the building. Every so often there came a buzzing noise from the sign.

'Shut the door,' Osorio said.

Malcolm did so, then looked at the younger man, his head thrust forward, the muscles in his jaws and neck standing out in knots.

'You saw Vince?' Malcolm asked.

Osorio nodded up and down as if speech was beyond him.

'Do you know what he told me?' he said at last. 'Do you know what he found out? All the big sell orders which came into the market that Friday and took it out of limit, the whole fucking lot of them were done for Durst Bank!'

'Durst Bank?' said Malcolm, not getting it.

'Fucking Durst Bank!' Osorio yelled, caught up a desk diary and flung it over the small office. 'Here we are, being swept down the river like pieces of shit, and all along the shots were being called by Durst Bank!'

Malcolm shook his head, but said nothing.

'A guy I consider to be a big friend, a guy who's just about to marry my kid sister,' hissed Osorio like a cornered mongoose, 'is Abel Eller's righthand man. His name is Ron Spirakis. I play squash with him three, sometimes four times a week. These last weeks what has he been asking me about? About oil! The bastard has been finding out everything he can about oil! Now I discover that Durst Bank conveniently came into the market and sold record volume exactly at the moment when we were long fifty million barrels for clients we were never going to see again!'

'Maybe your friend knew nothing about it?' ventured Malcolm.

Osorio's face showed signs of exploding. He snatched his phone and punched out a number savagely.

'Ron Spirakis,' he requested, his voice betraying nothing of his face.

After a pause, 'Ron Spirakis's office,' said a woman, then, 'just a moment, please.'

Osorio hit a conference button and Malcolm sat.

'Hi, Steve,' said Ron's rich voice.

'Ron, how's it been?' Osorio asked.

'Just fine,' Ron replied. 'Sorry about all your news, Steve. I know you're going through a rough time.'

'I'm rolling with the punches,' Osorio said. 'Listen, Ron, just because I'm living on the side of a volcano doesn't mean I can't keep in shape. How about some squash?'

'That would normally be fine,' Ron said. He hesitated. 'There's a lot going on in here, right now. Can I come back to you?'

'Sure, when?'

'Maybe sometime after the weekend?'

Osorio was holding a plastic pen in his left hand; he twisted it double.

'I was hoping for a game today, Ron,' he said, keeping his voice even, 'like anytime from now on.'

'I just can't fit that, Steve,' Ron said. 'I'm sorry, but there's another call holding. Can I get back to you?'

'Ron!' Osorio was fighting to stay in control. Ron Spirakis could always spare an hour for squash. 'I need to talk to you!'

'Steve, I'm sorry but it will have to wait,' said Ron in a tone which Osorio hadn't heard before.

Malcolm closed his eyes.

'Ron, I've only got limited time!' Osorio cried. 'You don't know half the trouble I'm in and I think a lot of it started right in the place you're working! Ron? Ron? JESUS!'

Osorio threw his head back. There was silence, except for the buzzing neon.

'My God, Malcolm,' said Osorio with exhaustion, 'is there no one in the world we can trust anymore?'

4

Wednesday 4.30 p.m.

Cristy Osorio was pale. Trembling with anger, she put the phone down, then closed her eyes to get herself back on leash. When she thought she had it right, she picked the receiver up again

179

and dialled the number, his private line which she was the only outsider to know.

'It's got to be you,' said the deep voice.

'It is,' Cristy said.

'Well, how's your day going? All sunshine and light like mine?'

'Ron,' Cristy said, 'I'll be through here in thirty minutes, I want to see you.'

'I see,' said Ron, sounding intrigued. 'Might I be permitted to guess about what?'

'I'd prefer to discuss it when we meet,' Cristy said.

'Am I confused, or are you and I having dinner tonight?' Ron asked.

'First I want to meet,' Cristy said.

'Tell me the time and place,' Ron said.

'One hour,' Cristy said. 'The bar opposite the GM building – we've had drinks there before.'

As Cristy stood on the subway platform waiting for an express to take her uptown, her anger began to subside. The call from Steve was one she had been expecting, but not what he had to say.

'Run that past me again?' she had said.

'Durst Bank,' Osorio repeated. 'Durst Bank were the prime movers behind the big oil move that Friday. While I was buying oil for these Gabriel people who have used Durst Bank all along, at the very same time they, or someone else going through Durst, were selling triple the amount of oil. It's got to be a fix. Durst Bank is where the information is.'

'And you called Ron?' Cristy asked.

'He hung up on me.'

'What did you say to him?'

'First I asked him to meet me for squash, and when I got the breeze on that suggestion – first time ever – I told him I needed to talk to him. Then he hung up.'

Cristy shook her head. 'Durst Bank is a big institution,' she said. 'Ron doesn't know every little detail that moves in there.'

'Little detail, huh?' Osorio laughed. 'You call a hundred million barrels of oil a little detail? It comes to nearly a week's OPEC production, for your information.'

'Ron is a corporate finance lawyer, not some sort of an oil

trader,' Cristy retorted. 'You also should know that he doesn't gossip about what goes on in his job.'

'He hung up on me, Cristy,' said Osorio. 'He knows what went on in there, he knows that someone has put me out to swing in the wind and he's telling me loud and clear: bye, bye, fellah, don't call me anymore.'

'You're jumping to conclusions,' Cristy said.

'Like hell I am,' Osorio replied. 'All these questions about oil! He's milked me dry for those guys in Durst Bank. He's like the rest, he's a dyed-in-the-wool bastard.'

'I don't like you when you speak like that, Steve,' Cristy said sharply.

'Well then go shove it,' Osorio had replied and disconnected.

There were no seats in the train; Cristy held a strap as they headed uptown. It was impossible that Ron had sat in her apartment two nights ago and let her talk on about Steve and GiltStock while he knew everything. Impossible. Who would Durst Bank be acting for anyway? Cristy felt herself ache at the hurt in Steve's voice, the sound of someone badly wounded.

Ron was waiting near the door; as Cristy entered the bar a table became free.

'Scotch on the rocks,' Cristy said.

'Make that two,' Ron said to the girl. 'What a pleasant surprise,' he said, smiling to Cristy.

Cristy had her approach prepared. 'I've spoken with Steve, Ron,' she said, holding his eyes. 'He knows about Durst Bank.'

Nothing in Ron's expression changed.

'Good,' he said.

'Good?' Cristy retorted. 'Is that all you can say? Good?'

Ron leaned towards her slightly. 'What would you like me to say?' he asked.

The drinks arrived; Cristy looked away and sighed.

'I'll start again,' she said. 'You and I, we think we have a relationship, correct?'

'Cristy,' said Ron, suddenly urgent, 'that relationship is the most important thing to me there is.'

'In that case,' Cristy said, 'you know me, the way I feel and operate, I'm a straight-up person, there are no shades with me, agreed?'

'I know you,' Ron smiled.

'I also understand business and discretion,' Cristy said. 'I'm not the type of woman who needs to be fed tidbits at the end of each day like a goldfish. But I think there are circumstances which transcend all that, particularly when close, personal relationships are involved. Quite frankly, I find it very difficult to accept that you and I can sit down for an evening after a good dinner, sipping our wine, supposedly sharing the same mood, the same thoughts, later the same bed, and all along you're sitting there laughing at me because you already know it all.'

'You're mistaken,' Ron said.

'It's deception!' Cristy replied sharply.

'I repeat, you're mistaken.'

'In what way?

'Do you think,' he asked, 'that I would ever laugh at you?' He tried to catch her hand in his, but she drew back.

'That's not good enough, Ron,' Cristy replied. 'There's business and there's friendship. I'm not talking now about our friendship, but about yours and Steve's. There's a man who has just been ruined. Did the people you work for have a part in that?'

'I am as concerned about Steve's situation as you are,' Ron said calmly.

'If you are, how come you didn't tip him off?'

'When people get into the trouble Steve is in,' said Ron, 'a lot of what they say has to be heavily discounted. I don't know what he's said to you, but he's had several very big shocks, including the cancellation of his wedding. Last week was to have been the biggest of his life, Cristy, instead he finds himself blown out, two steps from skid-row.'

'Are you saying that he's making all this up?' Cristy asked.

'The trauma he must be going through is appalling,' Ron answered. 'His head must be in bits.'

Cristy closed her eyes in exasperation. 'I know you're a lawyer,' she said, 'and I know lawyers never answer questions, but I just can't take this. I'm asking you straight out: are Durst Bank to your knowledge involved in whatever scam brought GiltStock and Steve Osorio down?'

'I don't believe,' said Ron slowly, 'that that question can or should be asked in that way.'

'I'm running out of leash, Ron,' said Cristy, now pale. 'Please answer me.'

'I have answered you.'

Her eyes blazed. 'Is this all something to do with the trip you made to Houston?' she asked acidly.

Ron's eyes blinked just once. 'Houston?'

'Well, thank you for your help!' Cristy cried. So saying, she jumped to her feet and emptied her drink over Ron's bald head. 'Thank God my eyes have been opened in time,' she cried.

'Cristy!' Ron cried and made to get up.

'Don't you touch me!' she yelled as the bar fell miraculously quiet. She grabbed her handbag and coat. 'And *never* call me up again, you understand, you treacherous shithead? *Never!*'

As Cristy left the bar without looking back and conversation resumed, a waitress came by and handed Ron a cloth.

'You can probably use this,' she said.

'Thanks,' he said, towelling himself. He held up his glass. 'I think I could use another of these as well.'

Fifteen minutes later he left the bar and hailed a yellow cab.

'Staten Island Ferry,' he spoke.

As they pulled away, downtown, a car swung across from the far kerb and in behind them.

CHAPTER SIXTEEN

1

Ron looked at the descending night as he joined the line to board the Staten Island Ferry. The night had been hastened by light rain, driving in from the Atlantic. Ron's feet were cold; his clothes smelled of scotch. The line of people moved forward through the terminal, Ron with them. Despite the rain, he opted for the lower, open deck at the stern of the squat vessel: the wind and weather during the twenty-minute crossing might remove some of the odour of Cristy's whisky.

The ferry rode up and down as they pitched their way out into the harbour. Ron felt rain on his face, turned up his collar and sought the shelter of a lifeboat station. Ten yards away from him were flimsy, concertina-like gates, drawn across the open deck, just feet above the churning wake. He put his hands on the side of the rolling vessel and looked back at the receding city, thousands of mega-watts pulsing through it, bringing it aglow. Cristy. Lovely, lovely Cristy. Cristy, how do we get out?

Ron moved slightly as a man wearing a hat joined him at the lifeboat station. Spray washed over the deck as they caught the top of a wave. In a perfect world you could be up-front, direct. This imperfect world which we're all prisoners in makes us devious and twisted, never meaning what we say. But in what other way could he have tried to warn Osorio of the killing zone he was entering than through Cristy? And what other way could he have told Cristy than the way he had?

Killing zone.

A trip to Houston, okay; a call to a troublesome old guy who was probably half crazy anyway, no problem.

But not the way it had turned out, not the unspeakable horror . . .

There had to be a way out. With Cristy there would be, she wasn't a rooted person; if they got married and he then suggested they try someplace else, Europe for example, Cristy would come. Straight away. Particularly if she knew. That just left his parents to consider. And the kids in college. It would be just about manageable with Cristy's salary to keep them going.

More spume hit the deck. Ron began to think of going inside. He excused himself, the other man turned as well, then Ron spun abruptly backwards as he was shouldered off balance.

'Hey!' Ron cried.

He crashed backwards, his hands out to save himself. The superstructure of the deck and the back of his head connected painfully. He felt a hand catch his throat. His jaw was forced painfully skywards, then a gun's cold muzzle sunk into the flesh of his neck.

Ron was trying to remember what cash he had on him when he felt his head jerked backwards further; out of the corner of his eye he could see a second man, who had something wrong with his skin. Then Ron felt both his arms grabbed and pinioned; the man with the gun moved right in to immobilise Ron's legs. Then with mounting panic, Ron saw a third figure, effectively completing the shield around him.

'What the hell . . . !'

There was agony and he felt cold steel rammed hard into his mouth, filling it. Then he heard the clicking click-click of a ratchet and felt his jaws breaking.

Ron could not move. Regardless of the gun, now he strove with all his might. They had forced his head back again and all he could see above him was a swinging lifeboat. He tried to kick out but could not. Then something was suddenly being introduced at the back of his open throat and despite his desperate attempts to cough and expel it, he could actually feel the slender tube as they passed it down his gullet, onwards down. He thought he would choke. He strained unmercifully, but all that now passed across his vision was the overcast night sky, heaving with the movement of the ferry. Then Ron smelled something else.

185

The sensation was appalling: whisky was going straight down the tube into his stomach. There was no taste, just an extraordinary feeling. With madness Ron tried to toss his head.

He heard a command but could not understand it. His head was released and came forward. Then he felt suddenly and appallingly nauseous and he thought his teeth would uproot such was the force with which they removed the steel gag and he gasped, but he was still held, and he opened his mouth to shout out, but he felt himself lifted and the next sensation was of falling, then struggling. Upwards. In total wet darkness. And seeing the receding stern of the boat. And screaming, CRISTY! CRISTYYYYYYYY!

2

U.S. Coastguard, Governors Island, New York
07th March. 00.50 hours

Preliminary Report

From: Patrol Boat 32-067, B.M. Scatelli in charge
To: Commander, Station New York, Governors Island

During the above tour of duty at 21.00 hours, we passed the entrance to Kill Van Kull.

As we approached the Bayonne Bridge we were making four knots, wind was light westerly, Force 2, causing a slight chop.

At approximately 21.05 hours, a hundred yards east of the Bayonne Bridge, our lights picked out what appeared to be a dark shape floating in the water.

We drew alongside this object and saw that it was a body. We hooked the body and with a pulley brought it on deck.

The body was that of a male Caucasian, middle to late thirties, fully clothed. By appearance the body had been in the water for between five and ten hours. We now know the man in question to be one Ronald Herbert Spirakis.

CHAPTER SEVENTEEN

1

New York

Thursday 7 March 8.00 p.m.

Osorio stopped at the door of the apartment. He turned. Cheryl, her mouth tight, nodded and gave a small smile. Osorio rang the bell. The door was opened by a man whom Osorio had not seen before.

'I'm Steve Osorio,' he began, 'is my sister . . . ?'

'Hello,' the man smiled kindly, 'I'm Bill Warner, I work with Cristy on the *Journal.*'

'Pleased to meet you,' Osorio said. 'This is Cheryl Leinster.'

Bill Warner closed the door, then steered them into a small bedroom nearby.

'How is she?' Osorio asked.

'Devastated,' Warner replied.

'I only got word an hour ago,' Osorio said. 'What happened?'

'It's still sketchy,' Warner said quietly. 'They evidently found him last night, but couldn't complete identification until early this morning. They then had to find the next of kin which wasn't easy. Cristy saw it on the news ticker in the office.'

'Poor kid,' Osorio said grimly.

Bill Warner nodded and whistled air out between his lips.

'Where did they find him?' Osorio asked.

'Somewhere in the harbour,' Bill answered.

'And how . . . ?'

'They don't know,' Bill said, 'they're doing the autopsy probably now. But let's face it, a guy who takes the Staten Island Ferry twice a day is found floating . . . '

'I don't get it,' said Osorio, shaking his head. 'Where's Cristy?'

'Inside,' Bill said. 'If you folks don't mind, I'll slip off, I've got to get back downtown, there's a paper to put to bed.'

'Sure,' Osorio said.

'Try and get her to sleep,' said Bill as Cheryl let him out the door.

Osorio walked past the kitchen, into the living-room. He saw Cristy looking at him from a chair; she looked small. Osorio stopped, then half turned.

'Cristy, this is Cheryl, I don't know if you've ever met,' he said awkwardly.

Cristy's mouth opened to speak but no sound came out. Her head went to one side but her eyes stayed on Osorio; like someone mute she stared at him.

'Oh my God, you poor kid,' Osorio said and went to her, sat on the side of the chair, put his arm around her. Cristy's hands had made a rope of a wet handkerchief.

'I saw him,' said Cristy suddenly.

Osorio looked at her. 'You . . . ?'

'There was a formal identification necessary,' Cristy said calmly. 'Who else was there? His kids? His parents?' She began to cry. 'They rolled him out and I saw him. He's so very cold down there,' she sobbed, shaking.

'You shouldn't have done that,' Osorio said. 'I would have gone.'

'No one knew where you were,' said Cristy. 'Besides,' she dried her eyes with a Kleenex from Cheryl, 'it's good to say goodbye.' She looked at Osorio. 'You look tired,' she said. 'Let me get you some coffee.'

'I'll get that,' Cheryl said.

'She's a nice person,' said Cristy as Cheryl went to the kitchen.

'It took me long enough to see it,' Osorio replied.

'The other night, Ron and I were here,' Cristy said, 'we were talking about you and all your problems. I said to him that what you needed was a good woman.'

'You were so right you'll never know,' Osorio said. He got up and went around, resting his hands on her shoulders. 'Have his parents been told?' he asked.

Cristy's head nodded. 'That's another thing,' she said. 'I don't know what money there is, but Ron would be so worried if he thought they were going to have to leave that place in Vermont. He was so happy for them there.'

'Two weeks,' Osorio said softly, 'in two weeks, everything has changed for everyone.'

Cristy's tears ran and suddenly there was the little girl in Abilene again, her eyes red from crying when she'd lost something.

'And to think that his last memory of me was a bad one,' she said.

'What are you talking about?'

'After you called and told me that Ron had hung up on you,' she sniffed, 'I had a showdown with him.'

'A showdown?'

Cristy nodded pitifully. 'When he told me nothing,' she said, 'I threw a glass of whisky over him and told him it was finished between us.'

'He would never have believed you,' Osorio smiled. 'He was the most level-headed guy I ever met.'

'Then, what happened to him?' Cristy asked.

The telephone rang.

'It's for you, Cristy,' Cheryl said. 'Dr Someone, I didn't catch it.'

'It's the autopsy,' Cristy said, getting up. 'The doctor in the City coroner's office is a friend.' She took the phone. 'Hello?'

Osorio and Cheryl stood there and watched as slowly Cristy's face shrivelled in bewilderment.

'That's just not possible,' she was saying, 'that's just not possible.' Then, 'Thanks for calling, Si. Yes, I'm fine. Yes, my brother's here. 'Bye.' She sat down abruptly.

'What was that about?' asked Osorio.

Cristy was fighting for her breath. 'Alcohol,' she gasped. 'He had five times the tolerable level of alcohol in him.'

'Alcohol?' Osorio said.

Cristy nodded, unable to speak. Cheryl poured strong coffee into three cups.

189

'So they'll say he either fell over or jumped,' Osorio said. 'Were there any signs to indicate he was assaulted?'

'Not yet,' Cristy answered faintly. 'That was a preliminary call, but they're saying he was drunk.'

'That's not Ron,' said Osorio.

'Of course it's not,' whispered Cristy. 'But it's the verdict that they're going to give. Death by misadventure. His whole life spent upright and doing the right thing and it all ends in New York Harbour, drunk.' She began to cry. 'That's not the man I know, that's not the man I love,' she sobbed. 'What's happening, Steve? What's happening?'

'Sssh, calm yourself, Cristy,' said Cheryl and caught her hand.

Osorio tried to concentrate. 'How bad was this quarrel you had?' he asked.

Cristy shook her head miserably. 'I guess pretty bad. I saw red. I was shouting.'

'What exactly went before that?' asked Osorio sitting down.

Cristy closed her eyes. 'Nothing,' she replied.

'There must have been . . .'

'I mean nothing, as when Ron didn't want to play the game,' Cristy said with a great effort. She took her cup to her mouth with two hands. 'You didn't know him like I did. When he didn't want to answer questions, especially where his work was concerned, he could sit there and stonewall all night. I never knew anyone like him.'

'And what did you ask him?'

'Straight out I asked him was Durst Bank involved in the GiltStock trouble.'

'And you got a wall?'

'I got a wall, then I got mad,' Cristy said.

'The time before that, the evening you were here that you told me about just now,' Osorio said, 'what did you talk about?'

'I can't remember,' Cristy said.

'Yes, you can,' Osorio urged her. 'You already told me you said I needed a good woman at a time like this.' He could see Cheryl looking at him over Cristy's shoulder. 'Come on, Sis, think!'

Cristy took breath in through her mouth: her nose was blocked from crying.

'We were talking about my informant,' she said, 'the guy

190

who's been calling me about you and GiltStock.'

Osorio looked at Cheryl in frustration, then back at Cristy.

'What are you talking about?' he asked quietly.

'I'm sorry,' Cristy replied. 'I'd forgotten we haven't spoken.' She told them in a tired voice about the calls.

Osorio brought his hands together and pointed them at the tip of his nose; he looked at Cristy. 'Sis, I think you should go lie down,' he said, 'you're beat.'

Cristy nodded wearily. 'There's something you might do for me,' she said, holding out a key. 'It's probably illegal, but I don't care. This is the key to Ron's house on Staten Island; I had one to his place, he had one to mine. I've made out a list of things I want out of there before the vultures descend, his ex-wife being one of them, she'll be in from Cleveland tomorrow to get her hands on what she can.'

Osorio took the key. 'I'll do it tonight,' he said.

'I'm sorry to ask you with all the trouble you have yourself,' Cristy said. She looked ready to fold. 'I'd do it myself, only . . . '

'There's no problem,' Osorio said.

'I'll tell you more about the guy who called me up tomorrow,' Cristy said. She took a deep breath. 'There is still a story out there waiting to be written,' she said shakily.

'You're some kid,' said Osorio.

Cristy kissed him lightly, smiled to Cheryl, then went to the door and let them out.

Back in her orderly living-room, on her own, Cristy stared out the window where she could see the New Jersey Palisades twinkling on the night water of the Hudson. The same water that Ron drowned in, drunk, about twenty-four hours ago.

2

Staten Island, New York
Thursday 10.00 p.m.

Osorio had not driven across the Verrazano Bridge for years.

The sweeping concept in steel which joins Brooklyn to Staten Island swept out in front of them, the twin lines of its lights converging at the limit of vision. Cheryl's car was a Pontiac station wagon; although two years old it was little used and still smelled of the showroom.

'Nothing fits,' he said. 'Ron being drunk, Ron falling or jumping overboard the ferry, even Ron saying no to a game of squash.' He looked out the window right to Manhattan coming distantly into view. 'So who was Ron Spirakis? Was he the guy in Durst Bank who put this big oil scam together? Did he know of Gabriel Holdings, who also used Durst Bank? Was he maybe behind Gabriel, and if so, for Christ's sake why?'

'He could have been working under orders,' Cheryl said, 'saw what was happening to you, felt the pressure too much and then last night, after the row with Cristy, decided to end it all.'

'That might fit someone else's profile,' Osorio replied, 'but not this guy: he just wasn't like that.'

They crossed the crown of the bridge.

'You could always sue Durst Bank,' Cheryl suggested.

'I've considered that,' Osorio replied, 'try to join them in a conspiracy against GiltStock with persons unknown, try and find out if there was anything that Ron knew. Trouble is, Sol Ansbacher says an action like that could take years to get into court. I've got less than three weeks to the bankruptcy hearing.'

'How are your finances?' asked Cheryl quietly. 'I mean, are you totally cleaned?'

'I'm as burst as the water melon that bounced off the truck,' Osorio replied. 'The bank have got their hands on everything, except some pictures I have. I'll need to turn them into cash to fund my legal fees.'

'That's all?'

'I had an account in Miami,' Osorio sighed. 'Most of it went earlier in the week so that GiltStock could open again in that latrine off Fulton Street.' He patted his pocket. 'Apart from the five grand I've got in here, everything else I have is now owned by Manhattan First.'

They left the bridge, then the highway and wound uphill on streets with lawns in front of wooden-fronted houses. They checked street names, then numbers and eventually pulled up in front of a house, two stories, one of a row on an incline. The windows of the house were dark.

From the trunk Cheryl took two large liner-board boxes as Osorio let himself in.

'He lived here with his first wife,' Osorio said. He pressed a switch and lights came on everywhere. 'According to Cristy she's piranha.'

There were rooms either side of the hall door, one leading through to a dining-room and back to the kitchen. A staircase ran directly from the hall.

'Let's see what we want,' Osorio said, 'then let's get the hell. If not, with my luck we'll be busted.'

'This was his study,' said Cristy, walking into the room right of the hall and dragging her boxes with her. 'What sort of papers should we take?'

'Whatever we see,' Osorio replied, letting down venetian blinds with a slap. 'Cristy can sort them out.'

There was a desk against a wall with a tier of four drawers down one side. Osorio tried them but they were locked. Beside the desk were two full bookshelves and a built-in wooden press. He opened the press: shelves of books and periodicals presented themselves.

'I'll take these,' he said, lifting half a shelf into one of Cheryl's boxes. 'What items did she specifically list?'

'I've got, a tie-pin,' said Cheryl reading, 'gold cuff-links, books.' She leaned against the desk. 'Poor girl,' she said, looking at Cristy's list but not seeing it. 'She really loved this guy, didn't she?'

Osorio had already cleared the press; he shut it and began to top up the box with books from the shelves.

'I'm not sure, Steve, that she wants all the books,' Cheryl said.

'We haven't time to sit around and review them,' Osorio said, scooping a whole shelf into the second box. He straightened up. 'We're breaking and entering here,' he said. 'Why don't you get what's on your list, then we can go, okay?'

'There are some clothes items,' Cheryl said. 'A large rock-like paperweight.' She turned behind her. 'This must be it. Gee, it's heavy,' she said lifting it, then, 'here's another key.'

Osorio took the small key, squatted down and fitted it into the lock above the desk drawers. The key turned and he slid the drawers open one by one.

'That's peculiar,' he frowned. 'Why lock empty drawers?'

Cheryl shrugged. 'I'll go upstairs for the clothes,' she said as Osorio stood up.

'Steve, did Ron smoke?'

Osorio turned. Cheryl was standing beside a table near the door.

'No,' he said.

She shrugged, then pointed to an ashtray on a sidetable: the twisted butt of a cigarette lay where it had been smothered. Relocking the drawers, Osorio cast around. He could hear Cheryl going upstairs as he made a last circuit of the study. Bric a brac on a sideboard were all swept into the box.

'That's it, Cristy,' Osorio murmured. 'Anymore you negotiate for.'

He went to the hall door and opened it. Overhead, Cheryl's footsteps crossed a room.

'I'm through down here,' he called up, 'I'm going to load.'

He walked the short distance to the station wagon with the first box, clicked open the rear hatch, turned and then stopped, rooted where he stood. In the upstairs room of Ron's house, in perfect silhouette, two figures struggled the other side of a thin curtain. One was a man. The other, her face covered by his hand, was Cheryl.

Osorio covered the distance from road to house in two strides. Three bounds took him to the top of the stairs. Foot outstretched, leg rigid he smashed the bedroom door backwards, saw Cheryl's bulging, terrified eyes and charged. The second man behind the door swept his gun hand down but Osorio was going fractionally faster than the man had judged and the barrel struck him painfully but not decisively between neck and shoulder. Osorio stumbled, righted and whirled as the gun began to be readied. Savagely he caught the hand at the wrist, swung him around left to right, brought his own left hand over the gun, turned it back and leant with such manic force that there was a snap. The man screamed and his useless fingers opened. Osorio kicked him deep between his legs, then as the man began to soundlessly bend, Osorio brought his two hands down in one powerful fist on the back of his head.

'STEVE!'

Osorio could actually hear the air whistling; he rolled; the knife sang past him. Like something on springs Osorio came off the floor, the fingers of his right hand splayed rigid. They caught assailant number two near his thyroid and drove him back gagging to the window. Osorio hit him with a closed fist first near the left ear and second with a piledriver into the face which propelled the man backwards through the curtain and with a huge crash out through the bedroom window.

Osorio's breath came in laboured instalments. Cheryl and he stood there, heaving, staring at each other. There was a sudden squeal of rubber from the street as a car left the kerb at speed.

Osorio came alive first.

'The desk downstairs,' he panted. 'They had emptied it before we got here.'

'One of them must have been outside the whole time,' Cheryl said.

'We've got to get out of here,' Osorio cried.

Cheryl was behind him at the top of the stairs. He crashed down, grabbed the remaining box and ran to the station wagon. He flung the box in, not daring to look back at the shattered window, or what was in the front garden, or the neighbouring houses where lights had come on.

'I'll drive . . . ' he began, then looked around him wildly. With dread he realised that he had not checked upstairs for anyone else. Mouth dry he ran back, took the stairs six at a time and collided at the top straight into Cheryl.

'Are you alright?' he shouted.

She nodded. 'Let's go.'

'What the hell were you doing?' he asked as she joined him in the hall.

'One red, silk dressing-gown,' she panted and held it up.

Osorio grabbed her hand and made for the car; Cheryl was powered along, the dressing-gown floating out behind her like a sail.

CHAPTER EIGHTEEN

Dutch Tremaine's office left the visitor in no doubt as to who was king. Windows, everywhere, enormous soaring windows through which, on one side, the stacks and smoke of New Jersey appeared across the Hudson and on the other Manhattan went about its business, the skyscrapers of midtown thrusting upwards like plants gone to seed in a gigantic window-box.

Here, over the years, had sat the chairmen of mighty corporations, heads of state, members of European families with royal blood in their veins, and self-made men worth billions, all of whom wanted their banking business handled by the man whose name had long been synonomous with wealth and Wall Street and money.

Armchairs of leather surrounded a low table of burnished copper. Tremaine waited politely as Jay Cox reunited his coffee cup with its saucer, then recrossed his legs, the lower portion of each rotund calf correctly hidden by black sock. Beside Cox, Jacob Landey, President of Man First Bank, leaned back and awaited the answer to the question which Dutch Tremaine had asked of the chief executive of First Com, Man First's new broker, the newest on the Street.

'Pretty well, Dutch, pretty well,' said Cox at last, his face indicating that he had taken the question very seriously. 'We're now . . . established. We're new, but we're not the new boys anymore. It's not yet two weeks but people are already dealing with

First Com as if we've been around for ten years.' Cox's face, the oval behind the oval glasses, nodded with assurance.

'We've filled the GiltStock slot, in other words,' said Dutch Tremaine.

Cox's face showed him to be unhappy with this logic. 'I prefer to see this another way,' he said. 'I think it's better to forget that whole GiltStock affair, you know? I think that the time was right, absolutely right, for a really . . . professionally run and backed operation. No doubt about it. The experience is proving that theory, I do believe.'

Tremaine shifted his weight in his chair. 'Okay, I take all that on board,' he said, 'but as a yardstick, earnings-wise basically, how does it unfold, one on the other?'

'Do you mean,' queried Cox, 'what are our earnings right now compared to what GiltStock's might have been, were it around?'

'Precisely, that is precisely my question,' said Dutch Tremaine.

'Well,' said Cox with some caution, 'it *is* early days, and budgets and full reporting aren't all completely up and running yet, and everyone is just settling in, but it is going to cost us between twelve and fifteen million a year to open the doors, that's, say, a quarter of a million a week, and in our first two weeks, well I guess we will about equal that in earnings.'

Cox sat back, his hands laced over his waistcoat, his face composed in an attitude of well-earned contentment.

'Projecting that out,' said Jacob Landey quietly, 'that would leave the year just breaking even.' He looked briefly at Tremaine. 'I think GiltStock were doing better than that.'

Cox cocked his head. 'This is week two,' he said patiently as if the bank president might only be hearing about the whole venture for the first time. 'You've been presented on a plate with something that otherwise would literally take years of effort and money to get where we now are.' He looked to Tremaine for confirmation.

'Sure, sure,' Dutch Tremaine said, 'but GiltStock, were it still in place . . . ?'

'GiltStock was going to make ten million this year,' Cox said. 'I told your guys that six months ago.'

'Ten million,' said Tremaine. He got up and strolled, hands in pockets, to a wall of glass where he turned, his white hair catching the sun's rays. 'Let me explain, Jay, how we see this thing from up here,' he said. 'I mean, I have no doubt that First Com under your stewardship can do just as well as GiltStock did under Osorio's. You've got the same team. There's no doubt . . . '

'No doubt,' Cox affirmed.

' . . . in my mind that this will be done. But,' said Tremaine, 'we just don't see First Com as an "as you were" set up. Man First is one hell of a bank. We're worldwide. We've got to use that for First Com, get the synergies working, I mean like straight away.'

'That's good, Dutch, that's what brought me to you, the concept, the global concept,' Cox replied. 'I'm in a planning mode on this one already. I'm asking questions like, where do we see ourselves in three years from now, and I'll sure as hell need some answers.'

Dutch Tremaine exchanged glances with Jacob Landey.

'Look, ah, Jay,' Tremaine said, 'we don't view First Com as coming to us on a plate, there's a tail, like a seventy million dollar plus tail which is left by the whole GiltStock thing, you understand?' Cox made to take issue, but Tremaine went firmly on: 'We're a big, popular bank, our share price is very important to our stockholders, naturally. We keep a very close eye on our earnings, you understand me? It's always been our belief that GiltStock's ten million a year, in our hands would be more like twenty.'

Cox smiled as if indulging a child. 'So you want me to start making, week by week, the equivalent of twenty million a year, and you want this to happen right away?' he asked humourously.

'Yes.'

Jay Cox's face began to show a battle between irritation and disbelief. 'No matter how good the set up is, or the people are, Dutch,' he said, 'it takes time to get accepted. People don't just ring up with all their business, they need time.'

'You've got a bunch of some of the highest-paid people in America sitting on hardware that cost a fortune,' Tremaine snapped. 'They're paid what they're paid because they are meant to be better than everyone else. If they're better that means they should be making more money than everyone else. What's the delay? Three years from now, horse-shit! Now is when we need these earnings, sir, now!'

198

'They are the best . . . ' Cox began.

'Durst Bank's earnings are due out next week,' Tremaine went on. 'The word is they'll be up twenty percent.'

Cox made a gesture of submission.

'I was told you guys play the fastest game in town,' Tremaine boiled. 'As of right now I've seen faster games of checkers.'

Cox closed his eyes for composure. 'The right mix in something like this,' he said flatly, 'is a lot of big commission business which in itself leads to plenty of opportunities. I'm repeating myself, but that takes time. On the other hand, if you're saying to me, earnings is all . . . '

'You got it!' Tremaine smiled as if everything was suddenly and miraculously solved. 'You got it in one, Jay.'

'It will mean loading our activities more in favour of trading for our own book . . . ' said Cox.

'I like it,' said Tremaine, leaning over and slapping the trader on the shoulder. 'Let's see some real numbers, okay?' He stood up again. 'Just one thing, Jay.'

Jay Cox, now also on his feet, paused uncomfortably.

'You see this place here?' said the banker, draping himself around the smaller man's round shoulders and gesturing around the room. 'You know what got this place?'

Cox's eyes held the other man's, enquiringly.

'Religion,' nodded Tremaine, answering his own question, 'religion, Jay, and right at the top of the pile is the one and only commandment of this religion. Know what it is?'

Cox shook his head.

'Thou shalt not fail,' Tremaine said. 'Remember that one, Jay, and if you're in any doubt as to whether or not that commandment is the right one, take a walk down the gutter after work today and ask the first guy you see lying in it whether I'm right or not. The chances are, his name will be Steve Osorio.'

CHAPTER NINETEEN

1

New York

Friday 8 March 10.30 a.m.

In the King Cole Bar of the St Regis Osorio had to blink several times before he found Sol Ansbacher.

'Sorry I'm late,' Osorio said.

Sol inclined his head sympathetically and called a waiter.

'Steve,' the little lawyer said, 'we've been in conference about your case this morning.' He ran his tongue inside his lower lip. 'Let's just say, there are times to stay and fight and there are times to run away. Everything we see in your case seems to point to the latter option.'

'Are you worried about getting paid?' asked Osorio.

Sol made his mouth curve down until it looked like a lemon slice in his burnt-custard face.

'I know you'll pay me, however you do it,' he said. 'But is there any point in going into court, either to defend what looks like an open and shut case against you, or to file suit against a major financial institution?'

Osorio closed his eyes, then drank from the clear water which the waiter had brought.

'There has been a concerted attempt to bring down the price of oil for the last six months,' he said quietly.

'So you keep telling me,' Sol said.

Osorio held up his right hand, showing skinned knuckles.

'Sol, last night two guys tried to kill me. The night before that the most sensible, level-headed lawyer in New York drank two bottles of whisky and jumped into New York Harbour. Two weeks ago I was president-elect of NYMEX and worth maybe fifty million dollars, today I'm lucky if I know where the price of my next meal comes from. But I've still got my hands and my head, there's still blood in my veins and I can think straight again. All these things were done by someone afraid of losing a lot of money.'

'But who?' Sol asked reasonably.

'I've tried to speak with people I know at NYMEX,' Osorio said. 'I wanted to tell them about the selling initiated by Durst Bank in oil, about how Durst Bank may have tried to rig the market. I couldn't even get to speak to anyone higher than a secretary, for Christ's sake.'

Sol's head was shaking left to right.

'Unless you can give me something solid, Steve,' he said patiently, 'you would honestly be better spending your money on wine, women and song. That way you might have some fun.'

'Jesus, Sol, give me a break!' Osorio exclaimed. 'Man First have ended up with my business, I want them sued. The Arabs used a Durst Bank cheque to open their account with GiltStock, while at the same time Durst Bank were selling oil in the millions of barrels and using their top lawyer to pump me for information. If all that doesn't add up to a case, then what the hell does?'

Sol Ansbacher filled his chest with air, let it out, then leaned forward solicitously in the bedside manner of someone who has learned how to convey bad news.

'Steve,' he said gently, 'you know those positions you took for the Arabs were in excess of the speculative position limits authorised by NYMEX?'

Osorio sat back. 'We didn't exactly report them all, if that's what you mean,' he replied, moistening his lips.

Sol's head was shaking. 'I got a call an hour ago from a good friend in the New York Attorney's office, Steve,' he said.

Osorio looked at the little canary head in disbelief.

Sol nodded grimly. 'It's not my friend's area,' he said, 'but it looks as if the Feds are being pressurised by the CFTC in

Washington to move against you.'

'Jesus Christ!' Osorio managed to say.

'I'm not trying to scare you,' Sol said, 'but if I were you, I'd be thinking ahead in terms of arranging my bail.'

2

Friday 1.00 p.m.

Cristy went about her apartment mechanically. Normally someone who relished fresh air, today Cristy could not face the prospect of leaving the familiar surroundings, the rugs, the polished floors, the whitewashed walls. Her grief had overwhelmed her. Like a fever, it had taken her over, and although she could think and talk and rest her mind from its agony for small spells of time, the deep-boring realisation of how life would be from now on – for ever – was never more than a breath away.

Cristy jumped as the phone rang.

'Is Mr Steve Osorio there?'

It was a woman's voice.

'This is not Steve Osorio's number,' Cristy said.

'Oh,' said the caller. 'I'm sorry. I tried to reach him at a firm called GiltStock, but when I eventually got through someone told me they had moved. I got this number through the operator; there are only a few Osorios listed in New York.'

'That's right,' Cristy said. Then: 'I'm Steve Osorio's sister, can I help you?'

The woman began to talk. Instinctively Cristy reached for a pen and began to write. The woman kept talking. Cristy wrote, nodding, encouraging her. After twenty minutes Cristy had covered ten pages in shorthand.

'Just give me a number I can reach you at,' Cristy said, then wrote it down.

It took her another ten minutes to read through her notes. Shaking her head, she dialled another number.

'GiltStock.'

'Is Steve Osorio there?' Cristy asked.

'I'm sorry, he's not here at the moment. Can I help you?' Malcolm asked.

'This is his sister,' Cristy said. 'Can you ask him to call me as soon as he gets in. Please say it's very urgent.'

3

Friday 2.00 p.m.

The street off Fulton Street where GiltStock had relocated was one-way. Osorio paid off the cab and began to walk. He had the feeling of a fish caught in a net: events way beyond his control were pulling him inexorably. Feds. Bail. He shook his head. He had to stay ahead of them. To allow them to dictate things would mean certain ruin.

He was within thirty yards of the office. He was passing the entrance to a deli; suddenly he felt himself caught and propelled inwards. Turning savagely as he was dragged, Osorio brought his fist up to strike.

'Don't!' shouted Malcolm.

'Jesus Christ, what are you doing?' asked Osorio as the store fell quiet.

Malcolm was pale and worried. 'I had to stop you,' he gasped. 'Come on in the back.'

They walked past the food counter to where there were chairs and tables.

'Two coffees,' Malcolm said and sat down heavily.

'Stop me from what?' asked Osorio.

'Steve,' Malcolm said, 'you're not going to like this.' He fell silent as two coffees arrived.

Osorio's face was twisted. 'Stop me from what, goddammit?' he asked again.

'Right at this moment,' Malcolm said, 'there's a federal attorney and two cops sitting in your office.'

Osorio closed his eyes.

'They're acting on information they received from the CFTC in Washington about breaches of regulations regarding position limits in the oil market,' Malcolm said. 'They're up there waiting for you, Steve. They've got a warrant with them for your arrest.'

'Sol already warned me,' Osorio said tonelessly. 'I just didn't think they'd move this quick.'

They sat in silence.

'What are you going to do, son?' Malcolm asked at last.

Osorio pushed his untouched coffee to one side.

'Malcolm, I'm not going in there and letting those fucking goons put handcuffs on me,' he said. 'They'd kill me, you know that.'

'Where will you go?' the older man asked.

'Somewhere out of town,' answered Osorio, thinking aloud. 'Sooner or later they'll find me in Cheryl's. The bank have the place in Boca Raton.' He focused on Malcolm's concerned face. 'Jesus, I don't know where I'll go,' he said.

'You're welcome to stay with me,' Malcolm said. 'We've got countryside up there, the Hudson, some darling streams if it's fishing you're after. Come and stay with me, son, I'm too old to give a shit about anyone except the people I like.'

Osorio concentrated on the table.

'You don't need this sort of hassle, Malcolm,' he said quietly. 'You've been a better friend to me than I can ever say. But we've come to the end of the road.'

'I'm not complaining,' Malcolm said.

'You're such an obstinate old son-of-a-bitch,' Osorio said. 'You could get a job someplace else. There're no marks for valour in this game, you know.' Their eyes met. 'Let's call it a day, okay?'

'Whilst we've still got a customer on board, I stay with the ship,' said Malcolm firmly.

'Who have we got?' Osorio asked.

'Miss Singer,' Malcolm answered and watched as Osorio smiled and shook his head. 'You won't believe this, Steve, but she's still holding all that oil you put her into.'

'I don't believe it. What price is oil?'

'Fourteen bucks a barrel,' Malcolm replied, 'and it's going lower.' He clicked his fingers. 'With the cops coming into the office and all, I nearly forgot,' he said. 'Call your sister. She said it's urgent.'

They stood up.

'I'll be in touch, Malcolm,' Osorio said. 'Even if I knew where I was going, I wouldn't tell you where. I think it's better that way. But I'll be back, I'll be back to GiltStock.'

The two men embraced; Osorio blinked: he didn't want the older man to see his eyes.

'I know you will, son,' Malcolm said, 'I know you will.'

4

Friday 3.30 p.m.

Cristy sat in a dressing-gown; she looked tired and drawn.

'Her name is Jen Cassavantes,' Cristy said. 'She was calling from Houston.'

Osorio sat on the edge of his chair, Cheryl on the arm. Outside, a grey March day had begun to lash rain against the windows.

'She told me she did temporary secretarial work for a geologist named Gerhardt,' Cristy said, reading from her pad. She looked up. 'Gerhardt was murdered in his office two weeks ago.'

'*What?*' Osorio's face was ravaged in bewilderment.

Cristy sighed. 'I'm afraid so. Cassavantes says that Gerhardt wrote an article based on his experiences in Japan when they were exploring for oil there, claiming that the present find is very exaggerated. She says you invited him to come to New York for a dinner.'

'My God!' said Osorio running a hand through his hair. 'It was to have been part of my speech at the oil dinner, *"The Myth of Ishikari Bay."* Do they know who killed him?'

'Evidently not,' Cristy said. 'It's being treated as a case of armed robbery: Gerhardt surprised them and was unlucky.' She shuddered. 'They strangled the poor guy.'

'Holy Moses,' said Osorio.

'Steve.'

He looked at Cristy.

'There's a connection,' she said in s small voice.

'How, a connection?'

'Houston,' said Cristy flatly, her mouth a straight line. 'Ron lied to me three weeks ago. He told me he'd been to Vermont to see his parents, but he'd been to Houston.'

Osorio looked at Cheryl, then back at his sister. He stood up.

'Let's hold everything,' he said, his eyes blazing. 'Let's hold everything right here. This is not some new planet we've all just landed on. Ron Spirakis may have been a lot of things, but a murderer he was not.'

Cristy looked up helplessly.

'People are dying for a reason,' Osorio said. 'It's because they know something.'

They looked at him, Cheryl enquiringly, Cristy as if she might cry again.

'Let's look at what we know for a fact,' Osorio said quietly. 'Durst Bank are big sellers in oil, *the* big sellers. A man in Houston called Gerhardt writes a crazy article questioning the fundamental reason for oil's fall – the Japanese oil find. No one takes any notice of Gerhardt until he gets in touch with me and I decide to liven things up at the NYMEX dinner using his material.'

'But how did Durst Bank know?' Cheryl asked.

'Through Ron!' cried Osorio. 'I let him read my speech before ever I knew Durst Bank were bears of oil! And now I can see clearly what happened. He came back and asked me all sorts of questions about my speech, about seismic, about the whole issue. He was probing, for God's sake!'

'Why didn't he try and warn me?' asked Cristy, trembling.

'He did!' Osorio said. 'Anonymously!'

'Anonymously?' said Cheryl.

'Who was the guy who's been calling you up at the *Journal*, trying to steer you in certain ways about the big oil story?' Osorio asked.

'The person who's been calling me had a weird voice, a thin voice,' Cristy said. 'Ron spoke totally differently, he had a deep voice.'

Osorio shook his head. 'It was Ron,' he said. 'Ron Spirakis could put on any voice he cared to, imitate anyone, you know that.' Osorio faced them, his hands out as if to grasp something.

'When you confronted him about his knowledge, Ron stone-walled – to protect *you*. What Ron didn't realise was that he had been tumbled. Someone discovered his connections to me, maybe even heard him calling you up in a funny voice, who knows? They pumped him full of whisky and threw him in New York Harbour.'

'How do you know it's Durst Bank?' Cristy asked. 'You have no proof it's them, you have no proof that Ron called me up or that what happened to him the other night wasn't in fact an accident.'

Osorio looked at her darkly.

'Whoever has been selling oil, causing it to fall in price, has been synchronising their movements with Jap announcements about the find,' Cheryl said. 'You may remember that was the result of my market analysis on the subject,' she said to Osorio drily. She went on: 'If what you say is true, then it's axiomatic that the Japanese also want the price of oil to fall. How can you explain that?'

Now Osorio's face glowed. 'You tell her, sis,' he said, 'you tell her.'

Cristy took a deep breath.

'Apart from wanting the price down because they're the world's biggest importers,' she said, 'the Japanese may easily have had an important short-term objective. They saw the rise and rise in Saudi politics of Prince Saleem, a man particularly known for his anti-Jap feelings. They may have panicked. What would happen if he got the top oil job? Japan could be fighting for it's oil again. Twenty-six percent inflation like in '74? Another oil shock? They're paranoid at the best of times, so think of the effect that would have had.' She nodded. 'It's the story my mystery caller put me on. It's the angle I was following.'

'So they decide the best way to hurt the Arabs is in their pockets,' Cheryl said. 'They rig the market, using Durst Bank as their agent; they exaggerate the size of the find and every time, just before they make an announcement, Durst Bank go massively short.'

'They over-succeeded,' Cristy said. 'Saudi has dropped Saleem, but the bear market in oil still goes on.'

'I got in their way,' Osorio said, 'so they bust me.' He looked at Cheryl. 'Gabriel was a fabrication!' he cried. 'It had no other function than to discredit and silence me.'

The rain beat the window in squalls.

'I'm going to Houston to talk with this Jen Cassavantes,' Osorio said.

'I've never been to Houston,' said Cheryl.

'No way,' Osorio said. 'You saw what happened out in Staten Island, these people aren't playing. Besides, my new friend the federal attorney is now on my tail. I'm a wanted man. I'm going to have to be able to move quickly. I stay on my own.'

Cheryl positioned herself in front of him, her back to Cristy.

'I want to see this thing through,' she said, smiling from between clenched teeth. 'I can move as quick as the next, you know. You seem to forget I've spent the last seven years trading commodities.'

Osorio made as if to argue, then he shook his head. He went to Cristy.

'I want you to be careful, sis,' he said. 'Abel Eller and whoever else is in this thing may assume you know too much for your own good. Do you have anything to protect yourself with?'

Cristy nodded and sniffed.

'I still have the little pistol Brent gave me' she answered.

'The toy with the pearl handle?' Osorio asked. 'Does that thing work?'

'I don't know,' Cristy said, her eyes brimming. 'I'm sorry I'm like this. I just can't stop crying.'

'Don't upset yourself anymore,' said Osorio, putting his arm around her.

'All I can see is his face,' Cristy wept. She lay her head against him. 'What's going to happen, Steve? What's going to happen?'

'Do you remember when we were kids?' Osorio asked, rocking her. 'Do you remember how much part of the great outdoors we were living in those trailers? When there was a storm or anything, our home on wheels used to shake and rattle like a bitch. Do you remember how scared we were when that happened, especially the bit between the lightning and the thunder? Do you remember the flash of lightning, then the silence, the gap before the big noise starts?'

He looked at Cristy but his eyes were someplace very far away.

'I remember our mother telling us to count during that gap,' he said. 'We'd been sitting there scared after the bright flash had lit up the night, and she'd say, "You kids count now," and we'd say, "why?" and she'd say "because God is counting, that's why".'

Osorio squeezed Cristy tight.

'Right now,' he said softly, 'God is counting.'

5

Saturday 2.30 a.m.

Cristy stood in the window of her living-room and looked out, over the streets and houses and the water. She could not sleep. Only the desk light was on in the room; she stood at the edge of a pool of light.

There was a frost outside, beyond the glass; inside, it was warm but further inside, inside Cristy, she felt cold. The place of her grief had now been taken by something glacial, sometimes a fear, sometimes an anger. The fear came when she thought of the spectre of the time ahead, stretching into an infinity of loneliness. That was something they now shared together, Ron and she. Infinity.

She looked out, unseeing. Everything was changing. Arrangements would be made, property assigned. Where you had been intimately part of something, now you were an outsider looking in.

And in a way Cristy now felt an outsider in the relationship she had shared with Ron. The face she knew had been replaced with the face she had identified in the City Morgue: not warm and jolly but impossibly white. However hard she strove to replace this image, to call up the memories of the good times, all she could come up with was this dead, marbled face.

Who had he been anyway? Certainly not just the happy, parent-loving lawyer that had come across. Had he spied on them all? Reported everything that Steve had told him as a friend?

Cristy took a deep breath. Closing her eyes she used all the strength she had left to banish the image of the face in the morgue. She recalled Ron's laughing voice; his happy face followed.

She covered her face with her hands and for five minutes recited the prayers she had learned as a child. She prayed to God. To God's Mother. She prayed to her own mother whom she had never known but had long imagined as a beautiful angel. And she prayed to Ron Spirakis who, if there was a heaven, she knew was up there, looking after her.

But the stern stuff that her teachers had called cussedness and for which Brent had whacked her ass red, not recognising his own obstinacy in female form, this now had bubbled up; anger competed with fear for a place in her emotions. She was an Osorio. She was descended from women who rode horses bareback, urging them with strong, unclad legs and hunting food with men on equal terms. She was a survivor, born of survivors. Her blood ran quick and rich and when she had to stand and fight she did.

Opening the pad with her notes she began work.

On Riverside Drive, the solitary lights from the apartment shone down. To the mottled-skinned occupant of the parked car who had watched them come on thirty minutes before they were a source of hypnotic attention.

PART THREE

CHAPTER TWENTY

1

New York
Friday 8 March 11.15 a.m.

NYMEX was heaving. Swells of noise, great breakers of pande-
monium, washed up and out from the pits and around the walls.
The turbulence was most violent in crude oil, the eye of the
maelstrom, where a ceaseless whirlpool of frenzied bedlam had
been going on for ninety minutes.

Vince Carpenter stood at the First Com oil position like the
captain on the bridge of a pitching ship. Feet apart, a phone
crooked between his left shoulder and ear, he watched as, an
arm's length away, over three hundred jostling and screaming
men and women flailed their arms on the carpeted, tiered steps
of oil.

There was a great baying and Vince tingled from head to toe.
In all his years working with GiltStock he had never felt quite as
good as this. Even on the day when oil had gone limit up and
Osorio had sat on the biggest ever position, even then the buzz
hadn't been like now. Vince hadn't believed the market then in
the way that he did now. Or almost did.

'Holy sweet mother of God!'

Max looked like a mercenary on his way home from the front.

'Benvenuto just bid twelve ninety on a hundred thousand barrels,' he panted, 'and he was fuckin' eviscerated!'

'Did you get on?' Vince asked.

'Yeah, sure,' said Max. He tore sheets from his pad, time-clocked them and threw them on to Vince's ledge.

Vince spoke to his cradled phone. 'Sold you a hundred at ninety, Jay,' he said. 'Working four.'

'Don't take all day,' said Jay Cox and clicked off.

'If we don't fill,' said Vince to the perspiring Max, 'Suck will have our guts.'

Max took a huge gulp of air, then bawling he clawed his way back into the action.

Vince took out his position book and opened it where he had First Com's oil positions neatly listed. He scanned down the ordered columns. They had gone short when oil was sixteen, then two days later there had been the meeting in the First Com boardroom.

'All the signs are that this is a bear market, *the* bear market,' Jay Cox had said. 'Let's get in on some of the pickings. What do you think, Vince?'

'I've never been an out and out bull of oil,' Vince replied cautiously. 'I was never happy when Steve went long at twenty-one.'

'I know,' said Cox, looking pained at the mention of the name. 'But what do you think?'

'Why go against a trend?' Vince shrugged. 'What's going to make oil go up? Sell the bitch.'

Cox raised his eyebrows, faint crescents above oval glasses. He turned to the other person at the table, a man of about twenty-four or -five, with brown hair which came to his shoulders and wearing wire-rimmed glasses like Cox's.

'Jean-Paul?' Cox said.

Jean-Paul Peterschmidt was First Com's latest recruit and, at two hundred thousand basic, one of the more expensive. Originally French, he had worked for five years on Wall Street with a European bank, earning himself something of a reputation as a chartist. Now he looked at the chart in front of him on the table and made a very French expression with his mouth.

'Before twenty it was anybody's game,' he said with a strong American accent. 'Since twenty it had to break seventeen to confirm the trend.' He shrugged. 'Now ten dollars is the number.'

The statement seemed to galvanise Jay Cox.

'Ten dollar oil,' he said. He looked at Vince, then back to the Frenchman. 'You're right. The fundamentals aren't going to change. People don't want oil. We've just had the mildest winter in a hundred years. A U.S. destroyer was sunk in the Persian Gulf two days ago and oil *lost* fifty cents, for Christ's sake!'

Vince found himself nodding.

'Ten dollar oil!' Cox cried. 'Ten dollars might be dear! Historically, it's outrageous! Ten bucks could look a rip-off in six months!'

'Or three,' said Peterschmidt enigmatically.

Just then the door opened and the three men stood up as Dutch Tremaine walked into the room.

'Just thought I'd come and see how things work in the cockpit, Jay,' he smiled. 'Hope you don't mind.'

'Be my guest,' Cox said. 'You haven't met Jean-Paul Peterschmidt, I don't believe, our new state-of-the-art chartist. And this is our man down on oil, Vince Carpenter.'

Tremaine shook each man's hand.

'Sit down, gentlemen, sit down,' he said. 'Please go ahead as if I wasn't here.'

Cox gave the two bottom lugs of his waistcoat a little downward tug.

'We're talking oil, Dutch,' he explained. 'I guess we've been evolving a target.' He looked at the Frenchman.

'Ten dollars,' Peterschmidt said, obviously remembering his previous success with the phrase. 'Ten dollars is the number.'

'What's oil now?' asked Dutch Tremaine.

'Fifteen, sir,' answered Vince.

'We're short almost two million barrels at sixteen,' Cox smiled. 'That puts us two big ones in front.'

'I seem to recall the GiltStock debacle taking place at around twenty,' Tremaine said. 'What happened to the dollars between twenty and sixteen?'

Vince looked at Cox who looked at Tremaine and frowned.

'We weren't being as aggressive then, Dutch,' he said, 'as you may recall.'

Tremaine just nodded.

'But we've got a pretty good view of where it's all at, right now,' Cox continued with a smile, 'and the best chartist there is on Wall Street says the big number is ten dollars.'

As Cox was now looking pointedly his way, Vince cleared his throat.

'I'd go for ten,' he said. 'But I just wouldn't like to say when.'

Cox looked to Peterschmidt. The Frenchman held up three fingers.

'Three months,' said the two-hundred thousand a year man.

Cox leaned back, satisfied.

'We're ready to act on this, Dutch,' he nodded. 'We're ready to build.'

'What are the numbers?' Tremaine asked pleasantly.

'Five million barrels? Maybe six?' said Cox.

'It's fifteen dollars a barrel now and it's going to ten, you tell me,' Tremaine said. 'That means it's going to fall by five bucks. Six million times five bucks gives thirty million. Being a little tame, aren't you?'

'There are position limits, Dutch,' said Cox with a little gesture of his head as much as to say that Tremaine should know.

'Yeah, I know, but there are ways around everything if you try hard enough,' Tremaine said. 'I mean we've got operations and clients all around the globe who might like a slice of this. We've got offshore accounts.'

'You want us all to be on the run from the Feds like Steve Osorio?' joked Cox, then froze as he saw Tremaine's face.

'You've got an operation here,' Tremaine said slowly, 'that's cost me a lot of money. You tell me oil is fifteen and set to go to ten. You're the experts.'

'I know, but . . . '

'I listen to what happens on Wall Street,' said Tremaine. 'I hear that Durst Bank have been selling oil for the Japanese. I hear they've been short from thirty, all the way down. Do you think that Abel Eller let that kind of opportunity slip? Do you think he stood there selling oil for the Japs and didn't sell some for himself?' Tremaine spread his big hands out flat on the shining table. 'He's been making a fortune selling oil,' he said harshly, 'and using it to buy up stock in my bank.' He slapped the table hard. 'What in hell's name is wrong with us taking a twenty million barrel position? Or twenty-five? There are a hundred different ways we could hide it.'

'Nothing *wrong*,' Cox said. 'But we're talking exposure . . . '

'I thought we were talking about the ten dollar oil,' Tremaine snapped.

'Sure,' Cox replied, 'sure, Dutch.'

Tremaine got to his feet. 'You carry on, boys,' he said, 'don't let me disturb you. I know you've got work to do.'

So saying he had left the room, his white hair around his head like a gleaming aurora.

The bedlam blasted Vince back to ground zero.

'Filled two hundred thousand at twelve-eighty,' Max panted and time-clocked the trades before grunting back into the fray.

Vince spoke the execution into the phone, then neatly wrote it into his book. The cumulative position of First Com in oil, done through a web-like series of interlocking accounts, came to twenty-two million barrels short, that is, twenty-two million barrels of oil sold at higher prices, but oil which First Com did not own or had not got.

If Vince felt a shudder of unease a bit like that of two weeks ago, he surpressed it. This was the bear move of the era, and no one on Wall Street had a better position. Vince licked his lips. He had even broken the one rule, the promise which he had made to Osorio all those years ago. A broker high in the World Trade Center was holding a hundred thousand barrel short position for a Mr Carpenter whom he had never met.

Vince sighed.

Twelve dollars seventy just traded.

Two dollars thirty to go.

2

New York

Saturday 9 March 12.30 p.m.

Malcolm Finch paused for the traffic streaming on to Fifth Avenue. It was warm but Malcolm wore his Burberry. Automobile fumes swirled in front of his head, causing the Plaza to bend and sag somewhat, then the lights flashed WALK WALK and Malcolm was off again, walking up Fifth with Central Park to his left.

Events, in a way, had beaten Malcolm. One day he was planning his exit – and in fairness, he couldn't leave Steve before he came back from his honeymoon – the next day he was lying on his back in the dark, sucking oxygen from a plastic cup.

In the following days a strange thing happened to Malcolm. Out of hospital at his own insistence, (there was nothing wrong with him, for chrissakes), he suddenly realised that he cared for GiltStock and Steve Osorio a lot more than he had ever imagined. He put his money up without a second thought. When that was swallowed up and they moved offices down to Fulton Street, just Steve and he and a kid and the girl, to Malcolm it was like old times again. He mattered. He was back to being half of the people who mattered in GiltStock. They had been here before and won. They would do it again. The new, tiny office was somewhere that Malcolm could feel more comfortable, the rent was manageable, there was no silly bullshit dining-room with waiters and people costing a fortune making puddings.

In their new environment Malcolm, in his own mind, had taken a trip back in time. Wasn't this what he had done as a younger man? Fought the odds? And . . . retirement? Well, hell, who wanted to sit out in a boat getting wet when there was a job to be done!

Malcolm paused in mid-stride to admire a flower display in a shop window on Fifth. With Steve away, Malcolm's enjoyment with things had gone up several notches. Sure it would be all uphill at GiltStock, and the cops were watching the place day and night for Osorio, and sure all of Wall Street and the media were beside themselves with glee following not just a bankruptcy anymore, but a manhunt! So what? *Some* business would be done, and now here was Malcolm making a client visit. A client visit! He smiled as he walked. How long was it since he had visited a client?

After ten years in GiltStock Malcolm had a mental image of Miss Singer: it was of a blousey lady in her early sixties. Still, he thought as he passed the Getty Building, she got the markets right quite a lot of the time. And she never stopped asking to see Osorio. What did she want to see him for? What did it matter? Hell, they had few clients now, suddenly they needed the Miss Singers of the world.

Fifth Avenue was sunny. Malcolm looked at his watch. He had

come in specially, breaking his weekend to make the visit, as he reckoned he needed to be in GiltStock every moment during business hours. Ten minutes here, then back to Grand Central for his train home. Malcolm turned into the apartment building on his right.

'Take the private elevator at the other side of the lobby please, Mr Finch,' the concierge said, having telephoned upstairs. 'It takes you right to the top of the house.'

Malcolm made a face. Surprise one. He had imagined Miss Singer in a dark, rear apartment somewhere, not in a penthouse with its own elevator. He stepped in through doors which had been activated elsewhere. Miss Singer's elevator was decorated in light blue pastels; a watercolour which looked familiar filled the back panel and light for the ascent was provided by a miniature chandelier. Malcolm smiled. Surprise two.

The doors reopened and Malcolm's eyes met two faces: one, a grandfather clock, the other, a man of fifty in a dark suit, white shirt and grey tie, standing in an attitude of attentiveness.

'Good afternoon, sir,' the man addressed Malcolm.

'Good afternoon to you,' Malcolm responded and looked around him. Surprise three. He was in the hallway, not of a New York apartment, but of a gracious country mansion. Several levels of the building must have been used to create this sense of height and space; underfoot there were large tiles of red and yellow; overhead, at least fifteen feet up, hung a magnificent, cut-glass chandelier; the walls were wood-panelled to halfway and above the panelling were rows of oils.

'So the young pup sent the old dog!'

Malcolm turned. Double doors had opened and between them, sitting in a wheelchair, was a diminutive lady with silver hair.

'Miss . . . Singer?'

Surprise four.

'Come on in and sit down, Mr Finch,' said Miss Singer, turning herself around and leading the way into a huge room with views from three sides over Central Park and midtown Manhattan. 'Have a drink. What's your poison?'

'Do you have a beer?' asked Malcolm, sitting. He looked at his hostess in wonder; she was seventy-five if a day, but she wasn't dressed old: she had on an elegant blue dress, white flowers chasing through the blue, buttoned to the neck, half sleeves showing thin but firm arms. Her face skin was very fine and pale, almost translucent, drawn tightly back over visible bones. But her eyes stole the show: bright blue, they never wavered, always stayed in command.

'We have everything here,' Miss Singer replied. 'And I'll have a little pink, Willie,' she said, twirling herself around. There were two chandeliers in this room and behind Miss Singer stood a black Steinway grand. Art covered the walls.

'This is a beautiful place you've got,' Malcolm observed.

'If you must live in New York, you may as well do so in some comfort,' Miss Singer said. 'I would have preferred the country, myself, but my father insisted I live in New York.'

'Your . . . father?' said Malcolm, taking his beer from Willie's tray.

Miss Singer smiled as the butler placed a pink gin on a table beside her.

'Ephraim Singer,' she said. She looked at Malcolm. 'You're no spring chicken, Mr Finch. Surely you remember Ephraim Singer?'

Malcolm paused, his beer in mid-air. He knew he looked stupid, but if Malcolm was anything he was honest. He shook his head. 'I'm afraid . . . ' he began, then something twanged inside his head. 'Wait a second!' he cried. 'The retail king! Ephraim Singer, the retail king!'

'That's him,' Miss Singer beamed. 'I haven't heard anyone who could trip it off like that for ages.'

'It just came out,' Malcolm said in wonder, 'like something you learn and never forget. Ephraim Singer, the retail king. Why, when I was a kid I guess I must have heard that said a thousand times.'

'Your good health, Mr Finch,' said Miss Singer and together, eyes sparkling on each other, they drank. 'I contracted polio when I was fifteen,' she said, smacking her lips. 'My father devoted his life to trying to get me cured – he reckoned the best medical facilities were here in New York, so I guess I got here and never moved.'

'When was that?' Malcolm asked.

'Nineteen thirty,' Miss Singer replied. 'Another reason was that he actually liked to see his property. When we bought this place we were the highest building around.'

Malcolm sipped his beer; looking out over Central Park; sunshine streaming down; some trees beginning to bud. Something began to dawn on him.

'And . . . commodities?' he ventured.

'Oh, I like to dabble a little in lots of things,' said Miss Singer mischievously. Then she shook her head and her mouth became grim. 'But I detest losing,' she said with venom, 'de*test* it. It doesn't happen very often, but when it does, boy do I get angry.'

'So I expect you're pretty angry with GiltStock these days,' Malcolm said openly. 'We put you into oil.'

'When I say I get angry,' Miss Singer said precisely, 'I mean angry with me, Mr Finch. I'm the one who ultimately says do it, not the broker. He makes a sales pitch, but I make the decision.'

Malcolm nodded and smiled. 'I wish all our clients were as generous,' he said. 'Usually in the client's mind it's him who makes the profits, but the broker who makes the losses.'

'I don't consider the oil position as a loss yet,' Miss Singer said sternly. 'I've got a fifteen million dollar negative open position, but I haven't yet got a loss.'

Malcolm coughed sharply and blew beer froth out of his glass.

'Fifteen million dollars?' he spluttered. 'With respect, you're nothing like that, ma'am. I looked at the figure before I came up here – you're losing eight dollars on a hundred thousand barrels, that's eight hundred thousand bucks.'

'I didn't just use GiltStock,' said Miss Singer impatiently. 'My father always said you should spread your business around.'

'So you bought . . . two million barrels?' asked Malcolm incredulously.

'I think it all adds up to that,' Miss Singer replied and took a sip of pink gin.

'And you held them all?'

'That was another thing Ephraim Singer taught me. Only lightweights sell out when things get rough. If you've got the guts and the money hang in there and add like hell when you think the market has turned.'

Malcolm sat back and stared as his dawning took another great leap.

'I tried to contact that youngster Osorio,' Miss Singer was saying. 'This is the time to discuss tactics, not to run like rabbits and hide.'

221

'Steve has big problems, ma'am,' Malcolm said.

Miss Singer nodded grimly. 'Don't we all, don't we all,' she said. She reached under the table beside her and pressed a bell. 'Now, Mr Finch' she said, 'if you would care to join me, I'm just about to have some lunch.'

Malcolm was about to protest when the butler reappeared, wheeling a large table set with silverware for two and tall glasses.

'It would be a great pleasure,' he said with genuine feeling.

'When we're through,' the old lady said, 'we can then sit down and have a look at this hand that the Good Lord has dealt us.'

Three hours later, back on a still sunny Fifth Avenue, Malcolm's head was buzzing as if he was walking in a cloud of honey bees.

CHAPTER TWENTY-ONE

1

Sunday 10 March

Oil. Osorio looked from the plane window. Utah was thirty-five thousand feet underneath, its saline lakes a deep blue in the brown of the earth. Oil. Black and viscous, flowing through all their veins. The most traded commodity on earth. The one Osorio had been reared on. And Cristy's commodity, dear Cristy, so lonely now that Ron was gone.

Oil. Black and venemous, spurting out of holes dug with men's sweat and blood. Brent's oil and Malcolm's, back in New York, trying despite his age to hold something together that Steve Osorio had given his life to.

Oil. Black and damned. Oil had ruined GiltStock, given Dutch Tremaine a business and made Osorio a fugitive from justice. Would oil now, in some way give Osorio a chance to strike back?

Houston had been humid as usual. Through the airport Osorio had expected any second to feel a hand on his shoulder. He'd even travelled under a false name.

But nothing had happened. They went straight to the Marriot and met this wow of a kid named Jen with legs to the moon. She had big, beautiful eyes, sort of yellow-brown, and a mane of black hair. What had been the story between her and a sixty-five year old geologist?

'He was a really nice old man,' Jen said. 'And very lonely. He was very proud of the fact that his article had been published and that you had taken an interest in it. He asked me if I would like to go with him to New York.'

'The NYMEX dinner,' said Osorio.

'I told him sure I'd go,' Jen said. She had long finger-nails, painted white at the tips. 'Then I read he'd been murdered.'

'What a shock you must have got,' Cheryl said.

'The article itself is pretty general,' Osorio said. 'It really just asks questions. Any idea where he might have put the seismic details on Ishikari Bay that he referred to?' Osorio asked.

Jen shook her head.

'That's the point,' she answered. 'I went to his office to try and find just that. When I got there I was told that all his papers had already been taken. But that morning's mail had arrived, including the latest copy of *Key Stone*.' Jen fished in her bag. 'Here it is. Right there on page two is a letter from Mr Gerhardt saying that his article had been based on inaccurate facts and that he now accepts that the Ishikari find is a good one.'

'Just like that,' said Osorio grimly.

'So he'd been mistaken,' Jen said. 'Okay, but where are all the charts gone that led him to make the mistake? I tried to get into his apartment, but the same story, the place was cleaned out. I even called his sister to see if they'd gone to her but no dice. I decided then that the whole thing really stinks, so I tried to contact you.'

'He had a sister?' Osorio asked.

'He wrote regularly to her,' Jen replied. 'She was his only relative. Her name is Mrs Ruby Stumpf. She sounds a bit weird.'

'And she knows nothing about charts or papers?'

'Nothing,' Jen replied. 'I thought she might since Mr Gerhardt went out to the coast a week before he died.'

Osorio and Cheryl exchanged glances.

'Did Mrs Stumpf tell you that?' Cheryl asked.

'No, Mr Gerhardt did,' said Jen. 'But here's her number if you want to call her.'

'Thanks for all your help,' Osorio said as they stood up.

'Is there really a connection?' Jen asked. 'Between his murder and this Japan story? Or am I imagining it all?'

Osorio looked at her young face. 'I think Mr Gerhardt died because he knew too much,' he said quietly.

Jen smoothed her skirt which ended well above her knees.

'I hope you find whoever did it,' she said. 'He was a really nice old man.'

Her eyes held Osorio's with interest for just a second, then she hitched her bag on her shoulder.

'Do you know what he said to me the last time we spoke?' she said. 'He said when all this became public that the price of oil would shoot up by ten dollars a barrel.' She smiled. 'I don't understand exactly what he meant, but it stuck in my mind: he said it would be the bear's requiem.'

Oil, beating through the earth. Powering the plane. Fuelling the globe. Oil. Osorio looked to Cheryl beside him, her eyes closed, her face perfect as she slept. Would oil be what brought them together? He felt a rush of tenderness. He brought his hand up and gently stroked her hair. How had he missed her all this time? She was made of something unique and like a fool he had missed seeing it. What he thought to be her coldness was simply the device she put between herself and the world so as to get on with her life. There was real depth there, a real, loving person who, when she chose, would stay with her choice until the end. She was a still, deep river that made Carly look like rain running down a window-pane.

But was he too late? Was he simply a project in her life, or had he a chance?

'I've been such a fool,' he whispered.

The plane's engines changed pitch as they began the descent into San Francisco.

2

San Francisco

Sunday 5.00 p.m.

The last time Cheryl had been on a cable car in San Francisco was in high school when they had all joked about the men with their waist-length hair tied up with ribbons.

> *San Francisco*
> *Beautiful city*
> *Where the women are strong*
> *And the men are pretty.*

Now lurching up almost vertical Powell Street, hanging from a strap, Cheryl watched the long-haired conductor issue tickets and wondered what it might be like to live out here. Clean San Francisco, none of the hassle or dirt of the Big Apple; chilly San Francisco this evening, becoming chillier as they passed the Fairmont and breasted Nob Hill. She looked across at Osorio, tie loosened, shirt sleeves rolled, hanging, face to the wind, his black hair whipped out behind him. At the airport she had seen Friday's closing prices in New York on a monitor: oil at twelve fifty. Cheryl leaned out sideways from the car and the wind caught her hair and suddenly, miles below, she could see the velvet blue seductiveness of the Bay.

They left the cable car at the top of Hyde Street and walked one block west to Larkin. A call from the airport had established Mrs Stumpf to be at home. Her house was one on a quiet hill, a small tidy garden, the cheerful red stone of California in the walls. Osorio rang the bell.

'Yes?'

The voice came from the side of the house; a woman's head peered: Osorio saw eyes telescoped behind framed bottle ends.

'Mrs Ruby Stumpf?'

'Who are you and what do you want?' She wore khaki slacks and gardening gloves. Each arm was bare to the elbow, sinewy and black with hair.

Osorio took a step forward. 'I called from the airport . . . '

Then the dog appeared: pink-jowled and froth-flecked, an ink-black Doberman, restrained by the leash connecting him to his owner.

'Are you trying to sell something?' asked the woman. Her hair, salt-and-pepper grey, was parted and combed like a man's.

Osorio shook his head and stood his ground. 'We're looking for Eric Gerhardt's sister.'

226

'I'm sorry, but I don't talk to people who walk in off the street. Please leave.'

'Mrs Stumpf,' said Osorio, 'if you'd just . . . '

'Are you deaf or just stupid?' the woman asked. 'I don't know who you are and I want you off my property.'

Osorio didn't move. 'We've come a long way to see you,' he said.

The dog growled and strained.

'Do you want me to let this animal loose?' the woman asked.

Osorio crouched down and began to make soothing noises. Immediately, the Doberman's growl changed to a less threatening pitch and it began to move it's tail-less hindquarters from side to side.

'Mrs Stumpf,' Cheryl said, 'you really have nothing to fear from us.'

'Nor you from me, it would seem,' said the woman, looking down in disgust at the dog which was now licking Osorio's face. 'Have you any idea what it's like to live alone in this jungle, have you?' she asked. 'You tell me I have nothing to fear. What do I know? Sure you're both young and handsome and plausible. But so are twenty-five million other people living in this State, and that includes the ones who are permanently under the influence of controlled substances and spend their time prowling around, looking for easy targets like widow women living on their own.'

'Mrs Stumpf, we would like to talk to you about Eric,' said Osorio, getting to his feet.

'Eric? Eric lived all his life and when he died, it now seems he didn't even have a proper policy. I mean, explain that. At least Gunther Stumpf who only sold ice-cream off a bicycle in Union Square, at least when he went the way of all flesh he left me a house to live in, a twenty-five thousand dollar policy, and a business. But, Eric . . . '

'Some people are like that,' smiled Osorio.

The dobermann whined for Osorio's attention.

'Shut up!' cried Mrs Stumpf and the animal cowered. Her eyes narrowed. 'Am I by any chance wrong?' she asked with sudden hope. 'Is this the call you read about in books and magazines, the one where the widowed sister is out of the blue informed that she's the new owner of six oil wells?'

'I'm afraid not,' Osorio said.

'I didn't think it was,' said Mrs Stumpf in resignation. 'So what do you want?'

'To talk about Eric,' Osorio said. 'To ask you some questions.'

'Police? I.R.S? F.B.I.? Sheriff's office? Bounty hunters? Health Department? Trade Descriptions? Media of any kind? Do you work for any of the aforementioned?'

'No ma'am,' Osorio answered.

Mrs Stumpf turned to Cheryl. 'How about you?'

'Right now, I'm out of work,' Cheryl replied.

'You sure you don't work for a newspaper?'

'I'm sure.'

Mrs Stumpf's headshake could have meant anything. A busload of tourists went by, then a car, driven slowly.

'I don't trust newspapers,' she said. 'I hate their prying.' She sighed. 'You'd better come in, but you'll have to excuse the place; I don't have many visitors.'

They followed her around the side of the house, past early vegetables in a plot and through the back door. Immediately there was a deafening baying. They were at the back of a cluttered hall, the far end to the front door; there was a staircase at halfway, but everywhere there were dogs and upright pianos.

'What did you say your names were?'

'Cheryl and Steve!' Osorio shouted.

'This is Cheryl and Steve,' Mrs Stumpf said. 'Now shut up!'

There was instant quiet. Dark, slavering forms crouched ready between banisters or wound fiendishly in and out among the pianos.

'I breed them,' Mrs Stumpf said. 'They're complete fools as you obviously know, but they look savage.'

Osorio looked around in wonder; from this position alone he could count ten pianos.

'And the pianos . . . ?' he said.

'I buy them, I sell them,' the woman answered. 'How many people nowadays understand the importance of overstrung?' She played a chord on the nearest instrument and her mouth curved downwards. 'That's what happens when they don't get played,' she said. They passed through the hall and into a front room, home to four further pianos, where large, rustling boxes stood on the floor.

'Pups,' Mrs Stumpf said as Cheryl inspected. 'Two hundred dollars the dogs, one fifty the bitches, take your pick, you'll pay twice that price downtown and they won't have half the pedigree.' She stood with her back to a mantelpiece. 'Okay, that's not why you came to see me.' She half turned and indicated a glass preserve jar on the mantelpiece behind her. 'By the way, that's Eric.'

Osorio stared. 'He . . . '

'They sent his ashes in a gold-leaf casket,' Mrs Stumpf replied. 'I got seventy-five bucks for it in Chinatown.'

Osorio looked at Cheryl who hurriedly had taken renewed interest in the box of pups. He looked at the dull ashes through the glass and thought of Jen with the wonderful legs and what she would think if she knew the old guy she liked was sitting up like this in a room full of dogs and pianos.

'Mrs Stumpf,' Osorio began, 'I'm here because, like your brother Eric, I have an interest in oil.'

'Hah!' Mrs Stumpf's cry caused a hitherto unnoticed dog to scuttle from the room. 'Oil!' she said with zest. 'Did you know my brother? You certainly couldn't have known him as I did, over fifty years ago. We lived not ten minutes from here, you know, in Daly City? Our father had a steady job in insurance, but Eric – all that boy was ever interested in was rocks.'

'Geology?' Osorio ventured.

'Go into his bedroom and all you saw were rocks with labels everywhere,' Mrs. Stumpf said. 'I've got photographs from that time, somewhere . . . ' She turned her head as if listening for something. 'However . . . '

'Eric told me about some seismic data he had,' said Osorio quietly, 'charts. They've not turned up in Houston. We badly need them. We've come to you for help?''

'To me?' said the woman. 'How can I possibly help?'

'I thought, maybe, you could suggest where else I might look?' Osorio replied carefully.

Mrs Stumpf's tiny, pin-prick eyes were evasive. 'I don't know how I could,' she said, half to herself. 'I . . . never saw him.'

'Anything at all might help.'

Mrs Stumpf appeared to be studying the innards of a piano. 'Such as?' she asked.

'Any papers, documents, files for example, which might relate to oil,' said Osorio.

Small eyes fixed on Osorio. 'Could there be anything in it for me?' asked Mrs Stumpf softly.

'There could,' said Osorio, quickening as he realised he had her. 'There could be something for everyone.'

'Like when?'

'I can't say,' he said. 'All I can promise you is that if you help us and there's money to be made we won't forget you.'

Mrs Stumpf sat on the lid of a keyboard, her eyes taking them in, her rough hands scratching at her hairy arms.

'He came here – last month,' she said quietly, 'never told me he was coming, just turned up like you did today.' She looked at nothing in particular. 'I don't know how many years it had been, must have been a dozen, he came out fair dues when Gunther died, but not since. Funny things families; if there's anything there at all I guess you burn it up when you're kids together, then all that's left is duty.'

'I understand,' said Osorio.

'I mean it's not as if I expected anymore,' Mrs Stumpf said distantly. 'We had a happy childhood, good memories, I can remember my parents just as if they'd been here today. That's what I do at nights now: I remember those old days and the people who are dead and gone. Funny thing is, when you remember them, they aren't dead anymore. Isn't that peculiar? As long as you remember someone, they never die, for you they live. The problem is, if no one is left to remember you, then you really die. That's awful, isn't it? When that happens, there's no spark at all, no current, no memory, no life, nothing. That's when you're really dead.'

'Your brother very badly wanted me to have those charts,' Osorio said.

Mrs Stumpf looked at them, then seemed to reach a decision. She walked to the back of the room and lifted the top lid off a piano. She reached down and withdrew a parcel wrapped in yellow plastic.

'This is probably what you're looking for,' she said. 'He gave it to me, asked me to put it someplace until he asked for it back.' She looked at the parcel quizzically. 'Funny thing is, it's been lucky for me,' she said. 'Every piano I put it in gets sold. The other day I had to jump into a truck to get Eric's damn parcel out.'

'May I?' asked Osorio, his ears buzzing.

'Help yourself,' Mrs Stumpf said.

The plastic wrapping was gritty to the touch; Osorio placed it on top of a nearer piano and Cheryl came to stand beside him as he peeled it open. Inside were two large yellow envelopes, one bulging, the other slim, both sealed. Osorio looked enquiringly at Mrs Stumpf who shrugged; inserting the tip of a pen in the top corner of the bulging envelope, Osorio ripped it across the top then shook out the contents: a number of chart-like documents slid along the piano.

'Is that what you're looking for?' asked Mrs Stumpf.

'Yes,' Osorio answered, and stretched one of the documents out like an accordion.

'What do they mean?' asked Mrs Stumpf, pulling hair at her chin.

Osorio opened the slimmer envelope. Here were several pages, stapled together. Osorio read them once quickly, flicking each page, then again, slowly. 'If what this says is true,' Osorio said slowly, 'then it means your brother was right. It is going to be the bear's requiem.'

CHAPTER TWENTY - TWO

1

I am Eric Gerhardt, geologist, of Houston, Texas. Of my own free will do I make the following statement:

I have extensively studied the seismic and other geological data which has been disseminated in relation to the oil find known as the Ishikari Field, off Hokaido, Japan.

In June of 1984, I was employed as a seismic engineer by the then fledgling Hokkaido Oil Company, an organisation with little knowledge of or experience in oil exploration.

Part of my brief was to oversee the shooting of seismic tests in Ishikari Bay. The only westerner present, my activities were very strictly monitored and I was forbidden to remove any copies of seismic charts from Otaru.

As I considered this prohibition unwarranted and outside the terms of my contract, I secretly removed copies of all the seismic shot over a five-week period, principally as a protection for myself.

I have now studied the seismic data released by Hokkaido Oil which was allegedly shot in 1984 and I have read with incredulity the claims that only now, with advanced computer and other equipment, have the seismic attractions of the area become apparent.

I can say categorically that the seismic data released by Hokkaido Oil bears NO RESEMBLANCE WHATSOEVER to the seismic shot under my supervision, the originals of which I attach. Furthermore, the seismic charts released by Hokkaido Oil are, to my mind, not charts of Ishikari Bay, but charts of parts of the Forties Field in the U.K.'s North Sea.

It must follow from the above, that if the seismic charts are false, so also is all the subsequent data, including drilling reports, analysis of

232

core samples held at Otaru, testing reports and estimated reserves, although why deception should be practiced on such a scale I have no idea.

What is needed now in relation to the Ishikari Field, is an examination by a totally independent geologist, on site, of all the evidence normally associated with an oil find of this size, including logging reports and core samples.

It is my belief that the area where oil is now meant to exist in huge quantities is an area of dense and extensive shale, a structure which does not permit the existence of oil in any quantity.

I have expressed these views in an article published in Key Stone, *a New York geological magazine. Within the last two days I have been told that unless I retract my views in writing to* Key Stone, *I will be the victim of unspecified threats.*

I am depositing these papers in safekeeping with Mrs Ethel Stumpf, my sister, who lives in San Francisco.

If someone other than myself is now reading this it means that I have paid dearly for what I know to be the truth about Ishikari.

Eric Gerhardt, Houston, Texas, 11 February

2

San Francisco

Sunday 10 March 6.00 p.m.

Malcolm walked through the small lobby of the Donatello, found the elevators and allowed a bellhop in gloves to press the button for him. Malcolm stepped in, hit floor five and leaned back to look at himself in a gilt mirror.

He looked as tired as he felt. He couldn't handle impromtu transcontinental plane journeys anymore. He had been sitting on his stoop in Dobbs Ferry, threading flies to a line when Sol Ansbacher had found him.

'I don't even know that he'll call me,' Malcolm said.

'Well, if he does, give him that piece of news,' Sol said.

Osorio had called fifteen minutes later.

'You should know, Steve, that Sol's just been on,' Malcolm said. 'There's some more bad news.'

'How bad?'

'Because the Feds are after you for fraud, Man First Bank have persuaded the Federal Bankruptcy Court that the bankruptcy hearing should be brought forward. Something about time being of the essence. It means you're now slotted for hearing next Monday.'

'*What?*'

'I'm afraid so, Steve,' Malcolm said. He could imagine Osorio's tight face three thousand miles away. 'Steve, there's something else you should know,' Malcom said. 'It's about Miss Singer.'

'Not now, Malcom,' said Osorio, his voice flat.

'Steve, this is something you'll want to hear,' Malcom said, and then, looking out at the sun's cold beams spreading over his wooden porch, he told Osorio.

'She's worth how much?' exclaimed Osorio.

'Maybe a couple of billion dollars,' Malcom said. 'I've had her checked out. She's the sole beneficiary of the Ephraim Singer Foundation – have you never heard of Ephraim Singer, the retail king? – which owns high blocks of property in midtown. One guy I spoke to reckoned that the Ephraim Singer Foundation was the wealthiest owner of real estate in New York, even bigger than Trump.'

'How come she's been playing commodities through a relatively small outfit like GiltStock?' Osorio asked.

Malcom shook his head to Cheryl. 'She's nuts about you,' he replied. 'Now she's just rarin' to get her money back from this oil market.'

'How rarin'?' Osorio asked.

'If she recoups her losses she'll go fifty-fifty on the profits of any proposal we put to her,' said Malcom.

'We need to talk,' Osorio said softly. 'We need to talk today.'

'Today?' Malcom said. 'You're in San Francisco. Who'll look after GiltStock?'

It was Malcolm's turn to get up and walk around the sitting-room of the small suite. Outside, San Francisco had becom suddenly dark; Cheryl had drawn the drapes.

'It's some story,' he said at last.

'Just imagine what it will do to oil!' Osorio said fiercely. 'No Japanese oil! Take that scenario away and you remove the factor that's overhung the market for a year! The Japs have been manipulating the market down on an oil field that never existed!'

'But why?' Malcolm asked.

'The Japs saw Prince Saleem move nearer and nearer to the top oil job in Saudi Arabia,' Cheryl answered. 'Saleem was violently anti-Jap, so Tokyo panicked. They probably first tried normal diplomatic channels, then when those failed, decided the only way to make the Saudis get rid of Saleem was to hurt them – hard. They brought oil down through news of their phoney find. It worked. The Saudis squealed like hell, but they fired Prince Saleem.'

'And Durst Bank are involved?' said Malcolm.

Osorio nodded. 'They may be. Their traders handled the actual selling in New York. But it also represented a fantastic opportunity for Abel Eller to solve his own financial problems: Durst Bank may have begun to sell oil for the bank's book as well. Eric Gerhardt's article which showed the oil find to be a phoney, my proposed speech to the NYMEX dinner, Ron Spirakis's attempts to warn me through Cristy, all these things would have threatened Abel Eller's vital plan.'

'Good God,' Malcolm said.

'Abel Eller is riding this bear for all he's worth,' Osorio said. 'He thinks he's going to make one of the great twentieth century fortunes in the process. But he's still depending on oil going down. It's like a huge spring. If it turns – and nobody thinks it will – that fortune can be ours. You say Miss Singer will give us the seed money. That's what we need! From here I go to Japan and prove Gerhardt's allegations to be right. You get back to New York as fast as you can, Malcolm, and start setting this thing up. You tell Miss Singer that the oil bear is leaving town.'

Malcolm looked alarmed.

'Forget it,' he said. 'You can't achieve anything in Japan. I spent three years in Tokyo after the war, working in counterintelligence. I know the Japs. What you're thinking is insane.'

235

'Who in Japan would be responsible for setting up a deal like this?' Osorio asked him.

'Probably an offshoot of the *koan-ikka,* the Japanese Secret Service,' Malcolm replied reluctantly.

'I never knew they had a secret service,' said Osorio.

'Next to the Israelis, they have probably the best secret service in the world,' Malcolm said. 'No one ever talks about it or even mentions it; in Japanese logic that's eminently sensible: after all, it's secret.'

'And are the *koan-ikka* capable of mounting operations like this oil scam?' Osorio asked.

'Undoubtedly,' Malcolm said. 'But now, if what you tell me is correct, the most important thing for them will be to withdraw without being discovered or losing face. They are ruthless. They'll sacrifice someone who'll be seen to have made a huge mistake over the oil find. Over a period of time they'll feed out news to the market which will slowly reverse everything they've said over the past year.'

'Steve can't wait that long,' Cheryl said. 'Next Monday the opportunity which this Gerhardt information represents may be lost for ever in a New York courtroom. Once Steve is formally declared bankrupt he's finished.'

Osorio hunkered down beside Malcolm.

'I'm going to try,' he said quietly. 'We may lose, but if we win, we'll win bigger than we ever dreamed.'

'You're insane,' Malcolm said. 'You'll be a dead man.'

'Insane, that's just it, isn't it?' Osorio said. 'They would never in a million years think that anyone would be crazy enough to go in there and try and prove Gerhardt right.'

Osorio clenched both fists. 'Somewhere over there is the *negative* information we need,' he said. He squatted to a briefcase and came up with an envelope. 'Listen to what Eric Gerhardt wrote. "It must follow that if the seismic charts are false, so also is all the subsequent data, including drilling reports and analysis of core samples." '

'How would you know where to go?' Malcolm asked.

'According to Gerhardt, all the core samples and logging reports are kept in Otaru,' Osorio said. 'Gerhardt was obsessed with this so-called find, he had been researching everything about it, he's even provided a map.'

'I cannot tell you how dangerous this is,' Malcolm said, shaking his white head. 'To have anything to do with the *koan-ikka* or their agents, particularly in Japan, would be suicide.'

'It's the only way,' Osorio replied.

'Tell the world about Gerhardt!' Malcolm cried. 'Show the press the seismic, tell them everything! Give yourself up to the Feds, but don't do what you're thinking!'

Osorio was shaking his head.

'It wouldn't work,' he said. 'So these are seismic charts? So what? Of where? Of Ishikari Bay? Why not of Brooklyn? Or Queens? And who are you, Mr Osorio? Ah yes, you're the guy who the cops are looking for, isn't that so? Would you care to read this thirty-five page indictment?'

Cheryl looked at Malcolm, sitting apprehensively, and then at Osorio.

'What's it better to be?' he asked softly. 'A guy who shot for the stars and failed, or a guy who stands up, pathetically, in a New York courtroom, surrounded by lawyers he can never pay, waving sheets of paper written by a dead man?'

Malcolm opened his mouth to say something, but Cheryl caught his eye.

'What do you say?' Osorio asked her softly.

Cheryl got to her feet.

'I guess I say, when do we leave?' she answered with a smile that was halfway happy, halfway sad.

CHAPTER TWENTY - THREE

1

Tokyo, Japan

Tuesday 12 March

Honolulu, the Tropic of Cancer, the endless vastness of the Pacific. Narita. On a train into Tokyo, passing houses built so close together you couldn't split them with a razor; and the green netting of driving-ranges; and factories, factories; and rice fields; and stands of bamboos and long tubes of tea bushes which snaked up the side of little hills.

Tokyo. Faces. Not Texas faces or New York faces or even the kind you expect in Chinatown. Smooth faces, unlined, unstubbled, clean, exotic, menacing if you wanted them to be. Eyes. Sphinx-like, cat-like, lidless, cryptic, cut upwards into cheek-bones of taut hide.

Hair. Black, straight, round whorls, neatly cut and regimental distance over white, always white, collars. Heads, thousands of them, hundreds of thousands, bobbing along, eyes to the fore, except for the briefest instant when they slid off course for the double-take of the *gaijin*, the outsider.

Humid Tokyo evening. An after-dinner stroll. Osorio, although he was taller than Cheryl, because of his physical mobility, the way he carried himself, looked compact not tall. Too tall for a Japanese, yet not a towering American. Skin not white like a

European, nor bronzed, nor even yellow, but . . . almost a light red. And his eyes. Sweeping almonds, they defied an instant category. These are great-grandma's eyes, here they are in Tokyo, first Osorio to walk down the Ginza, who's to know that the two grand I have in my pocket is the whole farm and fortune?

In Osorio's room, the curtains were drawn back to reveal a tiny spotlit garden on a balcony outside.

'Let me fix us a drink before I turn in,' Cheryl said.

She went to a mini-bar and took out two scotches. She clinked ice into tumblers and poured the drinks.

'Thanks,' Osorio said.

'Cheers,' said Cheryl.'

Osorio looked over at her: she held her drink in her lap and was looking away in thought.

'You look beautiful when you do that,' he said.

'Do what?'

'When you narrow your eyes and think like this,' he said and tried to imitate how she had looked. 'What were you thinking of?'

She caught one side of her cheek with her teeth. 'You really want to know?'

'Sure,' he replied.

'I was wondering,' she answered, 'how a guy like you could ever fall for a woman like Carly Tremaine.'

Osorio filled his chest with air. 'How the hell do I know?' he said and looked out past her. 'You're going along at a certain speed, everything in synch . . . ' His flat hand cleaved through the air. 'She intoxicated me,' he said. 'I really believed she'd be there through thick and thin.'

Cheryl's face showed only mild interest.

Osorio licked his lips. 'Cheryl,' he said, 'what you've done for me, I'll never forget. You made me pick myself up.' He leaned forward and took her hand in his. 'But right now I feel more than gratitude,' he said.

Cheryl looked at him for a long time. Then she finished her drink and stood up.

'I'm sorry, Steve,' she said, 'but I need time to think.'

'I'm in love with you,' he said. 'We're right for each other. I know it.'

'See you tomorrow,' she replied.

There was a soft click as the bedroom door closed behind her and Osorio stood looking out at the aerial Japanese garden.

2

Tokyo, Japan

Wednesday 13 March a.m.

They checked out at six.

Tokyo Station at seven-thirty was like going to the Superbowl: dense crowds of commuters swarmed around them as they made their way to a ticket-office where a broad-shouldered oriental leaving the counter collided with Osorio, nearly knocking him.

'*Shistu-rei,*' the man mumbled and hurried on.

They bought tickets to Sapporo and then faced into the throng again, making their way to the platform for the north-bound bullet train, the *Shinkansen*. In the carriage they bought small flasks of hot green tea and watched Japan dashing by. Three and a half hours later they changed to a slower train at Marioka and after a brief glimpse of the Pacific at Hachinohe, they arrived in Aomori at three in the afternoon where they changed again for Sapporo.

Cheryl dozed as the train plunged in and out of tunnels which ran under the hills on the most northerly peninsula of Honshu.

'*Kippu-o-Haiken-shimasu.*'

The ticket-collector stood there, immaculate in cream linen suit and cap, his face unlined, his eyes feline. He punched the tickets, bowed and moved on. The rhythm of the train was comforting beneath them. There were half a dozen other people in the carriage, all Japanese. They pulled into a place called Mori and Osorio got off and walked down the platform before jumping back on at the last moment. Nothing happened, no one had followed him off anymore than they had done on half a dozen evious occasions during the day.

Osorio looked out at rice fields stretching to densely wooded untains, snow flecked at their peaks. People working in some the fields, their backs bent, their heads covered by straw hats d cotton veils. The water of the rice fields flashed in the dying 1, then all at once there was darkness as the train whipped o another tunnel on its northwards way and the rhythm of el on steel became more resonant. This time by its length, orio guessed that they were in the Tunnel of Seikan which red beneath the Straits of Tsugaru, the thirty-mile piece of ter which separates the rest of Japan from Hokkaido.

Soon they would be in Sapporo.

CHAPTER TWENTY-FOUR

New York

Wednesday 13 March a.m.

Bill Warner's face was composed at it's inscrutable best. (
worst, depending on your point of view. Cristy fought the urg
to get up and run; she crossed her legs, joined her hands in h
lap and smiled.

'I'm okay,' she said, 'believe me. I'm much better doing som
thing than just sitting around.'

'It's your decision,' said Bill, 'it's whatever you want to do.'

'I want to come back to work,' she said.

'If you want to come back to work, that's fine with me,' B
said. 'But if you want to take off somewhere to the sun for te
days that's equally fine. I understand the shock you've had.
don't want you ruining your health.'

'I know what I'm doing,' Cristy said.

Bill picked up a few typewritten pages, then looked at h
over the top of his glasses. 'I've read this,' he said quiet
'There's no way we can run it.'

Cristy made to speak, but Bill was shaking his head. 'Th
White House are on the verge of concluding a breakthroug
agreement with the Japanese on opening up their market to
whole host of U.S. goods. The vibes coming down from the se
enteenth floor say, back off if you haven't got anything rea
substantial, what you're doing is not appreciated.'

Cristy blinked to keep back her tears.

'This is a *news*paper,' Bill said, 'my job is to edit *news* stori
that you wonderful people come up with. Please depersonali

his, but Prince Saleem, Ron Spirakis, a dead geologist named Gerhardt, none of them are news anymore. Oil is twelve. Great! That's good for industry, isn't it? That's the story I want, not a fairytale by some nut who says there's really no oil at all in Japan, and what they've been flaring off, I guess, is bottled gas.'

Cristy looked at the ceiling, then back at Bill. 'I think you're making a mistake,' she said. 'I think you'll end up regretting it.'

'That may be so,' replied Bill Warner firmly, 'but that's the way it is right now.'

Cristy sat, motionless, looking fixedly at a pen-stand on Bill's desk. Behind her, outside, she could hear the newsroom of the great newspaper at work, phones ringing, people calling to each other.

'Okay,' she said, suddenly bright again, 'ours not to reason why. I guess all at once I'm free as the breeze.'

'That's more like it,' Bill smiled and nodded. 'You still sure you want to come back to work?'

'Sure, I'm sure.'

'Well, there's something juicy here that deserves the Cristy Osorio treatment,' Bill said.

'What's that?'

Bill reached for a file. 'A defence contractor who lives in Long Island and who's about to be indicted for embezzlement,' he said. 'I'd like something on his personal lifestyle angle, the guy was into private zoos among other things.'

'Sounds fun,' Cristy said and took the file. 'I'll get right on to it.'

'And Cristy?'

Cristy looked up.

'No hard feelings about oil?'

'Oil?' Cristy frowned and pinched the bridge of her noise. Olive oil? Corn oil? Cod-liver oil? Why should I have hard feelings?' she smiled at Bill.

'Get outta here!' he laughed and watched fondly as she got to her feet. 'By the way, Cristy?'

She turned.

'What does Steve think of the Houston geologist?' Bill asked.

Cristy looked at Bill for a moment, then shrugged and smiled.

'He says the guy was crazy,' she replied, then made her way back to her desk.

CHAPTER TWENTY - FIVE

Sapporo, Northern Japan
Wednesday 13 March 9.00 p.m.

Sapporo: a modern city, laid out in a grid. Near the station, across a wide street of cobblestones criss-crossed by tram-tracks, they found a car-rental office, just closing. There was a frost, much colder here than Tokyo; Osorio drove the small Toyota downtown until they reached a flashing sign which read 'Hotel Rich'. They paid cash for two rooms, more cubicles than rooms, with pre-fabricated bathrooms that had lost their way en route for installation in airplanes. The corridors were narrow, the lights dim. Their rooms were on the eighth floor and the windows were of the soundproofed variety, not designed to open. A single elevator was at one end of the corridor, at the other was a door marked with a red EXIT sign in English.

Osorio sluiced cold water on his face, then drying himself, stepped out of the plastic bathroom and went to the window. There was no noise, just a silent, night-time Sapporo. He thought of Cristy, back in New York, waiting for the news, and Malcolm, also waiting. He threw down the towel and went to his jacket for Gerhardt's report. Frowning, he went through each pocket; twice he checked them. Discarding the jacket he went to his leather grip and up-ended it: among his things, the fatter of the two envelopes fell out. Opening it, he sifted through maps of Otaru, press-cuttings dealing with Ishikari Bay, seismic and other geological data, but not Gerhardt's handwritten report, not the damning indictment of Ishikari with its seismic charts attached

ore urgently now, Osorio cast around the small room, the
throom, his bag, his jacket once more. He went to the corri-
or and rapped on Cheryl's door.

'Gerhardt's report,' he said. 'It's gone.'

'You had it in your inside pocket,' Cheryl said, her face con-
rned as she opened the door.

'Not anymore,' Osorio said. 'I mailed a copy to Cristy, but the
iginal plus the two sets of seismic have disappeared.'

'Have you any idea how you might have lost them?' Cheryl
ked.

Osorio's eyes flicked. He saw a face in his mind's eye, but it
eant nothing, as yet it had no place.

'I'm not sure,' he replied as they left the room.

In the street there was the real sound of traffic and a city on
e move, reassuring after the non-noise of the sealed hotel.
isiness on Wednesday night was brisk in Sapporo. They passed
opfronts with western-style mannequins, department stores
en late, an artist selling his paintings from the pavement, clap-
ng his gloved hands to keep warm. Osorio, walking on the
lls of his feet, could have been doing this all his life, a native
Hokkaido, out for a late night stroll; it was Cheryl who stood
t: hopelessly non-oriental, long and willowy, her fair hair all
ound her shoulders, she walked like an exotic female goddess
me amongst the little people.

They crossed Odori Park, the heart of Sapporo, and wan-
red three blocks west before they found a restaurant among
e forests of neon signs, all in indecipherable Kangi.

'It's the first time I've thought neon to be pretty,' Cheryl said.

'Next time you should bring your easel,' Osorio said.

'Next time, I will,' she replied.

The restaurant was a grill where chefs cooked fish and sticks
chicken and livers over coals. Inside the door was a stuffed,
-and-a-half foot brown bear, standing upright, his massive
oulders hunched forward in attack. Osorio and Cheryl were
ated beneath him as the chef at the other side of the grill
iled broadly.

'Make sure he doesn't move,' Osorio said.

'*Higuma,*' the man grinned, then in broken English, 'bear of
okkaido, national symbol.'

They ate grilled tunny and chased it down with jugs of beer.

245

Cheryl lighted a cigarette.

'Tomorrow's the big day,' she said.

Osorio nodded tightly.

'How long do you reckon it will take us to drive to Otaru?' she asked.

'About an hour,' he replied.

'You're uneasy,' she said.

Osorio watched as the chef skewered a sparkling fish and flung it gaping on red-hot bars. A face again intruded on his mind's eye.

'There's a lot riding on it,' he replied.

'Of course there is, but we'll pull it off,' she said. 'This is your territory, rocks, oil, this is what you know.'

'I'd personally prefer if this warehouse was in Abilene,' Osorio replied.

'We've still got all Gerhardt's data, his maps, his description of the offices and warehouse,' Cheryl said. 'All we have to do find out what's in there and we have the commodity story of the century.'

'Or we don't,' Osorio said. He blinked; the face flashed.

'Steve,' Cheryl said, 'I just want to say something. In Tokyo, I wasn't trying to trade. I just want to do what's best for both of us, okay?'

Osorio looked into her frank, grey eyes. He ran his hand up and over hers on the counter.

'Sure,' he said. 'I hope, however, that my position in the matter is clear.'

Cheryl nodded and smiled.

'Honeymoono?' asked the chef, grinning.

'Yeah, sure,' Osorio said, 'some honeymoon.'

'*Higuma*,' said the chef, pointing to their guardian behind, 'bring *ko-un*, luck to honeymoono.'

They recrossed Odori Park, a long rectangle running thirteen blocks east to west, and walked away from downtown Sapporo. They strolled until they came to a river and turned left, walking for ten minutes. At a bridge where the water was checked by small dam, goldfish the size of two-pound trout were feeding.

'Malcolm wouldn't believe this,' Osorio laughed.

The sidewalks had thinned out as they reached Sapporo Station Plaza and turned back downtown for Hotel Rich. Cheryl stopped.

'I thought he was closing,' she said and pointed to the far side of the wide street.

There, on the opposite corner, lights still blazed through the venetian blinds of the car rental office. Osorio thought of the missing envelope and again he saw a face which he couldn't resolve. They crossed. The car hire office had two windows; in one, a potted plant inside had caught the bottom of the venetian blind and created a space of about an inch. Osorio dropped to his knees. Cheryl watched as he looked up at her in puzzlement, then peered in again.

'Jesus!' he said and beckoned.

Cheryl hunkered down and stared in and up. Her eyes met Osorio's. Simultaneously they stood and began to walk rapidly downtown.

'Don't run!' Osorio hissed. 'But it's him, isn't it?'

Cheryl nodded, her breath short. 'Definitely,' she said.

'Same face, same breadth across the shoulders,' Osorio said. He held his hand up to his face. 'I looked at him this close in Tokyo Station when he nearly knocked me. Ever since I missed Gerhardt's report, that guy's face has been going through my mind.'

They passed a dark Japan Air Lines office and recrossed the road.

'What are we going to do?' Cheryl asked.

'We've got to get out of the hotel, out of Sapporo,' Osorio said. 'He's obviously getting details of our car.'

The lobby of Hotel Rich was deserted as they made for the elevator.

'Can you drive one of these cars with a shift up on the wheel?' Osorio asked.

'I can drive a truck through a mango swamp,' Cheryl said.

Osorio handed her the Toyota keys.

'The fire exit is at the left hand side of the building,' he said. 'Bring the car around to it, I'll meet you there in three minutes with our things.'

Cheryl held the keys between her teeth as she wound her hair into a plait, then tucked it inside the collar of her shirt. The elevator door opened and for a second they looked at each other. She leaned forward and kissed him on the cheek.

'I'll be there,' she said.

The eighth floor was quiet. In his bedroom everything was as he had left it: bedside light on, contents of his bag on the bed. He checked the bathroom, then packed at speed. He tried to relax, tried not to think of where the man in the car hire office was. He eased open the bedroom door and edged out. The corridor was empty. In Cheryl's room he could smell her perfume; for an instant he stopped to savour it, then packed her things and hurried on, a bag in each hand.

It was ten yards to the elevator; he would ride it down seven floors, then take the fire stairs to the street. Osorio put the bags down and pressed the button. He had half turned when he realised the doors were opening, registered in one ten-thousandth of a second that something was wrong and ducked. The oriental in the elevator tried to use his gun muzzle as a club. It sang over Osorio's bent head. Osorio did the only thing he could and rammed him head to chest back into the elevator. The car shuddered on its pulleys and the doors hummed to close. Osorio was on top. He felt manic, heaving muscle beneath him. He realised dimly that the gun had fallen outside the elevator. There was machinery noise and they began to descend. The squat man on the floor whipped his black head up and back and caught Osorio square on the nose. Osorio powered blindly though his pain and caught lank hair. He pulled as the other man tried to bring his knee up in a savage thrust, but the car allowed no room for the blow to be effective. Osorio tightened his grip on the hair and yanked down savagely, simultaneously driving his fist for the exposed throat.

'AAH!' the man exclaimed.

They crashed backwards on to the control panel; the elevator briefly stopped, then began to rise. Osorio chopped downwards for the back of the neck with his left hand, then felt his air go as his opponent grabbed his shirt collar and tried to lever his head down to his own. Releasing his grip on the man's hair, Osorio brought both his fists crashing into the eardrums beneath him. There was a scream and his attacker seemed to fall.

The elevator had stopped again and the doors hummed open. The two bags stood there and Osorio realised that they were back again on floor eight. He could only have turned his back for an instant, but he heard a guttural cry, then felt his neck pinioned. He couldn't move. The man behind was drag-

248

ging him into the corridor, then, through bulging eyes, Osorio saw the objective: the shining gun lying in the corridor. Osorio tried to catch at a heavy chair to halt their progress, but they continued for the gun, inexorably. Screwing his face a millimetre to the right, he sank his teeth into yellow wrist.

'AHHHHHHHH!'

Backwards they tumbled and fell. The oriental sprang viper-like for Osorio's neck, his hands claws. As they rolled down the corridor, Osorio wrenched free, swung half a revolution away and kicked for the head. His opponent gracefully dodged the kick, came to his feet and grabbed the foot but Osorio kicked with his free leg in a high arc, connecting with his heel to the man's jaw before falling. With a grunt of pain the oriental went down on one knee. Osorio leaped to his feet and hit him with a piledriver full in the face. He watched as the man hurtled backwards and crashed against a bedroom door shattering it inwards with a tremendous detonation of sound as it struck the hollow wall of the bathroom within.

Osorio stood there, panting. The oriental lay in the doorway of the bedroom, face upwards, stone cold. A small Japanese in night attire appeared from the room. He stepped over the unconscious figure, caught his leg and pulled him outwards. Then with a bow to Osorio, he returned to his room and closed the shattered door.

Osorio took the eight floors of the fire stairs in great leaps, the bags in his left hand, swinging down the steel rail. At a black door with a chrome cross-bar he readied, then kicked it outwards. He crouched, ready to spring. The door made a loud scraping noise as it flew open. In the alleyway was a garbage skip, ready for collection. Then he saw the red Toyota, its roof gleaming in the street lights and Cheryl at the wheel, looking urgently towards him.

'Let's go!' he gasped as he jumped in beside her.

She just pointed.

At the top of the alleyway, twenty yards away where it joined the street, a helmeted figure clad in black leather and astride a large motorbike had appeared. The alley was slightly downhill from the street. Osorio winced as Cheryl gave the car full throttle in the stationary position. The motorbike was probing into the alleyway with unhurried confidence.

'The gears . . . ' Osorio started to say.

The bike was ten yards from their front fender when Cheryl jumped her foot off the clutch. As if hurled by a gigantic spring, the car shot forward, engine screaming, bowled the bike to the ground and became momentarily airborne at the top of the alley before it hit the road with a crash.

'Jesus!' Osorio cried.

She swung them past the front door of the hotel, nipped through a green light going orange and then gunned, engine roaring, in the direction of downtown.

'How many of them did you see?' Osorio shouted.

'Three,' Cheryl cried. 'One went into the hotel.'

'He's accounted for,' he panted. 'Have you any idea where you're going?'

'No,' she replied, 'have you?'

Cheryl's seat was back, her legs comfortable on the pedals, her arms straight to the wheel. They reached Odori Park and she brought the Toyota sweetly through its gears, making a right at speed, again beating the lights by a second. They were now going due west, the park to their right. They passed a western-style church, Cheryl taking them along at near sixty in the outside lane. Osorio looked back several times at the street behind, then found a map in the glove compartment.

'If we go right at the end of the park,' he said, reading, 'and then keep north for about ten blocks, we should connect with the main highway for Otaru.'

They paused thirty seconds for lights at the end of Odori Park, then went right, under a railroad. After two blocks they were forced to turn left again.

'Take the next right,' Osorio said.

The street they now entered was tree-lined and dimmer than the avenue which they had left. They were halfway down it when without warning, behind and to the right, there was an explosion of light, and the single lamp of a powerful motorbike dissected the rear window.

'Shit!' Cheryl said and changed down, looking for extra speed.

The bike, at least 500 cc's, pulled alongside the passenger door and Osorio drew his breath in sharply as he saw the man on the pillion for the first time: like the front rider he wore an all-encasing black helmet with a chin guard; unlike the front rider he was currently pointing a gun, two-handed, straight at Osorio.

'Get out of here!' Osorio cried.

Without discussion, Cheryl jumped the car on to the wide pavement outside the Hokkaido Museum of Art, paused for all of half a second to judge the traffic, then flung the car across the road, in front of a steaming, horn-blaring truck. Miraculously they made it and were singing along the next block, a flow of traffic separating them from where they had been.

'Give me oil trading any day,' Osorio said.

Cheryl pitched them into a drift left, rounded a corner, then screeched right. She flattened the accelerator and five blocks of quiet streets tore past.

'They're on us again,' said Osorio through gritted teeth.

The single light could be seen some way behind, but closing.

Around another corner, Cheryl very nearly bought it when a bus appeared from nowhere, but obligingly stood on its nose as they screamed by. A bridge loomed up and they passed beneath it, then suddenly they passed a sign and were on a dead straight road, lawns and trees both sides. Without warning they hit a steel speed ramp and jumped, then crashed back down, the Toyota's chassis hitting the road with a squeal of metal.

'We're in a school or institution of some kind,' Osorio said.

They were tearing down an avenue lined both sides with poplars. There were buildings across wide expanses of parkland. Looking back, Osorio could plainly see the bike now, thirty yards back and readying. He could actually see the pillion man's gun poking up over the front rider's shoulder. Every fifty yards or so they hit another ramp and the sinews in Cheryl's arms stood up as she tried to hold them on course. The motorbike, no less, also flew in the air, coming down, rear wheel first with a burr of rubber.

Osorio's hands clawed beneath his seat. He felt plastic covering and tugged. The wheel-changing kit of the Toyota had never been opened and smelled new in its shiny black pack.

They hit another ramp and the car roof seemed to come down and whack their heads. They were fast approaching a T-junction and Cheryl crashed them into third in preparation for the turn. Osorio tore open the ribbon which bound the kit; his hand closed on the steel jack. He didn't have to look to see the bike, it's light horribly close.

Cheryl was beginning the drift, righthanded, and the bike's front wheel was level with the car's back window. Osorio depressed the window button just as the man with the gun straightened his arms. Osorio brought himself up on the seat and shoved his whole upper body out the open window. They were turning right, the weight of the car changing. The bike was turning as well and Osorio could see yellow flame spurt from the pointed hands, but the shot at the angle was well wide, and now the bike rider had completed the turn and was beginning another run.

The wind whipped Osorio fiercely. The bike was five yards out from the car and almost level. The pillion-man took careful aim. They hit another ramp, almost together. Osorio felt the frame of the car bite painfully into him as they crashed down. For an instant the car was level and the bike was still airborne or its front wheel was. Osorio readied the jack above his head, then launched it. In a blur it spun for the bike. With immaculate precision it pierced the spokes of the wheel. There was a hideous noise of thrashing steel. The result was spectacular. The bike performed a loop, slow motion almost, backwheel vertically over the front. Two figures rolled like pins to Osorio's fast receding vision, there was an awful scraping and then a small explosion and sudden, vividly orange flames.

Without pausing, Cheryl brought them in and out of a number of turns, over road ramps, past buildings, and out again into the quiet traffic of night-time Sapporo.

'Where to now?' she asked as they sat, heaving, looking at each other.

Osorio's face was pale. 'Now we go to Otaru,' he said.

CHAPTER TWENTY - SIX

Lloyd's Neck, Long Island

Wednesday 13 March a.m.

It was a lovely day on the North Shore. Some daffodils thrusting through; sun with a hint of warmth; the sails of yachts out on Long Island Sound, pitching gently up and down among the white tops.

The builders had long since gone. The ballroom with it's carved wooden eaves – cherubs supporting their ship's prow – and its flounces of delicate whites and blues, was like a bride waiting patiently for her first night. The sprawling Tudor residence nestled in its cliff gardens; the creeper which clung to the walls still lacked any suggestion of green, but covered the great house in a protective web.

Dutch Tremaine felt omnipotent. Showered, shaved, dressed and coiffed, he sat in the sitting-room of the master-suite and looked out at the lovely day. The helicopter which had arrived on the top lawn forty-five minutes before sat there. Let them wait. This was power, the pulsing certainty of a winning hand, the promise of victory with all the testicle-tightening, body-tingling exquisiteness that went with it. *Barrons* had said it all the day before:

'*Anybody who counted Manhattan First out of the Wall Street stakes is just about to get their fingers burnt. This old bank has shaken off its problems, sharpened its controls, and got itself a sexy portfolio of new investments. Under the stewardship of the legendary Dutch Tremaine, Man First has taken on board some of the hottest commodity people in* *town – most of them the old GiltStock team. With first quarter rumoured to be around the $100 million, that's twice last year's, you could say that old Dutch is shooting for the moon again.'*

The unblemished sea scene confirmed to Tremaine the right-eousness of unfolding events. First Com had already taken $60 million clear out of the oil futures market and had a current open position of twenty-five million barrels which, when ten dollars a barrel or thereabouts was reached, would give a further profit of over $60 million. In New York in the last two trading days, Man First stock had moved up four dollars to $38 and looked set to go higher.

Through the open windows Tremaine scented the day with pleasure, then moved downstairs.

'Is it any wonder this was Gatsby's favourite spot?'

As one, the three men rose from the fire.

'When I was a kid I used to dream of putting the air out here into bottles and selling it in New York,' Tremaine smiled, flapping his hands to tell them sit.

All three men renewed their appreciation of the view.

'I got a call this morning,' said Tremaine from the window, 'from someone close to Schumann Ellis.'

Mention of the influential brokers made Jacob Landey raise his eyebrows. Tremaine turned; sunlight caught the silk woven into his Italian-cut suit.

'They're putting us at the top of their buy recommendation list next week,' he said.

Landey's face took on a stupidly crooked grin and he rose his arms up, then dropped them in the manner of a dying seal.

'You've done it,' he laughed. 'I never had any doubt, but you've done it.'

'What are we traded this morning?' asked Tremaine as he sat.

'Thirty-nine bucks bid, sir,' answered William Maldonado. 'And on good volume. I think some of the bigger pension funds are moving back into us after an absence of over two years.'

'We had the raw material,' Tremaine said, 'all we needed was the will.' His face shone. 'This is just a beginning, gentlemen.'

'But what a beginning,' said Maldonado. 'If our price makes the forties – and it looks highly likely – we're talking major acquisition again.'

'Any move from the mystery buyer?' asked Tremaine sharply.

'Not that we can tell, sir,' Maldonado replied. 'If it's Mr Eller, then he's keeping his head down.'

'Very good,' Tremaine said, smacking fist to palm, 'down to cases. What's the exact turnout going to be, bottom-line-wise for the quarter?'

'Depends on a few things, Dutch,' said Landey carefully. 'If we could cut the quarter now, we'd be talking $110 million. That's without taking unrealised First Com profits which come to another $60 million. Most of that comes from oil.'

'I know,' Tremaine said. 'What's oil this morning?'

'Eleven dollars and fifty-five cents a barrel traded and offered,' replied Joseph Pappas, speaking for the first time.

'Our new investments will strengthen the balance sheet picture,' Landey went on, 'but we haven't yet resolved the treatment of the GiltStock business.'

'Meaning?'

'Our preferred strategy,' answered Landey, licking his lips, 'is to treat the Osorio loan as the price it cost us to set up First Com. In that way we could write it off over a period. However Broadhurst Colridge, as auditors, see the Osorio loan as a bad debt which we must deal with this quarter.'

Tremaine winced in displeasure.

'Then we value First Com and add that as a gain,' he said.

'An extraordinary item, sir,' Maldonado said. 'It would come below the line.'

'Lean on them, Jacob,' Tremaine growled. 'I'm not going to have Broadhurst Colridge or any bunch of fag accountants fucking around with one of New York's greatest banks, understand?'

'Understood, Dutch,' Landey swallowed.

'With respect, sir.'

Tremaine turned to Pappas.

'While we're all happy with events,' the lawyer said, 'particularly the media reaction and the way our price has moved, we must not lose sight of the underlying factors.'

No one spoke.

'If you remove the contribution of First Com,' Pappas continued, 'you have a first quarter profit of around $50 million. Were the $70 million Osorio loan to be written off against that, we'd show a loss of $20 million for the period.'

'What's the point of such a hypothesis?' Tremaine snapped.

'We *have* a first quarter profit of $110 million. The Osorio thing *has* to be amortised like any other acquisition.'

'Our core banking business hasn't had time to really show its improvement,' Pappas said. 'It's stuck where it was last year. The entire extra earnings occur because of the fall in oil and the positions taken there.'

'You object to that?' asked Tremaine.

'It makes us vulnerable,' replied Pappas. 'Vulnerable if oil turns, vulnerable in the coming quarters when we can't repeat the same performance for the market. They'll mark us back down – heavily.'

Tremaine led with his jaw. 'Wrong on both counts, Joe,' he said coolly. 'One, even if oil turns, we'll be out. The objective is ten bucks, but Cox knows that every asshole on Wall Street is also looking for that number. Our positions will be out, we'll be flat before ten dollar oil is ever reached. Two, Cox has got the start that people only ever dream of. He's going to squirrel away the other $60 or $70 milion that he's going to make, then dribble it out over the next few quarters. During that period the synergies between First Com and Man First, worldwide, will have started to yield. The earnings will be maintained and the market will love us.'

'And the stock will be riding high enabling us to buy earnings again,' chimed Landey. He tapped a file on the table. 'There are a couple of little banks I have in mind just begging to be taken.'

There was a discreet knock, then Oliver, Tremaine's butler, entered, bearing a tray.

'Where do we stand, exactly, on the GiltStock Osorio business right now?' asked Tremaine, declining coffee.

Jacob Landey took up his cup. 'GiltStock has filed under Chapter Eleven,' he said, 'and continues to trade, or to try and trade, somewhere down off Fulton Street, I understand.'

'They've got people there?' Tremaine asked.

Landey shook his head. 'Just an old guy called Malcolm Finch,' he answered. 'I believe he and Osorio started out together. They're doing nothing. From what we hear, it's very much all founded on hopes of filing suits that no one seems to be able to run with. I mean, no one has seen Osorio since the Feds started looking for him.'

'These law suits,' Tremaine frowned. 'Do we have a liability?'

256

Landey shook his head. 'Two weeks ago Osorio was screaming that we had set him up to get his business, or some such crazy notion. Since he's gone underground, there's been nothing further.'

'The bankruptcy hearing is now on Monday, sir,' Maldonado said. 'If he shows, the Feds put cuffs on him. If he doesn't show, he'll be declared a bankrupt and we help ourselves to his assets.'

'But we still drop $70 million,' Pappas said.

'Steve Osorio,' said Tremaine, ignoring Pappas's remark and getting to his feet. 'There was always something there I didn't like, that I couldn't quite put my finger on.' He chewed his lip and looked out the window. 'I think it was his eyes,' he said, 'there was something in there . . . savage, animal almost, anyone know what I mean?'

'Still had one foot in the reservation?' Landey ventured as they all stood up.

'Could be,' Tremaine said, 'could be,' then walked with them to the french windows and watched them cross the lawn to the waiting chopper.

Tremaine sat by the fire with the file which Pappas had left opened on his knee. He never heard her behind him. Suddenly his view of the fire was blotted out and he smelled perfume.

'Guess who?'

He caught her hands tenderly and turned. Carly's white-gold hair, her perfect face, her long body in a suit of tailored, blue linen, was enough to make any father happy.

'Where did you come from?' he laughed.

'I was over in Huntington,' Carly smiled. 'Rather than drive straight back to New York, I called Oliver to check you were here.'

'He never told me,' Tremaine said.

'I told him it was a surprise,' Carly said.

'Well it sure is,' Tremaine said. 'Now I won't have to eat lunch alone.'

'Can we walk in the gardens first?' Carly asked. 'I'm all big city smoke and smells. I want air.'

They left the house by a side door, through a conservatory where a gardner worked on seed-trays, out on to a sheltered lawn. The statue of a nymph graced a corner where rhododen-

257

drons budded. Ducking beneath branches they emerged on another lawn which seemed to sweep for miles down to Long Island Sound. Carly shook her hair out and the wind tugged and teased it.

'I saw the ballroom,' she said. 'It looks beautiful.'

'You haven't been here since it was finished?'

She shook her head. Tremaine stopped and caught her elbows.

'You've no regrets about anything, have you, baby?' he asked with concern.

'Of course not.'

'I mean, I didn't force you to do anything, events took care of themselves, right?'

'Sure.'

Tremaine looked at her, then screwed his face up in anguish.

'You're not crying, Carly baby, are you?'

'It's the wind on my contacts,' she said, and linking him again, began to walk.

'We were just talking about it earlier,' Tremaine said, 'the business aspect of the whole thing, I mean. Of course, Osorio is now a fugitive from justice and he's blown right out of the water financially, but I couldn't help thinking to myself, there was something not right there. You know what I mean?'

Carly nodded as she saw little sails come into view.

'Then it came to me,' Tremaine said, laughing. 'Osorio always had one foot in the reservation. Isn't that right? He's still a goddamm injun.'

Carly threw her head back to the sun.

'Once an injun always an injun,' Tremaine said. 'He tried to take on the system, but it broke him, the poor fool. He hadn't got the essentials in his blood to make it up here.'

'Can we talk about something else?' Carly said.

The downward gradient of the lawn became steeper and now Carly could make out the texture of the waves, each foaming spume-head, racing like lions for the shore. She blinked back the moisture from her eyes. It was the Indian she had really loved. That she would never forget. The bronze-bodied, black-haired, vital Indian, sitting with his golden-haired squaw in a reservation all of their own.

CHAPTER TWENTY-SEVEN

Otaru, Hokkaido, Japan
Thursday 14 March 3.30 a.m.

He narrowed his eyes as they hurtled along. One of the Toyota's headlights had been put out of action in Sapporo, so now their passage through the countryside was illuminated by a single beam piercing the night.

It was an undulating land they crossed, sensing rather than seeing the volcanic mountains to their left, the cliffs and the sea to their right. Cheryl kept her foot to the boards; Osorio kept checking behind. There was an occasional truck, the lights of a train out between them and the cliff, darkened villages which they sped through, but no lights behind.

Signs in Kangi and in Romaji spelled out the decreasing distance to Otaru. There was an enormous sign depicting a wildlife park complete with Hokkaido bears. They passed a stud-railed paddock and saw horses grazing, climbed sharply from a valley and at the hilltop paused for a moment to see the lights of Otaru beneath. At that moment, the clouds parted and a half moon became perfectly reflected on what seconds before had been darkness.

'Ishikari Bay,' Osorio said.

Houses slipped by as they eased downhill, then traffic lights. Gerhardt's notes had all the data: the address of Hokkaido Oil's offices, built in grey granite, and behind them, the laboratory where the drilling reports were kept, and the warehouse where the sea-bed rock was stored after analysis. Osorio knew the procedures intimately. How you drove in the core-bar. How you examined the sample for traces of oil – praying, just praying for a trace. How you jealously hid such samples from outside eyes. In the black night of Otaru, Osorio could see the cores of sandstone in Brent's rough hands, brittle, brick-coloured sponges of porous rock, their chips of limestone winking in the Texas sun.

They parked two blocks from the harbour and faced east. They could see the wharfage from which the rigs, twenty-five miles out, were serviced; the piles of steel on the pier; the shining, inverted silo which would house the drilling mud.

Their eyes were on the darkened outline of the granite building fronting Pier 4, one hundred yards away. The foyer of the offices could be seen from the quiet street: a middle-aged security guard, inside a glass door, behind a desk; a single elevator; the offices above him and the buildings behind him dark. Cheryl opened the window slightly and as she did the breeze picked up a notch and caused plastic bunches of flowers tied to the streetlamposts to rattle.

'How long do you think we have until they catch up with us?' she whispered.

'Not long,' answered Osorio. 'Minutes perhaps.'

He closed his eyes for a moment in the way that a believer might in prayer. Faces hurtled in on him incoherently. Great-grandma Osorio, black and wisened, came to do her bit. There's Brent, there's Malcolm, there's Ron. There's Dutch Tremaine, laughing. Why is he laughing? And just as strangely, there's Carly, crying. Why? The oriental face seen in Tokyo station and Sapporo completed the collage.

'Let's do it,' Osorio said and they both got out.

Walking in the shadows but keeping to the side opposite the office, Osorio made his way towards the harbour.

Cheryl crossed the empty road. She had changed in the car into a white silk blouse and a skirt which she had hitched at the waist making it tight and nine inches above her knees.

Osorio passed opposite the office foyer, continued on until he was out of the line of vision, then crossed. Using doorways for protection he crept back up the street on the office side. He saw Cheryl approach. She had let her hair down around her shoulders and unbuttoned her blouse to halfway. She had unbelievable legs. She walked nonchalantly down the street, her hips

winging, then at the lampost immediately outside Hokkaido Oil
ne paused, leaned against it, kicked a shoe off and brought her
oot sliding up the other leg as if to examine a toe. In the pool
f light of the dark street, the vision made even Osorio swallow:
ne long legged, beautiful girl, her hair tumbling forward as she
ent, her blouse billowing out to show the thrust of her breasts.

There was the click of a lock. Cheryl studied her foot,
bsorbed. Osorio reached to the small of his back and withdrew
ne wheel brace which he had strapped there. A door could be
eard to open, out of Osorio's sight. There was a man's voice.
)sorio inched to the cover of a gateway and readied. He could
ee Cheryl drop her shoe to the ground and then sensuously
ub her right knee against her left thigh.

'*Goyo-de-shoka?*'

The guard's back was suddenly presented.

'*Goyo-de-shoka?*' the man asked again, 'can I help you?' as
Cheryl turned to him, smiling languidly.

She winced as Osorio brought the brace down, then took it as
)sorio dipped and caught the falling body in a fireman's lift.
'hey hurried into the foyer. Osorio dumped the man in his
hair, swivelled him around so that from outside he would
ppear to be asleep, uncradled the phone beside him and took
he brace from Cheryl. She nodded once. The door from the
oyer opened to a corridor. 'I'll keep watch from back here,' she
rhispered. Osorio stepped through into the darkness. It took
alf a minute for his eyes to adjust, but even then he could see
lmost nothing. The corridor ran straight, doors either side.
'he lab had to be at the other end. Then the core warehouse.
ilently he edged along, wincing whenever the rubber of his sole
queaked on the plastic tile underfoot. He felt the brace at his
ack and the torch which he didn't yet dare to use. He walked
ideways, his left hand outstretched. Then abruptly the corridor
nded.

Osorio ran both hands up and down in front of him and felt a
ound handle. He turned it and it clicked open with what
ounded like an explosion. Now he was in another corridor, run-
ing in the same direction, but here there was more light, a pool
ast through a glass door, halfway along. Osorio crept. He could
ear noise, a man's voice, chattering in Japanese. A man talking
n a telephone. The voice laughed and reverberated into the

hall where Osorio stood, flattened by the wall, the wheel-brace ready. Then normal tones resumed and Osorio leapt the pool of light.

There was a sudden silence. Osorio froze. He heard a telephone receiver being replaced, then light quadrupled in the corridor as a guard opened the door and emerged. Osorio crouched to spring, but the guard went to another door and entered. Probably a toilet. Trying to take his breaths without noise, Osorio continued on.

There was a further door and then more darkness. He was conscious that time was ticking away, that the people they had thwarted in Sapporo would be regrouping. He chanced the torch. He was in the laboratory. Rows of presses; silent counter with instruments; straight ahead had to be the door of the warehouse. He hurried to it. A wooden door. Locked as he tried it. A mortice lock. Praying that this internal door was not wired to an alarm system Osorio inched the brace into the door-frame between lock and jam, and leant on it with his full weight.

A deafening crack which had to be heard in Tokyo rang out. He was in a bog of sweat, but there were no sirens or bells and the door had swung inwards. Again he probed by torch. The concrete ceiling of the warehouse. He stepped in and closed the door. Metal shelves. Rows and rows of them. And on them wooden boxes, all with handles on each end. Padlocked. Each box numbered in white paint. Dozens of them, all with different numbers.

Osorio caught the handle of the nearest box and pulled it out. Placing the torch on its side he inserted the tip of the brace into the lid of the box and levered. The lid ruptured with a crunch. He put his hand in until he touched what he knew would be there. Sick with anticipation he took out the handful of rock and shone the torch on it. The smoothness of coal-black shale reflected dully in the torchlight.

Osorio stood there, nodding. His heart was double-pumping. Shale! The most dense rock known to man. Three hundred million years old. Non-porous. Non-permeable. Solid as iron. Barren of oil.

The lights came on.

Lights but no noise.

Osorio straightened from where he had crouched and crept

back towards the door. Still nothing. He inched the heavy door open: the lab was also now fully lighted, but there was nobody. He walked through, the wheel brace in his left hand. Through the next door to where he had seen the guard.

Nothing, no sound.

He opened the door a crack: more lights, everywhere ablaze, but empty. Two bounds took him to the security man's office. He saw a chair, a desk. There was a smell of tobacco.

Osorio ran the rest of it to the foyer. It seemed every light in Otaru was on. The reception desk lacked its unconscious occupant. Sick now, Osorio, a goldfish in a bowl, even lights outside were on, but still he kept going, powered by hope, driven by it, clinging to it, hope was everything to him now.

And then he saw what he had dreaded.

The Toyota, drawn up outside the offices. Cheryl standing beside it on the kerb. Her chin was up, pointing for the stars, her head was back, held by her abundant hair. Blood trickled from a scratch in her throat, blood which seemed to shimmer in the lights from the building and from the street. And the long knife drawn horizontally across her throat also shimmered. And the barrel of the sub-machine gun shimmered, pointing steadily over the shimmering roof of the car for Osorio's head.

Osorio slowly put his hands on his head.

'Okay,' he nodded, 'you win.'

CHAPTER TWENTY - EIGHT

1

New York

Thursday 14 March a.m.

Malcolm picked the phone up and hit the flashing key.

'GiltStock,' he said.

'Malcolm, baby, this is Tony,' said the unmistakable voice of Tony Quacks.

'Hi, Tony, how are you today?' Malcolm said.

'I'm real good,' replied Tony Quacks. 'Malcolm, I just had a note from my accounts people telling me that ten million dollars just arrived into us from Chemical Bank, credit GiltStock. Is this right?'

'Oh, I'm sorry, Tony,' Malcolm said, looking around the tiny, empty office, 'we've been really busy. I asked them to send you some money because I think we might want to do something in oil and I'd like you to have the business. I should have told you, sorry, it clean slipped my mind.'

'Forget it, forget it,' said Tony Quacks cheerfully, 'glad to help. What are your ideas in oil?'

'Oh, nothing spectacular,' Malcolm said, 'just a client with more money than sense, I expect.'

'Not an Arab, is it, Malcolm?' Tony joked.

Malcolm's laugh was deep and rich. 'I think I'm too old for these Arab clients,' he answered.

'What's the news on Steve?' asked Tony Quacks when he had
nished laughing.

'I don't know, Tony,' replied Malcolm with just the right
egree of regret. 'I expect he'll show up eventually.'

'I expect so,' said Tony Quacks sombrely. 'Hey, Mal, I gotta
o, but how about lunch someday?'

'Sure,' Malcolm said. 'I'll have my girl call yours.'

Malcolm replaced the phone and sat looking into space. What
teve had told him in San Francisco had been like something
ou read about, injected straight into the vein: he had gone
round doing what was needed like a guy who's just discovered
or the first time that he's in love: he did things mechanically, he
miled the whole time, but his extremities, like the ends of his
ngers and his toes, kept tingling so much that he had to
cratch them. It was like swimming after a lot of beer: you knew
ou were getting wet, yet you felt nothing.

GiltStock was busy like tombs are busy, but Malcolm didn't
are. Marilee had gone uptown to pick up a message so the
uter office was still. The kid had gone to interview someplace
lse, leaving Malcolm on his own, but he relished the – if it
ere possible – additional quiet of the place. His euphoria bub-
led somewhere just under his skin. The last time he'd had that
eeling was the very first time he'd met Steve Osorio.

Malcolm's eyes saw the price of May oil on the screen in front
f him. It took him several seconds to register what he saw.
linking, he picked up his phone and called a floor broker on
he Merc.

'Is that a good quote for May oil?' Malcolm asked.

'Ten ninety offered? Sure is,' the broker replied. 'Just had the
hit sold out of it through eleven. Aren't you short, Malcolm? If
ot, then you're the only person on Wall Street who isn't.'

Malcolm put down the phone and steadied himself. He felt
ke the epic gunfighters of old, the ones who had survived to his
ge only because they were the best, now called out to a dusty
treet at noon to face the lynching party. He hit the tie-line.

'Hi, GiltStock!' said Tony Quack's man on NYMEX to the
sual background of noise. 'Long time! Tony told us you might
e calling. Welcome back, Malcolm!'

'Thanks,' said Malcolm pleasantly. 'Trading quote on the
1ay?'

'Just a minute, Mal.' There was the usual shouted exchange
'Ten eighty-five, ninety,' came the quote.

'Buy a million at ninety,' said Malcolm, ears now tingling as
well. There was nothing like this. Nothing. Trout, sex, grand
children, nothing measured up to this.

'Mal, you bought a million at ninety,' came the execution
from the floor.

Malcolm noted it, then hit an outside line.

'It's Malcolm,' he said.

'Ten dollars ninety cents a barrel just traded on the May,' said
the voice on the other end.

'I know,' Malcolm said, 'that was us.'

'So this is it, this is where it happens or not. We buy a million
barrels every two cents down from here, and if it breaks ten
bucks and nothing happens, then we pack our bags and check
into homes for the destitute elderly.'

'It won't, and we won't,' said Malcolm with a confidence that
amazed him.

'Any word from Japan?'

'Nothing further,' Malcolm replied. 'We're all just sitting
around, waiting.'

'Eighty-eight just traded. Go to, Mr Finch, and let me know
when you want more money,' Miss Singer said.

2

New York

Jay Cox rarely went down on NYMEX. To Cox the real power was
always somewhere upstairs, the cockpit whence all ideas and
moves originated. Down on the floor were mere operatives,
bawling prize fighters, picked for their ability to perform essen
tially mechanical tasks in crazy conditions. The floor simply
reacted; upstairs was where creation took place.

Cox showed his pass and made his way across the huge audi
torium towards crude oil. Although down here he felt ill at ease

ere was something good about coming to the place where the ecisions which had made such a fortune had actually been nplemented. The underfoot litter, the wild surges of bodies, nd the wall of noise were all part of the process which had rned First Com into the hottest property on Wall Street and e most important division of First Manhattan Banking orporation.

Although his basic employment contract – negotiated during at hectic weekend – started him at a basic five hundred thou- nd, bonuses based on profits would quadruple that, and when are options were kicked in, Cox would be looking two point ve million straight in the eye. And then there were the extras: e use of company assets, or assets which although listed some- here in the Man First balance sheet had long since drifted into utch Tremaine's personal estate: the jet, the yacht, the houses l over the world, tickets for anything, no matter how impossi- le, tables in restuarants, limousines which waited around the ock . . . the list went on and on, and Cox liked it.

He heard Vince Carpenter before he saw him. The oil pit was robbing, the booths around it a frantic relay of information, as eople with twenty-foot-long phone extensions screamed orders to the market. On the winking red board behind, Cox could e May oil at ten dollars and sixty-six cents last traded. Vince's ice had a pitch and place all of its own: Cox approached the rst Com stand, guided in, as it were, by sonic bullhorn.

'Jay, we are honoured!' Vince bellowed.

Cox inclined his oval head in a smile. 'Busy?'

'It's like trading a dream,' Vince replied. 'You sell it, it goes own, you buy it in, you make money. It's hard to imagine this uff was once forty bucks a barrel.'

'Any news in the market?' asked Jay Cox.

'Nah,' Vince said and curled down his mouth. 'Listen, you uld tell this market that the Russians had taken the Saudi wells nd pumped them into the Persian Gulf, and oil would dip on e news.'

Light reflected on Cox's rimless glasses. 'That may be so,' he id quietly, 'but our objective is in sight.'

'You mean . . . ?'

'I mean we cut and take our profits,' said Cox, looking from ft to right as he spoke like a spectator at a rodeo.

267

Vince rocked back slightly. 'Hey, Jay,' he murmured, 'you know something that I don't?'

'Of course not,' Cox answered.

'Look, I agree with our plan,' Vince said, 'but this market isn't going to stop at ten dollars a barrel. The whole fucking world is short, nobody wants the stuff, we're talking seven dollars now, maybe lower. Take some profits by all means, but don't take them yet.'

'The financial graveyards are full of people who waited too long to take their profits,' Cox retorted.

'Jay,' said Vince, squaring himself, 'what's going to make this market go up?' He fell silent as a clerk pushed between them, then he took Cox's elbow and turned him into the booth. 'I mean, we're so far in front, Christ, think of the really massive fortunes that have been made over the years, it's the guys who grit their teeth and stay in there who are the winners.'

There was a panting behind them and the sound of a time clock being punched. Max stood there, his curly black hair glistening, his shirt stuck to his chest.

'Ten sixty-five and a seller,' he gasped. 'Hi, Jay, you comin' to work in the zoo?'

Cox smiled. 'It looks rough out there,' he said. 'What's the story?'

Max butted his head forward. 'This market is like the guy in the Marines who's makin' his first parachute drop,' he said. 'He's standing at the door of the plane looking down thirty-five thousand feet and he turns to the instructor and he says, "which way we goin, sir?" and the instructor puts his hand on his shoulder and gives him a little push and says, "down, son, we're goin' down."'

Cox laughed good humouredly.

'I'll give you fellows a real laugh,' Max said. 'I was just beside Tony Quack's guy and I couldn't help overhear something. You know that oil he's been buying today? You know who it was for?'

Cox frowned.

'Who?' Vince asked.

'It was for fuckin' GiltStock!' cried Max, slapping his leg with his hand.

'Jesus!' exclaimed Vince. 'We better double up, Jay. If GiltStock are buying oil, soon it'll be given away for free.'

'Who in GiltStock bought the oil?' asked Cox sharply.

'Old Malcolm,' Max said and shrugged, 'who else is there?'

Cox's small eyes were darting.

'Why is Malcolm buying oil?' he asked.

'Why don't we call him up and ask him?' suggested Vince and picked up the phone.

'No!' Cox held both hands up. 'We can't have anything to do with them, not whilst Man First are suing them for seventy-five million bucks, it might prejudice things.'

'Okay,' said Vince. 'See if you can get anymore on that,' he said to Max who nodded and shuffled back to the pit. 'What are you thinking, Jay?' he asked.

Jay Cox was blinking at speed.

'I don't know,' he replied. 'For some reason I don't like what I hear.'

'Don't worry about it,' Vince said. 'Somebody's got to buy or there's no market. The fact that it's Malcolm is just coincidence.'

'But who is he buying for?' Cox asked.

'Who knows? Who cares?' Vince said. 'Maybe he's hallucinating.'

'Let me see your position book,' said Cox.

Vince took the book from his inside pocket and opened it.

'Twenty-eight million barrels?' Cox said.

'Twenty-eight million four hundred thousand to be exact,' Vince confirmed.

Cox snapped the book shut and handed it to him.

'At ten dollars sixty, start to buy,' he said softly. 'Nothing too obvious, just nice and quietly, start to take them out.'

'The whole position?' queried Vince.

'The whole position.'

'But, Jay, I really think . . . '

'I don't care what you think,' Cox retorted. 'I'm giving you an order.'

Vince sighed. 'Very well. You do realise this is going to take several days?'

'Of course.'

'Would you not consider leaving, say, a five or six million barrel position in there, just something to have on board for when he breaks ten dollars?' Vince asked.

'Do what I said,' Cox replied, 'and don't horse around.'

'Yes, sir,' Vince said.

Jay Cox nodded once, then began to retrace his steps over the floor. The litter, the noise, the physical confrontations taking place all around him now appeared ugly. He wanted the peace of the big boardroom five blocks away where the dimensional problems of running the fastest growing brokerage on Wall Street could be sifted and sorted in appropriate tranquillity. In five days' time he was due in London to look at office property. Then it was on to Frankfurt, another location to be viewed for First Com's expansion, then to Monte Carlo for a well-earned weekend before coming home. Of course he had the Gulfstream to do this loop: that was what he liked the most: two pilots and a stewardess at his beck and call, perpetual motion, instant communications, money oozing out of every pore. He paused at the edge of the floor and looked back. Here is where it had all happened. Right down here, in the litter and the smell and the shit. Cox shook his head. Ten dollars sixty-five again traded May oil. Soon Vince would start to haul in the short positions and Jay Cox's future would be as solid as bedrock.

He walked from NYMEX to the elevator. Everything had gone as planned. So why, as he stood there waiting, did his mind's eye insist on recalling the face of Steve Osorio?

Irritated, Cox stepped through the opening doors.

CHAPTER TWENTY-NINE

1

Hokkaido, Japan
Thursday 14 March 7.30 a.m.

was three hours since they had left Otaru.

Their captors had numbered just two: an oriental with hair to s shoulders and a thick black beard, he gave the orders to a naller, more stereotyped Japanese. They had taped Osorio's ands behind his back. His feet were bound. He was made to neel and his joined wrists were lashed to his ankles. A rag was uffed into his mouth and a tape run half a dozen times around s head. No violence, no malevolence, just the calculated exe- ation of unspoken orders. Like mutes they turned to Cheryl nd repeated the procedure on her, working unhurriedly in the ley, beside the core warehouse in Otaru.

One by one they were lifted, almost gently into the Toyota's unk, first Osorio, then Cheryl. Osorio had caught a last impse of the lights of Otaru before the lid had been slammed.

Three hours, minute by minute recorded on the phosphorous ce of Cheryl's wrist watch, which Osorio could just see. It was ke the inside of a sealed drum: no light, no form. It was impos- ble to judge speed, all that could be discerned was whether the ar was stationary or moving, for when it moved, each bump and ip of the road came crashing up through the chassis and rought the tin lid harshly down on their heads and shoulders.

Trussed like a chicken, gagged, suffocating, Osorio battled t
keep his mind clear. The eyes of the bearded man who gave th
orders were expressionless, half-lidded. But there was an econ
my of movement and a physical competence which Osorio coul
respect. Where were they being brought? Depression floode
through Osorio as he realised that he had failed. This weighe
almost more heavily on him than the physical danger. Tomorro
was the hearing in New York: in his absence he would becom
with one stroke of a pen, a financial non-entity.

In the nightmare time became suddenly meaningless. The ca
was on a road, a highway by the sound of other traffic. It was da
light, seen through a tiny pinhole near the trunk latch
Although he battled to prevent it, Osorio slept, dimly hopin
that he would wake. It was a half sleep: he was always aware c
their predicament, but sleep relieved the discomfort of his con
torted position and made time pass more quickly.

Once they stopped for gas: Osorio could actually hear the l
quid flowing to the tank down a pipe somewhere near his head
he tried to shout, to kick; he heard voices, laughter, the engin
restarting; then the mesmerising drone of the car took over an
he dozed again.

He looked at Cheryl's watch and saw the digits for noon. Th
next time he looked, although it felt that only minutes ha
elapsed, it read nineteen-thirty. The pinprick of light began t
dull. Another day in Japan was ending.

The car crossed a sharp bridge or hillock and Osorio felt himse
rammed against Cheryl as they were both bounced up an
down. He could feel the angle of the car change to a climb. Fc
thirty minutes they went upwards, and by the occasional spin c
the car wheels, Osorio could tell they were on a track rathe
than a road. The angle of their climb became more acute so tha
they were both pressed against the trunk latch. The car's whee
spun on stones, they jerked to a stop, freewheeled back, the
booted upwards again, the stones spinning up and spatterin
the chassis. Again they spun, stopped. The car was slewed to th
left and its engine killed. Osorio could hear the door open, the
his eyes were blinded as a light flooded into their sudden
opened cell.

Osorio lay there, blinking. There was a torch and lights fron

272

another car pulled up close behind. Osorio could see someone reach in, catch Cheryl and lift her easily out. Osorio saw the flash as a knife appeared and severed the tapes which bound her ankles, then the tape which had joined her hands and feet. He felt himself caught and pulled. Helpless, he rolled and hit the stoney ground with a jarring crash.

'Yanero!'

For a second Osorio looked up and saw the bearded man's eyes blaze with anger at his subordinate, then the knife came out again. Carefully he inserted it between Osorio's ankles and sliced. Blood flooded painfully into the joints. Another sweep of the knife and Osorio could stretch himself straight. He lay there, wincing, still gagged, his wrists still bound, taking the maximum time.

They were clearly on the side of a mountain; there were pine smells, and the smells of herbs, lavender and vanilla, strong on the night air. No noises that Osorio could hear; he tried to concentrate his hearing function fully, searching the boundaries of their situation for traffic sounds, voices, any background, but there was nothing, wherever they had been brought, sound might not have been part of their new environment.

As if to emphasise their isolation, the bearded leader cut off both their gags. Cheryl stood there, hands bound behind her, blood stains on her torn blouse, her skirt and on her bare legs.

'Are you alright?' Osorio asked.

'I'm okay,' she answered, but he could hear the pain in her voice. 'What are they going to do with us?'

'Aruke!' ordered the leader in answer, 'walk!'

Osorio led the way upwards in the direction pointed. Past the front of the car there was a moment when he considered diving downwards, rolling away from them and dividing their attention, but he looked back and saw the impassive eyes less than a metre away, and behind the leader Cheryl stumbling along, the rear gunman's hand guiding her from behind.

They made their way in this fashion for an hour. The climb was exhausting, not because of the gradient which wasn't excessively steep, but because of the continual need to preserve balance in total darkness without the benefit of arms. Each new step was a threat.

Osorio heard Cheryl cry out and pitch forward. He turned

and tried to make her out, barely discerning the white of her blouse.

'Cheryl!'

'I can't see a damn thing,' she said getting up.

Several times Osorio's foot came down wrong and he fell twisting involuntarily to take the fall on his shoulder. Each time he was righted from behind by a strong hand which grabbed him before he struck earth.

'*Kocchi-da!*'

Osorio stopped and felt a hand on his back. The leader said something to the other man, then repeated, '*kocchi-da*, this way.'

They were guided off the track, sideways through knee-high bushes. Osorio's eyes still strained to see anything but black forms. The bearded oriental must have been equipped with some extra facility, for now he walked beside Osorio, his hand on his shoulder, guiding him like someone taking their grandpa for a stroll down the Boardwalk in Atlantic City.

Again Osorio considered trying to take him. He could possibly do it since the man was downhill from him. They stopped and the leader grunted something to his invisible companion. Cheryl came into view.

'Hi,' Osorio said grimly.

'This is a fun way to see Japan,' she said before her guide turned her around so she and Osorio were both back to back.

Osorio could hear the rasping sound of the binding tape being unwound, then he felt the flesh of Cheryl's hands as both their wrists were bound together. In the black night he laced his fingers with hers.

'*Suwarre!*' the leader ordered, 'sit,' and pushed them, always gently, downwards.

'Where do you think we are?' Cheryl asked.

'Not far from Otaru,' Osorio answered. 'My guess is that we've been driving in circles all day.'

Cheryl's breath came out in a shudder.

'They're so damn . . . impersonal!' she said, a break in her voice.

Osorio could see the leader, less than a metre away, squatting silently, and his companion with eyes glued to Cheryl.

'Do you speak English?' Osorio called.

The oriental looked but did not react.

'You understand me, don't you?' Osorio said. 'You under-
tand what I'm saying. Ishikari Bay.'
There was no reaction.
'We know there's nothing there,' Osorio said. 'But it's not just
s that knows it, we have friends in the United States who know
verything, we've told them all about Eric Gerhardt and what he
rote and the fact that the seismic produced by Hokkaido Oil is
fake. Whatever you do to us is a waste of time. It doesn't matter
f you kill us, the secret is out, the whole world is soon going to
now that the Japanese have no oil and never did. So what's the
oint of all this, why not just let us go and look after yourself?'
Slowly the leader reached to his pocket and came out with
omething flat and square shaped. He squatted beside Osorio
nd there was a rustle of paper, then a snapping sound.
'*Taberu?*' the man asked. 'You want?'
'What's he doing?' Cheryl enquired.
'I'm not sure,' Osorio said, then he laughed shortly, 'but I
hink the bastard is offering me chocolate.'
'*Oishii',* ' the leader said, 'it's good.' To demonstrate, he
opped squares into his own mouth, then held two more an
nch from Osorio's lips.
'My grand-daddy once had an old horse,' Osorio said, ignor-
ng the oriental. 'It's name was Jeff. One day the horse doctor
ame and said there was nothing for it but Jeff had to go to
leep. You should have seen grand-daddy – he was more upset
han if he was told it was him, not the horse. He told the doctor
o wait and went into the house and came out with a whole bag
f peppermints. I was little more than a baby but I can remem-
er him feeding Jeff great handfuls until the bag was empty.
'hen he said goodbye to the horse and went into the house and
could see he was crying.'
'I can't see these guys shedding a tear,' Cheryl said.
'It's the only difference,' Osorio replied.
'You talk a lot about your family, don't you?' she asked.
'I guess I do,' he answered.
'It's good,' Cheryl said, 'it's a reserve, a sort of inner
trength.'
'Don't you think of yours?' Osorio asked her.
'I do, but I think in a different way,' she said. 'I think I'm
nore independent than you are, that's not necessarily better, it's

275

just the way I am. I love my father particularly, but he wanted a daughter who could stand by herself, totally self-sufficient. In a way some emotions had to go in order to achieve that.'

The two orientals watched them, legs tucked underneath guns beside them on the ground.

'What are your regrets?' asked Cheryl quietly.

Osorio didn't answer immediately.

'I suppose,' he said eventually, 'that for a very long time, confused happiness with money.' He sighed. 'After that, I regret that I blew it, that I nearly made it, that I let a lot of people down. I regret that we lost, that they won. I regret that very quickly everything seems over, that I may not see home again, or enjoy the company of my friends one last time. I regret that next week, if there is a next week, I'll be here and not in New York to defend myself.' He paused and felt the outline of her back pressed into his. 'I regret above all,' he said, 'that there hasn't been the time for you and me to develop what I think we have going for us.' He worked his fingers gently up and down on hers. 'What are your regrets?' he asked.

Cheryl didn't reply at once. Then in a steady voice she said, 'I wanted someday to have a child.'

They turned their heads half a revolution and briefly their cheeks touched.

Six feet away the leader was eating chocolate. Stars had come out to relieve the darkness of the night. The trees overhead suddenly rustled with a breeze that must have come from somewhere high up the mountain.

CHAPTER THIRTY

New York

Thursday 14 March 7.30 p.m.

It was just before the rush hour. Cristy sat watching the train doors close at Times Square, then they lurched on uptown, the spray-can crazy, multi-coloured carriages swaying with each twist and bend of the tunnel.

At 96th Street Cristy crossed to the platform for the uptown local. It all now depended on Steve. 103rd Street and 110th came and went. Malcolm whom she'd never met sounded like the kind of friend you could do with. And who was the mysterious financial backer they had found?

At 125th Street Cristy crossed the steel footbridge and descended into Broadway. That morning she had taken lamb from the freezer; she would cook a casserole and drink some wine.

Everything now depended on Steve. But Cristy felt unable to concentrate fully on Steve's task, to worry about the danger he might be in. It wasn't that she did not care: it was that whenever she tried to concentrate, Ron's dead face popped into her internal vision.

That day in the office she had taken out a yellow pad and tried to go over her handwritten article on the forbidden topic: oil, Japan, Durst Bank. But even though it read well, even though it would rank among the legendary pieces if ever it saw daylight, she still had not been able to concentrate.

There was a wind into Cristy's face as she walked uphill. She was alone on the hillside avenue, walking towards Riverside, the high tower of a church ahead jutting up in sharp silhouette against the red evening sky. She walked purposefully. The kerb to her left was lined with parked cars; the door of a house opened and a black man came out with a bag of garbage; a car door opened and a woman emerged with dry cleaning held at arm's length.

Cristy was halfway up the hill when something happened. She stopped abruptly, frowning. Although she suddenly didn't want to, she turned around and looked back downhill, back in the direction of the 125th Street subway which she had just left. The black man, the garbage, the woman, the dry cleaning. Empty street. Some kids she hadn't noticed. But there had been something else.

She resumed her walk for home.

Cristy's apartment, fifth floor, looked on one side down at the Hudson, at the other, on to the street. She entered the lobby, dark tonight, fuse gone, emergency lights on weak yellow glow which made the mail boxes dark and ugly. She called the elevator. The doors slid back and stronger light suddenly illuminated the lobby, making the elevator seem a safe haven. She entered it and pressed five.

Then her mind, up to now drifting, not concentrating, suddenly clicked into place.

A car parked on the hill. A grey sedan. A man at the wheel. Parked in the same place as the evening before.

There were three doors on the fifth floor between the elevator and Cristy's apartment. Lights okay up here. Her feet echoed on the wooden floor. She hadn't eaten, waited all day at her desk for Steve's call, watched the oil market like a hawk, talked to poor old Malcolm, hurried home in case Steve would call, hadn't thought of anything but the forbidden story which would be so vital, she had worked it out, line for line in her head all the way home on the train, composing phrases as she walked uphill, and then, for no reason she could rationally fathom, the grey car with its single occupant had become suddenly important.

Cristy opened her hall door, threw her coat and bag on the chair and switched on the lights. The kitchen was off the hall. Then a bathroom. Right to the living-room where she worked, overlooking the Hudson. Left to her bedroom, its window over-

278

ooking the street. Her bed, a big brass affair which she had bought years ago, stood opposite the window. She wanted to close the drapes. She walked to the window and looked down into the street.

There was the car, a hundred yards away. She could actually see the man. Cristy realised she was standing at her window, lights on behind her, projecting her silhouette. Hastily she drew the drapes.

In the kitchen she went mechanically about the task of preparing supper. Steve was what she must think about. Steve in Japan. He would call any minute. Steve was in Japan, proving the oil find to be phoney. Steve was in Japan. Ron was dead. Cristy was on her own in New York. With a man sitting outside her apartment, watching her.

Cristy got to her feet, drew in her breath and walked purposefully across the hall to her bedroom. She brought a chair to a cupboard, stood and took down a bag. On the bed she unrolled the oily rag: the tiny gun, so small it fitted in the palm of the hand, winked as its pearl handle caught the lights.

To leave the room Cristy had to cross the window. Not wanting to, but drawn to the danger like a rabbit, she opened the drape an inch. At exactly that moment a car driving up the street illuminated the car Cristy knew to be there: she saw the head and shoulders in black relief.

Abruptly, her predicament overwhelmed her. She ran from the bedroom, the pistol in her hand. Everywhere there were curtains she jerked them to close. At the hall door she checked the chains and treble-locks. She stood in the hall, chest heaving, the only sounds her heartbeat and a faint hissing from the kitchen of water coming to the boil.

She began to weep with fear. Never had she felt so alone. Beyond the bright floral yellows and reds of the curtains, in the street, sat evil. With flawless timing – Ron dead, Steve away – it had come. What could she do?

Once, years ago, in the desert storm of a Texas night, a dog had come and howled for refuge, so near her, just outside the flimsy wall of their trailer, that Cristy had screamed with terror and jumped from her bed into Steve's. As she clung to him and he turned and shared his warmth with her, the howling dog had melted into the night and vanished like the dew on a cactus.

Morning was what Cristy now prayed for.

She poured herself a double scotch. From a drawer in the kitchen she took a bottle and swallowed four sleeping-capsules.

In the bedroom she lay clothed, face down on the covers, and waited for oblivion.

CHAPTER THIRTY-ONE

1

Hokkaido, Japan
Friday 15 March 5.30 a.m.

With every second the quality of daylight improved. Each new moment brought a changed sense of proportion. Despite the hopelessness of the situation, the beauty of the location was undeniable. They were up in a land of mists and scents and running water, with sheer drops on either side of them, plunging valleys, other mountain tops at indeterminate distances below and a silence only now begining to be broken by the chorus of the dawn.

Osorio got stiffly to his feet. The bearded oriental was helping Cheryl up, her hands, like Osorio's, still taped behind her back. Looking left Osorio could see the companion adversary now with the sub-machine gun held waist high and pointing at them. The leader approached Osorio. He held car keys in his hands and was wiping them with a cloth. Carefully, holding them with the cloth, he slipped them into the pocket of Osorio's jeans. So careful, everything they did. Even the tapes had left no marks that Osorio could see on Cheryl's ankles. Like apples, not to be bruised. Except for Osorio's unceremonious decanting from the car boot, no untoward violence. The textbook protocol for dead meat.

'Why are they being so careful with us?' Cheryl asked.

'We're being set up for some kind of accident,' Osorio said. 'It's going to appear natural; they don't want any evidence that we were captured.'

The leader took out his roll of tape. Expertly and quickly he gagged them both. Then he wound the tape twice around Cheryl's neck, making a dog collar of it, snaked it out six feet and duplicated the collar on Osorio. Their eyes met and, despite the gag, Osorio saw Cheryl smile. Joined at last. Albeit by tape on a Japanese mountain. Nearly made it, we did. Nearly blew them all out of the water. You and me. We're for each other, always have been. We're the same mould, the same spirit, us two. What a laugh fate must be having now, seeing us revealed fully to each other only now, with everything ticking away so fast. In this beautiful morning. We've both just discovered love.

With a single inclination of his head commanding them to follow, the leader began to walk up the mountain.

The track rose through spectacular stands of trees. Gradually the pre-dawn was giving way to the morning proper and Osorio could feel the heat of the sun on his face as it began to burn through the mists. They crossed streams some of them knee deep and scalding, volcanic spigots from deep in the earth. Any opportunity to run for it had been effectively neutered by the strong tape which joined their necks. They continued upwards slowly, never rushed, the bearded Japanese ahead waiting with infinite patience and occasionally helping Cheryl over difficult terrain, the one behind at a safe distance with the sub-machine gun, never speaking, his finger never off the safety catch.

A dramatic sunrise was taking place all around them. Every so often their upward path would breach the cloud and they could glimpse the panorama which they were part of. Mountain tops thrust upwards from white clouds to the limits of a great fluffy sea. Through these soft white clouds rose the hot steam from the thousand rivers which coursed downwards. Birdsong was full-throated. The vegetation either side of the endless course began to change: fir now gave way to ash, then to sycamore, then to birch with luminously white barks, and then to small forests of bamboo, tubular and upright, more like growing steel than living tree.

Suddenly the ground levelled and they stopped. They had come to a clearing, paused for breath and looked back once more. Beyond the mountains and the clouds, beyond the white sea of mists and steam, the sun was climbing up out of a real sea. A dazzling yellow orb lifting inch by inch, the life-giver returned. At the same moment, they both heard the sound. Osorio turned, jerking Cheryl's head as he did. Some primal mechanism sucked all the blood from his face. The sound was repeated, a powerful grunting which echoed. The man with the gun had positioned himself to one side; the leader put his hand on Cheryl's shoulder and steered her and Osorio higher, towards the back of the clearing.

Osorio was pouring sweat. He heard the grunting again, deep and angry and now he could suddenly see what they were being led to: a pit had been carved into the hill, ten feet deep at the front, twice that behind, lined like a stockade with upright pointed posts. Five paces from the lip the grunting increased to a roar and the head and shoulders of a massive brown bear reared into view.

'*Aruke!*' the Japanese snapped.

Osorio stood, his body touching Cheryl's. She looked at him, her eyes brimming as, at the same time, they both realised what was going to happen. Behind there was the click of a gun breech and Osorio could see the snout of the sub-machine gun levelled at them less than six feet away. They approached the pit.

Two bears, brown and huge, were prowling their area with impatience and occasionally standing on rear legs to bellow with rage at the humans above. Long pieces of white bone littered the pit, whose floor was strewn with dung. At the back of it, built into the stockade, Osorio could see a heavy door. There was a foul animal smell. The leader unsheathed his knife.

When man first lived in jungles he was equipped with valves deep within him, a support kit juiced by adrenalin which ensured his survival as king amongst the beasts. The oriental cut the gag from Osorio's mouth then the tape at his throat and wrists. All Osorio's neck hairs stood on end. He brought phlegm from his throat to oil his mouth.

'Don't move in any way,' he said hoarsely to Cheryl. 'And when I do what I'm going to do, just remember to lie absolutely still.'

'Lie?' she said, having spat the gag from her mouth.

Osorio saw the Japanese slice the tape from her throat. The

gunman with the two-foot-long sub-machine gun had it pointed for Osorio's head and his finger on the hair trigger.

'That's right,' said Osorio, quietly, but urgently. 'And no matter what happens now, remember that I love you.'

The Japanese leaned to put the knife between her wrist tapes. There was a period of perhaps half a second when part of his body was between them and the barrel of the gun. With the madness of the jungle Osorio leaped, arms apart, clutching both Cheryl and the Japanese in his embrace, powering all of them over the lip of the pit and into space.

They hit the ground together. Immediately Osorio could see the bears rush. He sprang to his feet the same time as the bearded Japanese who still held his knife. The bears were almost on them. Cheryl lay face down, inert. The Japanese was shouting something, screaming. Osorio was a foot from him.

'*Kocchi-e-nagete-kure!*' the Japanese screamed up. 'Throw it!'

The larger bear came in first. The gunman outside tossed in the sub-machine gun and the leader flung his knife away to catch it.

'*Steve!*'

As Osorio bent for the knife the second bear tore the flesh and muscle from his left shoulder in a single sweep. Simultaneously there was the chattering of a gun going off followed by the terrifying roar of a wild animal in pain. Osorio's grizzly paused and turned. The Japanese had shot the larger bear in its underbelly and it had reared up and was bellowing in agony, flapping the hooks of its claws around it's head.

The Japanese took his chance and leaped for the locked door. He plastered the lock with shot from close range, but his turned back was an opportunity which the second animal was not going to miss. As the wounded bear continued to roar in bewildered pain, its companion covered the space to the Japanese in a bound and took him at the neck, just as the man was turning to fire. Osorio lay on the ground watching, still thinking in terms of the knife. The sub-machine gun spun like a walking stick across the pit. The door of the pit had swung outwards, but it was too late for the bearded Japanese, who was now gripped, face to face with the giant animal. The man never had time to scream. The animal ripped his throat like tissue paper, flung him to one side and lumbered on all fours through the open door.

On his knees Osorio could still hear the larger bear's roars of pain. Then the sub-machine gun spoke once more. There was quiet. There was a sudden terrified scream from somewhere outside. There was renewed quiet.

Birdsong errupted, but might have been in progress throughout.

Osorio passed out.

2

Steve.

That's my name.

My old man called me Steve after an old black guy who had once worked for him over in Abilene. Old black Steve was as strong as a big mule and Brent said he was the best friend he ever did have. He died in a freak sort of way: under a jacked up truck, looking for a rattling noise, down came the whole thing and crushed him dead, although Brent didn't find him for an hour.

I adored that guy, my old man. I can look at myself and see him in there. Sure, we fought and scrapped and the day I told him I was getting out he hit me one on the jaw and the bump's still there. But there's no rancour. I'm proud of him and I think he's proud of me.

Steve.

You've got to dream.

This is a country where dreams happen, so if you don't have a dream, it can never happen for you.

The Osorios dreamed plenty. Way back in the mists of time, I don't know where exactly we came from, injun mixed with some sort of a conquistador grandad liked to think, but way back there I'm sure the men and women whose flesh and blood I am, I'm sure they dreamed of being free, not just unshackled, but free in the way that money and possessions make you free. Really free.

Steve.

I dreamed big and I was free.

Playing behind the trailer, I dreamed. I dreamed we'd have water when we were dry. I dreamed we'd hit oil, but we moved on. I dreamed when Ma died that Brent would get another Ma and move her in and then we could have some good cookin' again. But he didn't and the cookin' was nothin' good, and there were long nights when me and little sis were all that was there, and sometimes I would have been really scared if it wasn't for the dreaming.

Steve.

All you need is guts and imagination and a little luck. It sounds simple, but look around and see how many other people got all three.

There were days when I was a kid that I worked until I nearly fell down. My limbs were strong, but compared to the steel in Brent's arms, I had just green sap. He pushed me pretty hard and I don't resent that. In the evenings we'd eat out of cans, sometimes we'd go to a diner, have a beer, it wouldn't be long until I'd have my face down on my arms, I couldn't hold my head up, I sometimes went to sleep for hours like that, and he'd laugh at me like I was a baby, he'd laugh out loud, and he'd call my name to see if I could hear. Steve. I'd hear it from wherever I'd gone. In it would come, floating in from out there somewhere. Steve. I could sleep for ever and still hear that name, my name, called in from the waking world, intruding in on my peace, never waking me really, a line into where I'd gone, something tangible in the big infinity, something to hold on to, a comfort, a good sound, I still can hear it now, Steve, it's alright, even though you're asleep there's no more pain, and when you wake the sun will be up, warm on your face, and side by side we'll have another day, Steve, we'll have another day.

3

'Steve.'

Osorio was held and water was sluiced into his mouth.

'You've got to wake up. You must make the effort,' Cheryl said.

The left side of his whole body was numb. With a gigantic act of will he opened his eyes and kept them open. All his left shoulder was covered in a bandage of white silk.

'Where . . . ?'

'The bearded one's dead,' she said. 'The other ran off in blind terror.'

He jerked his head to keep awake. They were still in the pit. Cheryl stood there in her skirt and brassiere; her face was smeared with blood and dirt; the sun beat down hotly.

'We must get to the car,' she said urgently.

Somehow she got him upright, then clutching the gun and inserting her shoulder in under his good side, they swayed out the gate. Osorio looked back at the bodies of the leader and the huge bear. Swarms of flies rose and fell about their wounds.

They began their descent of the mountain. Osorio's head began to clear. At a cool stream he sank down and drank.

'How bad is my shoulder?' he asked.

'I've cleaned it out pretty good,' she replied. 'It's raw but not too deep. With disinfectant and some shots you'll be fine.'

The water seemed to revive Osorio.

'Do you think you could use that gun if you had to?' he asked.

'Steve, I've just shot a seven-foot grizzly,' Cheryl replied.

Osorio winced in pain.

'What we're looking for is still in Otaru,' he said, then continued down the mountain. 'And time isn't on our side.'

Descending through the trees and the rising steam from hot streams was like coming down from another world.

Cheryl knew that if she started to think she was finished.

She tries to guess at that very moment what price was trading in oil.

CHAPTER THIRTY- TWO

1

New York

Friday 15 March 10.15 a.m.

Vince Carpenter picked up the payphone twenty yards from the entrance to NYMEX and punched the number.

'Carpenter,' he said to the broker twenty floors above, 'take a day order. Buy fifty thousand barrels of May oil at ten sixty-six or better.'

'It's sixty-eight traded and bid,' the broker replied.

'I know,' said Vince and hung up.

Walking back into the huge auditorium was like entering a circus of the surreal: each writhing ring with its complement of bawling artistes; performers from some Dali-esque land, exclusively in New York for five and a half hours only.

Vince shouldered through the confusion, making his way to the First Com pitch. Vince was tired. He had woken the night before and been unable to get back to sleep. His mind was involved in continuous evaluation of his personal position in the crude market: short a hundred thousand barrels of the May at an average price of fourteen fifty. You didn't need to be a maths wrangler to work out the profit with oil at ten and a half. Yet the actual realisation had not taken place, oil had never traded below ten sixty-three, and that was a couple of days ago when, like a train coming into Grand Central but stopping unexpectedly within sight of the platform, the market had simply stopped at ten sixty-three, despite the universal expectation that it was headed much further down.

Jay Cox's orders for the huge Man First position were all in there at ten sixty; Max was poised to savage the market at that price. But Vince's personal order was in at ten sixty-two, and when the market had stopped a cent over his limit he had felt little apprehension. He was going to get out with the guts of half a million bucks. The money was firmly committed in Vince's mind: a hundred and fifty grand to be put aside for the kids; a couple of hundred grand for a new house, up the river, they'd seen a place with two acres and a small lake that was still only an hour and a half by train; a trip to Europe; bits and pieces including a boat; half a million got accounted for pretty quickly.

He raised his limit the next day to ten sixty-four. It never traded. Sixty-five traded, but not sixty-four. The same story today: ten sixty-eight trading May oil: Vince trying to buy at sixty-six. That was what was keeping him awake. It was slipping away from him. He looked at the board as he approached oil. Ten sixty-nine just traded. Shit. Should he raise the limit which he'd just given? Relax. This market isn't going anywhere. Still, how could he afford not to take this profit? Five steps from the pit, he made the decision. Make it a market order for half the position, just take it out. He turned back towards the door and walked straight into Benvenuto's floor man.

'Hi, Vince, what d'you make of it?'

'It's goin' down,' Vince said and spread his hands, 'where else has it got to go?'

'That's what I think,' the broker said. 'Did you see the New York Times this morning? The Sheikh of Dubai has cancelled three new 747s he had ordered from Boeing to fly his racehorses around the world. He says with oil at these prices he can't afford such things.'

'My heart bleeds for the guy,' Vince said, 'but if he'd asked me, I'd have had him short and the horses could go first-class.'

Benvenuto's man laughed and slapped Vince on the arm before carrying on for the pit. Vince turned once again for the door.

'Vince!'

Max was at the pitch, holding a phone over his head.

'Suck,' mouthed Max.

Vince pushed through, irritated that Max had spotted him. Ten seventy traded.

'Hi, Jay,' he said.

'Vince, what the fuck's going on down there?' demanded Jay Cox.

'Relax,' Vince said. 'It's having a little run on the upside, but it's done that all the way down.'

'Sixty-nine traded and offered,' roared Max, now on the pit.

'Sixty-nine now offered,' Vince relayed. 'There's nothing to worry about. It's business as usual.'

'It's beginning to look like it's bottomed on the chart,' Cox said.

'Is that what Peterschmidt says?' asked Vince.

'He won't commit himself yet,' answered Cox with more than a hint of irritation, 'but for me it's looking like it's bottomed.'

Vince ran a pencil over the day's trading so far, drawn in by Max on their own chart.

'No matter what way you look at it, Jay,' he said, 'it's still in a dive.'

'Maybe so, but we need to raise our buy limits,' Cox said. 'We're too far off the pace at ten sixty. We need to start hooking them in right now.'

Vince swallowed and his hundred thousand buy order at ten sixty-six with the broker twenty floors overhead came popping up in his mind.

'We've got a very big position, Jay,' he said, 'we don't want to spook this market, there's an awful lot of people very short.'

'It's oversold,' Cox persisted. 'Anything could happen.' The board winked sixty-nine traded and Max roared seventy from the pit.

'Is that seventy traded again?' asked Jay Cox.

'And a seller over,' Vince said.

'You sound like you have a position in there that you're trying to protect for yourself,' said Cox sharply.

Vince's laugh was a little hoarse.

'Wish I had,' he said. 'I guess the job of taking out twenty-eight million barrels for the firm has made me a little nervous, that's all.'

'We're getting out,' said Cox firmly. 'Buy five million for a start at ten seventy or better, right now, understood?'

'Understood,' said Vince. 'I'll be back to you.'

He threw the tie-line back on the shelf and beckoned at Max.

'Seventy traded again,' Max said as he arrived. 'Tony Quacks doing the buying.'

'Quantity?'

'Million barrels.'

Vince blinked. 'Could it be GiltStock again?' he asked.

'It could be the Sheikh of Arabee,' Max replied.

They both heard the trade from the pit at the same time.

'Jeez, seventy-two traded and bid!' Max cried. 'We've got some stops in there!'

'Look, I got to go to the head!' Vince cried.

'Sure,' said Max and shook his head knowingly as he clawed back into the action.

As Vince ran out of the auditorium, ten seventy-two traded again.

2

New York

Friday 10.30 a.m.

Sol Ansbacher sat back in his chair and looked across his size-able office at nothing in particular. The call which he had just concluded had been with a man he had known for twenty years, a lawyer named Henry Ewel, someone who knew how to go for the jugular and whose client was First Manhattan Banking Corporation.

Their conversation, after the small talk, had been to the point.

'Anything you want to tell me about our mutual appointment on Monday?' Henry Ewel asked.

'What should I want to tell you?' Sol enquired.

'I thought that maybe I could be of assistance in some way,' the other man said, then added, 'strictly between us, of course. I mean this thing can be done nice and quietly if your man would, for example, just agree to co-operate and admit his liabilities to my client. Why make life anymore difficult than it is already?'

Sol had smiled at that one. There had been zero contact between himself and Ewel in the six days which had elapsed since Man First had succeeded in pulling back the date of Osorio's bankruptcy hearing to Monday. What the offer of help just made really meant was something like this: have you received instructions from your client? In other words, I know the Feds can't find him, but do you know where he is? Put otherwise, is he going to show on Monday at two-thirty? And if the answer to that question is affirmative, is he going to spring any surprises on my client which might make life uncomfortable for me?

'My instructions are pretty clear,' said Sol enigmatically.

'So he's coming along and you'll defend?' Ewel asked.

'I don't want to say too much out of court, Henry,' Sol said, 'but let's just say that I think your client is far from the snow-white lily that has been presented in this whole affair.' Then he said quickly, 'Look, sorry, but I've got a call coming through I need to take, okay? See you Monday,' and he disconnected.

Like all lawyers, Sol was in it for money. That's what he told himself. He was nearly sixty, happily married, spent at least three months of every year in Palm Beach, soon he'd increase that out to four or five, let the younger bloods in the firm have their heads. Sol's whole life had been one of detached judgement. He'd handled divorce cases years ago, and some criminal law too, where you learned to keep a steel band separating your head from your heart. When he'd moved from Queens into Manhattan in the fifties and become a corporate lawyer, he had found this detachment to be not of less importance. Money was what mattered. In a new client's case, up front. You never let your heart take over or your brains go to work for some poor slob who trailed his ass into your office with a case full of holes and no money.

Sol therefore found it strange at this late stage in a highly successful career to have just given an old colleague an earful of undiluted horse about a case coming up in the Federal Bankruptcy Court in three days' time, where Sol was meant to be representing a man whom he had not heard from for ten days, from whom he had no instructions, who was the subject of a Federal warrant, who had been at the centre of Wall Street's juiciest scandal of the year, and who was undeniably, uncontrovertibly blind bust.

Sol shook his small head in disbelief and looked at the thin file on his desk.

The trouble was, and it amazed Sol to admit it to himself, that even at this late hour, he still believed in Steve Osorio.

CHAPTER THIRTY-THREE

Otaru, Japan

Friday 15 March 8.00 a.m.

His bleeding had stopped but the disinfectant which Cheryl had bought and decanted into his wound was the singularly most painful thing he had ever experienced.

Their dash down the mountainside in the undamaged car had confirmed what Osorio had suspected: they were less than fifty miles from Otaru.

They stopped at a clothes trading stall, just opening and bought jeans and sweat-shirts.

It was eight-thirty when they got to the warehouse.

There was a new guard in the foyer. He frowned as they walked straight in, then flung his hands up as the tall, blonde-haired woman swung the machine-gun on him.

They marched him down the empty corridor. The guard turned once to protest, but the look on Osorio's face made him change his mind.

'There's no one here,' Cheryl said. 'The place is deserted.'

They came to the door which Osorio remembered; the night before there had been another guard behind it. Osorio kicked it open and pushed the uniformed man through.

Their breaths rasped in the empty corridor. They pressed on.

The next door was partially open so that the lights of the laboratory could be seen to be on.

'Careful,' Osorio mouthed.

They jumped through, the terrified guard still ahead of them, his hands on his head.

Osorio blinked. The rows of presses were open whereas last night they had all been closed. He looked at Cheryl, then back at the room. All the laboratory equipment was gone.

'Christ, they've cleaned the place out!' he exclaimed. He ran down the row of empty presses. 'They've taken the records!' he cried.

He shoved past the man, running for the final door, the warehouse. He had forced this door twelve hours before. He stood, terrified to believe. The concrete ceiling of the warehouse. Metal shelves. Rows and rows of them. Totally empty.

'They've cleaned the place out,' Osorio repeated, choking, looking from Cheryl to the guard as if the uncomprehending oriental might be able to help. 'They've taken all the proof.'

Cheryl bit her lip.

'There were hundreds of boxes with core samples here the night before last!' Osorio cried. *'They've removed the proof!'*

Seeing Osorio's ravaged face, hearing his anguished roar, the oriental guard feared the worst for himself and fell trembling to his knees.

It was then that Cheryl saw the discarded book lying wedged at the back of the opened door.

CHAPTER THIRTY - FOUR

1

New York

Monday 18 March 10.55 a.m.

May oil on the screen showed ten seventy-four just traded. Malcolm had known from early on it would be no ordinary day.

Six o'clock had seen Malcolm up and walking the bank of the little tributary he hadn't fished for years. Come to think of it, he hadn't been up to walk at that hour for years either, and that was his only regret as he strode along, scenting all the good things that only happen at that hour. There was a spectacular dawn powering up from behind the hills which completed that part of the valley; birdsong was at full throttle; a trout even rose a foot out of the water for an early fly and Malcolm could see every scale of its long body, glistening like silver-leaf in the sunshine.

Ten seventy-four traded again, a small green digit winking in a black sea.

He came down the Hudson on the train, still drinking in the day, utterly calm and composed despite the earth-shaking nature of what he knew was about to happen. Making money itself was something Malcolm admitted that he had become indifferent to. He had ridden the switchback of hope and despair so often that the prospect which every player dreams of, the Really Big Killing, no longer tantalised him, just remained an image, out of focus, somewhere out there where the sky meets the sea.

So the fact that for a week Malcolm had been painstakingly assembling a long position in oil which was quite mind-blowing in dimension, where a younger, keener man might have felt occasionally giddy, Malcolm sailed flat along the surface, conscious that no matter what happened, his real enjoyment had been in the implementation, the building itself, the brickwork.

Ten seventy-five traded.

He had used all his knowledge, accumulated over forty-three years on Wall Street, to put it together. He had opened accounts with seven different brokers, using variations on his own name and Miss Singer's, and then seven bank accounts for these names, all in different New York banks. He had sat sipping a beer provided by her manservant and listened with mild incredulity as she had given instructions on the phone for each of the new bank accounts to be credited with an initial ten million dollars. Seventy million, just like whistling.

Ten seventy-six traded, then seventy-five, then seventy-six again.

From the tiny office in GiltStock he had started the great task, buying every two cents down as agreed, sometimes in GiltStock's name, sometimes using a new account, sometimes calling Miss Singer to go in herself. Always for a million barrels. Fully margined in cash. The position grew as the market slipped towards ten sixty.

'Where would you start to take in shorts, Mr Finch?' Miss Singer had asked. 'Say you're spectacularly short, and have been for four or five dollars, where would you hook them in?'

Malcolm scratched his belly.

'The market is looking for ten bucks and lower,' he replied eventually. 'Ten bucks will be a major point and every sucker who ever learned to spell short and oil and who knows how to use a telephone will be looking to get out near ten.'

He sipped his beer and saw the old lady in a brilliantly bright red dress looking at him, her head cocked to one side like an exotic bird.

'If I was mega-short,' he continued carefully, 'I'd be getting out long before that point. In fact I'd assume that the *other* smart asses would be looking at ten fifty or thereabouts, so I'd start buying in even before that, like ten sixty.'

'Let's assume we're the ultra bright guys,' said Miss Singer, 'let's say there's no one brighter around. So we've got to out-guess everyone, even the smart ass who's ahead of the posse and who's going to buy at ten sixty.'

Malcolm laughed. 'Okay, I'll go for that,' he said.

'Therefore,' Miss Singer said, her eyes shining, 'it's going to turn somewhere in the sixties, therefore *that's* where we need to complete our business.'

'We've got forty-five milion barrels on board all the way down from ten ninety-six to the present price of ten sixty-eight,' Malcolm said.

'So we complete all our business tomorrow,' Miss Singer said. 'Double up and get everything on board before the markets close.'

Ten seventy-six just traded again. Malcolm had been buying solidly for an hour. It was going to be no ordinary day. He grabbed the phone as it rang.

'Malcolm, it's Tony,' said Tony Quacks.

'Hi, Tony.'

'What gives, Mal?' asked the broker.

'What gives where?' Malcolm responded.

'Come on,' said Tony Quacks, 'there's somethin' happening in oil and I'd bet a brick of gold to a ping-pong ball you know what it is.'

'Swear to God, Tony,' said Malcolm seriously, although his face was beaming from ear to ear. Back at the centre, that's where GiltStock suddenly was, the mover again.

'There are rumours,' Tony Quacks says, 'some of them are crazy. A guy rang me earlier on and told me that Venezuela was going to announce it had run out of oil.'

'Off the wall,' Malcolm said, enjoying himself scandalously.

'Have you seen the volumes that are trading?' asked Tony Quacks. 'They're unbelievable.'

'Unbelievable,' Malcolm grinned.

'I see Steve Osorio somewhere in this,' pressed the broker.

'Steve?' Malcolm gave his sad little laugh. 'If Steve shows up here he risks having the Feds take him away,' he said.

'Well,' Tony Quacks said, 'I just hope that all this oil you bought through us for whoever, I just hope for your sake, this time it goes up.'

'It does look kind of strong this morning, doesn't it?' Malcolm said, and made his cheek pop out with his tongue. 'Sure does,' said Tony Quacks. 'If it goes over ten dollars eighty, a lot of people are goin' to start scrambling like hell. Hey, shit! Ten seventy-seven traded and bid oil! I gotta go!' 'See you, Ton,' Malcolm smiled.

Quietly he dialled a number. 'Seventy-seven traded and bid,' he said softly.

'Hang in there, Mr Finch,' said Miss Singer. 'Now tell me once more *exactly* what young Osorio said when he called.'

2

Rotterdam, Holland

Monday 5.00 p.m. European time

Piet Seydlitz would normally be on his way home. But thirty years in the oil business and you learned the days to take off early and the days to sit tight. In a business where the cargo you had just bought might tomorrow be worth substantially more or less due to international incidents completely outside your control, you didn't panic easily, but you used the tools of your trade to finesse the profits which you daily coaxed from the black liquid which each day washed and slopped around the world.

As a trader of oil, Piet sat in an office in Rotterdam's Coolsingel and bought and sold tankers of oil as they sailed from the Middle East to Rotterdam, or oil already in tank in Rotterdam, or oil on the sea or in tank or in barge anywhere in the world where the seller was someone reputable and the price was right.

Piet's customers were the oil majors, worldwide, always hungry for a cheap cargo. He found himself a customer at a price, went and found oil somewhere below that price, then flogged it on.

However, in some instances, if oil looked a bargain, Piet's

Rotterdam oil house bought the oil before they had a customer and simultaneously hedged the transaction, which is to say, sold it forward, mainly on the New York Mercantile Exchange.

Now Piet lit his twenty-fifth tiny Dutch cigar of the day and hit a button which put him through to Joost Van Ulzen, his direct superior who worked from an office on the floor below.

'*Heeb je de olieprijzen gezien?*' Piet asked. 'You've seen oil?'

'Ten eighty has just traded on the May,' said Joost, reading from his desk screen. 'What do you think?'

'I think there's something happening,' Piet answered. 'I'm up in the apple tree and I feel the *takken*, the branches shaking.'

'What's our position?'

Piet sucked at his cigar.

'We're short five million barrels on NYMEX,' he said, smoke pouring from his nostrils. 'We put them on to cover the three Kuwaiti cargoes we bought five days ago.'

'You want to lift them?' asked Joost, knowing exactly the answer.

'We may have to be long overnight,' Piet responded.

Joost Van Ulzen laughed.

'It wouldn't be the first time,' he said. '*Ja akkoord.* Go ahead.'

Piet picked up another phone and punched a thirteen digit number.

'First Com,' came the response with a blare of noise.

'Hi, Vince,' said Piet cheerfully. 'I've got a buy order for you.'

3

New York

11.30 a.m.

Cristy's head was clear, much clearer than it had been two hours before.

At nine she had awoken, fully dressed and groggy. She took a step towards the window, then changed her mind and stood for fifteen minutes in the shower. Too much imagination, that was the problem, too eager to see old ghosts at every turn. After the shower she had eaten an enormous breakfast and felt immeasurably better. She was a morning person, like all the Osorios, she remembered grandfather that way, cracking the joints of his fingers impatiently as he waited for his workman to show.

Since she didn't want to rush into work, arriving late and flustered, Cristy had dressed in jeans and a thicknit and strolled up to Riverside Park. If she called in she'd get all her messages, get embroiled, when what she wanted now was a morning to herself of total peace.

Sun nearly warm, some squirrels playing, a lovely view across the river. Cristy sat alone on a wooden bench. For over an hour she drank in the sun, wondering about Steve and oil and what was going to happen. Like a car nosing over the edge of a cliff, oil looked set to crash through ten dollars a barrel. Steve. Come on home, big brother, and let me write this thing.

Her apartment was a five or seven minute direct walk. Instead, drawn by something she could not identify, Cristy walked north through Riverside Park for fifteen minutes, eventually coming out at the point where Claremont Avenue runs into Tiemann Place and 125th Street. This was the route she took each evening from the subway; the route she had taken the evening before.

She turned into Claremont Avenue and began the walk uphill. Cars were parked as usual along the kerb, no spaces free. Kids played. What had she seen the evening before? Absolutely nothing. Irrational fear. Silly. Where had the grey sedan been? Around here on the uphill avenue. Right. There. Cristy stood rooted. Ten yards away, on the other side of the road, a man was looking fixedly at her from the open back window of a grey car.

Cristy screamed. She turned and ran downhill. She saw a yellow cab cruising down Claremont Avenue. She jumped into the roadway, her hands waving at the same instant she heard the grey car's tyres screech as it left the kerb. The cab came to a jolting stop a yard from her.

'Hey, lady, you're crazy!'

Cristy dragged the door open.

'I'm off duty!' the cabby cried.

'This is an emergency,' she gasped.

'Where do you want to go?' asked the man, an Hispanic, his eyes wide.

'Away,' she panted. 'Downtown.'

'Downtown,' the man sighed and hit his meter.

She made herself look back, but she could no longer see the grey car. She shook violently as they stopped at the lights for Broadway. They eased downtown. As if a shroud was winding round and round her, Cristy felt herself immobilised by terror. She looked out the cab window: every noise was sinister and ugly. Traffic was six or seven deep behind them . . . There was a grey sedan over there . . . STOP! . . . She wanted to scream.

'Lady, where do you want to go?'

Cristy blinked. How could she go home? She could visualise her apartment. Empty. She would have to open the door, then lock it behind her. She could ask the porter to come up and do it. What about the fire-escape outside? Easy for anyone to have slipped in. There were walk-in cupboards big enough for a man to hide in.

'Lady, where to?' the driver repeated.

'Don't stop, drive on,' Cristy blurted, scanning left and right until she was dizzy.

'I told you, I'm meant to be off duty.'

'Drive!' Cristy cried.

'What kind of an emergency is it if you don't know where you want to go to?' the driver asked.

The police? What could she tell them? A strange man looked at me from a car? She bit the back of her hand. It was all her imagination. She made herself look out. Just normal traffic. No grey sedan. She was going crazy.

'LADY!'

Cristy jumped. She realised they were stopped.

'This is as far as I go,' the driver said. 'That'll be five dollars.'

The cab pulled away; Cristy saw that she had been dropped outside Columbia University. She climbed the steps. The wide gravelled forecourt of Columbia crunched underfoot, students walking, some hand in hand, she had to get to a telephone, to call someone. Bill. She'd call Bill. Bill would come up for her. She was nearer the main building. She had done a course in journalism here years ago. She tried to remember where the phones were. She couldn't think. There was no telephone she could see, so she walked purposefully across a hall, towards a corridor. Around a corner, two phones were both occupied. There were stairs. She thought she remembered phones up there. She was going to chicken out. She couldn't go up. She had to. Ascending, step by step, looking back down to the hall, by the curving stairs, not many people . . .

'AAAAH!'

Cristy slammed back to the wall at the top of the stairs. The man into whom she had walked as she looked behind, stepped forward solicitously.

'Are you . . .?'

'I'm fine,' Cristy panted, 'I'm sorry,' then she turned and hurried on, her clothes quite wet, stuck to her belly and the small of her back. She was in a corridor, no windows, dimly lighted, empty of people, walls with enormous paintings, darkened with age, wood panelled, wood underfoot, and telephones, two of them, right at the end, two cubicles, unoccupied. Fifteen paces. No sounds anywhere. Ten. She began looking for money. The phones were in a sort of recess. She had remembered them right. Shaking uncontrollably, Cristy put down her bag, breathed in and out with purposeful regularity, thumbed in a nickel and took three attempts to punch out Bill Warner's direct number.

'Bill Warner,' said the familiar voice.

'Bill,' said Cristy, suddenly ridiculously relieved. 'Thank God. It's Cristy.'

'Cristy? Where are you?'

Cristy swallowed and tried to stop the shivers which had now come. 'I'm up in Columbia,' she gasped. 'I can't explain, but I need to see someone, I need to talk.'

She heard the footfall and dropped the phone out of raw fright. The outline was at the end of the corridor, no doubt, same shape although she couldn't see his face. She opened a door blindly and ran the length of another corridor. This one was narrower, empty, long, how many times in dreams had she ran along such corridors, except now, unlike in dreams, it was coming to an end. There were stairs of marble and she flung herself down them, catching the handrail with her left hand, feeling her flesh caught by steel knobs set in the wood. She was lost now but she kept running. Through a large room with notices, a man smoking a cigarette, she fancied she could hear feet on the stairs she had just taken.

303

She ran through a door, stopped, chest heaving, realised she was back outside, half-ran, half-walked back for the traffic and Broadway. She looked behind, thought she saw someone move behind a tree. Cristy took the steps down to Broadway in twos. It had begun to drizzle and she vainly waved taxis, then began to run uptown, people on the sidewalk looking at her. Her feet hurt now, so she kicked her shoes off and ran with them in her hands. She had to phone Bill again. Running, she tried to look back and find a coin all at the same time. She dropped one shoe, then as she tried to grab it, dropped the other. At 120th Street she saw a phone, a hundred yards east under the dark north wall of Columbia. The rain in her face she ran for it, oblivious of wet feet, of her hair plastered down on her face, of her heart hammering at a rate she had never known. Looking back she had an imperfect view of the rain-swept street, but no one was running like her, there was no one creeping up behind.

Thirty yards from the warm payphone she began to walk. She had abandoned all rational thought and had to get back on course. Her money was out as she reached the phone booth. She concentrated on pressing Bill's number correctly. She was concentrating so hard that the hand took almost a second to register. It snaked in over her shoulder, terminating the call.

Cristy whirled. Her right hand went to her bag. She saw a mottled face, brown eyes. Her fingers closed on the cold handle.

The explosion was outrageous for such a small gun. It propelled her assailant backwards as if on wires and left a smoking hole in her bag.

There was the sound of people running.

Cristy threw down her bag and began to vomit.

4

here was a lull in trading. After two hours and fifteen minutes
tivity during which May oil, the most traded month, had risen
price from ten dollars sixty-eights cents a barrel to ten eighty-
o and then slipped back to its present level of ten eighty, there
as now a brief pause, an involuntary time-out, during which the
t became unusually quiet.

Vince picked up the phone, looked around him and dialled
e number. He didn't dare go outside to the payphone. This
arket was on a knife's edge and could go either way.

'Carpenter,' he mumbled.

'Still working those hundred thousand barrels,' said the bro-
r seventeen floors up. 'It's not easy. Volume's thin and there
en't that many sellers around.'

'Raise the limit,' Vince said. 'Hook them in at ten eighty or
tter.'

'I'll try,' responded the broker, 'but you may not get on at
at price.'

Out of the corner of his eye Vince could see Max approaching.

'Sure, sure,' Vince said loudly, 'I'll be right back to you,' and
ung up.

Max's head was shaking.

'Gone dead, all of a sudden,' he said. 'I'm afraid to say any-
ing out there – I get the impression this market is waiting for
mething.'

'We've been in freefall for ten dollars,' Vince said tersely,
wenty if you go back to last year. There's so much oil around
at no one wants it. Yet this morning we get a lousy twelve cent
se and all of a sudden everyone's going around with End of the
cking World written all over their faces.'

Max gave his usual shrug.

'It could be oversold,' he said.

They both turned as the pit erupted. Max was up there in two
ounds.

'Seventy-nine trading oil!' he shouted down.

Vince nodded I told you so. He hoped the business bein done was for him. He watched while, as a wind rises and falls o a lake, the noise level in crude oil again began to build. H could hear Max bellowing, pulling in the First Com position, li tle by little.

'Seventy-nine traded and a seller!' Max bawled.

Vince smiled. Everything was alright again. He shook his hea as he listened to the wall of sound. A twelve cent rise and they a behaved like it was the end of the fucking world.

5

New York

12.15 p.m.

Cristy felt exhausted but calm. The office she sat in was dirty an cramped. There was a glass-panelled door and outside it th noise of the precinct station continued unabated. As Cris looked out, a man in handcuffs was led to a holding cage, th door opened and Bill Warner came in. He appeared to be ha ing difficulty breathing. He removed his glasses, wiped then put them back on again.

'Are you alright?' he managed to say.

She nodded gamely.

'Look,' Bill said, 'I've heard about the experience you've bee through, and I know it's apalling, but I've got to talk to yo about something.'

Cristy looked at him, not knowing what to expect.

'Your brother,' Bill said, sitting down. 'He showed up twent four hours ago at the U.S. embassy in Tokyo.' Bill shook h head as if he couldn't believe it himself. 'He called our corr spondent there and said he had a log book from Hokkaido C in Otaru which shows the whole Jap oil find is a fake. He the challenged the Oil Ministry in Tokyo to deny it.' Bill moistene is lips. 'An official called Ziro Takahashi at first denied the hole story, but then went home, sat in his bath tub, and cut his rists. Oil stocks are expected to collapse when Tokyo opens ter today.'

Cristy's face registered no surprise. Instead she reached to her ocket and brought out some sheets of paper.

'I've already written it, Bill,' she said.

Bill Warner read it, looking progressively as if he might burst. The door opened and a detective put his head in.

'Miss Osorio's lawyer is here,' he said.

'We're nearly through,' Bill said to him. He looked down gain at her article. 'This is . . . sensational!' he said.

'It's true,' Cristy responded.

'You realise what this means?' Bill said. 'You realise what this going to do to the market?'

'I have a fair idea,' Cristy said.

Bill did his breathing routine again. He stood up.

'This we're going to go with,' he said grimly.

'Don't let me down,' said Cristy in a small voice.

'You just leave this one to me,' Bill said. At the door he raightened his tie, then turned and winked at her as the detec- ve ushered in her lawyer.

6

New York

2.00 p.m.

utch Tremaine threw the file on the copper table and snorted t Jacob Landey.

'Fire the bastards,' he said.

Landey made little thrusting motions with his head.

'We can't do that, Dutch, not without a stockholders meet- ig,' he said. 'Also, I've spoken with Maldonado this morning nd he reckons that any public row with our auditors would be

307

very adverse for our stock.'

Tremaine stood up and began pacing.

'If it wasn't for First Com's performance,' he said, 'we'd be reporting the bank's first quarter loss in over thirty years and all because of GiltStock.'

'Something else has happened that you should know,' said Landey, wincing.

Tremaine's desk intercom buzzed.

'Mr Tremaine?'

'I told you I didn't want interruptions,' Tremaine snapped. He turned and glowered at Landey. 'Go on.'

'There was some sort of incident in Tokyo yesterday,' Landey said. 'A Government official, in the Ministry for Energy, killed himself. They're expecting a huge fall in oil exploration stocks. Like a twenty percent fall. We've got some big positions in there, Dutch.'

'How much will it cost us?' asked Tremaine, his mouth ugly.

Landey took a very deep breath.

'The fall is probably just temporary,' he replied shakily, 'but we could be looking at thirty million bucks.'

'*Thirty million?*' shouted Tremaine. 'We've lost thirty million dollars in the Tokyo stock market?'

'It's still a paper loss, Dutch,' said Man First's president, 'the market could recover.'

'Just hold everything for a minute,' said Tremaine venomously, 'you're sitting there and telling me that someone in the Jap Government kills himself and the oil sector falls twenty per cent? What's the connection?'

'Like I say, it's not yet clear . . . ' Landey muttered.

'This is too much,' Tremaine murmured, running his hand through his hair. 'That idiot Pappas said we should have some of the action out there, but this . . . ' He slammed the switch of a desk intercom. 'Get Pappas,' he snarled.

'He's actually right here, Mr Tremaine,' came the secretary's voice. 'He says he needs to see you urgently.'

Tremaine straightened as Joseph Pappas walked into the office. He looked grey.

'I've just heard about this Tokyo fuck up . . .' Tremaine began.

'Can we leave that for a moment, sir?' Pappas said.

'Leave it?' Tremaine said, his eyes narrowing.

'Sir, Man First shares are down over a dollar and offered ower,' Pappas said. 'We've been trying to get through to tell ou. There's a story going around that we're going to post a whopper of a loss for the quarter.'

'And?' Tremaine hissed, knowing there was more.

'Wells Fargo just unloaded a million units of our stock at $36 share,' Pappas said. 'All we can find out is that the buyer is an ffshore trust fund based in Panama.'

'Eller?' asked Tremaine in little more than a whisper.

'I doubt it, sir,' Pappas replied. 'If it was Eller, I think he ould have shown his hand by now.'

Tremaine filled his big chest.

'Right,' he said, 'you meet fire with fire. First Com take all heir profits out of the oil market right now. We come out with a lazing performance for the quarter and worry about future uarters another day.' He hit the intercom. 'Jay Cox,' he napped.

He sat there, his eyes darting from Landey to Pappas.

'I'll want to hear some pretty plausible stories about this okyo fuck up,' he said.

'Sir?' said the voice on the intercom.

'Yeah, Jay you there?' Tremaine said.

'Sir,' said Tremaine's secretary, 'Mr Cox is watching some-hing on tv. He'll call you back in a moment.'

Tremaine blinked in puzzlement and looked at his watch.

'Ask what channel he's watching,' he ordered.

He got up as he waited for the reply and went to a walnut-onted cabinet which he slid open and he switched on the tv set here.

'Channel six, sir,' said the voice from the intercom.

As the other two men stood to see the tv screen, Dutch remaine pressed six with the yet unclear but already awesome ealisation that today was going to be one that he would long emember.

New York

2.30 p.m.

Sol Ansbacher felt isolated. He sat alone on the polished wood
en bench, his briefcase on the table before him and once agai
looked back to the doors of the courtroom: the bored cop wit
the big roll of gut standing back there yawned, removed his ca
and scratched his head.

Across at another table bending under the weight of files So
could see Henry Ewel, Man First's lawyer, in conference with n
less than three assistants. Immediately behind them Sol coul
recognise Dean Abercrombie, the comptroller of Man First an
a heavily shaven younger man with dark hair.

The clock on the wall behind the judge's bench was on
where time advanced by small jerks of the big hand. As So
looked at it another minute jerked by, the door to the judge'
chambers in the rear wall opened and a small man in a blac
gown emerged.

'All rise.'

Once more Sol looked back, but now the big-bellied cop wa
closing the outer doors. Sitting, Sol shook his head and pre
pared himself.

'The Federal Bankruptcy Court, His Honour, Judge Feli
Rheingold presiding,' the usher intoned.

The judge was the no-nonsense type. Severe black-rimme
glasses dominated a sallow, middle-aged face.

'This is a petition in bankruptcy,' the usher continued, 'th
petitioner, the First Manhattan Banking Corporation of Ne
York, the debtor, Steven Osorio, last known at 177 East 75t
Street.'

The usher sat. The judge turned without expression to th
team of lawyers and Henry Ewel got to his feet.

'Your Honour, I represent the petitioner,' Ewel said and sa
again.

The judge's gaze moved to Sol.

'If it pleases your Honour, I represent the debtor,' mumble
Sol.

Ewel rose once more.

'Your Honour, what you are being asked to judge this afternoon is, I am afraid, nothing more or less than an uncontested case of personal bankruptcy. It is also a sad case in which you will hear that a once respected member of the financial community, Steven Osorio, took advantage of the position of trust he enjoyed with my client, one of this city's most respected banks, to support a wild and ill-judged commodity position which essentially he had taken as a result of an infatuation with a female client.'

'Your Honour!'

'Mr Ansbacher?'

'Your Honour, I must strenuously object,' began Sol, the colour rising in his cheeks.

The doors of the courtroom burst open and everyone turned. There was commotion, people calling out. The judge glared angrily and raised his gavel. The cop struggled to reclose the doors and as he did so two people ducked into the courtroom under his arms.

Sol saw a woman, in her late twenties, tall with a strong, attractive face. Sol saw a man, familiar to him, his face drawn, his left arm in a sling. Sol stared as the man nodded his way.

'Your Honour, I'm Steve Osorio, I'm sorry I'm late.'

Everyone in the courtroom, except the judge, was on their feet.

'I accept your apology, Mr Osorio,' said the judge.

'I have something to give the court,' Osorio said.

The judge looked over his glasses at Osorio, then indicated towards Sol; Osorio handed over an envelope then, arm around his companion, he stood watching.

Sol took the envelope, ripped it, blinked, then stood.

'Permission to approach the bench,' he said, unable to contain the cinemascope grin spreading on his face.

The judge nodded and beckoned Henry Ewel to approach as well.

'What've you got there, Sol?' the judge asked irritably.

'It looks to me like a teller's cheque made out to the plaintiff here for seventy-two million dollars,' Sol beamed.

'Henry?' the judge said.

Henry Ewel made a face and looked at Sol. 'My client may

also insist on an undertaking from your client that no suits are contemplated against the bank. After all your client . . . '

'Don't waste my time. Henry!' snapped the judge. 'Is this the money owed to you or not?'

'Well, yes it it,' Henry Ewel answered.

Judge Rheingold brought his gavel down with a resounding thwack.

'Parties have resolved their differences,' he announced, 'the court rises.'

'All rise.'

Sol turned from the bench. Everyone was still on their feet but Osorio and the girl were striding for the now opened doors. Sol saw crowds of people in the corridor outside the court, the bursts from camera flashes and the arc lights of a tv unit. He shook his head in wonder.

He had never for a moment doubted Steve Osorio.

8

New York

2.45 p.m.

Jay Cox had insisted that no money be spared on the First Com boardroom. A west coast designer had been set at large and the result was an enormous, country club-type lounge, with wooden beams and leather and a vast fireplace and windows through which the only disappointment was that you overlooked the back of Morgan Guaranty and not a four-ball putting out on the eighteenth.

On his own Cox stood watching the television screen. The newsreader, although smiling, was also listening; now he turned to his viewers.

The newsreader: 'Now we're ready to go live to downtown Manhattan, to the Federal Bankruptcy Court where our reporter Jim Cook has that story we've been promising you. Jim?'

A new image filled the screen, that of a man in a Burberry surrounded by a lot of people.

The reporter: 'Thanks, Paul. I'm down here in the Federal Bankruptcy Court, where we've all just witnessed about the biggest surprise of the year. Rumours have been flying all morning concerning the whereabouts of GiltStock's Steve Osorio, wanted by Federal Attorneys on charges of irregularities in the oil market and also due here to defend his own bankruptcy petition.

'Osorio made a dramatic last-minute appearance in court and handed the judge a cheque for seventy-two million dollars, the exact amount he owes the petitioner, First Manhattan Bank.

'But even more sensational, Osorio has just released a statement which challenges Japanese oil authorities to deny that their oil find in the Ishikari Field is either non-commercial or non-existent.

'He's right here with me. Steve?'

As Osorio's face joined that of the reporter, Jay Cox covered the space to the boardroom table in a single bound and punched the NYMEX button. He drew back from the phone as noise at pain level hit his ear. He transferred to the loudspeaker and noted May oil on the screen at ten eighty-four.

'*Vince!*'

'Right here, Jay,' said Vince, 'yes, I've heard it, so Steve Osorio says Japan has no oil, so everyone here's gone fuckin' crazy, so what? Use this rise to sell more, Jay, don't be panicked . . .'

'Did you get those five out?' Cox hissed.

'No way,' Vince protested, 'you gave me a limit of seventy and it's jumped twelve cents in the last five minutes. Shit, eighty-six just traded!'

'Increase the five million to ten and buy them in for whatever you have to pay,' Cox commanded.

'Are you sure you want to do that, Jay?' Vince asked. 'A lot of this buying has come from Europe in the last thirty minutes. What do those guys know that we don't?'

'For Christ's sake!' Cox rasped.

'We'll do our best, Jay,' Vince said. 'Just remember, it took a lot more than a few hours to put this position together.'

Cox hung up and found himself looking at the screen with his mouth open. He actually leaned forward and rapped the glass with his knuckles, but May oil at eleven dollars a barrel even just winked at him. Cox lunged to the phone.

'*Vince!*'

'Eleven dollars traded and bid!' cried Vince.

'*Are we out?*' asked Cox, individual blood vessels throbbing in his neck.

'Of course we're not out!' Vince cried. 'I bought a half a million barrels at eleven, but there just aren't any sellers down here anymore!'

'You are to pay whatever price is necessary to close our entire position, is that absolutely understood?' Cox said, giving each word emphasis.

'I'll try,' Vince said, 'but the rumours doing the rounds down here are world-class crazy. I just heard that the *Journal* is coming out with a story which supports Osorio's allegations.'

'Keep buying and call me back,' said Cox, wishing he was someplace very far away.

He switched off Vince and hit the button to his secretary.

'Tell Jean-Paul Peterschmidt I need him in here,' he ordered.

Jay Cox valued his ability to be cool. Although he could see eleven dollars and four cents a barrel now trading for May oil on the screen, he walked behind his desk, over to the circle of plump leather chairs and sank into one, elbows on the leather arms, his finger tips supporting his chin.

Twenty-seven million barrels of oil sold short. Held through an intricate, international web. Each cent that oil went up meant a loss of two hundred and seventy thousand dollars. Somewhere deep in Cox's brain a nightmare scenario was ticking over: an almost childhood fantasy of terror where you can never get away from the monster: it was to be locked into a commodity with a huge position and to be unable to get out. He had a huge position. In oil. They weren't getting out. Cox felt an itch on the inside of his wrists and looked down to see little rivers of perspiration coursing from his palms.

'Mr Peterschmidt is out here, sir,' sang Cox's girl.

'Tell him come in,' said Cox, standing up and wiping his hands down his trousers. He tried to stop himself swallowing as the screen for May oil changed to eleven dollars and ten cents almost playfully.

Jean-Paul Peterschmidt came loping in, stacks of books under

314

his arm. Whilst his long hair and *dégagé* appearance had once seemed appropriate for Wall Street's hottest chartist, now Cox viewed him with unconcealed contempt.

'What's oil going to do?' Cox snapped without preamble.

The Frenchman went into shrug, put down his things and slowly opened out an enormous chart showing oil's price movements.

'We're into new territory,' he said mournfully.

'A clear break out of the downtrend?' Cox asked.

'Hard to say,' replied Peterschmidt. 'It's obviously going up.'

They both turned to the screen and watched eleven eleven trade.

'What's a crucial number?' Cox rasped. 'Where is the game for the bears definitely over?'

'I guess if oil went limit up today,' replied Peterschmidt, 'and then opened a further limit up tomorrow, that's the high twelves, you would start thinking major reversal.'

'Mr Cox, can you speak with Vince?' asked the secretary.

Moistening his lips, Cox turned on the loudspeaker and connected himself to NYMEX.

'Jay!'

Three hundred people screaming at the same time make a lot of noise.

'I'm listening,' said Cox, feeling dread.

'You won't believe this,' Vince shouted over the din, 'but oil is eleven forty bid!'

Part of Cox, the cool, thinking part, inclined his head to its usual angle and began a rational analysis of this information; another part, the part where the nightmares resided, began to go haywire.

'Eleven forty?' he managed to say.

'The screens are running half a minute behind!' Vince bawled. 'We've got three million barrels out, but every mother who ever sold a barrel of oil is now trying to buy back!'

Jay Cox looked wildly at Peterschmidt; the Frenchman had rolled out his lower lip. Jay Cox's jaw went from side to side and little specks of white spittle appeared around his mouth.

'Carpenter!' he hissed.

'Eleven forty-one traded and bid oil!' came Vince's voice. 'Jesus, I've never seen anything like this!'

315

'I swear you'll never work another day on Wall Street . . .'
Cox snarled.

At that moment the boardroom doors burst open and Dutch
Tremaine stood there, chest heaving.

'Are we out?'

A frozen tableau: the big man with the white hair in front of
the open doors, waiting for his reply; outside, the girl peering
in; Cox, his oval head inclined, something twitching over one
eye; the Frenchman, lip rolled out, eyes like a dog who hasn't
been fed.

'ARE WE OUT?'

'We're getting out,' Cox tried to say, then realised he hadn't
been on sound, and repeated, 'we're getting out.'

'Meaning?' Tremaine asked.

'We're out three million barrels, working the balance,' Cox
answered and tried not to look at the screen.

'Jesus Christ Almighty, have you any idea what's happening?'
cried Dutch Tremaine. 'Osorio is saying there's no oil in Japan!
Gig Hollis who's on our board is also close to *The Wall Street
Journal.* Some bitch has written a story claiming the same thing
and they're running it in the morning as their lead.'

'Eleven forty-four traded!' came Vince's cry.

'What does Osorio know?' Cox managed to say.

Tremaine was trying to get it under control. He lowered his
head and looked up at Cox with eyes that strained to leap from
beneath bushy brows.

'Man First shares have fallen to $30 dollars,' he panted. *'I
want those oil profits! I want them!'*

'Everyone is trying to buy, Dutch,' Cox said. 'We're doing our
best, but we can't do the impossible.' He turned to the pande-
monium coming from the little box on his desk. 'Vince! I've got
Mr . . .'

'Bought a million barrels, Jay,' cried an exhausted Vince, 'but
we're sending it up. Sellers are asking stupid numbers now and
they're getting them.'

'We mustn't send it into limit,' Cox said.

'Jeez, Jay, I'm not God Almighty!' Vince protested. 'I never
went for this ten dollar a barrel shit! Why don't you ask that
dumb fuck Tremaine how we get out? He pushed us in here!'

Cox turned to the bank chairman.

316

'I'm sorry, Dutch . . . '

'What are the other options?' Tremaine snarled, ignoring what had been said. 'How else do we cover this fucking thing?'

Cox closed his eyes.

'London is closed,' he said, trying to think it through, 'so we can't trade there. We're short of oil, so we could try and buy physical cargoes, oil in tank, oil on barge, oil in pipeline.'

'Do it! Do it!' Tremaine shouted.

'Eleven fifty-six just traded!' shrieked Vince.

Trembling, Jay Cox picked up a phone. For the first time since he could remember his mind was a total wipe, he had zero idea of the next step, brain-wise he was down.

'Jesus!'

Seeing what was happening, Tremaine flung the broker aside and grabbed the phone.

'Get me Pappas!' he bellowed.

'Mr Tremaine?'

Dutch Tremaine whirled around; the dark face of William Maldonado was looking at him with concern.

'Whatayuwant?'

'Sir,' exclaimed Maldonado, out of breath, 'I've been looking for you everywhere, I wanted to try and warn you.'

'Warn me?'

'Sir, you should be aware of something,' the bank's lawyer said.

Dimly, the big banker was aware of other people coming into the outside office, too many of them, he thought. He clung to the phone as if to life.

'Pappas,' said a voice on the other end.

'Our shares are trading at $27 right now sir,' said Maldonado gently, 'but you should know that Durst Bank have made a bid at $35 a share for our entire capital,' Maldonado said quietly.

Dutch Tremaine gasped.

'Jay!'

Tremaine saw Cox turn to the desk.

'Limit up oil, Jay,' said Vince, almost in a whisper, no need to shout now with the market closed.

'And . . . ?' Cox said.

'We got another million out on the limit,' Vince said, 'but the rest will have to wait until tomorrow.'

'Dutch.'

317

Jacob Landey had walked into the room.

'We've got some problems, Jacob,' Tremaine began.

'We sure have, Dutch,' said Landey with uncharacteristic assurance. He took the phone from the big man's hand and handed it to the staring Frenchman. 'Most of the board are out here, Dutch. We want you to come to a meeting.'

For a moment a flame flashed in the old eyes.

'Like right now, Dutch,' said Landey in a voice of steel.

Jay Cox watched in astonishment as the man who had recently burst into the room dissolved and was replaced by an elderly figure, suddenly stooping and shuffling as he was helped out by Maldonado.

'And Cox.'

Jay Cox turned.

'From this moment, you don't buy a bagel without clearing it with me, is that understood?' snapped Landey.

Jay Cox nodded. He was looking not at Landey, but over his shoulder, to the screen. He laughed stupidly and looked at Landey, then back at what he saw.

Although May oil was locked at eleven sixty-eight, limit up, the spot position, unfettered by limit restrictions, was trading at thirteen and a half dollars a barrel.

In the outside room, Cox's secretary had started to cry.

9

New York

3.00 p.m.

The silence was overwhelming. It was the silence of hundreds of people standing around, talking in normal voices under the unmoving digital price board. Men and women, mostly in their early twenties, stood chatting quietly around the crude oil pit, now empty of staff, oddly decrepit and strewn with the litter of earlier business. In the hundreds of booths where normally business was screamed back and forth, people sat disconsolately, unsure as to how they should behave now that the engine which powered everything had abruptly ceased. Even in the adjoining pits where coffee was traded, and platinum, and palladium, and gold and silver, activity seemed unnaturally curtailed as if the floor as a whole was holding it's breath for its most famous pit to re-open.

He had walked from the courthouse, leaving them all behind. Although his shoulder hurt like hell, he had refused any more pain killers, preferring a totally clear head to witness with relish what he knew he was going to see once in his lifetime and once only.

He had floated. Up Wall Street. Across Broadway. Seeing no one. Smiling with every floating step. The hugeness of the Twin Towers, their shadow, enveloped him.

Everyone has their place in history. Some big, some small. Old grandpa had his place, he passed along something in his blood to Brent, Brent is still making history way down there in the dust and heat, he passed it on to me.

The big elevator opened its doors and took him upwards.

No hard feelings, little fella? He shook my hand after he hit me. Good that, taught me to bury the rancour when you'd let the steam off. No hard feelings about anyone, not even Carly, just memories there, kind of sad ones, funny they should be sad since we had such good times together.

He walked from the elevator to the doors of NYMEX. As one, fifteen hundred faces turned to him. He began to walk.

No cries, no storms, not that this is the end of all troubles, no way, there's so much to be done, but for now there's a bewildering calm. I remember the night Sis came into the world. Wasn't all that long ago. Brent took me outside to the donkey pump, away from the caravan where our mother was yelling so loud that Brent would have had to take me to Houston if I wasn't to hear her. Later when she was through shouting and the midwife from Abilene came out to the door and smiled, Brent caught my hand and led me over. I remember that moment in time, I recall it maybe once a week, it'll always be there. The sky was black, every star there is was out, and we were there, a little group, happy, but what I remember most of all was the silence.

He cleaved through calm waters, black hair licking over white

319

collar, skin with the perpetual tan, eyes with a vital lustre. He walked with the assurance which comes from right, a man returned to his own ground, unhesitating, secure.

'Steve!'

Vince Carpenter was the first. He ran across the silent floor and shook Osorio's hand.

'I saw you on tv,' Vince said, 'but to see you back here – it's . . . it's just something else.'

'Thanks,' said Osorio. 'I guess you've had quite a day down here.'

Vince shook his head despondently.

'You wouldn't believe it,' he sighed, 'you honestly wouldn't believe it.'

Osorio's eyes were dancing.

'Yes I would,' he replied.

CHAPTER THIRTY-FIVE

New York

Monday 4.00 p.m.

Central Park basked in a sudden, unexpected warmth. All at once sunlight bathed everything, made the grass shine, brought people out, reflected on the face of the lake and caused the birds in the bushes and the trees to sing louder.

Sunlight streamed in through the elegant windows of the high apartment. It picked out the polished black wood of the Steinway grand, the gleaming silver on an antique table and the champagne glasses on the butler's tray as he quietly presented them, one by one. On a side-table, a market monitor winked.

'My God, look at oil!' Cheryl exclaimed. 'Fourteen dollars a barrel just traded on the spot month!'

'You should see what's happening in the physical market,' Malcolm said. 'It's going crazy. There's been a knee-jerk panic worldwide that's going to get worse in the short term.'

'What will happen to oil futures, Mr Finch?' asked Miss Singer.

Malcolm scratched his face. 'It's the kind of scenario that represents the best and worst in people's dreams,' he replied. 'For a lot of people who thought selling oil was the fast route to Fat City it's going to be a very expensive few days, that I can guarantee.'

'I understand there's an article in a certain paper tomorrow that we're not to miss,' said the old lady mischeviously.

They all looked at Cristy.

'I hope you enjoy it,' she said. She turned to Malcolm. 'What will they do in Japan after this?' she asked. 'Will we ever find out what really went on?'

Malcolm shook his head.

'They'll close ranks,' he said. 'They'll close them so tight that nobody – and that means nobody – will see inside. They'll essentially do nothing. The people who took the thing too far, who are now an embarrassment, they'll simply fade away.'

'You don't think they'll lose a lot in this market turnaround?' Cheryl asked.

'No way,' Malcolm answered. 'They achieved their objective when Saleem got fired – and that was three dollars above where oil is now. What they didn't bargain on was Durst Bank getting so much out of control.'

Miss Singer was dressed in a blouse of shimmering silver. She took her glass and raised it in the direction of the flickering market monitor.

'I was going to propose a toast to oil,' she said, 'but I really think that would be crass. Who wants to drink to something that comes out of a hole in the ground?'

'Or from out of a hole in the sea,' Cheryl said.

They laughed, Malcolm the loudest, a rich happy laugh which went on after the others had ended and then made them all start again. He looked at his frothing glass. 'Thank God I don't need oil,' he said. 'I come in by train and we burn wood in the winter.'

The three women burst out laughing again.

'We could drink to free markets,' Cheryl ventured.

'Or free spirits,' said Cristy quietly.

They looked at her respectfully.

'Each of us knows in their heart what's most important to them,' said Miss Singer. 'When you come through something like we have, life afterwards is never quite the same. We could drink to a million things. We could drink to courage, which I don't think it boastful to suggest is here in this room in some quantity. We could drink to loved ones whose example guided us through the darkest hours. We could drink to luck, to fortune, to the Almighty, to this city, to this great country, to this crazy little planet. We could drink to all these things, and given time, we probably will.'

322

Her eyes twinkling, Miss Singer raised her glass.

'But since the first toast is the most important,' she said, 'I would ask you to raise your glasses and drink with me to absent friends.'

AFTERWORD

SOME WIN BIG, SOME LOSE BIG, AS PLAYERS ASSESS AN OIL WORLD WITHOUT ISHIKARI BAY

By CRISTY OSORIO
Staff Reporter of *The Wall Street Journal*

NEW YORK. New York's Mercantile Exchange remained closed yesterday for the sixth day, as oil again went limit up. 'The spot has been as high as $21 a barrel,' said Tony Quagliano, a floor broker. 'The futures months are still way behind.'

If oil continues to rise, futures market limits may be increased to three dollars, NYMEX sources said.

In Rotterdam and London, two centres for physical oil trading, business has been hectic as buyers scramble to buy oil for twice the price it was a week ago. 'With New York locked in limit, the bedlam has moved to the physical market,' said Piet Seydlitz, a trader with De Graas Backhuys, a firm of oil brokers.

The cause for this sudden rise, the dramatic revelations last week in *The Wall Street Journal* claiming that Japan's Ishikari Oil Field is a fake, still remains shrouded in mystery. Following the suicide of Ziro Takahashi, a senior official in Tokyo's Ministry for Energy, shares in the oil exploration sector collapsed as rumours swept the market about the Ishikari Field. The disclosures based on allegations by Houston Geologist the late Eric Gerhardt remain unchallenged by either Hokkaido Oil or the Japanese Government.

In New York persistent rumours have been circulating about the involvment of Durst Bank in the whole affair. It is alleged by brokers that Durst Bank, acting both for unnamed clients and for itself, led the selling which caused oil to decline. The sharp rise in the price of oil has hit the bank hard, reliable sources say.

Durst Bank, long regarded as a hunter on Wall Street, may now become the hunted as analysts try to calculate just how much the sudden end of the bear market has cost it.

'Durst Bank will co-operate fully with any investigation which regulatory authorities may wish to make,' a spokesman for the bank said.

Elsewhere, Durst Bank's problems may be only beginning. Thousands of investors who lost money in oil are suing the bank in civil actions in New York which may take years to hear. Under federal antitrust law, any penalty handed down against Durst Bank by a federal jury is automatically tripled. Warns Sol Ansbacher, an attorney for the plaintiffs in one of the class actions: 'My case alone will cost Durst Bank three hundred million.'

In New York, a separate police investigation is underway to determine if there is a connection between the events in oil and the death last month of Durst Bank lawyer Ronald Spirakis whose body was found by Coastguards in New York Harbour.

The repercussions from oil's dramatic rise continued yesterday on Wall Street with the emergence of the Ephraim Singer Foundation as owner of nearly ten percent of the voting stock in Manhattan First Banking Corporation. The Ephraim Singer Foundation is a substantial property owner in Manhattan and is understood to have purchased large quantities of oil at last week's depressed prices. A spokesperson for the Foundation said they had been acquiring the position in Man First for the past six months for long term strategic reasons.

'This is fundamentally a strong bank which needs a young team at the helm,' the spokesperson continued. 'As the largest single shareholder, we will be making sure that this happens.'

Jacob Landey, Chairman of the Man First Board, refused to comment when asked if he had been asked to stay on by the bank's effective new owners.

First Com, the commodities brokerage and trading house which is the subject of an investigation by Washington's Commodities Futures Trading Commission, has still not reopened, giving rise to speculation that the new board of Man First Bank may decide to concentrate on its core banking business and dissociate itself from commodities.

First Com, established just five weeks ago, has valuable seats on commodities exchanges in New York, Chicago, London and Paris.

Neither First Com nor Man First could be reached yesterday for comment on its intention for these seats, but one name which was being mentioned on Wall Street as a likely buyer was that of rapidly resurging broker, GiltStock.